Also by Gary Paul Corcoran

The Trip Into Milky Way
The Last Love of Eleanor Sands
The Tribe
It's Always Christmastime In Cratchitville
Postmark: Paris ~ Destination: Unknown
The Twelfth Commandment

Afghan's Lipstick Warriors: Darkness Falls
Afghan's Lipstick Warriors: The Deadly Sins

From The Michael Devlin Series

South On Pacific Coast Highway
Love In A Dying World

With Gary Paul Corcoran

The Slow Train to Rishikesh
Purgatory: Origins

Afghan's

Lipstick Warriors

First Chronicle

Published by Stargazer Press
Charlestown, Rhode Island
http://garypaulcorcoran.com/

Printed in the United States of America
ISBN: 978-0-9971265-7-0

Visit us and blog with the author at
http://garypaulcorcoran.com/

To the women of Afghanistan,
this story was written for you,
with brave hopes for your freedom and happiness.

Author Foreword

To anyone who would dismiss this novel as little more than a fanciful confection, or worse still, a naïve and reckless manifesto, I will readily admit to having my own reservations. After all, what is the prospect that a multitude of Afghan women will rise up in arms against the Taliban? Or, in doing so, would not drive Afghanistan further into unwanted civil war, chaos and destruction?

And yet the alternative is so sickening to me — women enslaved again by a horde of brutes with their zealous beliefs — I find myself compelled to raise up my voice in protest. The horrendous images are not easily forgotten, that of women in burkas being led into stadiums and executed Mob style as their fellow citizens are forced to gaze on. It is revolting enough to me, the prospect of women being denied the right to an education and to work freely alongside men. In the course of human history, there is no greater miscarriage of justice than the one perpetrated by men upon the opposite sex. So, yes, I would rather see the Afghan women rise up in arms against their oppressors than to watch them being enslaved again, and the whole of Afghanistan marched back into the dark ages.

I feverishly wrote this novel in the spring of 2021, with the rapidly evolving events of the American troop withdrawal threatening to overrun the story at every turn. Will the yolk of Taliban barbarism once again oppress the whole of Afghanistan? As of this writing, the jury is still out, but one thing remains abundantly clear. In the ongoing struggle to build a free, fair and democratic Afghan society, women will be the ones who suffer most if the Taliban can retake power. This story represents my frail hope of holding back that tide. Never forget this simple truth, for it haunts the mind of every tyrant, despot and dictator. A tiger is only tamed for so long as it accepts the whip.

Afghan's

Lipstick Warriors

First Chronicle

Afghan's Lipstick Warriors
First Chronicle

One

The Panjshir River ran swiftly past the mountain village where Saarah Khalil lived, its clear and shallow waters skipping merrily over pebble and rock, as fresh as the snows that fed it from high up in the Hindu Kush. For as long as these peasant people could remember, they and their ancestors had toiled away in their fields, their fields always lush with crops and the bells of their flocks echoing daily up among the nearby hills and the snowcapped peaks forever towering over all the land. In a word, it was a fine place to live if a person did not mind hard work and a place where young hearts had always dreamed. And as much as there were wars and strife in this world, those things had rarely come to trouble this small corner of the earth.

Saarah was filled with dreams as much as any young heart and had stopped in the woods on her way home from school that day to sit atop her favorite rock and dream by the swiftly passing river. Soon enough, these waters would flow by lazily beneath a buzz of insects and summer heat, but now, in early spring, with the winter snow melting high up in the Kush, the shallow river rushed by with such a great roar, it nearly blotted out the whisper of leaves above Saarah's head.

It was nearly enough to blot out Saarah's every thought but she could always hear her dreams and was just then flying here and there around the planet, being brilliant and courageous and the talk of the world. In one moment, she was a scientist, having just made a great life changing discovery. In another, she was a doctor giving care and comfort to the poor. Then she was the first female president of Afghanistan.

Why not? There had already been female leaders in India and Pakistan and many other countries. Certainly the time had come for the people of Afghanistan to recognize that women were the equal of men. Her mother had told her it was once that way in Afghanistan and for the life of her, Saarah could not understand why it wasn't still that way now.

While busy daydreaming, Saarah gazed up at the late afternoon sky and spotted the moon through the rustling leaves. Or perhaps I will become an astronaut and go visit our companion orb one day. Naturally, I will have to hurry home to finish my studies so I can become a doctor and cure cancer and be the president of Afghanistan.

Saarah smiled to herself, imagining it all. As a young woman, the possibilities seemed boundless. Only six more months now and she would be off to college on a scholarship that her teacher Mrs. Farooq had helped her secure.

Saarah looked back at the moon and reached out a hand. It seemed so close, you could almost touch it. She remained there staring up into the sky, her vision of a journey among the stars having completely seized her heart until a sudden clang of farm equipment off in the distance broke the spell.

Reminded of her afternoon chores, she got to her feet and started off through the woods. Her father was a good man and never raised his voice but he was also quite serious, as men usually were in hardscrabble villages such as hers, and would not be happy if Saarah had failed to herd their goats and sheep safely back into the shed and milked them before darkness set in.

At the edge of the woods, Saarah spotted their family home nestled against the nearby hills with the snowcapped peaks towering up into the sky behind it and butterflies fluttering here and there among the fields and was very happy in her heart. Arriving home a short time later, she went in through the makeshift front door and found her mother Zeeana rolling out patties of naan beside their open brick oven. Zeeana had a pail of water beside her that she used to wet the dough before setting it down to bake and several pieces of the bread were already browning over the hot bricks.

"Hmm, smells good," Saarah said. "What are you making?"

"Qormah e Gosht. And your favorite Palaw."

"Narenj?!"

"What else?" Zeeana said.

Saarah lifted the lid of the rice pot and the sweet smell of saffron and orange peel filled the room.

"Hmm. Thank you."

Saarah kissed her mother and went off to drop her books in her room. From the outside, the home looked like any other mud brick structure, but her father had plastered the inside walls white and painted them a forest-green color along the top. He had also leveled the dirt floors nicely and covered them everywhere with rugs and the walls were adorned with tapestries and wooden shelves and hooks for hanging satchels and baskets and all manner of necessities that were part of village life.

Saarah's own room had a crude wooden bed frame and mattress that sat on the floor, one wooden shelf where she kept her books and two small alcoves built into the wall where she kept a vase her mother had given her from her own youth, along with a portrait of her parents at their wedding and a ceramic holder for burning incense.

Saarah set her books down and returned to the front room.

"Did you have a good day?" Zeeana asked with a look over her shoulder.

3

"Yes," Saarah said and explained everything she had learned in school.

Discounting the age difference between the two women, seeing them side by side, you could almost mistake them for twins. Zeeana had lighter skin and a broader nose, but otherwise, in their dark eyes and long, black hair and other facial features, they were nearly identical.

One other difference would immediately strike you in seeing the two women side by side. Where Zeeana exuded lightness of being and was quick to smile, Saarah's countenance seemed dark with passion. In Zeeana's case, it was perhaps due to the time she had spent in Kabul as a young woman, and also to the fact that she had seen a bit of the world but there was no question that Saarah came off as the far more serious of the two.

"Oh, must get on with my chores," Saarah said, suddenly remembering herself.

"Yes. No doubt you stopped in the woods again today."

"Yes. It is so lovely there."

Saarah was halfway out the back door when her mother called after her.

"It is okay, my dear daughter. It is good to dream. This life would be meaningless without them."

"Thanks, Momma."

Saarah continued out to the shed at the back of their house and found her younger brother Baddar had already herded the goats inside. She sat down on a stool beside him and joined in milking them. Baddar carried on with his task with barely a look her way. He had just turned eight but was already a serious soul, like his father. His shock of dark hair was forever a bit disheveled and his deep-set eyes always seemed to be squinting.

"What did you learn in school today?" Saarah asked.

"Allah rewards those who are reverent."

Saarah glanced at him.

"There is more to the world than the Quran, you know."

"Allah rewards those who are devoted."

"Oh stop. I have decided to be an astronaut and go to the moon once I am finished with college. What do you think of that?"

"Can you grow crops and herd goats on the moon?"

"I said stop it."

Saarah's younger sister Paksima had come in behind them just then and giggled.

"I want to go to the moon!" she said.

"That will be fun, yes?!" Saarah said. "We can reach out and catch the stars in our hands as we sail along."

Paksima giggled again and Saarah glanced at her with a smile. Paksima was six and sweet faced, but with haunting dark eyes that seemed to be saying, 'I will be utterly heartbroken if the goodness I seek in my fellow human beings does not actually exist.'

"And what did you learn in school today?" Saarah asked her.

"Oh, a lady from England came to talk to us about how she goes around the world helping other people and shared all these wonderful stories about other places and how we could go there too someday if we wished."

"Oh? I wonder why I did not see her."

"I think she came when you and Maanika went out for a walk at lunch. And then she left in a great hurry."

"She did? I wonder why."

"She said that she had gotten a call from Kabul but would be back next week to spend more time with all the students."

"And did you want to grow up and go all around the world helping other people and seeing new places like her?"

"Yes. She had this wonderfully big smile and seemed so kind and loving. I would very much like to be growing up just like her."

"What was her name?"

"Audrey."

"Well, that does sound very British."

"Yes. She told us that there are lots of people with lots of money who want to help young people just like us to fulfill our dreams."

Saarah darted another look Paksima's way while milking.

"And do you think there would be enough money to help us get to the moon?"

Paksima giggled.

"I do not know but we will ask her when she returns next week."

"And did she say exactly what day she would be coming back?"

"No. Just sometime next week.

Saarah had just finished milking one goat and was moving on to the next when she heard her father come into the pen outside. There were nickers and snorts from their horse as it was being unbridled.

He came into the shed a minute later to hang up a harness and some rope on the wall. He was tall and lean and had the weather-beaten face of a man who had spent years working out in the sun. His black beard was short and his green eyes intense. His bent nose spoke of the hardships he had endured in his still somewhat brief life, but the eyes were those of a decent and considerate man inside.

"Hello, father," Paksima said. "Saarah was just telling me that we'll be going to the moon next week."

Saarah admonished her younger sister with a look of her eyes while milking. Farzaad had glanced their way briefly before grabbing some hay and taking it out to the horse.

While milking the next goat, Saarah heard men's voices outside and quickly pulled the hijab up over her head. She could tell by the voices that these men were strangers, and not particularly welcome ones, by the sound of her father's voice.

Unable to stifle her curiosity, she stood up and leaned over to see who was there but quickly sat back down again when one of the men flashed a look her way. He was older, perhaps in his fifties, with a turban, a long, greying beard and one eye half closed. Saarah had been unable to tell if the eye was missing but it had seemed that way. The scowl on the man's face had struck Saarah more than anything else. There did not seem to be one kind thing about him. The other two men with him were also bearded and turbaned but younger in age.

When Paksima went to look too, Saarah grabbed hold of her arm.

"Stay here," she whispered.

"But I want to see."

"Ssshhh."

"Allah rewards those who are chaste."

"And enough with you, my young brother."

Saarah resumed milking while listening intently to the conversation outside. From what she could hear, it seemed as if the older man was admonishing her father.

The conversation had gone on for some time when Saarah sensed a shadow in the door to the shed and looked up to find all three men staring at her. They remained so for several seconds before finally retreating. The older man admonished her father one last time and they were gone.

Her father returned to the barn a short while later and acted as if nothing had happened.

"Who was that?" Saarah asked.

"Be sure to draw some water for the animals before you come in," he said and went out of the shed.

When Saarah returned to the house, her mother and father quickly stopped their conversation, and talk over dinner that evening was noticeably strained. Saarah kept stealing glances at her parents, certain that those three men were behind this unspoken tension but decided not to say anything more about it.

Later that night, with everyone in bed, Saarah heard her parents arguing. That they were doing so in hushed voices only served to magnify the heated nature of their discussion. Her mother, in particular, appeared to be upset.

7

In the morning, Farzaad went off early to work in the fields. Before leaving for school, Saarah cornered her mother in the kitchen.

"Please tell me what is going on, Momma."

Zeeana continued cleaning up in place of answering Saarah.

"Momma, whatever it is, I will find out sooner or later so you may as well tell me now."

Zeeana stopped what she was doing and turned to face her daughter.

"Do you know who those men were who spoke with your father yesterday?"

Saarah nodded.

"The Taliban, I think."

Her mother nodded back.

"And with talk of the Americans leaving, they came to say that they will be moving into the valley. They expect to have control of this area, perhaps as early as next week, and will be imposing Sharia law."

"So what? I'll have to stop going to school now and wear their stupid burka?"

"I do not know, Saarah. I'm as anguished as you are."

"Then we should just move away. I will do so personally, rather than submit to their disgusting beliefs."

Zeeana sighed deeply.

"And if I were a young woman your age, I would do the same thing."

Zeeana walked over and hugged her daughter.

"Let us wait and see what happens, okay?"

She stood back and looked into Saarah's eyes.

"Perhaps they won't come. This talk of the Americans leaving, so far it has only been talk."

Saarah shook her head.

"There is more, isn't there? I heard you and father arguing late last night. He's thinking to marry me off to one of them, isn't he?"

Zeeana sighed deeply again. Saarah pulled away in tears.

"I will flee this village before I let that happen."

Zeeana had to reach out and forcefully restrain her daughter from running off.

"Oh, my sweet daughter. Please believe me. I will run away with you before I ever let that happen."

Two

Saarah started off across the valley towards her school, fearing the worst. She knew enough about these men and their Sharia law to know that she might well be given to their leader by the village as a token of goodwill.

The thought of that vile old man having his way with her made Saarah sick. Never, she thought. Never never never never.

Growing more defiant with every step, Saarah broke out into a run and had neared the bridge that crossed the shallow river when she spotted her friend Maanika up ahead. Saarah called out and Maanika turned to wait for Saarah to catch up. Unlike Saarah, who let her black hair fall loosely about her shoulders, Maanika kept hers pulled back tightly beneath a brightly colored hijab, a habit that served to accent her thick eyebrows and prominent nose. And yet, what you noticed most about Maanika were her cheerful, wideset eyes and the ever present smile on her round face.

When Maanika saw Saarah's distressed state, a shadow fell over her perpetual look of mirth.

"What is wrong, my friend?"

Maanika listened with sincere concern as Saarah explained the events of the previous day, but a look of hope quickly returned to her face.

"I heard only yesterday that the Americans are not leaving. That their new president will not abandon us."

"I do not believe it," Saarah said. "Anyway, I saw those horrid men. They were here and I have no doubt they will return."

Maanika reached out a hand.

"We must have hope."

"Hope. What is hope if these men come and take over our village? I have more hope of flying to the moon tomorrow."

Hearing the word 'moon' come out of her own mouth, Saarah's mind was hurtled back to her fanciful dreams of the previous day. The world had seemed so filled with goodness but twenty-four hours ago, but all of that was shattered now.

"We had better go before we become late," Maanika said.

The two friends continued on their way to school and Maanika continued offering hopeful words but Saarah hardly heard any of it. All she could think of now was some means of escape. Saarah knew of other nearby villages, and even had family and friends in some of them, but that option offered scant hope. Once the village elders realized what had happened, they would simply send Saarah back home to her parents.

Throughout the day, Saarah's inner debate persisted and her thoughts turned often to that British aid worker. Perhaps she could help Saarah find a way. But if not, she would flee on her own. She would go anywhere and do anything before she would submit to that revolting old man with his one eye.

On her way home from school that day, Saarah again stopped in the woods and sat there with the river rushing by swiftly below her, only now in place of dreams, she found her thoughts riddled with worries and cares. She had to escape. The only question was how and to where.

When Saarah arrived home, she found her mother gone and her father out in back, shearing their sheep. In passing through the pen and into the shed, she could hardly look at him, suspecting what he planned to do.

She had been seated beside Baddar for some minutes, milking a goat, when she heard vehicles brake to a halt out in front. She saw her father look up once at the sound and go right back to work.

Presently, Saarah heard the sound of approaching footsteps and men's voices. She pulled the hijab up over her head and continued milking but kept stealing glances that way, dying to know who it was. The men were out of Saarah's sight but she heard them speaking in English.

Her father had continued with sheering the lamb in front of him as if no one was there. When he was finished with that, he wiped his hands and stood up to greet the men.

Unable to suppress her curiosity, Saarah leaned forward and peered outside. There were three men, one of them with his helmet in hand, speaking to her father, the other two standing back with their helmets still on. All three men had noticed the movement and looked Saarah's way. The one with his helmet off nodded courteously and turned his attention back to her father. The other two men kept staring.

Saarah retreated out of sight, uncomfortable as always with men staring at her like she was an object. At least the other soldier had been courteous enough to look away after nodding.

Curious about him, she had thought to lean forward again but heard her father arguing back, something about the Americans leaving Afghanistan and what choice would the villagers have then but to make peace with the Taliban? Saarah kept listening but heard only snippets of what was being said.

Finished with milking the goats, she passed through the pen on her way out to the front of the house. The two soldiers standing in back again stared at her disrespectfully but the soldier talking to her father barely glanced Saarah's way.

Out in front, she found three Humvees parked in the road, two of them with machine guns on top and soldiers manning them. A man sat in the front seat of the rear Humvee with the door open and two women stood leaning against the front of it. The women were all geared up in military fatigues with plated vests and ammo pouches and rifles strapped across their chests.

"Hi, I'm Natalie," the one with dark hair said.

Saarah walked over to greet her.

"Do you speak English?" Natalie asked.

"Yes. I'm learning in school. My name is Saarah."

"Hi, Saarah. This is Leanna."

The one with blonde hair held out her hand.

"How do women become soldiers in America?" Saarah asked.

Leanna shrugged at Natalie with a smile.

"You just have to beat up a couple of guys in basic training."

Natalie elbowed her. Saarah kept staring at them.

"I just heard my father say that the Americans are leaving."

The women shared another look.

"There's always talk of that," Natalie said. "But we never do. Why? Are you worried?"

Saarah looked away.

"What?" Natalie said. "Has the Taliban been around here lately?"

Saarah looked towards the house and back with a quick nod of her head.

"When exactly?"

Knowing her father would be furious with her for talking out of place, Saarah stared without answering.

"Yesterday?" Natalie said.

Just then, Saarah heard her father coming from around in back with the three soldiers.

"Yes, but please do not tell my father I said so."

Natalie and Leanna both reached out a hand.

"Don't worry. Your secret is safe with us."

"I must go then...It was nice to meet you," Saarah added and hurried off towards their front door, but not without a look back at the dark-haired soldier. He was busy talking with

13

her father and failed to look Saarah's way, a fact that only piqued her interest further.

With one last look his way, she went inside and fell against the closed door. Was he just being polite? Or was he really that uninterested in her? Saarah went off to do her homework, riddled with curiosity.

When Zeeana returned home, Saarah went out to help with making dinner. Earlier, once the Americans had driven off, her father disappeared somewhere and only came in as dinner was being served. Little was said over the meal, except by Baddar and Paksima.

Shortly after the dinner dishes had been cleared away, there was a knock at the front door. Farzaad gave Zeeana a look that Saarah knew to say, pull the hijab up over your head, take our daughters in back and make us some tea.

Farzaad answered the door and welcomed several men from the village inside. Salahuddeen, the village elder, was foremost among them. Even though he was only a boy, Baddar was allowed to remain with the men.

Bristling, Saarah paused with a look back from the entrance to the hallway, knowing these men had gathered here to discuss the fate of the village, and probably hers too. Saarah had an especially fierce look for Pazir, a young man who had long desired Saarah's hand in marriage, and with whom she had been wildly in love as a young girl. But time had extinguished those feelings. In fact, she had grown to despise him, almost as much as she despised the Taliban. Yes, Pazir was handsome, with pale skin and deep-set dark eyes and a sensuous mouth, but like Baddar, Pazir was pregnant with provincial attitudes and quotes from the Quran. His loftiest aspiration appeared to be that of becoming the village elder, while having Saarah play the role of his subservient wife. It made her sick.

Wait until you find out what the village elders have planned for me, Saarah thought to herself. That the object of your desires will soon be given away to a lecherous old

14

Taliban warlord, to play for him the subservient role you have so cherished for me. Saarah imagined Pazir yelping out loud, once this fact was revealed.

With a final glare at these men, Saarah disappeared in back.

A short time later, Zeeana appeared from the front room. Knowing her daughter's thoughts, she reached out a hand but Saarah brushed it away.

"I will run away first," she whispered.

"Please. Let us wait to see what happens."

"I already know what will happen."

"None of us know what will happen. Not for certain."

"I do…Did my father tell you that the Americans were here today?"

"No."

"No. Of course he would not tell you that part."

"Saarah. We have not yet had time to talk this evening. I'm sure he was planning to do so."

"Yes, well, just so you know, I spoke with two of their women soldiers…Yes, *women* soldiers," Saarah added for emphasis, "And they too tried to assure me that the Americans were not leaving, but I had already overheard father talking to the other soldiers and I know that they are."

"Saarah. All that the men of our village are trying to do is avoid a war."

"Of course. And sacrifice me in doing so."

Zeeana sighed, completely out of lies to tell her daughter.

Saarah stared past her now, straining to hear the men out in front. Pazir was squawking so her father must have let on about the Taliban leader's plans for her. As much as she had come to despise Pazir, at least he was putting up a fight.

Then Saarah heard Aarshin speak up in favor of cooperation.

"After all, the Taliban are our fellow Afghans. What is the harm?"

Saarah could see Aarshin's dark, wizened face in her mind, with its hawkish nose and black mustache. He was old enough to have been a mujahedeen and fight against the Russians, which accorded him an elevated degree of respect by the other men.

Then Maanika's father Bikram spoke up. He was generally a decent man, but he too expressed a desire to cooperate with the Taliban rather than start a war and destroy the village. Saarah saw his pointed, cat-like face in her mind and despised him too.

After much discussion back and forth, Salahuddeen finally spoke up.

"It is all good what you say but you do not cut the wheat until it is time to harvest. There is really nothing to do for now but wait and see what happens."

Sickened anew to hear these men sit around over tea and talk of women as if they were chattel, Saarah looked at her mother.

"Never," she said.

Saarah stared for another long moment before going off to do her homework.

The following morning, on her way to school, Saarah had neared the river when she saw three Humvees approaching from across the valley. When the vehicles came alongside her on the bridge, they stopped. It was the same American patrol that had visited her house the previous day and Natalie was one of the drivers.

"Hi," she said.

"Hi," Saarah said.

Saarah glanced at the dark-haired soldier sitting next to Natalie.

"This is Sergeant Rodriguez," Natalie said.

He leaned his head down a bit and nodded.

"We didn't say anything to your father," Natalie said. "But we thought we'd better keep a closer eye on things...Have you seen the Taliban again since yesterday?"

Saarah stole another glance at Sergeant Rodriguez and shook her head.

"But you would tell us if you had, right?"

Saarah stared for a long moment before nodding.

"I can tell that you're worried, Saarah. Did you have something else you wanted to share with us?"

Saarah stared for another long moment before shaking her head.

"I must go. Before I am late for school."

"Okay, but remember. We're here to help. Our outpost is just over the next hill. Anytime you think you're in trouble, come see us. It will be our little secret, okay?"

Saarah nodded.

"Good to see you again," Natalie said and started forward.

Saarah met the sergeant's eyes one last time and continued across the bridge on foot.

The following morning, Saarah again saw the patrol off in the distance but this time diverted her path through the woods to avoid another encounter. Several of the village men were watching from out in the fields and she did not want to arouse their suspicions.

On her way home from school, Saarah had again stopped in the woods to think when she heard gunfire from somewhere over the hills. There were several rapid exchanges, then silence, and then more exchanges. All of her worst fears were being realized. The battle had begun. The Taliban were coming.

Saarah headed home later, her thoughts focused more and more now on some means of escape.

In the morning, when she started out the door and off to school, she found the American patrol parked outside and Sergeant Rodriguez again talking to her father. Natalie was behind the wheel of her Humvee and Leanna was driving the Humvee behind her. The other soldiers were all sitting inside or manning the guns on top.

Not wanting to be noticed by her father, Saarah moved on but Natalie climbed out of the Humvee and intercepted her.

"Hi, Saarah. Just wanted to say hello."

Saarah's father took note of the exchange but went on talking with Sergeant Rodriguez. Natalie positioned herself so that Farzaad was at her back and could not see before handing a folded up piece of paper to Saarah.

"That's my personal phone number. We've been ordered to pull back."

Seeing the crushed look on Saarah's face, Natalie reached out a hand.

"We're not leaving. We're just pulling back to the next valley."

"In Afghanistan, that is the same as being in another country."

"I know. I feel awful about it. We all feel awful about it but you have my number now. If you're ever in trouble, just call me. Okay?"

Saarah placed the piece of paper inside her blouse and nodded.

"I'm sorry," Natalie said. "Things may get worse before they get better but I promise we're not really abandoning you. We just have new orders and have to follow them."

When Saarah failed to respond, Natalie reached out and squeezed her hand.

"I must go," Saarah said.

With a final look back at her father and Sergeant Rodriguez, Saarah started down the road.

Everything she had feared was truly coming to pass now. With the Americans gone, it would only be a matter of days, if not hours, before the Taliban returned and took control of the village.

Saarah touched her blouse, where the piece of paper was hidden away. At least there was some hope if she chose to escape. She wasn't sure how she would call Natalie. Her father had a cell phone but she was not allowed to use it. And even if she could somehow do so without his knowledge, there was rarely a signal in the valley. Her father often had to go over the next hill to make a call.

Well, whatever else, Saarah felt certain that the worst was soon to come. It was no longer a matter of *if* but *when*.

She had crossed the bridge and veered off towards her school when she heard the sound of motors behind her and looked back. The three Humvees had turned down the valley going west and soon disappeared from sight.

As Saarah continued on her way, she heard more distant gunfire from over the hills.

Three

All that morning in school, the quiet was broken by the sound of a running gun battle over the hills somewhere. From time to time, explosions went off and shook the walls and the students jumped in their seats.

At the noon break, with all the other girls filing out of the classroom, Saarah remained seated as if still working at her desk, then went up to speak with Mrs. Farooq the minute they were completely alone.

Like Saarah's mother, Mrs. Farooq was fair-skinned and had oriental looking eyes that made it seem as if she was always smiling, though on this day she was not. She wore a yellow and green hijab, draped loosely around her face.

"Yes, Saarah," she said. "What can I do for you?"

"I wondered if you knew anything about the British aid worker who came here to the village a few days ago."

"You mean Audrey?"

Saarah nodded.

"Yes. What did you wish to know?"

"If she was coming back."

"She said she was, though I doubt it now. Not with the fighting."

Saarah looked down at the floor, crestfallen. Mrs. Farooq lowered her own head to meet Saarah's gaze.

"What, Saarah? What is wrong?"

Saarah looked up.

"Everything." She wiped at her tears. "The Taliban are coming and will close the school for girls and everything will change."

"Saarah, my dear child. There is something else you are not telling me."

Saarah heaved an even bigger sigh.

"I think the Taliban leader who was here last week told my father he wanted to marry me."

"Oh dear God."

Mrs. Farooq pulled Saarah into her arms and rocked her back and forth.

"Come. Sit with me."

Saarah joined Mrs. Farooq in side by side chairs. Mrs. Farooq turned in hers and took Saarah's hands.

"I am truly sorry. About all of it. I know you have great hopes and dreams. And your scholarship."

"I already told my mother that I will run away first."

"Yes. Your mother is a good woman and I have no doubt she understands."

"I know, but she is not the one who will suffer. She is not the one who will have all of her dreams stolen away. It is only me."

Saarah brushed at more tears. Mrs. Farooq reached for her free hand and waited until Saarah had looked up again.

"If I share something with you, will you promise never to share it with anyone else?"

After a long moment, Saarah nodded.

"You must promise. Never. Otherwise I will have put my own life in danger, and those of my family."

"I promise," Saarah said.

"Then, if I were you, I would flee this village. I would get as far away as possible, before the Taliban come and this man can take possession of you. Because once he has married you, even the courts in Kabul will be reluctant to overrule his claims."

"But where can I go? That's why I had hoped to talk to this British lady. I thought maybe she would know a way."

"I have no doubt she would, but you must understand. For her to help an Afghan woman escape from an arranged marriage? And especially to one with a Taliban leader? She would be placing her own life in danger. If they found out, they would not hesitate to put a bullet in her head."

"Then what am I to do?"

"There is only one thing now. Go to Kabul. I can give you the name of an aid organization that will house you and help you to build a new life."

"But how will I get to Kabul?"

Mrs. Farooq sighed and squeezed Saarah's hands.

"If you are determined, I will give you the money for the bus fare but you will need to walk down to the next valley. If the villagers see you here, they will surely try to stop you. But from there it is only a matter of a day's journey and you will be in Kabul."

Mrs. Farooq squeezed Saarah's hands again.

"Remember. You must never tell anyone I've said these things. Even when you get to this aid organization, okay?"

Saarah nodded.

"Okay. And there is one other thing. You must leave soon. No later than tomorrow. After that, I fear the Taliban will have reached our village and there will be no escape."

When Saarah nodded again, Mrs. Farooq went to her bag and returned with the money. Before handing it to Saarah, she looked out the opened door to make sure no one was watching.

"Thank you," Saarah said.

"You will be in my prayers, dear child. Now please go out with the other girls before someone suspects us."

That afternoon on her way home from school, Saarah stopped in the woods and sat by the river, considering her plans. There was not much to consider. As Mrs. Farooq had said, there was little time left. If she did not leave by tomorrow morning, the window for escape might well have closed. She considered leaving that very minute but there was only one bus down the mountain each day and she knew from prior experience that it usually left the village below theirs around midafternoon. That meant Saarah would have to pretend to be going off to school in the morning then sneak away. It was at least a four hour hike down to the next valley so there could be no delay or she would miss the bus.

Saarah returned home, torn by conflicting emotions. She felt anger for her father but still loved him, as she did her entire family. She would especially miss Paksima and her mother.

When dinner was done, Saarah settled down in her room and tried to focus on her homework. Zeeana came in and sat down beside her.

"How are you tonight, my daughter?"

Saarah looked up, thinking to act as if everything was okay but could not hide the emotions and threw herself into mother's arms. Zeeana did not say a word while her daughter wept. She just rubbed her back and waited until her grief was spent, then pulled back and brushed the hair from Saarah's face.

"It is all right," she said. "Whatever you need to do, I will support you."

Saarah nodded and threw herself into her mother's arms again.

The hours of the night passed by sleeplessly for Saarah. Several times, she nearly got dressed and slipped off early but suppressed the impulse. If she was not there in the morning, it would only give her away, whereas, if she went off to school, she would have at least eight hours before her father started to miss her.

It was everything Saarah could do in the morning not to hug her mother and break down in tears again. She gave Paksima an especially long hug before heading out the door.

Instead of heading off for school in the usual direction, Saarah followed the river down through the woods. Along the way, she hid her books among some rocks, then felt horrible about leaving them behind, but she could not afford to have anything slowing her down.

Beyond the woods, the shallow river ran through exposed terrain so Saarah moved up among the rocks and brush on the far side of the valley and worked her way downstream a good mile before coming back out into the open. Where the sandy soil alongside the river allowed it, she ran. Where there were trees and shrubs and rocks blocking her way, she pushed forward as fast as she could.

The valley narrowed into a canyon at its western end. The road then scaled up along the canyon walls with the river running farther and farther below it. Every now and then, a truck or car would pass by, snaking cautiously around curve and bend and sending rocks and pebbles cascading down Saarah's way. She often found her path impeded by rock formations and would gaze up longingly, wishing she could have taken the easier route but knowing the people passing by might well be from her village.

At one point, while climbing down alongside a falls, Saarah slipped and scraped her shin badly and was now burdened by this additional frustration. Had she taken the road, there was no doubt she would have made it down to catch the bus in time. Instead, she had increasing fears that the maddeningly slow pace would make her miss it.

After what had seemed like an entire day, Saarah came to a vista overlooking the next valley. It spread out for ten miles below her, the fields green with crops and surrounded by towering cliffs. The cliffs were pocked with caves everywhere and the walls of an ancient castle loomed over a town far off in the distance.

Knowing she might well run into someone from her village, Saarah avoided the road and instead made her way through the fields. A stiff afternoon wind had blown up and everything loose was fluttering about in the sky. Here and there, she saw villagers out tending to their crops but no one knew Saarah or had any reason to be suspicious of her passage. Whenever she felt no one was watching, she ran to make up for lost time.

As she neared the town, Saarah spotted a white Isuzu SUV passing by with a UN logo and ran towards the road with one arm waving. Saarah was hoping the blonde-haired woman sitting next to the driver was Audrey, the British aid worker. The man driving noticed Saarah through his rolled down window and alerted the woman, who then leaned forward and signaled for him to stop.

Saarah ran up out of breath. The driver glanced down at her bloody shin. The blonde woman had leaned forward to have a better look.

"Are you all right?" she asked Saarah.

"Yes…No…Are you Audrey?"

"I am. How did you know?"

"You were in our village a few days ago and met my younger sister, Paksima. Do you remember her?"

"I do, actually. Sweet child. But what on earth is wrong? Are you in trouble?"

Just then, a flatbed truck went by and Saarah ducked out of sight, having seen it was Aarshin and Bikram. Once they were well down the road, she stood back up and watched, unsure if they had seen her.

Audrey looked over her shoulder and back at Saarah. Her driver was watching in his rearview mirror.

The truck had gotten well down the road when it suddenly braked to a stop and started to turn around. Saarah jumped into the back of the SUV without asking.

"Please. We must go."

The driver looked at Audrey and she waved him forward. Saarah looked back and saw the truck was picking up speed.

"Please hurry," she said and got down out of sight.

Audrey was staring at her from over the seat.

"What is your name?" she asked.

"Saarah."

"And who are those men?"

"They are from our village."

"And why would they be chasing after you?"

"The Taliban are coming and my father was going to marry me off to one of them so I ran away."

"Oh dear," Audrey said. "And you think those men know this?"

"They must. I should be in school today."

"What do you want me to do?" the driver said.

Audrey was staring back at the truck.

"Hurry, I suppose. I doubt that truck can keep up with us."

"And then what?"

Audrey sighed.

"And where were you planning to go?" she asked Saarah.

"Kabul. I have money for the bus but I don't think I can take it now."

"No, I suppose not."

The driver darted another glance at Audrey and she waved him forward.

"And then what? Are we going to Kabul?"

"I suppose so. Just hurry."

The driver sped forward, leaving the truck farther and farther behind them.

They had neared the town when a Toyota truck going the other way quickly made a U-turn. There were four men in the truck, two in the cab and two in the bed and all of the men save for the driver were holding AK-47s.

"What on earth?" Audrey said. "Is it possible that these men from your village have called ahead?"

Saarah nodded.

"I know they have cell phones."

Audrey looked troubled.

"I don't know what we can do, Saarah. We are not armed. We are not allowed to be armed."

She lowered her head until Saarah looked into her eyes.

"We shouldn't even be helping you like this. Do you understand?"

Saarah nodded.

"I would gladly do so, if the decision were mine alone to make, but we are governed by certain treaties and protocols. And there is simply the matter of offending the village elders, where everything else we have worked for becomes at risk."

Saarah wiped at her tears.

"I will kill myself before I submit to that Taliban monster."

"Oh Saarah..." Audrey reached out to touch her arm. "Okay, just hurry," she told the driver and looked forward again.

When they encountered traffic in town, the driver began darting around cars. The Toyota truck was several hundred yards behind but doing the same. As Audrey watched, the flatbed truck came into view, well back of them.

Having reached the outskirts of town, the driver raced forward and passed the one car on the road ahead of him. The Toyota truck did the same. Half a mile farther on, Audrey saw the flatbed truck lumber back into view.

The driver flashed a look at Audrey.

"I don't see this working. We'll be coming to that checkpoint on our way down the mountain and there's no way I'm going to lose that Toyota truck before we get there."

He did a double take at Audrey.

"And once they hear the story, things will go badly."

Audrey looked back at Saarah.

"Well, there's no way I'm turning her over to them. We can't, John. We just can't. It's unthinkable."

They had gone on for another half a mile when Audrey spotted three Humvees coming the other way.

"It's a yank patrol, John. Pull over."

"Those bastards back there will be right on our ass in a minute."

"John! Pull over!"

As soon as they had come to a stop, Audrey jumped out and waved at the patrol. The vehicles were quickly upon them and went past a short distance before braking to a stop. Audrey dashed over to the driver's side window of the rear vehicle.

"We've got an Afghan girl with us. She's trying to escape from an arranged marriage to the Taliban and…"

The driver cut her off and pointed up ahead.

"Lead vehicle. You need to speak with Sgt. Rodriguez."

Audrey ran up to the lead Humvee and began to explain herself all over again.

"The men in that pickup coming along? They're after her and they are armed."

Natalie was driving and asked the girl's name."

"Saarah."

"Well Christ," she said and started to pull the Humvee across the road.

"Goddamn it, Montero, no!" Rodriguez said. "This ain't our fight!"

Natalie quickly had the Humvee parked across both lanes and grabbed her M-4.

"It is now."

She jumped out and paused at the open door.

"You can court martial my ass afterwards but this is not going to go down. Not on my watch. I gave that girl my word that we'd look out for her."

"Shit," Rodriguez said and jumped out with his M-4.

Saarah looked up and saw the sergeant instructing the second Humvee to turn around and the third one to get into position across the road.

"Get back in your vehicle and out in front of that Humvee!" Rodriguez told Audrey. "And keep that girl down out of sight!"

Rodriguez walked over to the Humvee that had turned around. Leanna was behind the wheel.

"You will be escorting these UN folks down the mountain. Watch for my signal. As soon as we've gotten this situation under control, you are to move out."

"What's going on, Sarge?" Leanna said.

"Specialist Montero has decided that this family squabble here is our business."

"What family squabble?"

"A runaway village girl. I guess they were going to marry her off to some Taliban bastard."

"Are we talking about Saarah?"

Rodriguez stared.

"Well real friggin' chivalrous of you, Sergeant. You know, if you don't mind, I'll personally put a bullet into a few of these assholes."

"You just stay right where you are, Becket, and follow orders."

John had gotten the UN SUV out in front of the Humvee and looked back at Rodriguez. Rodriguez waved for him to stop right where he was and then waved at Leanna.

"Get your nose on his ass and stand by."

Saarah had peeked up to see what was going on and Rodriguez gestured emphatically for her to get back down and out of sight. Leanna waved once to Saarah before she had disappeared.

Just then, the Toyota truck slowed to a crawl in front of the Humvees. Sgt. Rodriguez turned to face the truck with four other soldiers now standing beside him, including Natalie. When the driver tried to muscle his way around on the shoulder of the road, all four of them raised their weapons.

"Stop right there or we'll shoot!" Sergeant Rodriguez barked out.

The driver stopped and sat there glaring through the windshield. All four men in the truck looked ready for a fight.

Four

Sergeant Rodriguez motioned for one of his men to circle around to the back of the Toyota pickup. With that done and the hostiles surrounded, he motioned for Leanna and the UN people to move out. Rodriguez was watching in that direction when he felt the pickup truck lurch forward a few feet and whipped back around with his M-4 in the high ready position. All the soldiers had brought their weapons up and flipped their selector switches from safe to fire. The two privates in the gun turrets already had the .50 cals pointed at the truck, just waiting for the green light to shoot.

The man driving stopped and glared again through the windshield.

"Dundy!" Rodriguez called out. "Tell this son of a bitch to turn around and head back the way he came! And make it perfectly clear to him that this situation is going to go one of two ways! Either they are going to turn around as ordered and we all go our separate ways peacefully or they are all going to end up in body bags!"

Dundy, who spoke both Dari and Pashto, approached the driver side window and began to translate. As this was going on, the flatbed truck pulled up. Rodriguez motioned to another one of his men.

"Mason, cover that situation."

Rodriguez returned his attention to the driver of the truck, who was now in a heated back and forth with Dundy.

"Dundy, will you please tell him that this isn't up for discussion. Either he turns around and heads back to town or the shit's going to hit the fan."

As Dundy translated this, Aarshin and Bikram climbed out of the flatbed truck.

"Hey hey hey!" Rodriguez called out to Mason. "Tell those dudes to get back in their truck!"

Mason motioned with his rifle but Aarshin and Bikram kept coming.

With a quick look down the road towards Kabul, Rodriguez cursed under his breath. A truck was coming up from that direction and more vehicles were approaching from the direction of town. Meanwhile, Aarshin and Bikram had walked up, unarmed but talking away a mile a minute. The whole situation was quickly getting fubar.

Knowing these men personally from Saarah's village, Rodriguez called out to Dundy again.

"Tell these dudes in the pickup to hang loose for a minute! And any movement deemed a threat to us, they will be shot! And Natalie, you make sure they obey my orders!"

Already bristling, the men in the pickup truck really looked pissed to see a woman pointing an M-4 their way. Rodriguez grabbed Dundy and headed over to deal with Aarshin and Bikram.

"Find out what they want," he told Dundy.

The two villagers had gone on for a good thirty seconds when Rodriguez cut them off.

"All right, all right. What the hell's their problem?"

"They're saying that those UN folks ran off with a girl from their village and that we allowed it to happen."

"All right. You tell them that we don't know anything about a village girl. We saw these men in the pickup truck following the UN people in a hostile manner and intervened. And that I personally looked inside their SUV and there wasn't any village girl in there. Okay? End of story. Go ahead. Translate."

Dundy did and Aarshin went off again.

"He says they saw her get into the vehicle," Dundy said.

"Well, you tell them, maybe they did, but she wasn't there when I looked so she must be back in town somewhere. Now they are to get back in their truck and turn around and go back the way they came."

Having heard Dundy's translation, Aarshin and Bikram just stared. Rodriguez gestured with his rifle and the two men slowly turned back towards their flatbed truck, but not without several angry looks over their shoulders.

Rodriguez returned to the pickup truck with Dundy.

"Okay, you tell these assholes again. Turn around and head back to town. And don't get any wild notions about chasing those UN folks down the mountain because we'll be sitting right here, waiting for them. And that includes going forward. They are not to harass the UN people anytime, anywhere, under any circumstances, period."

Rodriguez signaled for the Dundy to translate.

He did and the driver started arguing back. Rodriguez cut him off again with his rifle and pointed back up the road.

"He has about five seconds to comply with my order or I'll take that as active resistance and dust them all right here."

As Dundy was translating that, Rodriguez called out to Mason.

"Let's start clearing this road! Get that flatbed truck turned around and headed for town!"

Rodriguez looked back at the driver of the pickup, waved one more time with his rifle and watched as the man reluctantly began to turn around. And with both the flatbed and pickup truck headed on their way, the platoon got their two Humvees off to the side of the road and waved for traffic to move through in both directions.

With that done, Rodriguez climbed into his Humvee and called ahead to Leanna.

"Where are we, Becket?" he asked when she answered.

"Just cleared the checkpoint, Sarge, and headed down the mountain."

"And is it your assessment that your package is now safe?"

"I would say so, yes sir."

"Then have them pull over and get that UN agent on the phone with me."

"You got it, sergeant."

Rodriguez ended the call and climbed out to face his team.

"Well, that was fucked up."

"Totally F'd up," Mason said. "And I can pretty much guarantee you that it will be even more F'd up by the time the sun comes up tomorrow morning."

"Yeah," Rodriguez said with a look down the road. "The fact is, out of respect for local customs, we ought to be running our asses back up there to sort this out with Saarah's family."

"Yeah, well, that ain't going to happen," Mason said. "Not unless we're taking the 1st Cavalry in with us. The Taliban are crawling all over that mountain now."

"Yeah, roger that."

Rodriguez' eyes drifted over to Natalie.

"Sorry, sergeant," she said. "You can go ahead and start the packet for a court martial if you want but I was not about to let those villagers enslave that poor girl."

Rodriguez stood there nodding his head and looking from face to face.

"Well, the bottom line is, we're in this thing together now. Meaning, we have one story and we stick to it. Don't matter what those villagers saw, the girl wasn't in the UN vehicle when we pulled it over. Period."

Rodriguez looked from face to face again.

"Anyone have a problem with that?"

"Hell, it's their word against ours," Mason said. "I don't see a problem."

"Everybody?" Rodriguez said.

There were shrugs and nods all around. The phone in the Humvee rang while they were standing there. Rodriguez turned to Natalie before taking the call.

"And just for the record, Montero. You ever pull that shit again and I will court martial your ass."

"Duly noted, sergeant."

Rodriguez nodded and sat down to answer the call.

"Sergeant," Leanna said. "I have that UN agent Audrey here."

"Okay. Put her on."

After the introductions, Rodriguez explained what their cover story was for the girl.

"Meaning, the wrong people see that girl in your SUV and this thing could blow up in my face. Now I covered your ass and I need you to cover mine. Are we perfectly clear on this, Ms. Audrey?"

"I know exactly what to do, sergeant. There's a shelter in Kabul run by an Australian aid worker. She's a good friend of mine. Once I drop Saarah off there, it will sever any connection to our vehicle."

"Yeah, well, that all sounds real good but you just make sure the girl's up on our story too. I don't mind doing the valiant thing here but if this situation ever goes sideways on us, our whole company could end up in the stockade. Understood?"

"Understood. I'll make sure not a word is said about your involvement."

"Good. Now please put Specialist Becket back on the line."

"Well, thank you again for doing the valiant thing."

"Yeah, sure. No problem."

Leanna was back on the phone a moment later.

"Go ahead, sarge."

"If you're all done, turn around and head back. You'll find us here at the same coordinates, making sure these village assholes don't go and try something else funny."

"We're on our way."

34

"We'll be waiting."

Leanna ended the call and climbed into the backseat with Saarah.

"Are you okay?"

Saarah nodded. Leanna looked up at Audrey.

"Okay, get my number into your phone."

With that done, Leanna looked back at Saarah.

"These folks are going to help you find shelter in Kabul. You already have Natalie's number and Audrey has mine. If anything comes up and you need help, just give one of us a call, okay?"

Saarah nodded.

"But remember. You can't tell anyone that we were involved in your escape. Do you understand?"

Saarah nodded again.

Leanna looked back at Audrey.

"And the same goes for you. If any of this goes sideways, you don't know us from Adam."

"Sgt. Rodriguez has already advised me of that...Thanks so much for all your help anyway. I know it's been a bloody mess for you folks but it's really, truly appreciated."

"Glad to help."

Leanna patted Saarah on her thigh.

"I know this is tough for you, kid, but sometimes we have to close one door before another one opens. You're a bright young lady. I'm sure you have a great life waiting up ahead of you. Just keep looking forward. And stay in touch, okay?"

Saarah nodded.

"Okay, let's move out," Leanna said.

She climbed out of the backseat and waited until the SUV had started down the mountain before climbing back behind the wheel of her Humvee.

~~~

That afternoon, the minute Aarshin and Bikram had arrived back to the village, they went searching for Farzaad and found him at work in the fields. He took the news of his daughter's disappearance stoically. Perhaps there was a bit more flint in his green eyes than usual, but his weather-beaten face showed no other sign of emotion. Farzaad certainly wasn't about to tell these men his true feelings, that he had never wanted to marry his daughter off to this Taliban leader. To Farzaad, they were all scum. It was only out of concern for the entire village that he had considered this marriage. And now, thanks to Allah, the decision was out of his hands.

"The Americans lied to us right there on the road!" Aarshin said. "Betrayed us! I told you long ago they were useless infidels! They have no respect for our people and our customs!"

Farzaad listened while staring off towards the distant hills. The sound of gunfire had been growing closer every day, a reminder that a confrontation with the Taliban was not far ahead, and that whenever they returned to claim the village, there would be trouble. Their leader Akmad Husseini was unlikely to believe that Saarah had escaped on her own. He would assume the family's complicity.

"Well?" Aarshin said. "What are you going to do?"

Farzaad looked back at him.

"What would you have me do? Rush down to Kabul and search the entire city for my daughter?"

"Well, we should do something! Confront these American dogs! Make *them* find her and bring her back! If she is not here when the Taliban return, they will drag us out onto the road and shoot us one by one until they have what they want!"

"Then let us concentrate on what to do about that."

"There is nothing to do! We must find your daughter!"

Farzaad stared at Aarshin, thinking the man a fool for believing the Americans were worse than the Taliban. Nothing was sacred to those dogs, save for their own power and zealotry.

"Well?" Aarshin said again.

Farzaad threw his hoe down.

"Let us go talk with Salahuddeen and see what he says."

Farzaad joined the men in their flatbed truck and together they headed down the valley. Salahuddeen's house was across the bridge and nestled against the opposite hills. They found him sitting on his front porch when they drove up. Aarshin brought his truck to a stop and the men climbed out.

"Praise be to Allah," Aarshin said, approaching the porch.

"Praise be to Allah."

All three men bowed their heads before taking a seat. Salahuddeen acknowledged the men in return and resumed staring to the north, where the snowbound peaks of the Hindu Kush stabbed into the clear blue sky. Strands of white hair escaped from beneath his black turban and were a fitting match to his short-cropped, salt and pepper beard.

Whatever else you could say about the man, his expression barely changed from minute to minute. He may as well have been chiseled from the surrounding sandstone. He had the vigilant eyes of a hawk but a hint of kindness and compassion bled through his stoic gaze.

Knowing the men had come with something on their minds, Salahuddeen continued staring off in the distance until Aarshin broke the silence and explained the matter to him.

"Well?" Aarshin said when he was done. "Don't you agree that Farzaad should go find his daughter? Otherwise we will all killed!"

"And what do you think?" Salahuddeen asked Farzaad.

"What I think is unimportant. The girl is gone and I have no suitable daughter to replace her. Paksima is barely six years old."

"You see?" Aarshin said. "Farzaad will do nothing to save us!"

"I seem to remember you having a daughter," Salahuddeen said.

"That is not the point! This Akmad has become obsessed with his Saarah!"

"How do you know this?"

"One of his men told me."

"Ah. So you have spoken with them. Then perhaps you can reason with this Akmad."

"There is no reasoning with him!"

Salahuddeen looked over at Aarshin.

"Then what is the point of this discussion?"

Salahuddeen turned to Bikram.

"And what do you say, my friend?"

"I agree with Aarshin. It would have been best had the Americans not allowed Saarah to flee from us, but now that it is done, I must agree with Farzaad. It will be impossible to find his daughter and bring her back to the village."

Aarshin practically shrieked in response.

"Farzaad must bring her back! There is no other solution to this problem!"

Salahuddeen waved his hands out across the valley.

"Please show me where there is a problem. All I see is peace and quiet."

"Ugh!" Aarshin said. "With all due respect, this is nonsense!"

"You are right, Aarshin. It is nonsense. As I have already told you, you do not cut wheat until it is ready for harvest."

"You can speak these words of wisdom all you want but they will mean nothing when the Taliban come."

"And when they come, we will explain what has happened and offer them another bride...If it comes to that."

"If it comes to that," Aarshin said. "There is no question it will come to that!"

"In which case, you and your wife must discuss giving up your daughter to keep the peace. All the men in this village must be willing to do the same."

"And in the meantime?" Aarshin said.

Farzaad stood up.

"In the meantime, I have crops to till."

It was getting on into late afternoon the next day when a caravan of trucks and SUVs rode into the valley. The truck beds were spilling over with Taliban soldiers and all of them were firing their weapons into the air. There were flags waving and a general sense of menace.

The caravan pulled to a stop in front of Salahuddeen's home first thing.

"Praise be to Allah," Akmad said as he walked up to his front porch.

"Praise be to Allah," Salahuddeen said.

Akmad sat down next to him. A dozen or so men had gotten out of their vehicles with their weapons and stood facing the house.

"I have come to pay my respects to the village elder."

Salahuddeen nodded his head in response.

"It will fall upon you to make sure that the rest of the villagers respect our authority."

"I will do my best of course."

"You will do more than your best. As of this moment, we are imposing Sharia Law and you must make sure that your people respect our edicts."

"I will do my best of course."

Akmad stared

"Is this an attitude of disrespect I hear from you?"

"It is not a matter of respect or disrespect. It is only a matter of observing the will of Allah."

"I am the will of Allah in this village now! Do you understand?!"

"The will of Allah abides in righteousness. That I understand."

Akmad pounded the butt of his AK on the ground and fumed.

"I have killed for less insolence."

Akmad stood up.

"And I would kill you this very instant if not for your role in this village. Think well on what I have said here. If you and the villagers faithfully obey my orders, there will be peace. And if not? If the rest of the villagers treat us with such disrespect?"

Akmad let that thought linger for a moment.

"Then there will be bloodshed before the sun goes down today."

"I am certain that everyone will fully cooperate with you."

Akmad glared for another moment before storming off.

Salahuddeen watched as Akmad climbed back into his SUV and the caravan raced off in a cloud of dust. The sound of gunfire and men shouting echoed across the valley. The unmoving snowcapped peaks stood as a backdrop.

The will of Allah truly does abide in righteousness, Salahuddeen thought. A thing this devil does not understand.

A few minutes later, Akmad and his horde were braking to a stop in front of Farzaad's home. Farzaad stood outside, having been warned of the Taliban's arrival by their gunfire. Zeeana was inside with her son and young daughter, relieved that Saarah had escaped but fearing what would happen when the men outside found out.

Akmad got out of his SUV and approached Farzaad, surrounded by a dozen of his men.

"Praise be to Allah," he said.

"Praise be to Allah."

"I have come to discuss my marriage to your daughter."

"Unfortunately, she has run away."

Akmad was instantly smoldering.

"What do you mean, she has run away?!"

"Just what I said. She went off to school yesterday morning, as she always does, but apparently made her way down to the next valley instead."

"And why do you just stand there doing nothing!? Why do you not go down there and drag her back home!?"

Farzaad explained what Aarshin and Bikram had told him in more detail.

"What am I to do? If their story is true, she is now in Kabul and how am I to find her amongst four million people?"

Enraged, Akmad hit Farzaad across the face with the butt of his rifle. Farzaad took the blow without a word and wiped the blood from his mouth before looking up again.

"Only a fool would believe this fantastical story of yours. You and your wife helped your daughter escape and I will give you two days to remedy this situation. And if not, we will start executing villagers one by one until your daughter is back."

Akmad spit on the ground before turning to leave. Farzaad watched the caravan turn around and race off, he assumed to find Aarshin and Bikram.

Five

Saarah sat in an open window of the shelter, pretending as best she could that the air blowing in from outside was a fresh breeze carried down from the Hindu Kush, not the exhaust fumes of passing cars drifting up from the city streets. She had spent her entire life in wide open spaces, a simple peace that had been exchanged for an ever present bustling city, with block after block of high-rise buildings, one of which was towering directly over her across the way.

A car honked somewhere down below and two men began arguing. The sounds of traffic echoed up incessantly, layered over by the blare of a TV behind her and the voices of those who were watching it. Ever since Saarah had arrived here the previous day, she had been in a state of shock, her spirit oppressed by all this jarring new sensory input. She longed to run away somewhere but there was nowhere to go.

Saarah leaned her head out a bit farther and looked down the narrow space between the two buildings, past the laundry hanging on a line, hoping to catch a glimpse of the distant mountains. She closed her eyes and pretended again that the passing traffic was actually the whisper of the wind in the woods of her former home.

Remembering her family, Saarah's heart jumped with fears. She had been told that she might not have news of them for weeks, if that soon. Once the Taliban took over an area, there was little hope of information passing in and out.

The goal of this shelter was to help women heal from their trauma and look forward to a new life, but Saarah's every thought was of the past. The horrors of Taliban oppression were all too real in this shelter. One woman had been burned with acid all around her neck and shoulders, an example to other women who would dare go outside without a burka on. Another girl Saarah's age had had her nose cut off for doing the same. And these were only the more visible atrocities. Most of the women were here because their families had been killed, and the majority of those had been used as chattel in the aftermath.

Saarah's own emotions wavered between guilt and anger. In one moment, she had visions of herself as a valiant warrior, riding in like Bahram and thrashing the Taliban. Then she was ready to rush back and surrender to her fate, rather than have her family suffer in her place. Then she was filled with rebelliousness again, preferring to burn the entire village to the ground than to submit to the Taliban.

On and on it went, leaving her with no peace.

Saarah heard a soft voice call out from behind her and turned to find Hunoon standing there with her infant son Parwaiz on her hip. Saarah had been assigned to Hunoon's room and Saarah was grateful for that much. Though of plain looks and simple nature, Hunoon had a kind heart and had immediately become protective of Saarah.

"Yes?" Saarah said.

"Cylyse was looking for you."

"What? Did she wish for me to go to her office?"

"Yes."

Saarah sighed and got down from the window.

"Okay. Thank you for letting me know."

Saarah said hello to her son Parwaiz but he just stared back with a blank look. Saarah had yet to see him smile. What horrors had he witnessed? She did not really want to know.

Saarah knocked on Cylyse's open door and paused there, waiting for her to look up from the paperwork on her desk.

"Oh, Saarah, please come in and have a seat, dear."

Cylyse offered Saarah a smile while finishing up with her bookkeeping. Cylyse's eyes were shaped like upside down crescent moons but the ends were forever crinkled up, as if in mirth. She wore a black and burgundy colored hijab loosely about her head that accented her auburn colored hair.

"That should handle it," she said, setting the paperwork aside. "Just busy pestering the Yanks for more money. Have to keep the funds flowing or we'll all find ourselves out on the street."

Cylyse offered Saarah another smile.

"So, how are we making out? Adjusting to things all right, are you?"

Saarah shrugged.

"Saarah," Cylyse said. "I know you're torn. Every woman who arrives here is torn. The Taliban leave us with such dreadful choices."

"Sometimes I feel that I should go back and accept my fate."

"I understand, I understand. And no one here would try to stop you, but I would beg you to take some time and think it over. I'm afraid you'd only be adding heartache to misery. As I promised, we've had our local people up there trying to get word out of the village but we've heard nothing yet. We will keep trying."

Saarah nodded.

"In the meantime, I've arranged for a group of you newer ladies to join me at a seminar this evening. It's put on by this wonderful lady who will be discussing the many opportunities at your disposal, from funding for education to various career paths out ahead. I'm sure you'll find it quite informative and helpful."

Saarah felt tears welling up in her eyes and looked away. Cylyse reached out a hand.

"I know, Saarah. It's still hard for you, trying to look forward instead of back, but you must try. From what you told me about your mother and father, I'm sure they'd want that too. Whatever hardships your village is about to endure? They will be enduring them anyway, with or without you. There's really nothing you can do that will make the situation any better. It is truly a blessing that you escaped at all."

Saarah wiped at her tears and nodded.

"Then you'll be going with us after dinner?"

Saarah nodded.

"Good, good. I'm sure you'll enjoy the evening. Women from shelters all around Kabul will be there and Benesh Nuristani is truly a remarkable woman. She too escaped the Taliban, you know. This was long ago now, during the last occupation. Made her way to Jordan and then England and ended up studying at Cambridge before coming back. There's no one better equipped to help you see the road out ahead."

Saarah nodded.

"Is that all, then?"

"Yes, of course. Unless there's something you'd care to share."

"No."

Saarah got up to leave but stopped at the door.

"Thank you."

Cylyse smiled and watched Saarah leave.

That evening after dinner, Saarah piled into the back of a long van with nine other women. Their shelter was in the Blue Zone, an area ringing the Green Zone that was not quite as safe but still much safer than the rest of the city. She stared out at the passing city, thinking that the people on the streets did seem to be going about their lives quite normally.

The seminar had been arranged at a government facility inside the Green Zone. They passed through a checkpoint and drove on for several hundred more yards before parking in front of a nicely painted colonial building. Cylyse guided everyone through an arched entrance and into a room teeming with other women. Amidst the hubbub, Cylyse exchanged a flurry of greetings before leading her entourage down a hallway and into a small auditorium. There were roughly a hundred women already seated or milling about the room and several more of them up on a stage, arranging chairs and microphones around a podium.

Having been led down an aisle between rows of chairs, Saarah settled into a seat and said hello to the young, dark haired woman sitting next to her.

"Kashm," the woman said, offering her hand.

"Saarah."

"Hi. Are you new here?"

Saarah nodded.

"And you?"

"Last week."

Saarah stared at Kashm, drawn in by her intense, dark eyes and fine-boned face. There was something both youthful and worldly about her. Even with her dark hair hidden beneath a hijab, she would have looked at home on the cover of a magazine.

"The Taliban came and took over our village," Kashm said.

"How did you escape?"

"My mother gave me a pack with some food and water before they came and made me run away. I had walked through the wilderness for two days before I came to a road and the American soldiers found me."

"How do you know what happened?"

"They came and told me two days ago."

"I'm sorry," Saarah said.

"Being sorry is pointless," Kashm said. "I'm tired of people saying they're sorry. There is only one question for women like us. Will we fight back or grovel like dogs?"

Saarah looked away, suddenly uncomfortable with Kashm and her statement. Yes, Saarah too had thought of fighting back, but when you put it in such stark terms, it all seemed so impossible. How were women to fight back? With guns and rockets? It was fine to fantasize about such things. It was quite another to actually pick up arms.

"And you?" Saarah heard Kashm saying.

Saarah looked back.

"You mean my village?"

Kashm nodded.

"Your village? Your family?"

"I don't know. I have heard nothing yet."

Saarah did not want to explain that she too had run away. It was only a reminder of the peril she had created for her family and the entire village.

The women on the stage had continued arranging things while they were talking and now a middle-aged woman stepped up to the microphone.

"Good evening, everyone, and welcome to the Women For Progress seminar on envisioning your new life. It has been my great pleasure to be both inspired by Benesh Nuristani's work and to work alongside her in building a better life for the women of Afghanistan. Every day for the past twenty years, she has risked her own life so women like you could have a better future. Will you please welcome my dear friend and inspiration, Benesh Nuristani!"

Ms. Nuristani stood up from a row of chairs and approached the podium as if she was completely unaware of the introduction and applause, and continued staring out over the gathering of women without the slightest sign of emotion. She was a short woman with a round, intelligent face, cradled by a camel colored hijab. She was neither beautiful nor unattractive. What you noticed most about her was the somber air. It was as if she knew there were women being maimed and abused all over the world at that very second and could never forget that fact.

She stood there staring out at everyone until the clapping finally subsided.

"I want to start tonight by sharing a secret with you, and that is, that women are the heart and foundation of every society in this world. Without women, societies everywhere would grind to a halt, Afghanistan included. Despite having been treated like second-class citizens for five thousand years, that is the power you possess."

There was silence.

"Your silence?" Benesh went on. "It is the same silence I am greeted with each time I address a new group of women. Women have been indoctrinated to think of themselves as subservient. It says in the Quran, righteous women are obedient. But I ask, why is it that we are called upon to be obedient? Every human being on the face of this earth owes its breath of life to the womb of a woman. Quite simply, the world would not exist without us, so it is my hope that tonight will be the first night in your new vision of what womanhood really means. Nothing in God's great creation says that you must submit to a man's will, except for the men who continuously repeat this fable."

Saarah looked around the audience and found every woman staring spellbound at Benesh, everyone except for Kashm. She had gotten her phone out and was browsing through pictures.

"Here," Kashm whispered, showing Saarah a photo.

Saarah glanced at the photo briefly before looking back up at the podium. The photograph was of a young Afghan woman seated in a house somewhere and holding a rifle in her hands.

"She was given to a Taliban warlord by her parents," Kashm whispered. "But after being abused by him for several months, she took his weapon and killed him while he slept. And then found refuge with a woman mujahedeen named Shararah down in Kandahar. What do you think of that?"

Saarah frowned while still staring up at the stage. Ms. Nuristani was continuing to speak and Saarah was trying to listen.

"Here," Kashm said, showing Saarah another photo.

This one was of an older, homely looking woman in a turban. She was also holding an AK in her hands and had a bandoleer of bullets crisscrossing her chest.

"That is Shararah. She was a legendary fighter against the Russians so none of the warlords dare to touch her."

Saarah frowned again, growing evermore perturbed in her effort to hear Ms. Nuristani speak.

"We should exchange numbers," Kashm whispered.

Saarah glanced at her again.

"I do not have a phone."

"Oh…I think they'll give you one after you have been here for a few days. Anyway, I'm in the Kah froshi Street Shelter. If you ever want to get in touch with me."

Saarah nodded and looked back at the stage.

"We need to fight back," Kashm added.

Saarah nodded without looking.

"I'm serious," Kashm said. "We need to fight back. If we go around begging for our freedom, we will never have it."

Saarah turned to stare at Kashm for a long moment before looking back at the stage. Another woman had just then taken the podium to discuss opportunities for education. She was followed by a woman discussing birth control, reproductive issues and feminine hygiene. All the while, Kashm's words kept rolling around in Saarah's head. We need to fight for our freedom. Yes, the warrior princess was a wonderful fantasy, but Saarah knew it was just that, a fantasy. She was never going to pick up a gun and start shooting people, no matter how disgusting they were or how much she hated them.

When the seminar was over, Saarah offered Kashm a polite goodbye and headed up towards the stage. She had hopes of speaking with Ms. Nuristani but a throng of women had already surrounded her. Spotting Cylyse at a refreshment table with some of the other women from their shelter, Saarah headed that way.

"There you are," Cylyse said, seeing her walk up. "So what did you think?"

Saarah nodded.

"I like her."

"It is all about having hope, Saarah. About having hope and finding a new direction We have no choice. What are we going to do? Just lie down and die?"

"No."

"Of course not."

Cylyse gave Saarah a gentle embrace.

"Trust me. I've been through this countless times, with countless other young women. It is so hard, what has happened to you, but life goes on and one day you'll find yourself so caught up in your new adventure, what's in the past will suddenly seem like a million miles away."

Saarah nodded. Cylyse smiled sadly and gave her another quick embrace.

"Here, try one of the Asabia el Aroos. They are heavenly."

Six

Returning to her room that night, Saarah found Hunoon seated on her bed, gently rocking Parwaiz back and forth in her arms. Hunoon continuously whispered soothing words in his ear but all he ever did was stare forward blankly.

Saarah said hello and sat down on her bed.

"Did you have a good time?" Hunoon asked.

Saarah nodded and stole another glance at Parwaiz. What kind of barbaric acts had he witnessed at the hands of the Taliban? Saarah realized her own two siblings might well be witnessing the same barbarism this very minute. The thought was enough to make all of Ms. Nuristani's inspiring words vanish into thin air. Saarah looked out the window with Kashm's words rolling around in her head again. So you dream of being a warrior princess and saving your village? Well here's your chance. All it requires is a willingness to pick up arms and spill blood.

"She gave me hope," Hunoon said, speaking of Ms. Nuristani. "I love to sew and with her help and the people here, I now have plans to open my own little shop when I leave in a few months. I know. It is a humble dream but I will be very happy just to have my own little workplace and to be able to take care of myself and Parwaiz."

"I'm sure it will be nice," Saarah said.

"Have you thought about your own dreams?" Hunoon said.

Saarah shrugged and shook her head.

"I cannot seem to think of anything right now."

"No. I understand. It is too soon. Your mind is still back in your village. It took me weeks before I could stop weeping over my dead husband. And still I weep at times when no one is looking, but it grows more distant every day. We must have hope or life is nothing."

Saarah nodded.

"I am tired," she said and went off to use the bathroom.

The following day, Saarah resumed her high school classes there at the shelter and was glad to be studying and learning again. But in every idle moment, she found her mind wandering. Sometimes she was there in the woods by the stream with the leaves whispering above her head. Then she would be worrying about her family. Then she was thinking about Kashm and the things she had shared.

Around and around it went. And the days passed. And still there was no word from her village.

It had gotten on into the second week of Saarah's stay at the shelter when one of the aides came and asked Saarah to join her in Cylyse's office. Saarah walked in to find Audrey already seated there. Cylyse waved at a free chair.

"Please, Saarah. Sit down...And close the door," Cylyse told the aide as she went out.

The three women were left staring at each other. Both Cylyse and Audrey tried to smile but there was no mistaking the grim mood.

"We finally got news out of your village," Cylyse said. "A man Audrey knows from a nearby village had passed through a few days ago and reported back to her."

Saarah looked from face to face.

"So? What is it?"

"I'm afraid it's not good news. I'm so sorry to have to tell you this but it appears that your father was killed."

Saarah leapt from her seat as if spring loaded and was halfway to the door when Audrey caught up with her. That led to a brief struggle before Saarah finally collapsed against Audrey's chest in grief. It was some time before she could finally gather herself and look at Cylyse again.

"Are you sure? Do you know for sure?"

Cylyse waved for Audrey to explain.

"Come. Please sit down," Audrey said.

Once Saarah was resettled in her chair, Audrey reached out and took hold of her hands.

"I have worked with this man for several years. I don't know how he does it but he comes and goes without the Taliban thinking twice about him. In this case, he was able to talk with someone in your village."

Audrey glanced at Cylyse and back at Saarah.

"I can assure you that he's both honest and despises the Taliban as much as we do. I've never known him to tell me an untruth."

"And so? What happened?"

"Apparently this Akmad was convinced that your father was hiding you from him, and when your father was unable to produce you, Akmad shot him."

This led Saarah to break down in wretched grief again.

"It is all my fault. All my fault. I should never have left."

"No no," Audrey said. "You can't blame yourself."

"No. It is. It is all my fault."

Cylyse came around the desk and kneeled before Saarah and both women spent the next several minutes doing their best to console her.

"It is," Saarah said again, once she had calmed herself.

Audrey stared at Saarah until she looked up.

"According to my contact, your father's last words were, 'I have no idea where my daughter is, but even if I did, I would never tell you'."

Saarah quickly looked away. Audrey waited until she looked back.

"Don't you see? He was willing to sacrifice his own life in order to make sure that yours wasn't stolen away."

Cylyse grabbed hold of Saarah's hands and shook them.

"You are his legacy now, Saarah. He gave his life to ensure that you had the gift of freedom and now everything you do must be to honor his noble gesture."

Saarah reached for a tissue on Cylyse's desk and blew her nose gently.

"And what of my mother? And my brother and sister?"

"Apparently this Akmad has moved into your house."

"Oh god oh god oh god, I never should have left."

"Sssshhhh," Audrey said. "This man was able to speak briefly with your mother too and she told him to be sure and tell you if at all possible, that she and the children were safe and for you not to worry. That you were to get on with your life and make the most of your new opportunity. She was praying for you but under no circumstances were you to come back to the village."

Saarah stared morosely down at the floor.

"Please," Cylyse said.

Saarah looked up at her.

"Please don't think of going back. I know how you feel. We've all made choices in this life that we come to regret. If only I had done this, if only I had done that, but there's no turning back the page. There's only going forward and you will have accomplished nothing by returning to the village now, save to ruin your own life...Okay?"

Without the least bit of enthusiasm, Saarah finally nodded.

"But is there not something you can do to free my family and bring them here to safety? I cannot stand the thought of..."

Saarah heaved a big sigh and looked down again.

"We have thought of that too," Audrey said. "And we will certainly be trying but it's unlikely that anything can happen now unless the Americans or the Afghan government fight their way back in...I wish I could give you a more hopeful answer, but that's the simple truth of it."

Saarah sighed again.

"Is that all then?"

The two women looked at each other and nodded.

"Then I'd like to go for a walk."

Cylyse reached out a hand.

"It's not particularly safe out there. Not for a single young woman."

"I need to walk. I promise I will not leave the Blue Zone."

"All right. It is your life, Saarah. We're not here to force anything upon you. We're only here to help."

"I know."

Saarah stood up and the two women stood up with her. She gave each of them a hug.

"I will not be gone long."

Cylyse looked anxiously at Audrey.

"I was on my way out anyway. I'll let the aides downstairs know what's going on."

Out on the street, Audrey gave Saarah another embrace.

"I will do everything in my powers to rescue your family. I promise, and I'll pass along anything new that I learn."

Saarah stared at her.

"You are not alone, Saarah. There are thousands upon thousands of young women and single mothers and whole families in the same position and all we can do is stick together. I know that is small comfort to you right now, but it is the truth."

Saarah nodded.

"Thank you. I know you took a big risk, rescuing me."

"It's okay. I was happy to help. I'm just so sorry that…"

"I know," Saarah said.

She gave Audrey another embrace, pulled the hijab up over her dark hair and turned down the sidewalk alone. Traffic rushed by her. Other pedestrians came and went but Saarah hardly noticed any of it. Her thoughts had been whisked away, in a collage of memories and longings, like the wind had often done to her on blustery spring days in the valley. Life had seemed so simple and straightforward but a few weeks ago. Now it was something she could hardly bear to face.

More tears welled up in her eyes for her father. He had always been something remote to her, and yet always there and reassuring, like the snow-capped peaks above the green fields of their valley. A fixture you could always count on, no matter the seasons, no matter the hardships.

Saarah thought of her father's final moments and heaved a great sigh of grief. I am so sorry, father. I am so sorry I made the choice that I did. I was being selfish, thinking only of myself, and now nothing will ever be the same again.

Saarah had walked many blocks, lost in her thoughts, when she heard someone calling her name. Saarah looked this way and that before noticing Kashm down the street, waving a hand at her. While Saarah waited, Kashm hurried up and gave Saarah an embrace.

"It is so good to see you! We are both still here!"

Saarah nodded. As before, she found herself filled with ambivalence about the woman. Her attractive, fine-boned face spoke of dignity and pride and all that was decent in this world, and yet on that night of the seminar, she had come off as completely wild and unhinged.

Well, whatever else Saarah thought of Kashm, she had yet to rush off in arms against the Taliban.

"And any news of your family yet?" Kashm said.

Saarah did her best to disguise her emotions but the effort failed miserably.

"Oh no," Kashm said with a reach for Saarah's hands. "Your family. They have been punished because you were not there."

Saarah brushed at the tears streaming down her face.

"Oh Saarah. I was so afraid of this," Kashm said. "Come, there is a little café just down the street. We will have a coffee and share our stories."

"I have no money."

"Do not worry. I do."

A minute later, the two women were settling into a quiet corner. Kashm quickly shared her story, just to break the ice. The Taliban leader had wanted Kashm for his bride and they would have killed her father for allowing Kashm to run away except that he also had a younger daughter to give.

"She was only twelve years old," Kashm said, concluding her story. "When I heard this, I wanted to rush back and spare her the cruelty but the women at my shelter convinced me to wait. You will come to your senses, I was told. Just give it a few days. I still feel guilty about my decision, but it is just as they said. If I had rushed back there, the Taliban would have simply made me a sex slave too. It would have done nothing to save my sister."

Saarah had listened silently to all of this, looking up occasionally as she fidgeted with the cup in her hands.

"And you?" Kashm said when she had finished.

Saarah took a sip of her coffee and set the cup back down.

"The same. The Taliban leader wanted me and demanded that my father go find his daughter, and when he could not produce me, they shot him."

Kashm reached for Saarah's hands again.

"I'm so sorry."

Saarah nodded and wiped at more tears.

"I'm so sorry," Kashm said again. "But does it not make you want to fight back?"

"Of course. I am as angry as you are. I would kill them all if I could, but they are only words, when this fight will take bullets."

"But there is a way we can fight back."

"You mean joining the Afghan Army?"

Kashm looked skeptical.

"What?" Saarah said. "A woman at my shelter was talking the other day of how our army is now training women to be soldiers."

"This program is not what you think."

"Then what is it?"

Kashm squeezed Saarah's hands

"Do you have time to come meet someone with me?"

Saarah looked at the clock.

"I should probably get back. I have been gone too long already."

"Just fifteen minutes."

Saarah glanced at the clock again.

"All right, but then I must be off."

She finished her coffee and joined Kashm in heading out the door.

"It is only two blocks down this way and around the corner."

Kashm eventually led Saarah down a quiet, tree lined street and to the door of a secluded compound. When Kashm knocked, a man in traditional dress opened a peephole and looked out at them.

"Hi Wahab. I have brought someone to meet Ariya."

Wahab stared hard at Saarah before closing the peephole and opening the door.

"I believe she is in the garden having tea," Wahab said.

As they walked along a stone path beneath the trees, the sounds of the city fell away and the wind whispered in the leaves above their heads and Saarah was transported back to a nearly forgotten time, when all was fine in her world. Then, just as suddenly, she saw the whole heartbreaking saga of her flight from bondage and how all that innocence had been stolen away. If not for Kashm, she would have fallen to her knees in grief.

It was in this state that she stopped with Kashm in front of a woman seated at a round table. The woman was in her thirties and quite beautiful but dressed in fatigues. She looked up from the newspaper in her hands with a smile.

"Greetings, Kashm. And who is your lovely friend."

"This is Saarah, Ariya, and I believe she is your long-lost sister."

That brought an even bigger smile to Ariya's face.

"Ah, I do believe we could be mistaken for sisters, yes."

Ariya held out her hand.

"Welcome, Saarah. Please, both of you, sit down and have some tea."

"Thank you," Saarah said, sitting down, "but we had coffee just now."

Kashm held up her hand too. Ariya set the teapot back down and looked from face to face. Her resemblance to Saarah was not exact but uncannily similar with her long black hair and black eyes and ruby lips.

"And so?" Ariya said, looking from face to face. "What brought you two here this evening?"

"Well, you already know my story," Kashm said. "And so it is with Saarah, only worse. They have killed her father."

"Oh, my poor child."

Ariya reached out for Saarah's hand.

"I am so sorry for your loss."

Saarah nodded.

"I know it is of little consolation to you now, but thanks be to Allah that you escaped from bondage to these dogs."

Saarah nodded. Ariya stared at Saarah until she looked back.

"You realize that I am Kurdish, yes?"

Saarah nodded again.

"Then you must know something of what we have endured at the hands of the Turks and the Iraqis. Whole villages wiped out. The grief of a thousand lifetimes. So much loss and suffering, there were times when I just wanted to lie down and die. But then each of us is faced with a choice, yes? Do we submit like dogs? Or do we fight back?"

Saarah stared down at her hands. Kashm and Ariya shared a look before Kashm spoke up.

"Saarah has heard of the women training with the Afghan Army."

"Ah, yes," Ariya said. "At first hearing this news, we too were hopeful."

With Saarah still looking down, Ariya snapped her fingers and an older woman appeared.

"Mojdeh. Please ask Irem to come join us."

The older woman bowed her head respectfully and returned to the house. Ariya smiled at Saarah and waited.

Some moments later, a young Afghan woman with long black hair and the face of a schoolgirl appeared. She was also dressed in fatigues.

"This is Saarah," Ariya said, introducing them. "Saarah, Irem."

Irem kissed Saarah on both cheeks.

"Kashm mentioned meeting you. I'm so glad that you came."

"Please, sit," Ariya said. "Saarah has heard of the women training to fight in the Afghan Army."

Ariya looked back at Saarah.

"Irem was one of those who joined."

"Perhaps you found this hopeful," Irem said to Saarah.

She nodded.

"Yes, so did I. The Taliban had bombed our high school, killing many of my friends and classmates, so I decided it was the only thing left to do."

"Why did you leave?" Saarah asked.

"Because the men never allowed us to fight. Because they themselves would never fight. The minute they heard Taliban guns going off in the distance, they would drop their rifles and run. The closest the women ever came to fighting was when they took us to this or that village and told us to stay with the women while the men discussed important matters with the village elders. Plus, most of the men resented having women soldiers among them. It was an insult to their religion. I had such high hopes in joining but grew more and more discouraged with each passing day."

"And so she came to join us," Ariya said.

"Women will fight to the death," Irem said. "Because submitting to the Taliban will already be like death for us."

Saarah had been staring at Irem this whole time but now turned to Ariya when she spoke up.

"I should confess, Saarah. I came here to Afghanistan at the request of the woman who owns this house. She comes from an old family and has money and power but fears for the future of all Afghan women, hers included. If the Taliban are able to impose their Sharia law again?"

Ariya held up her hands.

"So for this reason, we hope to build an all women military force here in Afghanistan and fight back."

Saarah kept staring.

"No, it will not be easy," Ariya went on. "I trained for six months before I was ever allowed into combat and we no longer have the luxury of such time. With the previous American president having set a deadline for leaving Afghanistan, I fear your people will be enslaved again before six months is up. We'll be lucky to have two or three months getting everyone ready to fight."

"Who is everyone?" Saarah said.

"Ah, yes. A reasonable question. And I'm afraid to admit that we only have a handful of women so far. But we have to start somewhere, yes? The question is, do you want to join us?"

"I don't know," Saarah said. "I have never used a rifle. I have never even touched one."

"Of course. It was the same with me before I began training. I will tell you this. A gun is a great equalizer. A man who can overwhelm you with his raw strength no longer has an advantage. Your bullets are just as powerful as his…Please don't think that I relish the thought of killing, but what these men do to women? They all deserve to die. Certainly, if they intend to treat you like slaves again, I will gladly join in killing them."

Saarah looked from face to face.

"I really should be getting back now."

Ariya smiled.

"Of course. You are a thoughtful woman, and that is good. This is nothing you should enter into recklessly. Because once you start, you must be fully committed. Any woman who picks up a gun with doubts in her heart will soon be dead."

Saarah looked at Kashm and stood up. The other three women stood up with her. Irem met Saarah's gaze.

"Kashm and I are Afghani, too. We share your doubts and fears, but also your hopes and dreams. Just imagine one day, showing this Taliban scum who's boss. There will be nothing sweeter."

Seeing that Saarah remained filled with doubts, Ariya kissed her on both cheeks and stood back to look.

"I notice you keep staring at my lipstick and makeup."

"I'm sorry, I..."

"No, it is okay. You see, all the Kurdish women warriors wear it. Mascara, rouge, we even paint our fingernails before going into battle. That way, if we die, we will still look beautiful. Besides, you should have seen how it drove those Daesh fanatics mad, to see that we were free from their religious oppression."

The women were left staring at each other again.

"Always good to see you, my friend," Ariya said with a kiss of Kashm's cheeks.

"Thank you for giving us some of your time."

"Please. You know I am always here for you."

"I will see you in two days then."

"Yes, we will be here preparing."

Irem kissed both Saarah and Kashm on the cheeks and watched them leave. Ariya was already back to reading her paper at the table.

"What do you think?" Irem said.

"She will not fight," Ariya said. "It is not in her."

"No, she will join us. I would bet my life on it."

Ariya looked up.

"We have all bet our lives on this thing."

Out at the gate, Wahab was waiting and opened it for Kashm and Saarah.

"What do you think?" Kashm said back out on the street.

"They are both very kind ladies."

"Well, they will not be kind to the Taliban...You know, there is another Kurdish woman fighter here to help train us. Kejal. She is truly a fierce one. Like all Kurdish people, she has lost so much, she has become like a caged tiger. Always pacing, waiting to strike."

They walked in silence until they had returned to the coffee shop. Kashm stopped.

"My shelter is down this way."

Saarah searched Kashm's eyes before kissing her cheeks.

"You have already decided to fight," she said, pulling back.

"Yes. And you?"

Saarah shook her head.

"To go, you must be prepared to die. And to give up on all of your dreams."

"Saarah, if the Taliban take power again, there will be no hopes and dreams left anyway. At least we will have died bravely."

"Yes, that much is true," Saarah said.

"Day after next. I will be here at eight in the morning. If you are not here, I will understand."

Kashm kissed Saarah's cheeks before turning down her street.

Seven

Saarah paused there once Kashm had disappeared, briefly taking in the bustling city before turning down the sidewalk the other way. She had not gotten two steps when a massive explosion went off over on the next block somewhere and threw her face down onto the concrete. Silence followed, with everything perfectly still. Then all hell broke loose, with people rushing by and sirens wailing and voices screaming in pain off in the distance. Saarah tasted blood in her mouth and knew she should get up but her body would not respond.

Then someone was at her side and speaking in English. A man's voice, a soft-spoken voice, unlike any other man's voice she had ever heard. Saarah felt his strong but gentle hands turning her over.

"Are you all right?" Clayton asked.

Saarah was able to nod, but not to mean that she was all right, only that she had heard him. She could not seem to gather her thoughts or stop the ringing in her ears.

"There was a bombing," he said. "Do you understand? An explosion?"

Saarah had to think for a moment before nodding again.

"Look, I have to go but can I take you somewhere quickly. Do you live around here?"

Saarah wanted to say that she did but could not remember even that much. She could not seem to remember anything.

"Okay, look," Clayton said. "I'll get you to someplace safe. My car's right here. Can you stand up?"

With Saarah barely helping him, he got her into the front seat of his SUV, closed the door and hurried around to his side. Saarah had collapsed against the door with her head on the window glass.

Clayton glanced at her several times while starting the car and pulling into traffic. More firetrucks and police cars went racing down the street the other way with sirens wailing.

Saarah heard the man's phone ring and his conversation with someone on the other end. Yes, he was aware of the bombing. He had been having dinner in the Blue Zone when it went off and was headed back to the base right now.

Saarah remained there with her head against the window glass, watching the world go by. People had gathered outside their shops and apartments and office buildings. Many of them were drifting down the street in the direction of the blast. There was a dazed quality to everyone she saw.

They had gone a few blocks when Saarah noticed the shelter.

"There," she said.

With a look back over his shoulder, Clayton braked to a stop alongside the curb.

"You're staying at this shelter?"

Saarah nodded feebly.

He got out and hurried around to her side of the car. Saarah nearly fell onto the curb when he opened the door. He caught her and fished around in his glove box for some tissues.

"Your mouth is bleeding."

He dabbed gently at her lips, then swept Saarah up into his arms and carried her up to the shelter door. Clayton managed to knock on it while still holding onto her.

Some seconds passed before one of Cylyse's assistants answered the door. She gasped and started speaking rapidly in Pashto.

"Do you speak English?" Clayton said.

65

"Yes, some. She is all right?"

"I think so. The blast knocked her over but I don't think she's seriously hurt. We were a few blocks away."

At hearing the word 'we' the assistant looked troubled.

"No, it's not what you think. I was having dinner when the blast went off and this young lady was standing outside the restaurant. Please, where can I put her down? I need to go."

"Oh, yes. Right here."

The assistant led him down the hallway and into a reception room.

"There," the woman said, pointing at a couch.

As Clayton was setting Saarah down, Cylyse rushed into the room.

"Oh my god, what happened?"

Clayton explained again.

"You should have a doctor look at her. She probably has a concussion. She may even be in shock."

"Yes, we will definitely have her looked at." Cylyse reached out her hand. "Thank you, Mr...?"

"Clayton."

"I gather you work for the American government."

He nodded.

"Is it bad? The bombing?"

"I'm not sure...Look, I'm sorry but I really must go."

"Of course...My god, this poor country."

Clayton nodded and was halfway out the door when he heard Saarah's raspy voice and stopped to look back.

"Thank you," she said.

"You're welcome...I'll try to stop by in a few days and see how you're doing."

A nurse was coming in as he was going out. She shined a light in Saarah's eyes and looked into her ears and took her pulse. Then Cylyse and her assistant helped Saarah upstairs and into her bed.

It wasn't until awakening the next morning that Saarah recalled the bombing and her father's death. Hunoon was there and asked if she was all right.

Saarah shook her head, not knowing what to say. She was still dazed and brokenhearted by all that had happened the previous day.

"What was the bombing?" she said.

"The Taliban set off a van filled with explosives. Thirty seven people were killed. Many more wounded. Nearly an entire block of the Blue Zone was destroyed."

While Hunoon was speaking, Saarah recalled the man and being swept up into his arms. Of everything about him, she remembered that the most.

Saarah looked over at Hunoon. She was gently jostling Parwaiz up and down on her lap.

"Cylyse asked me to tell you that if you were feeling well enough, she wished to see you in her office."

Saarah nodded and sat up, then paused briefly before standing up and going off to use the bathroom.

Arriving to Cylyse's office a few minutes later, Saarah stopped in the doorway. The two women stared

"Please, come in," Cylyse said.

Saarah did and sat down.

"How are you feeling?"

"Okay."

"Oh you poor thing. On top of everything else, this bombing."

Saarah nodded.

"Do you feel any need to get things off your chest?"

Saarah shook her head.

"It's really best to share your feelings, Saarah. After all that's happened the past few days, you must feel some need to talk about it."

Saarah stared.

"Very well. If nothing else, I would encourage you to get things down on paper. Keeping a journal can be tremendously cathartic."

"Cathartic. What is that?"

"Like when you feel better after crying?"

Saarah nodded.

"Writing helps you to get the grief from inside here, to out there, where you can see it all more clearly. Otherwise, the same thoughts and feelings tend to go around and around in your head."

"I will try."

"Good."

With nothing else to say, Saarah thanked Cylyse and went off to the kitchen for something to eat and then back to her room.

Gratefully, Hunoon and Parwaiz were off somewhere else in the shelter. Saarah felt weary and just wanted more sleep.

When she awakened, she was still alone and lay there on her bed, thinking about her encounter with Kashm and Ariya. It was such a momentous decision, this idea of going off to war against the Taliban.

Then the death of her father was back. That fact seemed unreal to her now, like a bad dream from which she could not awaken.

Saarah heard a car honk down on the street and looked towards the window. Late afternoon was turning to dusk with the usual bustle of the city. Saarah had almost grown accustomed to it in a few short weeks, but she had not forgotten her life back home in the least. This was the hour when her mother would have started a fire in their open oven and gone about preparing a meal, the faces of her family aglow in the dim light as they shared in their duties. Now, in place of those quiet routines, there was a sense of hurry in the air, with people rushing off to a restaurant or nightclub or to a friend's apartment to drink and laugh, responding to some residual Neolithic impulse to hold back the night.

Then the memory of the bombing was back. The Taliban were like the wild beasts in the night, prowling outside your cave. You never knew when they might come in and eat you.

Saarah had lain there for some time, going around and around in her head about these things when someone called out that it was time for dinner. Without any more clarity on her decision, she arose and went off to join the other women, first in prayer, and then converging together in the dining room.

Soon, they were passing around the Kabuli and Ashak and Bolani. There was talk of the bombing and how the treaty the previous American president had made with the Taliban had left the new president with little choice but to walk away from Afghanistan, and to leave the women to face all the horrors they had known in the past.

Saarah stole glances around the table as she ate. Some women were always talkative. Some seemed to be in shock and incapable of speech. Saarah had always been more introspective than outgoing, but now she truly felt like one of the traumatized ones, like a mason had taken up residence in her heart and was busy erecting stone walls around it, the walls growing taller and taller with every new sorrow.

Back in her room, Saarah sat down with one of her school books and tried to study but found it impossible. The decision before her had to be made. Could she go on as if the nightmare of the past few weeks had never happened? Or would she find there was no choice now but to become a warrior and go off to battle against the men who had ruined her life?

Saarah went to sleep with these thoughts and awakened the next morning, no closer to an answer. Thankfully she had another day to weigh her decision. It felt as if she had been marched off to face the gallows at dawn, only to be offered a chance at reprieve as the noose was being placed around her neck. You can accept certain death here, or go off to war, where you will likely die too, but at least there will be some hope of regaining your freedom.

As she sat in the classroom that day, this great dilemma continued to trouble her mind. How could you be certain at any given moment that you were making the right decision? Perhaps only later in life would you know whether or not you had missed the moment. And if you had? Saarah imagined that you would then be forever stuck on loop, wishing you could go back, wishing you had the choice to make all over again.

Saarah considered it in another, more practical way. If she joined Kashm tomorrow, she could always change her mind and return. Whereas, if she failed to seize this opportunity now, it might be forever gone from her grasp.

By the end of the day, the answer seemed perfectly clear to her. She had to go fight. If she did not, her days would be haunted over and over by that question. What might have been, what might have been.

Now that she had decided, another question confronted her. Whether or not to explain things to Cylyse. Perhaps it would be best to slip away without saying a word.

After much tossing and turning that night, Saarah arrived at what she thought was a reasonable compromise. She would go for a walk in the morning and leave a note on her bed, saying just enough to make it clear that she had left of her own free will, without explaining where she had gone. They might all be fighting for the same cause, but Saarah understood that she owed Ariya the discretion of silence.

In the morning, knowing that she was unlikely to see Cylyse and Hunoon ever again, Saarah had to repress her urge to hug them as if it was their last goodbye. Then, leaving the shelter, there was a last look back as she headed down the sidewalk, her mind still filled with ambivalence. For all her efforts to reason through the dilemma, she still did not feel certain that she was making the right decision.

Saarah had left the shelter at 7:30, wanting to make sure that she was there before Kashm and had been standing in front of the café a good fifteen minutes when Kashm called out from far down the sidewalk and ran in a great hurry to greet Saarah.

After a long hug, Kashm pulled back and searched Saarah's eyes.

"I'm so glad you came...But I can see you are still uncertain."

"How can you be certain?"

"Saarah. The future of Afghanistan is in our hands."

Saarah scoffed.

"I know," Kashm said. "I understand your skepticism, but that is what I believe. Think of it. Why do the Afghan government forces rarely fight with true bravery?"

"While watching the news there at the shelter, I heard many reports of them dying valiantly for our country."

"Yes, it is true. The best of them are good men but they rarely take the fight to the Taliban. It is simple. Life will change little for them under Taliban rule. They will have to grow a beard and hide the fact that they listen to music. But for us? Everything will be lost. We will be treated like slaves again and I will not accept that. I would rather die first."

Saarah stared back for a long moment before nodding her head.

"Yes. On that much we agree."

"Then why are you not fully committed in your heart?"

"In my heart, I am. It is in my head that I have doubts."

"What kind of doubts?"

"I do not know and it does not matter. I am here, so where are we going?"

"Oh, back to where we met Ariya and then off to a training camp. Other Afghani women will be joining us and Ariya and Kejal and Irem will be there to show us how to fight."

"Did Ariya tell you where?"

"No. She has insisted on keeping the location a secret. For our own safety. If anyone lets slip one word of where we are going, it could ruin everything. I don't think we will be blindfolded," Kashm added with a smile. "If that is your thought."

"No. I understand the need for caution."

Kashm could not help herself from giving Saarah another hug.

"I'm so glad you came."

"Okay, but let us go, before we are late."

They had gone around the corner and down the tree lined street some distance when they saw two Land Cruisers pull up to the gate of the secluded compound. Ariya appeared from inside with another woman and spoke with the driver of the lead Land Cruiser. Then both vehicles were waved in through the gate.

Seeing Kashm and Saarah approach, Ariya waited for them to arrive. The woman standing with Ariya was wearing fatigues and looked more Caucasian than Middle Eastern, with pale skin and wide set eyes

"You came," Ariya said to Saarah.

Saarah nodded.

"I am so glad."

Ariya gave her a hug.

"And this is Kejal. She will be one of your instructors."

Kejal viewed Saarah sullenly, as if to say, it would be better if you went back to cooking and sewing.

"Come, let us go inside," Ariya said. "We will have a quick briefing and then be on our way."

Nearing the main house, Ariya pointed towards a van parked on the gravel driveway.

"Please wait there. I will be with you in a moment."

Saarah and Kashm joined nine other women gathered beside the van. One of them was Irem. She kissed Saarah on both cheeks.

"I'm so glad you came."

Saarah stared back without comment.

"I know," Irem said. "You still have doubts, but I also know that you would have been haunted had you not come, yes?"

After a moment, Saarah nodded. Irem smiled.

"And before long we will be showing the Taliban who is boss. There will be nothing sweeter in this world."

With the two women staring, Ariya reappeared and called for everyone's attention.

"First thing, I must ask all of you for your cell phones. Where we are going must remain a secret so we cannot take any chances. One call made out of loneliness could doom us all."

Some willingly, some not so willingly, the women pulled out their phones and handed them over to Kejal.

"Saarah?" Ariya said when Saarah had failed to produce one.

"I do not have a phone."

"No?"

"No. I was never offered one at our shelter."

"Very well. Next thing, we will be journeying for three or four hours, depending on the roads, and then we will have the rest of the day to relax and get to know each other better and to adapt to our new surroundings. Then tomorrow morning we will begin our training. And I want you to know right now, it will be hard. For you to be good warriors, it must be hard. And you must be prepared to fight to the death. If any of you are not ready to make such a commitment, it would be best to back out right now."

Ariya looked from face to face and waited.

"Good. Then from this day forward, we are sisters in arms. Always faithful and never leaving one of our own behind."

Ariya went along kissing each woman on the cheeks and having a long look in their eyes.

"Everyone onboard then," she said. "And will be on our way."

There were three rows of seats in back with a pass thru to the seats up front. Irem was driving and Ariya sat across from her.

The women piled in and jostled for position. Saarah found herself seated directly behind Irem and by a window. Kashm sat next to her and Kejal next to Kashm.

Once everyone had settled into place, Irem signaled to the drivers of the two Land Cruisers and one of them started out towards the street. Irem followed behind him and the other Land Cruiser pulled in behind her. Wahab stood by the opened gate and waved goodbye to all three vehicles as they passed through.

The caravan quickly passed from the tree shrouded neighborhood into the bustling Blue Zone and continued northeast towards the snowcapped Hindu Kush. For the first time since Saarah had arrived to Kabul, she saw the vastness of the city. Everywhere she looked, neighborhoods rose up into the nearby hills, this seeming carpet of buildings and humanity framed by the distant mountains.

Here and there they witnessed more rubble left behind by Taliban bombings. There were regular military checkpoints and patrols coming and going and it was all very busy until they neared the edge of the city, when Kabul slowly but steadily fell away.

The lead Land Cruiser came to a crossroads and turned east towards Jalalabad. Farmland soon surrounded them and the distant mountains grew ever closer. Saarah heard voices behind her and looked back. Recognizing two of the faces from the seminar with Benesh Nuristani, she nodded politely and looked forward again.

"Kejal is a sniper," Kashm whispered to Saarah.

Kejal kept staring forward as if she hadn't heard the comment.

"Tell Saarah about some of your battles with Daesh."

Kejal leaned forward, looking even more sullen as she stared hard at both Kashm and Saarah.

"Do not talk of warfare as if it is a game. You don't win and go home to brag. Rarely have I left a field of battle without one of our own having been killed."

"But does not your heart beat faster, thinking you are about to kill one of these monsters?" Kashm said.

"Of course. But not in the way you think. I take no joy in killing another human being. When I am in battle, I am only thinking to protect my team. And hopefully to make this world a safer place to live."

"A better place," Kashm said.

"We can never make this world better by killing each other. But it can be safer."

Kejal leaned back again.

"Maybe I am wrong," Kashm said. "But I cannot wait until I start killing the Taliban. I want to crush them and watch them scurry like rats across the border into Pakistan. I would shoot them all in the back and never think twice about it."

She looked forward with a sigh.

"I was just a little girl then but I remember my parents celebrating because the Taliban had been defeated. Everyone was celebrating. There was music in the streets and people dancing and singing and fireworks going off everywhere. It makes me sick to think that such joyfulness will be stolen away from us again."

"Your people grew lazy," Kejal said. "It will take years and many will die before this war is finally over...If it ever is."

"It will be over when the women of this country decide to fight back. And *we* will remain vigilant, unlike these cowardly men. A few bullets and they run back to Kabul and hide under their beds."

Kejal smiled a rare smile.

"And you, Saarah? You say nothing."

"What is there to say? I must learn to use a rifle first. And then we will see what happens on the field of battle. It all seems impossible to me right now. I have never even shot a squirrel."

"You are wise to put first things first. You probably don't know this but most men who try out for the American Navy SEALs drop out before the end of training. Our training will not be nearly so hard, but it will be difficult, so we will see how many decide to quit before they are ready for battle."

Saarah noticed fields of red poppies alongside the road and the higher hills now turning green around them. Then they saw a sign saying Jalalabad was forty kilometers ahead and shortly thereafter, the lead driver turned left off the highway.

They had headed higher and higher up into the mountains and passed through Mitarlam when the highway came to a sudden end and the lead driver pulled to the side of the road.

"Wait here," Ariya said and got out of the van.

The drivers of the two Land Cruisers had also gotten out and the three of them stood there talking by the side of the road. After a short discussion, Ariya hugged both men and returned to the van. As Irem pulled back onto the road and continued up into the mountains, both of the Land Cruisers turned around and headed back the other way.

Irem made her way now along a narrow dirt road that wound precipitously along the steep slopes. The road went on and on and ever farther up into the mountains, with the land below them growing more distant with every mile.

They had driven on like this for nearly two hours when they came over a summit and a valley spread out before them, lush with crops and with a stream rushing swiftly through it. Saarah saw a small village off in the distance and the mountain slopes rising up above it and the sight of this seized her heart, the valley so nearly resembled her own.

Kashm saw her wiping at tears and grabbed her hand.

"I know. It is like seeing your own little village."

Saarah heaved a great sigh without answering and turned to watch out the window.

Irem continued up the valley and past the village and on for another five miles before turning left onto another narrow road and winding even farther up into the mountains.

They had driven for several more miles when the road came over a crest and into a smaller, even more secluded valley. The surrounding hills were steep and dotted with pines and the snowcapped mountains peeked out above them in all directions. And there, nestled at the base of the hills to the right, were two structures, one of them a single-story stone building with a red roof, and another structure a short distance up the hill, with weathered wooden planks and a peaked roof.

Irem pulled up to the front of the stone building and turned off the van. Ariya looked back over her seat and smiled.

"My fellow warriors, this will be your new home for the next two months. Let's all go inside and have a look."

Eight

The women grabbed their bags and joined Ariya in climbing out of the van. The day was brisk and cold and those not already wearing coats were quickly getting into them. A sign alongside the stone building read Elevation-1,840 Meters, another reminder that they were now deep within the Hindu Kush.

Ariya unlocked the door and waved the women into a long room with polished concrete floors. Two long tables were joined end to end in the middle, with six chairs along each side and one more at each end. There was also a large, stone fireplace against the wall on their left with wood stacked beside it.

At the far end of the room, a pass-through window looked into a kitchen and had another long table beneath it. There were also two doors at that end, one leading into the kitchen and the other one opening onto a hallway.

Ariya stopped in the middle of the room and faced everyone.

"Okay, first thing. Each bedroom has two beds so you must pick someone to be your roommate."

Kashm instantly grabbed hold of Saarah.

"She is mine."

Ariya smiled.

"All right, quickly. The rest of you do the same."

Once the ten women had paired up, Ariya led them down the hallway and assigned each of them to a room.

"Leave your things inside and join me back out in the main room."

Ariya was seated at one of the end chairs and Kejal in the other when the women returned. Irem was busy starting a fire.

Ariya waved for everyone to take a seat and waited until they were all settled.

"First, I will explain a bit about this place. It belongs to the same woman who owns the compound where we met this morning. It was built as a retreat for girl students back in the 1970s and was used as such until the Taliban made it forbidden. We believe we are safe here for now, but the Taliban are never that far away."

Ariya pointed at a large map that was pinned to an adjacent wall.

"That map shows who controls what areas in Afghanistan today. The green represents the Afghan government, the red Taliban and the orange contested territory. As you can see, most of the areas around us are government controlled, but for all we know, the Taliban could be over the next peak. Even with the coalition forces controlling Jalalabad, you will find the Taliban among the backstreets of that city. And from here to there is not such a great distance."

Ariya paused as Irem rejoined them. A fire now crackled in the background. Ariya searched each face around the table before continuing.

"This is what you can expect going forward. We will train for two months and then decide on where to attack. I know each of you will want to make your own village that target but this must be strategic. Think of yourselves as grass spreading outward. We clear an area and move on, clear an area and move on and all the while keep attracting and training new volunteers. Clearly, there are not enough of us here to win this war, but there are enough women in

Afghanistan to terrify the Taliban. We can only hope that as our exploits become known around the country, more and more women will be drawn to our cause. Men too, perhaps. They may be rare, but there are some who remember how it once was. Where you could praise Allah but still wear makeup and hold a job and listen to music and go dancing."

Ariya saw the skeptical look on Saarah's face and nodded at her.

"I see you already have doubts, Saarah."

"What if we are not welcomed by the people in a village? I am thinking of my own. Some of the men would be resentful to see women bearing guns."

"It is a legitimate question, but one that I think will be of little concern, since we do not intend to hold territory. Let me emphasize this point. We have one objective. Clear the Taliban from a village and move on to the next one, chasing them like a swarm until they no longer feel safe in that particular province. We are not here as occupiers. Some villagers may well sympathize with the Taliban, but if the Taliban is no longer present?"

Ariya shrugged.

"There will be nothing to argue about...That, indeed, is the whole point of our efforts. The villagers must be free to decide for themselves how to run their own village. And if they choose to live by Sharia Law?"

Ariya shrugged again.

"That is none of our business. As long as there is no national effort to impose such laws upon your people, you will be free to go to the next village or province, or wherever there is no Sharia Law."

Ariya looked from face to face.

"Understood?"

There were nods all around.

"Now," Ariya went on. "We will be training you in both conventional and guerilla warfare tactics. In areas where the Taliban are not an overwhelming force, we will fight them head on, but where they are, we will hit and run, hit and run, using the very tactics that they have used to destabilize the Afghan government and gain control of territories. Harass them again and again until they either flee an area or we are strong enough to eliminate them entirely."

Ariya searched each face again.

"Our strategy is simple. Diminish the Taliban to the point that they are no longer a risk to take over this country. However, our tactics must remain flexible and ever evolving. Each situation will require its own unique approach."

Ariya waved at Irem and Kejal.

"They are both very experienced in warfare and will be right at your side as we move forward so you needn't worry yourselves about these matters for now...Any questions so far?"

The women looked among themselves but said nothing.

"Very well. In a moment, we will go to a storeroom in back, where you will be issued a set of fatigues and boots, along with a field hat. This will be your uniform from now on. Each day will begin with running a mile, followed by some light exercise and breakfast. Then we will engage in whatever training is on the schedule for that day, then have lunch and conduct more training and exercises. Have no illusions. If you are going to defeat the Taliban, you will need to be harder and tougher and more determined than they are so our first objective is to build up your strength and stamina. Comfort will come only in brief moments, resting against a tree between battles, stopping here and there for something to eat. You will be tired every day. You will be dirty. You will find yourself wishing for the life you once knew, but at every turn, you must steel your spirit against these temptations. This battle cannot be measured against the pleasant memories childhood, of a lover you once kissed, or Sunday afternoon dinners with your family. This battle must be measured against the cruelty that will be inflicted upon you if the Taliban should ever take control again. Being forced to wear a burka, being denied the right to work or go to school. Being shot and mutilated for disobeying their orders. In short, being treated like less than dogs again. Are we all in agreement?"

The ten women nodded in unison.

"Good. Then let's go get outfitted, take a moment to become more acquainted with the facilities and make ourselves a fine meal before resting up for tomorrow."

With all of them on their feet and drifting off towards the hallway, Ariya spoke up again.

"Oh, I should mention one more thing. About prayer. We will make time in the morning and at noon and at night, but we will not be able to pray five times a day. You must understand that as warriors, there may be days when you won't have time to pray at all."

Ariya looked from face to face, waiting for each woman to acknowledge this fact before leading them on to the storeroom. When Kejal opened the door, Saarah marveled to see the rows and rows of uniforms stacked on the shelves. There were four sizes of fatigues and the women were quickly trying on the pants and shirts. Each woman was also issued a tan colored, long sleeve knit shirt to go beneath her fatigues.

In a bustle of activity, the women changed clothes and then chose from the pairs of boots lined up on the floor. Kashm was the first to lace up her boots and pull on her cap.

"Okay! I'm ready for lipstick and mascara!"

Ariya laughed.

"First you must learn to be an able warrior. Then we will talk about makeup."

With all the women dressed in their fatigues, Ariya led them out to the kitchen.

"As you can see, there is an actual stove that runs on propane and also a generator out back, which we will run as necessary in the evenings for lighting. We even have hot water for showers but don't think of spoiling yourselves. We will enjoy some small comforts as we train over the next two months but much of the time you will live out in the field, in order to accustom yourselves to actual battlefield conditions. At every step, you must work to become hardened soldiers."

The women stood there staring at Ariya.

"Well, all right. Enough of this talk of war for now. Let us eat and be merry."

After the meal, the women gathered outside on the porch and watched late afternoon turn to dusk over the valley. The snowcapped peaks blushed violet in the last light. Then the shadows of twilight rushed upon the world with a chill in the air.

Saarah was lost in her own thoughts. It seemed senseless to live in such a beautiful world, only to make war in it. She was still not entirely certain that she wanted to be a warrior, or if she could kill another human being, but she would train with the rest of the women and let time decide things for her.

Early the next morning, Saarah and Kashm were awakened by the sound of Kejal pounding on their door.

"Get up! Five minutes for prayers and then it's time for training!"

She continued down the hallway, knocking on doors. The two women looked at each other. It was still dark outside.

Following prayers, the women were allowed to use the bathroom and have some water before they were marched outside and ordered to run. Irem went out ahead of the pack, counting out steps and encouraging everyone along, while Kejal brought up the rear, barking at those who fell behind.

Saarah looked back once and saw two of the women bent over. One of them was throwing up. Kejal stood over both women, barking away.

"So this is what I can expect of you college students? How can you expect to be called warriors if you can't even run one mile?"

Kejal showed no mercy and soon had them running again.

By the time Saarah got back to the barracks, the line of women was strung out for several hundred yards. As each woman arrived, she collapsed on the porch. Kejal arrived with the last of the pack, still barking out orders.

"Soldiers?" she said. "You will need to be much tougher if you want to be called soldiers...But you did good for the first day. You all completed the run so let's give ourselves a pat on the back."

The women responded by eyeing Kejal warily.

Once all of them had regained their breath, Irem led them in jumping jacks and sit ups. When Kejal called for ten pushups before breakfast, there were groans and then laughter as some women struggled to complete even two of them.

"You see?" Kejal called out. "You think you are tough because you had to walk five miles each day to fetch water, or till your fields, or milk your goats but now you are using completely different muscles. And the only way to be mentally prepared for battle is to be physically prepared so let's see those pushups!"

"Tomorrow you will all do better," Irem said encouragingly. "Every day you will be stronger and better fit for battle."

With those struggling the most, she stood over their backs and helped lift them up until everyone had completed their ten pushups.

From nausea and sheer exhaustion, most of the women had little appetite for breakfast and sat there playing with their food more than eating it. Irem went around offering more encouragement while Kejal kept offering insults. Saarah understood why Kejal was doing this but still wanted to slap her.

Ariya, who was staying with Kejal and Irem in the wooden cabin up above, appeared after breakfast and gathered the women around her.

"The next thing we will do is issue each of you an AK-47 and the first thing you must learn to do with your rifle is take it apart and put it back together again. Come, follow me."

Ariya led the women back down the hallway, this time to a small, locked closet. Ariya personally unlocked it and stood back as Irem and Kejal passed out the rifles. Once each woman had one, Ariya locked the closet and waved towards the front.

"Come. Let us go back and sit at the table."

With everyone seated, Ariya turned things over to Kejal.

"Your rifles are not loaded and will not be at present except for target practice, but you must always act as if they are. In keeping with this, before you start to disassemble your rifle, make sure your barrel is pointed away from your teammates. There are too few of us already."

That got a smile from the women. With Ariya smiling back, Kejal placed a hand on the curved magazine of her own rifle and looked around the table.

"All of you, do the same."

She waited until all of them had duplicated the move.

"Now, press the magazine release lever like this and tilt it forward...Harder," Kejal added when some of the women struggled to disengage the magazine.

Ariya and Irem went around giving those who needed it a hand.

"Okay," Kejal said once all the magazines had been removed and were lying on the table. "Bring the action back like this."

She watched and waited until all the women had done the same.

"And now you visually check the gun to make sure that there are no bullets left in the chamber."

Kejal conducted her own inspection and then pointed the rifle in the air and pulled the trigger for good measure. She watched carefully until each woman had done this before going on.

"Okay, now set your rifle on the table like this and push this button back here."

Kejal waited until this action was completed.

"Now, keeping the button depressed, you pull here to remove the top of the rifle."

Ariya and Irem continued around the table, lending a hand to those who were still struggling.

"Now," Kejal went on. "Do you all see this spring? Push it forward and lift here and the assembly will come out."

Kejal again waited until everyone was done.

"Now, to remove the bolt, you pull it back and tilt sideways like this and remove it. You can also remove the firing pin from the bolt by spinning it like this until it pulls out...Finally, this is your cleaning rod."

Kejal showed them how to remove it.

"And in the butt of your gun, here, you will find a bore brush."

Kejal showed them how to open the trap door and pull out the nylon brush.

"You screw this onto your cleaning rod and use it to clean your barrel."

She shoved the rod and brush back and forth inside the barrel several times.

"When you are out in the field, it is important to keep your weapon clean and dry at all times. Therefore, a dry rag is good to have with you if possible. Now, you can disassemble your rifle even further than we have here, but for the purposes of maintaining it while out in the field, this is all you really need to know. If your rifle is no longer working and this level of maintenance does not fix it, you probably need a new rifle and a successful team will have no shortage of those. That is a natural function of warfare. As you terminate the enemy, you are constantly collecting their weapons."

Kejal looked around the table.

"Any questions?"

The women shook their heads.

"Okay, then it is time to put your rifles back together."

Ariya and Irem again moved around the table, lending a hand as the new recruits reversed the process. Saarah, who had always been good with her hands, had her rifle put back together before anyone else. Kejal checked the weapon and gave it back without saying a word. Ariya was passing by just then and patted Saarah on the shoulder.

Once every woman had her rifle put back together, Ariya stopped at one end of the table.

"Very well. To repeat, for the purposes of this exercise, none of your magazines was loaded but it is at this point that you would check to make sure your manual safety lever is on. Muzzle discipline is an essential part of good soldiery, and as part of that, always keep your finger outside the trigger guard and your safety on, unless you're actually shooting at someone. It is all too easy to be out on patrol and accidentally shoot one of your fellow soldiers. You could even be making camp somewhere and accidentally fire your rifle."

Ariya looked from face to face somberly, wanting to make sure that her point was well taken.

"Then if you all understand me, let's go out to our firing range and practice shooting."

Outside the door, Kejal and Irem showed the women how to properly use the sling of their weapon while on patrol then together they marched off towards the opposite side of the valley. Halfway there, where the grassy terrain rose up to a slight knoll, Ariya stopped.

"First we will exchange your empty magazines for loaded ones," she called out. "You have already practiced loading and unloading your magazine back at the barracks."

Kejal and Irem went down the line, making sure everyone had properly loaded the live magazines. With that done, Ariya held up her own rifle.

"Next thing, grab hold of the bolt charging handle, pull it back quickly and let go. This will ensure that your first live round is in the chamber. Then, once again, check to make sure that your safety is on."

Satisfied, Ariya nodded at Irem, who encouraged the women to get down into a prone position and aim at the targets directly across from them. Kejal and Ariya walked along behind the line of women, helping those who were not holding the grip properly and with getting the butt of their rifle tight to their cheek weld.

"Very well," Ariya said once everyone was set. She grabbed the pair of binoculars hanging from her neck. "You go first, Darsameen. And remember, focus on the front sight while steadily squeezing the trigger to the rear."

Darsameen was a stout young woman with a plain, almost manly looking face, and appeared at first glance to be someone who would make a splendid warrior, but her shot missed wildly.

There was laughter and offers of reassurance.

"Did you see what went wrong there?" Ariya called out. "Your rifle will kick whenever you fire so you must hold it more firmly. And remember what I told you. Squeeze the trigger gently."

While Kejal went over and showed Darsameen the right way to hold her rifle, Irem took a shot of her own and hit the target nearly on center.

"Like that," Ariya said. "Now try again, Darsameen."

Darsameen concentrated for a few seconds and fired again, missing the bullseye by several inches but at least hitting the target. There were applause and shouts of encouragement from the other women.

"Okay, now it is your turn, Esin."

Esin was in her late thirties and a Hazara, with that cheerful, oriental caste to her eyes. Being older and a nurse, she had already become something of a mother figure to the younger women. All of them watched as she focused on the target and missed the bullseye by about three inches.

"Very good," Ariya said. "Okay, you next, Hajira."

Hajira had once been a stunningly beautiful woman, but like the one Saarah had known at her shelter, Hajira had insulted the Taliban in some way and her reward was have acid thrown in her face. That she had once been so stunningly beautiful only made her fate seem all the more tragic.

Hajira had maintained her focus the entire time and fired, nearly hitting a bullseye. While the other women erupted in cheers, Ariya came along and patted her on the back.

"Very good, very good. You may end up being our sniper...Okay, your turn, Saarah."

As Saarah took aim, Kejal came to stand over her shoulder. Saarah focused all the more intently and heard great cheers erupt when she hit the upper right edge of the bullseye.

"Very good, Saarah," Ariya said. "It appears that we may have a stiff competition for who will be our sniper."

Feeling Hajira's stare, Saarah reached out and touched her arm. She could only imagine the horror of having acid thrown in your face and living the rest of your life like an outcast, and almost blurted out her thought, that you are such a brave and courageous woman, but decided it would only acknowledge what was better left unspoken.

Distracted in this way, Saarah had hardly noticed Ariya instructing Noushineh to take the next shot. To look at Noushineh's tiny body and pretty, olive-skinned face, you would have thought she was sixteen, not in her late twenties. The rifle almost looked comical in her grasp but she fired well and hit a few inches from the bullseye.

"Good, good," Ariya said. "I can see you're all learning just from watching each other...Okay, now it's your turn, Kashm."

Kashm too fired well, hitting a few inches from the bullseye.

"And now you, Tabaan."

Tabaan, who was also Hazara, focused her oval face on the target, firing without hesitation and missing a bullseye by an inch.

"Ah," Ariya said. "I can see the competition to be our sniper truly will be a fierce one."

Mahvash and Farzaneh, the two college students that Kejal had been harassing during their run that morning were called upon next. Saarah remembered seeing both women together for the first time and wondering what on earth would cause these privileged Pashtuns to join the fight. But Saarah had quickly realized that their lives as women would be no less oppressed by the Taliban.

Mahvash fired next, then Farzaneh, hitting in the second and third rings respectively.

Called upon last, Veeda glanced fiercely at the other women before shooting. There was always a fierce look on her ruddy face, a look that seemed to say, keep your distance. I will kill the first person who says the wrong thing to me. Saarah had learned from Kashm the previous night that the Taliban had held Veeda captive for a period of months, raping her repeatedly.

Veeda looked back at the target, aimed and fired without delay, hitting the second ring out from the bullseye.

"Very good," Ariya told her. "All of you, very well done. Tomorrow we will show you how to use your sight adjustment to hone in more accurately on your target but that is enough for one day. We must keep our live shooting to a minimum. The more live rounds we shoot, the more chance of a passing Taliban patrol hearing us and we're certainly not ready to take on the Taliban yet. For now, please properly clear your weapons and return your live magazines to Kejal and Irem."

Irem and Kejal walked among the women, again checking to make sure that all of them remembered how to unload and reload the empty magazines into their rifles safely.

"Okay," Ariya said when they were done. "It's on to a lesson in hand to hand combat!"

As the women started back towards the barracks, Veeda met Saarah's gaze with her ever-present fierceness before walking away.

Nine

Up ahead a hundred feet, Ariya turned to face the women. "Listen. On our way back to the barracks, let us pretend this is a search and sweep operation. We must use every opportunity to hone our warrior skills. Irem and Kejal, please show them the proper spacing."

The two women went along making sure everyone was standing roughly fifteen feet apart.

"This is the first thing you must learn about being on patrol," Ariya said. "Proper spacing. If you are all bunched together, you have made it easier for the enemy to shoot you. The same goes for explosives. God forbid that one of you should step on a mine or an IED, but the last thing you want is to wipe out the entire troop in doing so."

Ariya nodded and Irem and Kejal again went along, showing the women how to hold their weapons properly.

"The next thing you must learn is how to hold your weapon in the ready position. The enemy could be anywhere around you so you must always be prepared to fire back. Next, it is essential that half of the team faces forward while the other half faces back."

Ariya nodded at Kejal, who pretended to be taking the lead of the patrol while Irem pretended to be bringing up the rear.

"Now," Arriya said. "While keeping your focus forward and back, you will also be sweeping from side to side. And your team must learn to do all this at a synchronized pace.

Otherwise, you will soon find yourselves all bunched together again. Finally, it is important that each soldier maintains target discipline. Who is the enemy? Who are we attempting to engage? Imagine you are sweeping a village and a young girl suddenly jumps out at you. Mistakenly shooting her will cost you the support of the entire village. Or let's say you are out in the forest and stumble upon a wild goat or a fox. A bullet carelessly fired can give away your position *and* your advantage. These are the kinds of split-second decisions you must learn to make correctly if you wish to survive. Are we good so far?"

The women all nodded.

"Very well. Let us say that we have just attacked the Taliban near a mountain village but some of the men have escaped into the surrounding forest and you are giving chase. Imagine there are trees and shrubs all around you. You cannot see more than fifty feet in any direction. So, keeping everything else I have shared in mind, let us head back in formation."

Ariya drifted off to the side while Kejal and Irem went along offering further guidance to the women.

"Okay, Tabaan," Ariya called out from a distance. "You have just spotted me off through the trees. What do you do?"

When Tabaan raise her weapon and pretended to fire, the rest of the women turned that way and pretended to fire too.

"Wrong!" Ariya called back. "All of you! You have just compromised the entire team with your reaction!"

Ariya drifted back towards the women.

"Now, if I had fired on you, yes, the entire team would assume a defensive posture and return fire. Otherwise, your first reaction should be to alert the rest of your team. Show them," she said to Kejal.

Kejal pretended to spot Ariya and immediately got down on one knee while signaling to Mahvash, the soldier directly behind her.

"Like that," Ariya said. "Two fingers to your eyes and then point to where you saw the target. All of you must remain hyper alert to the entire team so that the minute one of you reacts and signals to the next soldier, that intel travels swiftly through your entire ranks."

Ariya nodded now at both Kejal and Irem.

"Okay, show them what else they did wrong."

Ariya backed away.

"You have just spotted me off through the trees. Now what do you do?"

As Kejal signaled again to Mahvash and the signal was passed down through the team, Irem got down on one knee and focused her rifle in the opposite direction.

"You see?" Ariya called out. "As part of your team turned its attention towards me, the target, Irem knew instinctively to cover your flank. You must have this drilled into your heads. Yes, five of you were initially tasked with covering your rear. However, in a firefight, with bullets going off everywhere, those roles may get all mixed up. The important thing is to react as a team. Always as a team. If you see that however many of you are focused in one direction, some of you must instinctively know to focus in the other. You almost never want to have everyone turned the same way."

Ariya backed off and waved for everyone to move on.

"Okay, let's try this again. Hajira. You have just spotted me off through the woods. Now let's see the whole team react."

This time, as Hajira got down on one knee and signaled to Esin behind her, the rest of the patrol reacted by taking cover in all directions.

"Perfect," Ariya said. "Now you are starting to work as a team."

She waved forward and they continued across the valley in their search and clear formation.

As they neared the barracks, Ariya let off a volley of bullets over their heads and all of them spun towards Ariya with their rifles aimed.

"My apologies!" she called out. "But this is what it would be like in a real-life situation! There would be bullets suddenly flying all around you! One of you might even have been hit or killed, but your reaction must never waver! Look at you! You're all standing up as if to say, please shoot me, and you're all pointed in the same direction again."

Ariya gestured with her hand at the women.

"Okay. Let's try this again."

They had walked forward another hundred feet or so when Ariya let off another volley of bullets, and this time the team maintained a proper formation.

"Much better, much better!" Ariya called out and walked back over to them. "You are beginning to have a sound foundation, but it is just a beginning. When the time comes to actually engage the enemy, there will be many unforeseen factors for you to consider. For instance, a solo Taliban fighter firing at you may seem like an easy target, so you give chase, only to find that you've been led into an ambush. Or you find dozens of men advancing towards your position but you hold the high ground and feel that you can neutralize their superior numbers. Or they hold the high ground but you have superior numbers. Then you must decide whether or not you can regain the advantage by flanking their position. This is where concealment and cover would come into play. Concealment is using stealth to advance on the enemy or to retreat, but where you are still vulnerable. Cover is getting behind a tree or a rock, something that will actually stop bullets. You can only fight for so long out in the open without getting killed."

Ariya acknowledged their consternation.

"No, there is no simple answer. No matter how much you train, every situation will be different. But that is why we train. Eventually, all your preparation will translate into muscle memory. You will instinctively know when to retreat, when to advance, when to shoot and when to hold your fire. Keep in mind, by the time we leave here and go into battle, you will have chosen a leader and that leader will be responsible for making threat assessments and ordering the proper reaction, and you must be ready to execute that person's orders without hesitation. You start arguing among yourselves and you will soon be dead."

Ariya went along high fiving all the women.

"For now, you've done well. Let's take a break and move on to the next phase of your training."

Back at the barracks, the women placed their rifles in their rooms, used the bathroom and hydrated again before proceeding over to a training area next to the building.

"Okay," Ariya called out. "As we learned in our training, firing a weapon is the great equalizer. No matter how big the enemy may be, you hit him with a few rifle rounds and he's dead. In hand to hand combat, it is not the same. Most of the time you will be at a distinct physical disadvantage. The men you encounter will have superior strength, so your only hope of success will be to counter that strength with superior tactics."

Ariya nodded at Irem, who pretended to be attacking Kejal. Kejal responded with a jab in Irem's throat, a knee in her groin and an arm twist that forced Irem to fall backwards. With Kejal's knee on Irem's chest, Kejal pulled out her knife and pretended to slash Irem's throat.

Ariya walked down the line of women and stopped at Noushineh, pressing the ends of her fingers gently to Noushineh's throat.

"*This* is one of the most vulnerable parts of the human body, even in a man."

Ariya then gestured in the direction of Noushineh's womb.

"But so is this area. Especially with men."

Some of the women could not help but snicker.

"Yes, a knee in the groin and a man will typically drop to his knees...Now, if you have him in this vulnerable position, the next thing you want to do is to finish him off."

Kejal helped Irem to her knees, placed both hands around the back of her head and pretended to slam Irem's face into her own knee.

"A blow to the nose like this will kill a man if done with enough force. It will certainly knock him out, allowing you to shoot him without threat to your own safety"

Ariya looked from face to face.

"Again, these techniques will help you to neutralize a man's superior strength, but don't be fooled into thinking it will always go easily. In hand to hand combat, nothing is off limits. Biting, eye gouging, fish hooking a man's mouth, using a rock or any other hard object within arm's reach. This is not a boxing match. There are no rules of engagement. You are in a fight for your life and must be prepared to do anything and everything in your power to survive."

Ariya waved a hand.

"For now, let's pair up with our partners and practice the techniques we have just shown you. Make it as real as possible without actually hurting each other."

As the women engaged, Kejal and Irem walked along offering further instructions. When Kejal got to Saarah and Kashm, Kejal pushed Kashm aside.

"You cannot do this like you're playing with a kitten. You must act like your life depends on it, because it will."

Kejal stabbed violently at Saarah's throat with her hand, then at her womb with her knee, then twisted Saarah's arm so forcefully that Saarah yelped and fell to the ground.

"I repeat," Kejal said with a knee to her chest. "This is not a game. Take what you are doing here seriously or you will get yourself killed, and possibly your entire team with you."

Kejal offered Saarah a hand up but Saarah pushed it aside and sprung to her feet on her own. When Kejal turned to move on, she found Veeda standing in her face. Veeda was a good five inches taller than Kejal and thirty pounds heavier.

"Maybe you would like to show me this same lesson," Veeda said.

With Kejal staring back, Veeda thrust her right hand at her throat, stopping only a fraction of an inch from striking her. A sarcastic smile spread over Veeda's tiger like gaze.

Ariya came over and intervened.

"Kejal is right. We must go about this as if it is life and death. But we must also remember we're a team," she added with a glance at Kejal. "Members of a team will fight among themselves from time to time, but they must never lose sight of their common cause."

Ariya gave both Veeda and Saarah a reassuring touch of her hand and continued on among the other women.

"All right. Everyone back to work. Reverse your roles and perform this same maneuver."

Once every woman had had her chance, Irem led the team in some light exercises and they broke for prayers and lunch.

Afterwards, the women were led down the valley to a hazard course and took their turns passing through it. It started with a belly crawl under barbed wire, then a knotted rope climb over a wooden barrier and a sprint through various obstacles on the other side. As each woman completed the course, she was instructed to pass through it again and by the third time, the team was completely exhausted. When Kejal waved for everyone to follow her on another mile run, they groaned in unison.

Back at the barracks, the women collapsed and lay there like beached whales. Ariya walked among them, offering encouragement.

"With each day, you will grow stronger, and as you grow stronger, the challenges will become easier. But enough for one day. Let us clean up and relax and have a fine supper together."

The women were again so exhausted after cleaning up that most of them just wanted to lie down and sleep. Having slogged through meal preparations, they gathered around the table, eating and talking.

At one point, Kashm mentioned the show, Afghan Stars.

"Finally, in season fourteen, they allow a woman to win it," Tabaan said.

"You are glad because Zahra is Hazara like you," Farzaneh said.

"Can we ever expect a Pashtun to vote for a Hazara contestant? Of course not but I was glad more so because she's a woman."

"Remember Setera?" Esin asked.

"Yes!" Tabaan said. "I was just a girl back then but the Taliban had just been driven from power and we were all so excited in my village to see that a woman could even compete. My older brother had to take our car battery down to a corner merchant and have it charged so we could operate our old TV. Even the toothless old men were gathered around to watch the show, eager to see if Setera would succeed."

"Because she too was Hazara," Farzaneh said.

"You should stop with this divisiveness. Saarah and Hajira are Tajik. Noushineh and Veeda are Uzbek. Esin and I are Hazara. So what? We were only glad because as a woman Setera was finally free to do as she pleased in this world."

"And then she danced in that final song and all the men went out of their minds," Irem said.

"Yes. And they've hardly let a woman compete ever since, let alone win it."

"I think Zahra wears too much makeup," Farzaneh said. "It is ridiculous. It is practically dripping from her face."

"I think it was much better in the early days," Mahvash said. "Now it is as if they are struggling to find anyone left in Afghanistan with talent."

"But I love Mujtaba," Kashm said.

"Well, yes, if you are a girl, he is very cute. But talented?" Mahvash gestured dismissively.

"I still love him."

"He should be on The Bachelor instead," Farzaneh said.

"Have you ever seen it?" Kashm asked Saarah.

Saarah shook her head.

"I believe the women were watching it one night at my shelter but I was reading a book and did not pay attention."

"That show is for fools," Veeda said. The table went silent. "In Badghis province where I lived, we had no hospitals for hundreds of miles. And if you were lucky enough to find one, it was filthy and ill-staffed. Half the children born, died on their way there, and many of the mothers with them. You were better off being whipped by your village mullah. This is how they cured you. Chase the devil from your chest with a rod. We had dust. Dust and hard work. And then the Taliban came along and took even that from us. That is the kind of life most people live in this country. And you have time to worry about this nonsense? You're all fools. All of you."

Mahvash and Farzaneh stared back. Tabaan and Darseema played with their meals. Saarah and Kashm shrugged at each other. Irem and Hajira continued to eat as if nothing had happened and Esin and Noushineh searched the other faces as if appealing for unity.

Meanwhile, Veeda stared back like a caged tiger.

Ariya, having watched this exchange unfold with minor concern, finally spoke up.

"We used to watch the show back home in Irbil."

Ariya looked around the table and back at Veeda.

"Is it foolish? Perhaps, but isn't this just the sort of thing we are fighting for? The freedom to do whatever we wish in this country? To watch whatever we want to watch without the Taliban police coming around to beat and arrest us?"

"I still say you are all fools," Veeda said. "But admittedly, that Fahim was kind of cute."

After a moment's pause, the other women broke out in laughter.

"Ah, so you have watched it too."

A faint smile crossed Veeda's face

"How can you avoid it? That show is everywhere in the shelters. I would have had to put a pillow over my head to ignore it."

"I will tell you what delights me," Kashm said. "To think of the Taliban going crazy over that show. What was it? Five years ago now, when they were planning to bomb the TV station? I hope their heads explode every time they see it on TV."

"That is like Daesh and our makeup," Ariya said. "They would see us with lipstick and mascara and painted nails and lose their minds. And we would quickly relieve them of their misery with a bullet to their heads...And you?" Ariya said, turning to Hajira. "You have said little tonight."

Hajira looked up, her beautiful face now deformed.

"I have only one thought. To rid my country of this Taliban scourge. And when they are finally all dead, then I will rejoice."

"Then you will never rejoice," Kejal said. "Because there will always be another Taliban fanatic, and another battle to fight."

"It is true," Ariya said with a sigh. "As it is in our country, the battle goes on. You can only hope to minimize them. But that is exactly why we must find moments to celebrate. Each of us may die in battle someday, but we should never allow them to kill the little joys we share as time goes by."

"I still cannot wait to start killing them," Hajira said.

Ariya looked seriously from face to face.

"And that time will come soon enough. Soon enough."

Back in their room later on, and talking by candlelight, Saarah asked Kashm if she knew exactly what had happened to Hajira.

"I'm not sure but I overheard Esin saying something to Tabaan about her entire village having been killed for fighting back against the Taliban, including her family, and when the Taliban warlord tried to force himself upon her, she spit in his face so he threw acid at her."

The two women looked at each other in the flickering light.

"We are the lucky ones," Kashm said.

"This is what you call luck?" Saarah said. "I ran away to save myself and got my father killed in doing so. And now my mother is someone's sex slave. I hardly feel lucky."

"No, you are right. I only meant to say, we haven't been taken down to Kandahar like Veeda and raped repeatedly, or had acid thrown in our faces."

"I know. There are worse things, but my heart still grieves every day."

"And mine too...Remember, Ariya had said that one day we will choose where to fight first and of course I want to go back and save my own village."

"Yes. I want the same. At least to save my mother and sister and brother. And to kill the man who killed my father."

"It will be sweet, won't it?" Kashm said.

Saarah nodded. She was reluctant to use the word sweet to describe it, but she would gladly kill that man ten times over.

Kashm noticed something moving outside the window and went to look.

"It is snowing," she said and climbed back in bed. "Good. Perhaps Kejal will not make us run a mile before breakfast tomorrow morning."

Saarah sighed.

"I'm tired," she said.

"Very well," Kashm said and blew out the candle.

Ten

It was again that gray hour before dawn when Kejal came down the hallway, knocking hard on everyone's door.

"Awake, everyone! Time to get up! Five minutes for prayer and then front and center!"

Groggily, Kashm crawled out of bed and went to the window.

"Everything is covered in snow. She cannot possibly want us to go running in these conditions."

"Up and on your feet!" Kejal was calling out in the hallway.

Following prayers, the women took their turn in the bathroom and hydrated with water out in the kitchen. Kejal and Irem were waiting for everyone at the front door.

"Let us go, team. Last one back from the run has to make breakfast."

"How are we to run?" Mahvash said. "It snowed last night?"

"Ah, I see," Kejal said. "So you think the Taliban will call a truce because it has snowed? Hey, everyone. Let us take the day off. We will play cards and get back to killing each other when the weather improves. Get used to it! The Taliban never rest! Even during the worst of winter, they are planting IEDs and attacking villages so if you want to defeat them, you must be tougher than they are. Now let us go!"

Grousing and grumbling among themselves, the women followed her out the door and off through the snow.

"Now you are becoming real soldiers!" Kejal said as the women straggled back from the run.

They were all bent over and catching their breath when Noushineh finally arrived and dropped to her knees.

"And you," Kejal said, "You have earned the right to make everyone breakfast."

Noushineh pushed to her feet and headed for the kitchen without saying a word. The other women stood up, shared a look and fell in behind her, their sense of shared destiny increasingly more powerful than any differences they felt. They knew they had to be a team now, joined in a common struggle, and stick together or die as one.

Once the breakfast dishes had been cleaned up, Ariya arrived with a small drone, a laptop and a solar charger. She waved for the women to join her at the table.

"Today, we are going up into the hills on patrol, where we will try to create a more real-life battle situation."

She held up the drone.

"This, as you can see, is a drone and it will be one of your key advantages over the Taliban...I have decided based on what I know of your backgrounds, that Mahvash and Farzaneh are best suited to be your drone team operators. You both have computer experience, correct?"

They nodded.

"Very well. Please come up here. Anyone have a complaint?"

The other women exchanged looks and shook their heads.

While Ariya brought the drone up into the air and hovered it over the table, Mahvash and Farzaneh joined Irem at the laptop.

"The two of you choose," Ariya said. "Which one of you wants to control the drone and which one the laptop?"

They looked at each other.

"You are more of a video game person," Mahvash said.

She took over the laptop while Farzaneh took control of the drone.

"For those of you who don't have experience with such things," Ariya said. "This is very much like playing a video game...Go ahead and show them," she told Farzaneh. "Move the drone around."

As she did, Ariya had Mahvash turn the laptop screen around so the other women could watch.

"You see? The drone will relay its images down to this laptop and Mahvash will then instruct Farzaneh to move the drone this way or that, based on what she wants to view. Imagine you are out on patrol and suspect the enemy is nearby. This drone will allow you to search for them with far less risk to your safety."

Ariya signaled for Farzaneh to bring the drone back down to the table.

"Now, the drone has an operational height of 500 meters but for most purposes, you will be hovering at around 150 meters. In a forest setting, like today, the enemy is not likely to spot it up through the trees so you can afford to hover even closer. Let us imagine you are approaching a village in open terrain and want to have an advanced view of the situation, you will likely choose to operate closer to maximum height, where the enemy cannot easily spot it. We have more of these but each team will only have one to start, so if the enemy shoots it down, you will not only have lost your drone, you will have lost the element of surprise. This charger will allow you to keep both the drone and laptop operational while out on patrol but it does need sunlight and time to charge, so these are factors you will have to keep in mind. It is unlikely that you will have a chance to plug into somebody's wall socket...Any questions so far?"

The women shook their heads.

"Good, then here is the plan for today's exercise. Once we are up in the forest, Kejal, Irem and I will break away and pretend to be an attacking Taliban force. Your assignment is to use what you have learned the past two days and this drone to find us. If you spot one of us before we spot you, we will consider ourselves dead and sit down so that everyone knows we have been killed. Or the other way around. Understood?"

The women nodded.

"Very well. I have chosen Veeda to be your team leader for today. Any objections?"

No one spoke up.

"Good. Then grab your weapons and move out."

The team headed down the valley for a mile and then north up a wooded slope beneath a crisp and brilliant blue sky. The snowcapped mountains peeked out through the pines here and there and the wind kept whisking clumps of snow from the limbs as they climbed.

They had gained roughly a thousand feet of elevation when they came over a crest and onto a plateau. Ariya stopped the patrol.

"Okay, you are to remain here until you hear gunfire. That will be your signal that the battle has begun. And a warning. We will be using live ammunition."

Seeing the looks of concern, Ariya quickly reassured them.

"There is nothing to fear. We will be shooting well over your heads but it is important to instill in you the real urgency of war. You must act today as if it is a matter of life and death. Veeda, as the leader, your primary objective is to protect your team while neutralizing the enemy. There is no perfect answer. Use whatever intel you can gather and make the best decisions possible."

Kejal and Irem had already turned away.

"Good luck," Ariya said before turning to join them. "We will discuss things once the exercise is complete. And remember. Wait for the sound of gunfire."

As those three disappeared to the east, the other women gathered together and exchanged looks.

"Is this not where we get down in a defensive posture?" Mahvash said to Veeda.

Veeda reviewed her and everyone else with her usual fierceness.

"Yes, but first we must establish a secure perimeter so spread out, as they taught us. And use a tree for cover. Mahvash and Farzaneh, you stay near me," she added before they could drift away.

With everyone in position, the women searched the woods around them with regular glances back at each other.

Most of five minutes had gone by when they heard gunfire and the bullets tore through the limbs above their heads.

"I think the bullets are coming from two directions," Tabaan said.

Veeda gestured at her throat while staring at Tabaan.

Tabaan stared back for a moment before pointing to her ear and off into the woods east and west. Veeda looked from face to face until all the other women had concurred.

With everyone in agreement, Veeda gave Farzaneh a nod and the drone rose up through the trees. Veeda noticed Hajira and Noushineh watching it and signaled for them to keep their eyes on the surrounding woods. Noushineh did so quickly. Hajira glared back before following orders but the message had been conveyed. Veeda was the boss, like it or not.

By this point, Farzaneh had guided the drone well above the trees and some distance to the east. Having found no sign of the enemy, Veeda signaled for Farzaneh to turn north. Veeda glanced over her shoulder to make sure the other women were maintaining their watch and turned her attention back to the laptop.

The minutes passed with no sign of the enemy so Veeda instructed Farzaneh to go up higher. The view from the drone widened out to a larger area but there was still no sign of them.

Veeda pointed to a nearby hilltop on the screen and whispered to Mahvash and Farzaneh.

"Let us send a patrol up to this position. It is always good to command the high ground and maybe a team will be better able to spot something from there."

"But how will we know what they know?" Mahvash said.

"You will signal to us and we will move the drone."

Mahvash made a sarcastic face and Veeda made one back.

Before dragging Mahvash and the laptop over to Esin, Veeda gestured for Farzaneh to remain vigilant and waved for Tabaan to join them.

"Do you see this high ground?"

Both Tabaan and Esin nodded.

"Take Darsameen and Hajira, secure this location and search for the enemy from that vantage point. If you spot them, then gesture in which direction. We will be watching you with the drone."

The two women started to move out.

"Remember to be vigilant," Veeda whispered after them. "Eyes in all directions."

As the four women moved off in a sweep and search formation, Veeda waved for Farzaneh to join her.

"Lock the drone into position over that site and help me to maintain our perimeter. You too, Mahvash."

Mahvash took the laptop and moved away a few trees. Farzaneh took the drone controls and did the same in the other direction. Veeda turned her attention from the departing patrol to the other women around her and then back to the surrounding woods.

A few minutes passed before Mahvash motioned to Veeda and pointed with two fingers at her eyes. Veeda scampered over to have a look at the laptop. The women had reached a gathering of rocks on the hill and were searching the terrain below them.

More time passed and Veeda had begun to reconsider her strategy when she noticed Esin gesturing up at the drone and pointing off towards the southwest. Veeda signaled to get Farzaneh's attention and pointed in that direction.

Farzaneh moved the drone in a southwest bearing until Kejal came into view. She was alone and moving from tree to tree towards their perimeter.

"Where are the others?" Mahvash whispered.

Veeda flashed a look her way and signaled for Farzaneh to take the drone higher. While the drone was ascending, Veeda stared off to the west again, thinking. When both Kejal and their own patrol were in the same view, Mahvash touched Veeda's arm to get her attention. Kejal was roughly two hundred yards off and still moving their way.

Veeda turned to Mahvash.

"Take Farzaneh and go explain to the others what is happening. I will take the other three and go ambush Kejal."

"Should not we be considering where the other two enemy soldiers might be?"

"It does not matter," Veeda whispered. "They are not anywhere nearby, according to the drone."

"They could be hiding and waiting to ambush us."

"It still does not matter. We must act."

"I think we should stick together. We are only putting ourselves at more risk by splitting up again."

"You are creating more risk by arguing with me! Now I'm ordering you to go join the other team and communicate the strategy to them."

Mahvash reluctantly turned to leave.

"And make sure Farzaneh keeps the drone directly above Kejal. It will help guide us to her. Then once we have neutralized Kejal, we will look to see where the drone is moving. If you have spotted Ariya or Irem or both of them, lead us that way. If we see the drone moving towards your position, we will know to rejoin you and we will resume our planning from there."

"And if you are neutralized along the way?"

"Then you can be in charge and do whatever you wish. Now go."

Veeda watched Mahvash leave before dashing over to Saarah's position and waving for Noushineh and Kashm to join them.

"Keep your eyes on the perimeter," Veeda whispered when she saw Noushineh staring. "All of you."

Veeda too kept searching the woods in all directions as she explained her plan.

"Any questions?" she said.

"Yes," Saarah said. "If you neutralize Kejal, how will we know it? And the other way around."

Veeda stared fiercely for a moment before looking off into the woods.

"May these Kurds be cut into a thousand pieces and devoured by dogs. This was no way to send us into war in the first place. We should have been given phones or radios or some way to communicate."

"But we do not have phones or radios," Saarah said.

"No, we do not, and what we do have, I will not speak out loud."

"We could knock on a tree with the butt of our rifle if we are successful."

"Fine. I will listen for that sound and you do the same. Now let us move out."

Veeda and Noushineh headed south with Noushineh providing rear cover. Saarah and Kashm headed north with Saarah watching their rear. She had one eye on Veeda and Noushineh off to her right as she backed her way along. So far, Saarah had not seen any sign of the enemy's tracks. There were advantages and disadvantages to having snow on the ground. On the plus side, it silenced your footsteps. On the down side, it left a track of your every movement.

Once Veeda and Noushineh had disappeared off through the trees, Kashm put a hand on Saarah's arm and stopped her.

"I think we should take cover and wait for Kejal to come to us."

"That is not how we agreed." Kashm shrugged. "And if they get into trouble?"

"They could get into trouble either way," Kashm said. "At least one team will still be alive."

"I do not agree but it is best we do something. If we sit here arguing, we will surely be dead.."

Kashm nodded at a fallen log twenty yards to their south. Saarah nodded back and the two women ran that way with heads down.

Once they were safely out of sight, Kashm turned with her back to the log and covered their rear. Saarah set her rifle atop the log and used a freshly fallen pine bough to camouflage the gun barrel.

Time passed. They watched and waited. Remembering the drone, Saarah looked up through the trees but it was nowhere in sight.

The minutes dragged on and Saarah was beginning to question the wisdom of Kashm's plan when something moved off through the forest. She carefully reached out for Kashm's arm. When Kashm turned to look, Saarah pointed off to the west. Kejal had appeared, about fifty yards away. There was no sign of Veeda and Noushineh.

Saarah sensed Kashm getting anxious and placed a hand on her arm. Kejal was still moving towards them tree by tree, her eyes and ears alert for any sign of the enemy. At the last second, with Kejal nearly upon them, Saarah jumped up with her rifle pointed.

"You are dead."

Kejal settled down with her back to a pine tree, staring. Saarah and Kashm ran over and crouched down beside her.

"Keep a look out," Kashm told Saarah and turned to Kejal. "Where are the others?"

"How can I tell you? I'm dead."

"We could torture you."

Kejal smirked.

"We are wasting time," Saarah said and knocked three times on the tree with the butt of her rifle.

"Veeda was right," Kashm whispered. "We should have been given phones or radios to communicate. Who knows what's going on with the others?"

Kejal was smiling now.

"I could still torture you," Kashm said with a smirk.

After waiting another minute, Saarah stood up.

"Let us leave her and go find Veeda and Noushineh."

"I think we should return to the rest of the team. They have the drone controls and laptop. We are blind without them and have no idea what we may find up ahead."

"Leave no one behind," Saarah reminded Kashm.

"Fine, but if we don't find them quickly, I say we should go join the others."

Kashm had another smile for Kejal before moving off.

With Kashm covering their rear now, she spotted the drone up through the trees and reached out for Saarah's arm. Saarah looked back and Kashm pointed up. The drone had hovered over them briefly but now started moving off in a northwest direction.

"They must be trying to guide us," Kashm whispered.

Saarah continued on point with Kashm covering their rear. A hundred yards farther on, they came upon Veeda and Noushineh. Both of them were sitting with their backs against a tree.

"What happened?" Kashm said, crouching down in front of them.

"We are dead, what do you think? Where were you?"

"We moved ahead for a while and then waited in ambush."

"So you did not follow orders."

"The orders were to kill Kejal, which we did."

"And got us killed in doing so."

"You got yourselves killed."

"Eh, you talk too much. Go join the others before they are all dead too."

"I'm sorry," Kashm said. "We did our best."

Veeda stared at her fiercely.

"We must go," Saarah said, seeing the drone head off towards high ground and the rest of the team.

Some distance ahead, they came to a clearing and saw the hilltop opposite them. Saarah revealed herself and waved. A moment later, Esin showed herself and waved back.

Resuming their search and clear posture, Saarah and Kashm moved across the clearing and climbed up through the trees to the hilltop. They found Irem sitting against a rock with the other women around her.

"Is she dead?" Kashm asked.

"What do you think?" Hajira said.

"So there is only Ariya left."

"She is only an observer," Irem said.

"She has already told us this but I don't think we should trust her."

Irem smiled.

"It is good that you are wary but on the grave of my mother, I tell you, the battle is over...Shoot off my rifle into the air," Irem added as the women looked to each other. "Ariya will appear shortly with her hands up."

"What do we have to lose?" Mahvash said.

"Our advantage," Tabaan said.

Irem just sat there smiling.

"Oh, fine," Kashm said. "Just shoot off one round."

Hajira did and the women got down behind the rocks to watch and wait. A minute later, Ariya appeared at the edge of the clearing with Kejal and Veeda and Noushineh at her side. Ariya pretended to wave the white flag and Esin waved back.

Soon, all thirteen women were standing together on the hilltop.

"For making so many mistakes," Ariya said. "You did well."

"Mistakes," Veeda said. "The biggest mistake was sending us out like this without the proper equipment."

"Yes, you should have had radios."

"Exactly as I said."

"And I heard you say it. Quite loudly."

Veeda looked fiercely at Ariya.

"Yes. As Irem has probably told you, I was just an observer today. While Irem and Kejal spread out, I stayed nearby and watched you with my binoculars."

"So it was a trap."

Ariya chuckled and put a hand on Veeda's shoulder.

"Like I said, you did good, but let me tell you what you did wrong. Or at least what you might have done differently. This is not to punish anyone. It is only to learn and become better, yes?"

With varying degrees of enthusiasm, the women all nodded.

"Okay, first of all, it was good that you decided to take the high ground, but failing some imminent threat calling you to do otherwise, it would have been wiser to take the entire team with you, then split up based on your observations from this superior vantage point."

"Just as I told you," Mahvash said.

"Eh," Veeda said. "With some form of modern communication, there would not have been these problems."

"You are right, Veeda, and let me assure all of you right now. Before going into battle, you will be given all the latest equipment. Everything the Americans have. Phones and radios. Night vision goggles. Plated vests for protection and magazine bandoliers. Remember too that each time you eliminate some of the enemy, you will be adding their gear to your own arsenal. Guns, ammunition, grenades. Whatever they have that you can use, you will confiscate. But that is for another day. For now, it was important to see how you would do without all these advantages. Even with all the latest gear, you may find yourselves in a firefight someday where you have lost your radio, or your night vision goggles. Where you will have to make do as best you can with less, like today. Understood?"

Again the nods came with varying degrees of enthusiasm.

"So yes, Veeda. There were many things you might have done differently. By splitting up your team before you had established a strategically superior position, you quickly lost control of the situation, but overall, you did good. You were decisive and took action. This is extremely important. As I told you at the start, there is no perfect solution. There is simply the best decision based on the intel you have at hand. What you don't want when under attack is to sit there and do nothing...Now, as to the rest. Saarah and Kashm, your ambush was commendable, but you broke a cardinal rule of good soldiery. You disobeyed an order. Yes, you killed one of the enemy, but you got two of your own team killed in doing so."

"They would have been killed anyway," Kashm said.

"You don't know that. But what we do know is that in a real firefight, you were not there to back up your own team members."

Kashm shrugged.

"No, it is true," Ariya said. "Otherwise, if I could fault your team for anything, it would be for too much talking. There is no easier way to get yourself killed than to sit around arguing with each other."

"If we had had these radios..."

"Yes, you will have all of that," Ariya said, cutting Veeda off.

Ariya looked around at all the faces again with a smile.

"I am proud of you. For the first time in battle, you worked fairly well together as a team. Now, let's go have lunch and afterwards we will find out who is our best shot with the sniper rifle."

Eleven

Spring had soon passed away and in long, hot summer days that followed, the women grew strong as warriors and evermore eager to take on the enemy. By virtue of her size and strength and steely resolve, the team had come to accept Veeda as their natural leader and Saarah had been chosen as their sniper on the basis of both her excellent marksmanship and stealth. From all her years growing up in the wild, she had learned to move through the fields and among the trees like the wind.

The rest of the women too had settled into their various roles, with perhaps the most important one being Esin as their team medic. Every team member carried a small medical kit on their vest, to be used on themselves if Esin wasn't available, but only she had a complete blow out kit, with tourniquets, packing gauze, Ace bandages, Sam splints, antibiotics, morphine, IV bags, sutures, quick clot, medical shears and chest wound gear for lung issues. As long as a bullet wound had not been fatal, Esin was equipped to treat any trauma, be it broken bones, stitching up major cuts, dealing with burns and giving CPR.

Every week, a man named Qammar drove up from Kabul with fresh supplies and brought along news from the world, and the most disheartening news of all was that the new American president had agreed to honor the withdrawal plan negotiated by his predecessor. That date was yet six months away but the finality of it had left nearly everyone in Afghanistan fearing the worst. It seemed to be only a matter of time now before Kabul fell and the Taliban retook power.

As promised, the team had been provided with all the necessary equipment, including radios for communication, combat helmets with night vision goggles and load bearing protective vests to go with their other gear. Veeda had also been provided with a satellite phone to stay in touch with Ariya and the outside world as needed.

After breakfast, everyone gathered out in front of the barracks and waited to receive instructions for that day's mission. Ariya appeared and went down the line, inspecting each soldier.

Satisfied, she stood back to face the team.

"Well, as we have discussed, this will be our final week of training. Yes, I know. I have seen it in your faces for weeks. You are eager to break camp and move on to the real fight but you must never forget the gravity of what lies ahead. Some of you will die in this struggle. That is the nature of war. People die, and not always on the other side."

Kejal went down the line passing out three live magazines to each woman. Saarah received one extra magazine for her Dragunov sniper rifle. She had become proficient at carrying both rifles and kept the AK slung over her back until it was needed.

Ariya looked from face to face.

"From now on, you will be carrying live ammunition and for today's patrol, Kejal and I have placed various targets around the area where you conducted your first patrol. Your goal is to find and terminate each of them. Are there any questions?"

There was silence.

"Very well, then. Everyone move out."

They marched down the valley on that hot summer day and passed over the now slow moving stream. The buzz of insects reminded Saarah of home and the dreams of her youth. She had planned to be a scholar, a diplomat, a doctor, an astronaut. Now she was a warrior, forced into that role by a simple truth. If the Taliban retook power, there would be no schools for women, no scholarships, no diplomacy, no dreams. There would only be those zealous brutes everywhere you turned, stealing from you your freedom and ordering you what to do.

She had considered at one point running away to Europe, or America, but Saarah had already run away once and would not do so again. If a person's freedom was not worth dying for, then nothing was.

Having crossed the valley, the team began climbing up through the wooded slopes. Here and there, a white cloud crossed the blue sky. The pines sighed above their heads in the heat of the day.

The team had learned long ago to be ever alert, ever watchful, ever listening and ready to fire and kill. To treat every moment as if the enemy might be around the next corner, and they did it well now.

When they reached the high plateau, Ariya turned to face them.

"The three of us will be higher up on the mountain, so as not to take fire. You are now trained well enough to know what to do. We will be listening in on our radios and afterwards will sit down to discuss the exercise with you. Good luck and God be with you."

As Ariya, Kejal and Irem headed farther up the mountain, Veeda gave some hand signals and the team spread out in formation, their movements now instinctively synchronized and cohesive. Without thinking, the women moved as if they were one organism, the space between them bending and flexing as the terrain required but never breaking its bonds, and with Saarah always roaming nearby, keeping a close eye on them as their over watch.

The team had swept one edge of the plateau for a quarter of a mile when Tabaan, who was on point, suddenly took cover on one knee. The other women quickly dropped and took cover too.

Tabaan pressed the call button on her radio and whispered.

"A hostile to the southwest at one hundred yards. Requesting permission to engage."

"Permission granted."

Tabaan took aim, fired one shot and hit the round metal target almost center on.

"Hostile terminated," she whispered over the radio.

"Roger that," Veeda whispered back. "Proceed with patrol."

All the more alert now, the team rose up and moved out again.

As Tabaan neared the downed target, Hajira, who was near the back of the team, suddenly dropped to one knee and signaled towards the northeast. Her action quickly rippled through the entire team, with everyone else taking cover and maintaining a lookout in all directions.

"What is our status," Veeda whispered over the radio.

"I thought I saw something move behind us."

"Direction?"

"To the northeast."

"Something," Veeda said, rhetorically.

"Something."

"It could have been a deer then."

"It could have been a deer."

Hajira was still staring off through the trees to the northeast. The seconds passed. The rest of the team kept stealing glances her way.

"Permission to explore, team leader."

"I'm not sure that's part of our mission today," Veeda said.

"Your call, but I know I saw something."

"Very well. Take Darsameen with you. The rest of the team, hold your positions, observe and give cover."

Hajira and Darsameen had moved forward but a short distance when they heard the muffled pop of Saarah's sniper rifle, followed by a bullet slapping into something solid and a deathly gasp off through the woods. For a brief instant, there was silence, then suddenly many guns were firing and a torrent of live rounds tore through the trees.

"What in the mother of god is going on?" Veeda called over the radio. "If this is part of the drill, I will personally be sending Irem and the two Kurds back to meet their maker."

"This is not a drill," Ariya called back. "I repeat, this is not a drill. You have engaged an actual hostile force."

Saarah clicked in over the continuing din of small arms fire.

"It was me. I spotted someone getting ready to shoot at Hajira and had no choice but to fire."

"Size and direction of this hostile force," Veeda said.

"Six Taliban that I can see, not counting the one I terminated. And to your northeast, as Hajira had said."

"Nature of their armaments."

"AKs with one hostile carrying an RPG and extra rounds in his pack."

While they were talking, the fusillade suddenly stopped and there was silence.

"Do we still command the hill in that direction?" Veeda whispered.

"I think so, yes."

"You think so."

"I have not seen any hostiles coming up this way. I am waiting for Ariya and the others to join me."

"Very well. Rear cover team, fall back, pivot to the base of the hill and report in as soon as you have locked that high ground. Farzaneh, fall back somewhere safe and get that drone in the air. I need more intel. Noushineh, you fall back too and give Farzaneh cover. Mahvash, you and that laptop stay here with me. The rest of you, fan out to our southeast. We cannot let these dogs outflank us."

Veeda sat there peering off into the forest, her mind furiously sorting through the various options. One thing was certain. This was for real now. This was actual combat, where people got killed.

"Where are you, Ariya?" Veeda whispered into the radio.

"We just rendezvoused with Saarah. Fifty yards up the hill and east of your rear team. No sign of the enemy. They must have taken cover. We will maintain sufficient elevation to avoid any friendly fire and provide support from this vantage point."

"Farzaneh, anything yet?"

"The drone is just coming up past the trees."

"Any day now."

"It is a drone, not a rocket."

In the silence, Veeda heard the muffled pop of Saarah's rifle again, followed by more yelling and return fire.

"What is going on?" Veeda said.

"I saw someone trying to make a call on his satellite phone."

"Is he dead?"

"He is not moving."

"Was he successful in making the call?"

"That I do not know. Possibly."

"Can you please just shoot all of them for us."

"The rest have taken cover."

Veeda sat there staring off into the forest again, waiting.

"I do not like this silence…Rear team, exactly where are you?"

"Up the hill and a hundred yards west of Saarah and the others. All secure here."

"I see them," Mahvash said.

Veeda scrambled over to her tree and looked at the laptop screen. Mahvash pointed.

"They have taken cover in this gully below the ridge."

While Veeda stared at the five surviving hostiles and considered her plan of attack, Farzaneh brought the drone up a bit higher and panned to the southeast.

"Mother of god," Veeda said.

She was quickly back on the radio.

"They are not alone! A backup team is pushing its way up the hill from the southeast! I'm counting at least twelve men! We need to secure that ridge before these dogs can join forces! Are you able to eliminate the five existing hostiles, Ariya?"

"I cannot see them."

"Can you see the drone?"

"Yes."

"Our target is directly below it. In that gully."

"There is fifty yards of open terrain between us and them."

"Okay. Rear cover team, I need you to proceed across the hill to their position and provide cover fire. Farzaneh, you stay back with Noushineh and keep your eyes on this situation. I'm proceeding southeast with the rest of the team to engage this backup force. The rest of you are to join us as soon as the initial hostiles have been terminated. We need to hold that ridge!"

Taking Darsameen, Hajira, Kashm and Mahvash with her, Veeda made a dash to the south edge of the plateau and stopped there to view the laptop screen. The Taliban backup force was still a hundred and fifty yards down the hill but had scattered well apart as they made their way up. Veeda keyed up her radio.

"We are about to engage these dogs from hell but will not be able to hold them alone. I have at least a dozen hostiles in my sights and they're scattered all across the hill. I need you to terminate the existing force *now* and provide us with backup."

Veeda ended the transmission, waved to the other women and they dashed together north along the ridgeline until they were centered above the approaching force. With another look at the laptop screen, Veeda signaled for the team to spread out left and right at ten yard intervals and take cover.

They had just settled in and taken aim when a firefight broke out to their left. The Taliban, unaware that a patrol stood above them, turned laterally across the hill in the direction of the gunfire, exposing their flanks. Veeda signaled and the five women tore into them with a shower of bullets. Four men dropped in their tracks and the remaining hostiles took cover, shouting among themselves and sending a wild volley of shots up the hill.

With the firefight ongoing to her left, Veeda called over her radio.

"Backup enemy force pinned down. A hundred yards below the ridge. At least four terminated. What is your status?"

Ariya called in a few seconds later.

"One hostile terminated. Preparing a grenade attack to flush out the rest or kill them in position."

"Roger that."

The women barely had time to brace themselves when the grenade exploded and the shock wave ripped through the woods.

Meanwhile, the Taliban men down the hill had abandoned all caution and were charging up the hill in a fusillade of gunfire and curses.

"We need backup!" Veeda called over the radio. "Repeat! We need backup! We cannot hold this ridge much longer by ourselves!"

With bullets slapping into the trees around her, Veeda took a grenade from her vest, pulled the pin and peeked out from behind her tree long enough to see where she was throwing it.

"Grenade!" she called out, then as soon as it had exploded, she called out again. "Return fire, but make your shots count! Our ammo is limited!"

She had turned to look back down the hill when one of the Taliban leapt up from below and bowled her over backwards. Before she could point her rifle and fire, he grabbed the barrel and held it to one side. When Veeda kicked back violently at his legs, hoping to knock him over, her helmet came off and the man stared down in astonishment.

122

"A woman?" he said, his astonishment turning to indignation. "You would insult Allah and the prophet Mohammed by using a gun?"

He had pointed his rifle when a shot rang out to his left and the back of his skull blew off. Veeda squirmed out of the way with a final kick of disgust at the dead body.

"May you die without leaving a son, you flea ridden mongrel!"

"You are welcome," Kashm said when Veeda looked her way.

Veeda pulled out her radio.

"Where is our backup force?! I repeat! Where is our backup force?!"

Ariya's voice crackled over the radio.

"We have just confirmed enemy status. All hostiles in the gully are dead. We are confiscating their weapons and ammo and will be headed your way. What is your status?"

"Enemy force everywhere on the hill below us and continuing to approach. I count at least seven hostiles terminated but more of them keep appearing. The gates of hell must have opened."

"Can you outflank them to their left?"

"I would love to, if I could find their flank. They are everywhere."

"We will engage their right flank, Veeda. If necessary, retreat to the south and let them take the ridge. Then we will be able to attack them from both flanks and their rear."

"Roger that. I would prefer not allowing them to take this ridge but we may have no choice."

"Understood, but remember. If you are attacking their left flank, we may be opposite you."

"Yes, we shall be cautious."

Veeda ended the call and scrambled over to Mahvash. She was alternately firing down the hill and ducking behind her tree to avoid enemy fire. The laptop sat open next to her.

As much as Veeda could see from both the drone and looking down the hill, it appeared that the enemy was still advancing while stringing out through the trees in both directions.

Veeda cursed and called on the radio again.

"At least four hostiles approaching your position, Ariya. Fifty yards out. It appears they are trying to flank us in that direction too."

Veeda clicked off and thought for a second before hitting the call button again.

"Everyone needs to retreat. You too, Ariya. You are about to be overwhelmed. We are abandoning this ridge. Farzaneh, I need you to provide diversion fire from your position. I want the enemy to think we are all retreating to the west. When I call back, you are to move up the hill to your north. Ariya, retreat two hundred yards along the hill to Farzaneh's position. We will try to clear their left flank and come in from their rear. And Saarah, please start shooting someone with that long gun of yours. We are on the move now."

Veeda waved to the other four women and together they turned tail towards the south. In the distance, off to their right, they heard Farzaneh let off several rounds. Moments later, they heard shouts and knew that the Taliban had taken the ridge. In that same instant, they had reached the southern edge of the plateau and leapt out of sight.

Having rolled down the hill some distance, Veeda scrambled back up and peered over the edge.

"Give me eyes," she said to Mahvash.

She had just scrambled back up with the other four women and opened the laptop for Veeda to see. With a quick view of the screen, Veeda called to Farzaneh over the radio.

"Farzaneh, I need you to fire again and retreat, fire and retreat while moving up the hill. Ariya, the hostiles have all cleared the ridge now. I count seventeen of them. Hold your fire until you hear our assault from the rear. I'm leaving Mahvash behind to monitor the enemy movements from her laptop. They outnumber us so this is our only advantage. As soon as you hear us fire, the battle is on. And God be with you."

Veeda clicked off and looked at the women around her.

"Spread out ten yards and move tree to tree until we spot the enemy. And Mahvash, I want second by second updates. Left, right. How many and how many yards. And quiet as the wind. Everything whispered now."

Veeda pointed at the screen.

"These four dogs right here. We will take them out first."

She looked from face to face again, nodded, and the four women moved cautiously up over the ridge.

In the stillness of the forest, Veeda heard a jay call. Insects buzzed in the dappled sunlight. The summer day had grown listless with heat, their battle gear heavy. The women moved forward slowly, covering each other as they did.

Mahvash's voice whispered over the radio.

"Veeda, one hundred yards ahead and to your left. All clear to your right flank."

Veeda signaled for her team to pivot forty-five degrees. They were now facing northwest. Mahvash's voice came over the radios again, updating the other women on enemy movements. Two Taliban were combing the lower edge of the hill. Ariya called in. Her team had retreated farther up the hill to avoid engagement until further word from Veeda.

Veeda signaled again and her team moved ahead one tree and then another one. Then Hajira suddenly raised her right hand and pointed.

Off through the trees, Veeda saw one moving. Then a second man appeared, and a third and fourth one. The team exchanged hand signals and moved ahead another hundred feet before stopping. The four hostiles were fifty yards away and blind to the danger at their backs.

Veeda turned her fierce gaze at the other women, pointed her weapon and nodded. A moment later, the stillness of the afternoon was torn apart by the bark of their rifles and the four men dropped where they were.

The jay let out a racket and took flight downwind.

Farther off in the distance, the Taliban had begun firing wildly and shouting, their commotion interspersed with the careful pop of friendly fire coming from up on the hill.

Mahvash called over the radio.

"Veeda, seven hostiles are rushing towards your position."

Veeda signaled and the four women took off running to the south with bullets ripping through the forest all around them. It seemed to be random fire, but being in flight, the women had no way of knowing for sure.

Once they had taken cover again, Veeda called in.

"Do we have their flank?"

"Move one hundred yards west and you will. But watch out, Ariya. I see two hostiles starting up the hill on your right."

"I have them in my sights," Saarah whispered back.

"Repositioning to the west now," Veeda said and clicked off.

She nodded and her team raced west along the edge of the plateau.

Up on the hill, the firefight was ongoing. Veeda signaled for her team to assume proper patrol spacing in an east/west line and they started forward tree by tree again while watching their flanks.

"That is one down," Mahvash said a moment later.

"One down?" Veeda called back.

"I'm talking to Saarah…And there, the second hostile is down."

"What is our status?" Veeda said.

"They're fifty yards to the other side of that brush ahead of you. Oh, wait. They just turned north towards Ariya's position."

"So we have their backs now?" Veeda said.

"You have their backs but they are moving fast to the north."

"Then we will move swiftly with them. Farzaneh, follow them with the drone and Mahvash keep us posted. We do not want to crawl up their backs."

"Roger that."

"And join the battle if everything else is clear."

"I will."

Veeda signaled for the team to maintain combat readiness in all directions and they moved out in a trot. Once they had cleared the wall of brush and could see clearly through the forest again, Veeda signaled for the team to stop and observe. They got down on one knee with their ears pinned back, listening for any sound of footsteps in the brush and pine needles. The hill was two hundred yards ahead and the enemy nowhere in sight.

"Veeda," Mahvash said. "They are still a hundred yards closer to the hill than you but moving north from tree to tree now."

Veeda signaled for the team to move out again.

Fifty yards farther on, Hajira dropped to one knee and the other team members dropped with her. She signaled with two fingers to her eyes and pointed north. Off in the distance, five of the seven men had come into view. Veeda keyed up her radio and whispered.

"Where are the other two?"

Mahvash called back.

"They have flanked far to the left and right. You are free to engage the five hostiles now in your sights."

Veeda paused to think before keying up her radio again.

"All right. We will terminate these five then split into two teams and chase down the other two separately.

The women nodded, took aim and quickly shredded the five men from the back.

"Five more down," Veeda whispered. "Fanning out east and west. You are clear to attack, Ariya. Repeat. You are clear to attack. There are only four hostiles still active below you."

"Three," Ariya said. "Saarah just took out one more of them."

"Very well. Let us end this thing. I am sick of both death and the Taliban."

"Agreed. Let us end this thing. And then we will talk. You do realize that we no longer have a home."

Veeda paused for a moment, considering those words.

"So be it," she said and clicked off.

Veeda signaled that she and Darsameen would move west. Hajira and Kashm were to move east. With an additional signal urging caution, the two teams headed out. Off in the distance, the sound of Ariya and her team engaging the enemy echoed through the forest.

Veeda moved forward fifty yards and stopped. There was no sign of the hostile.

"What is our status?" she asked Mahvash. "Mahvash?" she repeated when there was no answer.

"Sorry," Mahvash radioed back a moment later. "I was moving to a more forward position...I'm looking now. Looking...Okay, the one to your east is fifty yards up ahead. You have his back. I don't think he knows what he's doing."

"That is useful intel."

"Just terminate him...The other one has moved to join the attack on Ariya's position."

"All right. Guide Hajira and Kashm after that dog. Darsameen and I will dispense with this one and join the battle from the west."

"Roger that."

Veeda and Darsameen moved slowly from tree to tree until they spotted the other man. He was young and looked lost without someone to guide him. Veeda looked at Darsameen and shook her head. It was like killing a child. She took aim but hesitated again before putting two bullets into his back.

There was another long pause before Veeda keyed up her radio.

"It is done. We are moving out towards your position."

"Watch yourselves," Ariya said. "We have the last three on the run but they are still alive and armed."

"Headed which way?"

"Southeast. Back from where they came."

"We see them," Hajira said.

"We are on our way," Veeda confirmed and moved out with Darsameen on point.

When they stopped over the dead hostile, Veeda stood guard while Darsameen gathered everything useful. When she was done, Darsameen stood up and saw Veeda staring. She too looked down at the young man's face. He hardly had whiskers and could not have been more than sixteen. Darsameen took Veeda by the arm.

"He would have killed us if we had not killed him first."

Veeda looked at her and stared.

"Come," Darsameen said. "We must join the others."

Veeda nodded and gave rear cover with Darsameen on point again. A minute later, as they were nearing Ariya's position, they heard gunfire farther off in the forest.

"Status?" Ariya asked, keying up her radio.

"We are engaged with the three hostiles," Hajira radioed back. "But running out of ammo and in need of backup."

"We are on our way."

Saarah had been making her way down the hill this whole time and once all eight women had finally rendezvoused, they ran towards the gunfire. As soon as they spotted Hajira and Kashm, they dropped into a cover position. The two women were pinned down just below the ridge with bullets clipping off the trees and brush all around them.

"We have your back," Ariya called over the radio. "But at risk of taking friendly fire."

"Roger that," Hajira said. "Holding fire."

When they did, the return fire eventually stopped and silence followed.

Some moments later, one of the Taliban cautiously poked out his head. The women watched and waited until the other two had revealed themselves before firing. All three men quickly slumped over and stopped moving. Ariya signaled for the women to stop firing and the forest was silent again.

"Maintain alertness," she whispered and took Hajira with her to check the three downed men. Seeing that all of them already had bullets in their brain cavities, she didn't bother with adding another one and keyed up her radio.

"All clear here. Your status, Farzaneh, Mahvash and Noushineh."

"Moving your way," Farzaneh radioed back.

"Roger that," Mahvash said.

"Roger that," Noushineh said.

"Remain alert," Ariya said.

Hajira and Kashm appeared cautiously from over the ridge and gathered with the other women. They shared looks and glanced down at the three dead men. It turned their stomachs to see men up close with parts of their heads missing. All of the women were bloodied and bruised and looked stunned by what had happened.

They had been watching and waiting for another minute when they heard footsteps approach from off in the woods and collectively turned their heads. Seeing Noushineh raise her weapon with alarm, they spun back towards the ridge as a volley of bullets barked out behind them. Noushineh had cut the man down and everyone now stared at this latest dead body. It was lying half above and half below the ridge.

"What in holy hell?" Veeda said.

"He must have been one of the hostiles you shot down below earlier," Ariya said.

"Oh god no!" Saarah cried out and dropped to her knees.

Kashm lay there gasping through blood. Esin was quickly at her side and trying desperately to stop the bleeding but Kashm had taken a hit in the neck.

"Kill them," Kashm managed to whisper.

Her eyes turned towards Saarah.

"Kill all of them for me."

Before she could speak again, her chest heaved and her eyes glazed over. Saarah fell on her chest in grief.

"Oh, my dear friend, my dear friend!"

All of the Afghan women dropped to their knees around Saarah, having abandoned all caution.

The two Kurds stood back and shared a silent look. They had known this kind of grief far too many times already.

Ariya eventually placed a hand on Saarah's back and looked from face to face.

"It is my fault. We did not remain vigilant."

"No, it is my fault," Veeda said.

"It is everyone's fault," Kejal said. "In our gladness to see our team members return safely, we broke a cardinal rule."

Saarah looked up at them, her face and hands stained with blood.

"If not for her, I would never have been here."

The women embraced Saarah again, having no words to comfort her. Finally, Ariya encouraged Saarah to stand up.

"We must bury her quickly and move on."

"Not here," Saarah said.

"We have no choice. This place is no longer safe for us."

"No," Veeda said. "I will carry Kashm back to the barracks and we will bury her there. Where we all started and our hearts grew as one."

"I will help carry her," Hajira said.

"And I," Esin said.

"We all will," Irem said.

"Very well," Ariya said. "If you insist, but then we must leave the barracks as if no one had ever been there and move on."

"To where?" Mahvash said.

"We shall see. First, we must change into our civilian clothing and get back down from the mountain safely. If we make it that far, we will move to a safe house and consider our next move. I will call ahead and have Qammar come gather our battle gear."

Ariya looked from face to face, knowing from experience that the next 12 hours would be crucial to the future of the movement. There were those who grew faint in the face of such loss, there were those who grew more determined. By tomorrow morning, she would know what it would be with each of these remaining women.

Twelve

Daniel Silva, special assistant to the American ambassador on Taliban affairs, tapped lightly on his boss's door and parted it just enough to poke his head in.

"You called for me, sir?"

Ambassador Douglas glanced up from the document in his hands and waved at Daniel.

"Come in and have a seat. And close the door behind you."

On looks alone, Douglas made a fine ambassador. He was Ivy League from head to toe, with thick, graying hair and stately features.

As Daniel sat down, the ambassador pulled a classified report out of a drawer and passed it across his desk. Daniel glanced at the cover page, had a quick look at his boss and started to read. When he was done, he pushed the report back across the desk.

"When did this arrive?"

"Half an hour ago. The Taliban political leadership claim to have gotten wind of this overnight and are making a big squawk. What's your take?"

"Hard to say, sir. Has anyone tried to verify these claims?"

"Not to my knowledge. As far as I know, you and I are the only two people in Afghanistan who know a thing about it. Besides the Taliban."

"I assume the president has been briefed."

"Oh yes. Blackburn called from D.C., ready to hop out of his pants. If it looks like there's a rogue Afghan element out there we can't control, the peace negotiations unravel and we're back to daily bombings around the capital. Around the entire country. And there goes our graceful exit from Afghanistan."

Daniel shook his head.

"It doesn't make any sense."

"How do you mean?"

"There's nothing up there of value. Certainly nothing strategic. The only thing I can imagine is a local warlord getting into a turf war with the Taliban."

"Anyone come to mind?"

Daniel shrugged.

"Abu-Kar, but the last I heard, he was on good terms with them. That leaves one of our own agencies. Unless you can imagine the Afghan Army going up there to pick a fight on their own...I can't."

"So you think it's possible the Taliban leadership is trying to game us?"

"I don't know. As much as we don't trust them, I'm sure they trust us even less. Maybe they think we're playing them. I'd be happy to take an SP patrol up there and have a look around. If there was an actual battle, there ought to be evidence of it."

"No, no. I'm not about to put your life at risk over this nonsense. It's just a question of whether to call General Marshall over at Bagram or bring in the CIA."

"With all due respect to General Marshall, I'm not so sure the Army's our best call. Too much chance of word leaking out."

"Yes, you're probably right about that."

The ambassador leaned back in his chair and looked out his window.

"You know, back in the nineties, before the Taliban first took over, when I was still a young attaché with State, I remember meeting this Afghan gal at a cocktail party. Old blood. Proud as hell. Royalty somewhere back in her past, and with all kinds of money. She had built a retreat of some kind up that way. I'm guessing from the coordinates that we're talking the same general area. She used to take underprivileged girls up there on weekends and during the summer. Something like a camp for kids back in the States."

"Are you thinking she might be involved in some way?"

"No, I doubt that. The memory just jogged my thoughts. The Taliban had shut her down when they came into power, but maybe she's been operating it again. If so, there might be a caretaker up there who saw something."

"I can look into it, sir."

The ambassador looked back from the window.

"No, no. I'll follow up on that myself. If I can remember her damned name. In the meantime, why don't you take a ride over to Camp Eggers. See if the CIA has picked up on any chatter. And talk to them about sending a team up there. Just make sure they know to keep this off the airwaves for now. I was told to treat it with kid gloves. I'll phone ahead and let Simmons know you're coming."

"I'll head right over, sir."

The ambassador picked up the report and seemed to weigh it in his hands before handing it to Daniel.

"Hell if I take these Taliban people at their word. It wouldn't surprise me to find this was all a wild goose chase but best to check all the boxes. If this withdrawal turns into a debacle, the administration will get its nose bloodied in the next election. Blackburn is going perfectly ballistic over the thought, but of course that's his answer to everything."

Daniel smiled.

"I'll see what I can learn from CIA."

"And report in as soon as you're back."

"I will."

As Daniel went out the door, the ambassador leaned back in his chair and looked out the window again, doing his best to remember that Afghan woman's name.

Back in his office, Daniel called down to the military attaché and requested an armed transport over to Camp Eggers. It was barely a mile down the road, but other than for walking around the perimeter of the embassy building, or dashing across the street for something to eat at the local market, it wasn't wise to go anywhere on foot, even in the Green Zone. Anything to do with the American presence in Afghanistan and you had a target on your back. Intelligence had already thwarted one bombing attempt on the embassy that year.

Daniel placed the classified report in his briefcase, along with some other paperwork, and headed out the door.

Downstairs, his two-man escort was idling alongside the building in a black Suburban. Daniel climbed into the backseat and stared at the embassy as the driver took off. Someone had taken great pains to make the front of it look inviting, adding flowers beds and such, but it still had the appearance of a county jail more than anything else.

The driver raced down to Bibi Mahru Boulevard, turned right, then right again alongside Amani High School and left at the end of the campus. With one more quick right, they were pulling up to Camp Eggers and showing their IDs. A fine-looking, two-foot thick stone wall guarded the entrance, not high enough to exude paranoia, but high enough to keep a suicide bomber from conveniently penetrating the perimeter. A line of international flags waved in the breeze behind the wall.

Like any other overseas army base, the compound was comprised of both permanent and temporary structures. Over here, it looked like an overly tidy refugee camp. Over there, it could have passed for a Motel Six. All of the permanent buildings were done up in drab tan stucco.

The driver pulled to a stop in front of a building. What looked like a guard tower anchored one end. The roof was bristling with receivers. The adjacent empty lot housed two radio towers.

Daniel went in through the front door. An Army specialist was sitting behind a desk with his feet kicked up, as casual as could be.

"Hey, how's it going, Daniel?" he said.

"Good, Kurt. The station chief should be expecting me."

"Yeah, he called down a minute ago."

Kurt buzzed the metal security door and Daniel pushed his way through.

Simmons' office was up on the second floor. Daniel usually skipped the elevator but the door was open.

Lauren, Simmons' secretary, heard the elevator door ding and looked up with a smile as Daniel exited. Daniel smiled back with a furtive glance at Lauren's mouth. The whole thing seemed to be turned upside down and going the wrong way, as if someone had just told her an off color joke. She was a strawberry blonde with pale skin and lovely eyes but that mouth was enough to make you forget everything else.

"The chief's expecting you," she said.

"Thanks," Daniel said.

He knocked on Simmons' door and opened it part way.

"Good day, sir."

"Come in, come in," Simmons said. "And close the door."

Daniel did and sat down. Simmons stared while Daniel opened his briefcase. Simmons was handsome, in a stern sort of way, with steely grey eyes, a receding hairline and a slight gray mustache A pair of spectacles rested on his straight nose.

"What do we have here?"

"Oh, a bit of a situation. I'll let you read it."

Daniel handed the classified report to Simmons and sat back in his chair to watch. As Simmons flipped through the report, he increasingly looked like he had indigestion.

"You have any direct intel on these claims?" Simmons said, glancing up.

"No. That's one reason why Ambassador Douglas sent me over here. To see if you did."

"Haven't heard a damned thing. This is all news to me."

"Nothing on a rogue unit of some kind working up in that area?"

"Not a thing. You've got Army Special Forces and Seal teams working out of Jalalabad. But up in those mountains? I can't imagine anyone other than the Taliban having a reason to go up there. It has no strategic value...You planning to send someone up to have a look?"

"That was the ambassador's next question for you. He's reluctant to drag in the Army."

"Smart move. If you're trying to keep a lid on this thing, that's the last thing you'd want to do. You send an Army patrol up there and you'll quickly have it all over the evening news."

"That is definitely not what the ambassador wants."

Simmons studied him.

"If I'm reading this correctly, this thing blew up on you out of nowhere and your negotiating team's now sitting across the table from the Taliban with egg all over its face, looking like they can't control their own people."

Daniel nodded slowly.

"That would be more or less correct."

"And do I already have a green light to run a team up there or do you need to run this back by the ambassador?"

"I'd better check with him first. Let's say if I call you with a go, our code word will be cocktail."

"You say the magic word and I'll have a team on the way."

Simmons handed Daniel the report and Daniel started to put it back in his briefcase.

"Oh, did you need those coordinates again?"

Simmons tapped his forehead.

"It's all right up here."

Daniel snapped his briefcase shut and stood up.

"I'll get back to you shortly."

"Oh, one last thing," Simmons said as Daniel was opening the door. "If we're a go, make sure to put a call through to Doha. Let those Taliban assholes know you have someone heading up there to investigate. I don't need any fanatics hanging around taking pot shots at my men."

"I'll make sure their leadership team is informed."

They stared for another moment before Daniel went out the door. Simmons sat there drumming his fingers briefly before reaching for his phone and dialing an interoffice number. A moment later, a man answered his call.

"Clayton. I need you over here in my office. Pronto."

"I'll be there in a minute."

Simmons got back to drumming his fingers.

Clayton Dorn appeared some moments later from down the hallway. Lauren looked up from her desk and the two of them smiled through their awkward history; a one night fling Clayton had regretted the minute it happened. Drinks shared in a bar shortly after his arrival in country had led to clothes flying in Clayton's new quarters out back.

Like Silva, he hardly knew what to do with Lauren's mouth. Too, there were the colors. Clayton had never known another redhead to wear yellows and oranges. Redheads were supposed to wear greens and blacks and blues, not fire colors. Maybe a deep burgundy, but never yellow or orange.

And yet, Clayton still found himself aroused by her beauty and caring about her as a fellow human being. Lauren was a good soul and that counted for a lot with him.

He touched her hand in passing and opened Simmons' door.

"Close it," Simmons said.

Clayton did and took a seat.

"What's up?"

"Just hang loose here. I'm expecting a call."

Simmons sat there drumming his fingers and Clayton sat there watching him. Where Daniel Silva looked more like CIA in appearance, Clayton looked more like State, with his shock of blonde hair, pale skin and sensitive mouth. But he was ex Green Beret and had the cold gray eyes of a killer.

Simmons kept drumming his fingers and looking increasingly impatient.

"You ever been up to that Nuristan Forest area?" he asked Clayton.

"Can't say that I have."

"Well, you may be getting your chance here in a minute. Supposedly there was some kind of mischief up that way and I'm just waiting for the go ahead from State to send someone up there to investigate."

"What kind of mischief?"

"That's what you're going to find out...By the way, how are things going with that Mohammadi file?"

"The usual. Sometimes he provides useful intel. Sometimes it's useless. Based on one of his leads, I sent an SF team down to the Lashkar Gah region last week and it led to an ISIS-K cell. And that led to some terminations."

"Good, good. It may be a losing battle but..."

The phone rang and Simmons reached for the phone.

"Simmons, here."

"Sir, this is Daniel Silva, over at State."

"Hey, Daniel. What's going on?"

"Oh, just wanted to let you know that the ambassador is having a few dignitaries over for cocktails next week and wanted me to extend the invitation."

"Absolutely. Just send along the day and time and I'll be there. And be sure to thank the ambassador for the invite."

"Will do. I'll fax the invitation over to you in a bit."

"Great. I'll be sure to RVSP."

"That would be much appreciated. We'll talk soon then."

Simmons set the phone down and resumed drumming his fingers in thought.

"So? What's the word?" Clayton asked him finally.

"Oh, sorry. Yeah, we're on."

Simmons quickly explained the situation.

"Have you considered that it might be a negotiating stunt?" Clayton said when the station chief was done.

"It's always possible, but my gut tells me no."

"Any thoughts on who it could be?"

"Abu-Kar, maybe? He operates out of Jalalabad and has been trying to corner the arms trade in that area for years. He's definitely the only one I can think of who has the balls to take on the Taliban. And the resources."

"And you want me to go up there and have a look."

"Yeah. Are Bradley and Metcalf around?"

"Yeah, I think so."

"Good. Grab them and two more men for backup and go see what you can find out."

"Right now?"

Simmons nodded with a glance at his watch.

"There's enough daylight left and I'm eager to find out what the hell this is all about. I'll call ahead and make sure Sunny's waiting for you over at Karzai. And a couple of up-armored vehicles at Fenty."

Simmons scribbled the coordinates down on a piece of paper.

"That's where you're going...And look," he added as Clayton stood up. "Keep a tight lid on this. If you have to tell the shooters anything, make sure it's the bare minimum. State has been told to treat this with kid gloves so we'd better do the same."

"Understood," Clayton said.

On his way past Lauren's desk, he smiled and touched her hand again.

Down at the SP barracks in back, heads turned when Clayton walked in. Bradley and Metcalf and four other shooters were lounging around with their bare feet up, music playing. They were a beachfront cabana and a couple of those tropical cocktails shy of a Club Med vacation.

"Bradley, Metcalf, I need you and two more shooters for a mission. Grab whoever you want and meet me with a transport rig out in front."

"What's going on?" Metcalf said.

"I'll tell you on the way to Karzai. Let's go. The day's growing long."

Clayton headed back up to his office, pulled on his vest, grabbed his Glock and went out in front to wait. A minute later, his protection team raced around the corner. Clayton climbed in back with Rosen and Palmer. Bradley was driving with Metcalf riding shotgun. Bradley took off like they were taking potshots in Kandahar on a bad day. All four men were dressed in civilian clothing but geared up for war. Metcalf and Bradley were both dark haired, Bradley brooding and as serious as hell, Metcalf all smiles and pranks. Palmer and Rosen were both fair haired, Rosen ruddy faced and easy going, Palmer with a sarcastic exterior that masked a dead serious operator.

"So what's this all about?" Metcalf asked with a look back.

Clayton explained with as few details as possible.

"Did you hear that?" Metcalf said. "The Taliban got their asses kicked and went crying home to momma."

"I got their momma hanging right here," Palmer said.

"I thought you were supposed to be home on R&R," Clayton said to Rosen.

"I am. Leaving tomorrow. My sister's getting married and I'm taking an extra week while I'm there. Catch a little sunshine down on the Carolina coast."

"Lucky him," Palmer said.

Three miles later, they came to the Afghan checkpoint outside Camp Sullivan and Karzai International Airport. Bradley flashed his ID and the soldier waved him through. At the US checkpoint, Bradley stopped again, rolled down his window and showed his ID.

"Here with Agent Dorn in transport. There should be a bird waiting for us out on the tarmac."

The soldier checked his manifest.

"Your ride's on M6. Have a nice day, gentleman."

"Same to you, soldier."

Bradley raced down alongside the runway and pulled to a stop next to a helicopter. Everyone grabbed their gear and jumped out.

Sunny Piper, the pilot, already had the MI-17 warming up. The men all knew him from their decades of war and had been through every kind of hell together, from Fallujah to Helmond. Sunny had gotten the name from his rusty colored hair, freckles and ever-present smile. The gap between his two front teeth only served to accent the sunny appearance.

Clayton went forward and sat next to Sunny. The others got settled in back.

"Not your sorry ass again," Metcalf said to Sunny while slamming the cargo door shut.

Sunny laughed, brought the Sikorski up a few hundred feet and swung right over his shoulder, heading east.

The sprawl of Kabul soon dissipated into open countryside. The four shooters went on chirping away in back about war and women and backyard barbecues.

An hour later, Sunny was touching down at FOB Fenty. Jalalabad Airport was just to the other side of a chain link fence and some concrete barriers. There were cities in this world with more provincial looking airports, but not many.

"See you back here before dark," Clayton told Sunny on his way out.

As promised, there were two up-armored 4Runners waiting on the tarmac. Clayton took the backseat of one. Bradley climbed behind the wheel with Palmer riding shotgun. Metcalf and Rosen climbed into the other vehicle.

At the exit to Fenty, a soldier checked their names and manifest and made note of their departure time before letting them off the base. What armed forces personnel did after leaving the base was none of his business, or of much concern to anyone else there at command. It was only if folks didn't come back as specified that alarms started going off.

Bradley was quickly driving like they were in a jihad shooting gallery again. Clayton checked his GPS coordinates. Their destination was roughly fifty miles up into the mountains. He knew from experience that the road was decent as far as Mitarlam. Beyond that, they would be snaking along steep slopes with thousand foot drops. If you ran into a car coming the other way, one of you would have to back up for a mile.

They made Mitarlam in less than half an hour. Then it was as Clayton had anticipated, rough dirt roads with nothing around them for miles, sometimes running alongside shallow streams, sometimes climbing high up along the slopes. He kept checking his watch and the sun in the sky. The entire expedition would be fruitless if they didn't have at least an hour of daylight to investigate.

They had been driving up through the forest reserve for about ten miles when Clayton waved for Bradley to stop.

"I think that was it," he said, referring to an even rougher looking road they had just passed.

Bradley looked over his shoulder and back at Clayton.

"You sure about this?"

Clayton nodded and pointed again.

"I can't see any other way in."

Bradley radioed for Metcalf to back up and together they pulled onto the potholed road. Five miles up ahead, they passed by a village and then took another road left, higher up into the mountains.

Eventually, that road spilled out into a hidden valley. A stone building and wooden cottage were visible up ahead on the right.

"Here," Clayton said and had Bradley pull to a stop in front of the stone building.

"That looks fresh," Palmer said, pointing at a grave and grave marker.

Clayton nodded.

"So, is this our target?" Metcalf said.

"No, it looks like it's another mile up the valley."

He pointed ahead.

Following Clayton's directions, Bradley crossed the stream and continued up the other side.

"Here," Clayton said at the base of a wooded slope on their left.

Bradley looked back.

"You sure about this?"

"Pretty sure it's up there somewhere."

Clayton got out and started to climb up among the trees. The shooters did a weapons check and surrounded Clayton in a search and clear formation. When they came up over a ridge and onto a plateau, Clayton stopped and looked off through the forest.

"This it?" Bradley said.

"Somewhere in this area," Clayton said.

He put his phone away and walked ahead with the four men still surrounding him.

"Whoa," Metcalf said fifty yards farther on. He squatted down to have a look at something on the forest floor. "Blood."

"Shit, and somebody's skull parts," Rosen said.

The men fanned out a bit.

"Fuck, it's everywhere," Palmer said. "Taliban or not, somebody definitely got their clocks cleaned up here."

Bradley stooped down to pick up a spent shell casing.

"Looks like it's all AKs, too."

"Maybe these dudes were fighting among themselves," Metcalf said.

They had walked the plateau from one end to the other when Clayton stopped and stared off in the distance, thinking.

"We need to see anything else up here?" Bradley asked him.

Clayton shook his head.

"No. Let's go back down and have a look at those buildings."

Down below, the five men circled both structures on foot, peering into windows before ending up back at the grave.

"Dig it up," Clayton said.

"You sure about this?" Palmer said. "These people are pretty anal about disturbing their dead."

"Dig it up," Clayton repeated. "We're running out of daylight."

Grousing among themselves, the four men walked back to the 4Runners and grabbed their field shovels. Clayton sat down on a stone wall and kept watch.

Bradley and Metcalf took the first shift. When they grew tired of digging, Palmer and Rosen jumped in.

As the hole got down to chest level, only one man could conveniently shovel at a time so Palmer jumped out. Five minutes later, Rosen hit something solid.

"Pay dirt," he said and bent down out of sight. "Hey, the body's wrapped in some kind of a shroud!"

Clayton walked over to look. Palmer jumped in and helped with clearing off the remaining soil. Palmer was on the head end of the corpse and parted the cloth.

"Jesus Christ. It's an Afghani chick. In battle fatigues with a neck wound no less."

He looked up at Clayton.

"That wound was definitely enough to kill her."

Clayton nodded, his gaze fixed on the young woman's face, realizing he had seen her before, on the night of the bombing, talking with the woman he had taken back to the shelter. Clayton had noticed their conversation out on the sidewalk while he ate. And now she was here in this grave.

Coincidence? Maybe, but he doubted it.

Whatever their connection, he would definitely have to go back now and inquire at the shelter. He had been thinking to do so anyway. There just hadn't been the time, given the wave of ongoing crises but the other lady's beauty had never entirely left him.

Rosen and Palmer both straddled the body and parted the rest of the shroud.

"Chest wound, too," Palmer added.

"And friggin combat boots," Rosen added.

Metcalf was standing next to Clayton and looked over at him.

"A damned shame, huh chief? Nice looking doll."

Clayton continued staring down at the woman's face without comment.

"What's your take on this?" Bradley asked him.

Broken from his trance, Clayton shook his head.

"I have no idea."

He waved at Metcalf.

"Give Palmer a hand getting out. And you stand down by the feet, Rosen. I need to take a photo of her."

With that done, Rosen covered the body again before they helped him out. Fifteen minutes later, the grave was back to its original state and the four shooters walked down to wash off their hands in the stream. Clayton was waiting alongside one of the 4Runners when they returned.

"Still no thoughts on what happened here," Palmer said.

Clayton shook his head.

"Well, I'll tell you this much. If that chick was in civilian clothing, I'd think nothing of it. But in fatigues? And combat boots? And with combat wounds? That's just some weird kind of shit, no matter how you slice it."

"So, is that it?" Bradley said.

"Yeah. Let's head back to J-bad. And look, all of you. Not one word of this. To anyone. Understood?"

"Understood, chief. But if you ever figure out what went down up here, I for one would love to know."

Clayton was staring across the valley in thought. He nodded and the men climbed back into the 4Runners.

Thirteen

Twilight had settled over Kabul by the time Sunny touched back down at Karzai International. While he busied himself with shutting systems down on the helicopter, the five men gathered their gear and jumped out onto the tarmac. An Iman was calling the faithful to prayer somewhere off in the city. The snowcapped Hindu Kush rimmed the distant horizon, glowing in various shades of lavender and white in the fading light.

Clayton paused outside the cargo door before closing it.

"This is classified," he said to Sunny.

Sunny winked with a smile. Clayton closed the door and joined the other men in the Suburban. Bradley raced full speed back to Camp Eggers and stopped in front of the station. Clayton got out and paused with the back door open.

"Definitely some weird shit," Metcalf said.

"Yeah, but just remember. Not a word of this to anyone."

"No worries, chief. I'm sure it'll be all over the evening news soon enough."

"Maybe, but just make sure it's not one of you leaking it."

Clayton closed the door and Bradley headed around in back. Clayton went up to his office and called Simmons. Simmons answered after two rings.

"I'm back on the ground. Are you still in the office?"

"Still here."

"I'll be right over."

Heading down the hallway, Clayton crossed paths with Adelman, a fellow operative. Adelman was like the frat boy everyone had come to hate. Always acting like he was one up on you and sticking his nose where it didn't belong.

"Burning the midnight oil, huh Dorn?"

"Just wrapping up a report for Simmons."

Adelman smiled and raised his eyebrows, waiting to hear more.

"Gotta run," Clayton said and kept going.

"Always playing your cards close to your vest, huh Dorn?"

Clayton waved without looking back.

Lauren was gone from her desk when he turned the corner, sparing Clayton another awkward encounter. To say he felt ambivalent about Lauren was an understatement. Set aside the odd mouth and she was a beautiful woman, erotic in that pale-skinned, redhead sort of way, and as loyal as a homeless mutt. He felt like one heartless son of a bitch for rejecting her but what could he do? There was no escaping a man's emotions.

Clayton tapped on Simmons' door and let himself in. Simmons looked up expectantly from his desk.

"So? What do we know?"

Clayton settled into a chair across from him.

"There was definitely a skirmish up there. And a pretty major one from the looks of it."

Clayton explained what he had seen and showed Simmons the photograph of the corpse.

"We walked that plateau from end to end and the signs were everywhere. Flesh and blood, spent shell casings, explosives of some kind. Everything you'd expect."

"But not one corpse."

Clayton shook his head.

"Nothing to suggest that coalition or Afghan troops were involved?"

"Going by the shell casings we found, no. Everything was 7.62 mm, so AKs."

"What the hell then? I'd go with my original theory, that a warlord like Abu-Kar had picked a fight with the Taliban, except for that female corpse you found."

Clayton shrugged noncommittedly.

"Come on, out with it," Simmons said. "You think this woman was involved in the battle?"

"Maybe. Going by the freshness of the grave, I'd probably have to say yes."

"And the uniform? It definitely looked like Afghan Army issue?"

"There weren't any insignias, but I would say it was sourced the same, yeah."

"Okay, so let's say for the sake of argument that an Afghan force went up there and took on the Taliban."

"Then we're left to explain the empty casings. The Afghan Army started phasing out AKs back in 2008. There may be a few of them still floating around among the ranks, but if this was a regular army unit, we should have found a lot of spent 5.56 rounds mixed in with the AKs. Definitely not AK casings alone. And even with that, you're left with why they would bury the body up there. It doesn't make any sense."

"Then what's *your* theory?"

"I really don't have one."

"Come on, Clayton. This is what we get paid to do."

"Oh, I've gamed it out in a number of different ways, just like you, but it's still nothing that makes sense."

"Okay, let me run this one by you. Let's say a regular Afghan Army unit did go rogue. They *have* been training women, which would explain her presence. And let's say they were savvy enough not to use regular army issue weapons. AKs are a dime a dozen in Afghanistan and you figure they've watched our special op teams ditch their M4s during a mission so they won't leave their signature behind."

"Then you're back to explaining the body."

"Maybe they just thought it was the best place to hide it. Hell, if they went rogue, they wouldn't want to be caught dragging a dead body around with them."

"It's still a big red flag. And even setting that aside, you're left to explain why an Afghan unit would go rogue in the first place. They're not exactly known for their courage."

"Yeah, it's definitely a major head scratcher, no matter which way you spin it. And you never thought to drag the body back with you?"

"We have the photo. And the body's still up there if anyone wants to exhume it. I just thought, in this country, with the scant records they keep? What's the point? Forensics isn't going to help you."

"Yeah. Best to let State deal with that question…Okay, let's get back to the two buildings. Were you able to make any sense of that?"

"Not really. There were footprints all around the place but I wrote it off to whoever had buried the body. The inside of both buildings looked untouched. I'm guessing it was some kind of retreat in the past. Possibly even the present. I don't know how else to explain that larger structure. It had the looks of a barracks."

"Yeah. We'll have to follow up on that angle. I can't see you burying a body up there without some kind of connection."

Simmons leaned back in his chair.

"You know, this Afghan woman warrior thing isn't without precedent. Take that Hukmina down in Kandahar."

"Yeah, but she's a one off. And it was a very different Afghanistan when she took on the Russians."

"Come on. Malalai Kakar? She had some balls, taking on the Taliban the way she did."

"And for which they promptly put a bullet in her head."

"Yeah, but I stick by my point. This warrior princess thing goes way back with these people. It's part of their mythical tradition. Frankly, I'm surprised we haven't seen more Afghan women picking up weapons."

Simmons sighed and came forward in his chair.

"Well, I suppose I'd better go report in to the ambassador. See how this mess fits in with the administration's *'we've got to get our asses out of Afghanistan and leave it to the Afghanis'* company line."

Clayton stood up in response.

"Anything more I can do for you tonight?"

"No, just follow up on that facility. My gut tells me there's a connection."

"I'll see what I can find out."

"Thanks. And thanks for chasing this story down."

Simmons placed a hand on his phone and smiled. Clayton got the message and left. Simmons had the ambassador on the line a moment later.

"Preston. Wondered if you'd mind me stopping by for a drink and a chat?"

"Not at all. Come right over. It's been a while since we've had a chance to catch up."

"I'll be there in ten."

Simmons called down for an escort, stuck the classified briefing into his briefcase and headed out the door.

Over at the embassy, the Marine guard out front wished him a good evening and opened the door. There was another Marine inside the vestibule with a locked security door behind him. Per protocol, Simmons signed in and was buzzed through.

"The ambassador's expecting you," an aide said at the elevator door.

Simmons was ushered into a study on the second floor. The ambassador was seated by a window, reading a dispatch. He stood up and shook Simmons' hand.

"Can I get you something to drink, Ted?"

"A splash of Scotch, if you have some."

"Right here."

Douglas walked over to a credenza.

"Straight?" he said over his shoulder.

"Please."

Douglas returned with two lowball glasses, handed one to Simmons and sat down in the adjacent wing backed chair. The two men saluted with their glasses and drank. A view of the city spread out before them.

"So?" Douglas said. "What do we know?"

Simmons explained the facts as they had been explained to him, without offering a hint of his own theories.

"That body buried at the facility has my curiosity up more than anything," Simmons added. "You have any idea who owns the place?"

"Haven't the slightest," Douglas said while staring out the window. "But we'll definitely look into it."

"I already tasked Clayton with following up on that angle. Shouldn't be too hard to find out."

Douglas nodded while continuing to stare outside.

"*You* have any theories?" Simmons said while studying his profile.

Douglas looked over.

"Oh, that's more your line of work. My job is just to keep the peace and implement the president's policies."

"That still leaves us with explaining this away to the Taliban leadership."

"That's true. And what would you suggest I tell them?"

"It doesn't matter what I suggest. You're the ones wanting out of Afghanistan..."

"The president's goal is to depart this country peacefully. Twenty years of involvement is quite enough. It's time to leave Afghanistan to the Afghanis."

"Respectfully, Preston, but history's not going to be kind to us. Why are we drawing an arbitrary line in the sand here? Our presence in South Korea has been going on for seventy years."

"That's an advanced country with a longstanding border dispute, not a civil war. It's hardly the same situation."

"It was anything but an advanced country seventy years ago. Besides, we have troops in harm's way all over the world. Somalia, Mali, Niger. Hell, we've been in the Balkans for longer than we've been in Afghanistan. Why are we so ready to turn tail and run from this commitment?"

"Look, Ted. I know how you feel. After Camp Chapman. Well...let's just say you boys have a lot of skin in the game, but the previous president signed a peace treaty and the current one feels duty bound to honor it, however much he feels it stinks. We tear it up now and we'll just have more dead American soldiers and a blemish on the honor of the United States."

"What you're going to have is a whole bunch of current and former enlisted men wondering why the hell they came over here to die. Just like in 'Nam."

"Ted, at some point, these people have to learn to fight for themselves. Our only objective at this point is to make sure the Afghan government can properly defend itself."

"All you're doing is handing it over to the Taliban on a platter."

Simmons downed the rest of his Scotch and stood up.

"I'm sorry, Preston, but you folks are dead wrong on this one. This country needs us. All the decent people in this country need us. I'll say it again. Think of all the blood and treasure we've spent, and we're just going to turn tail and run? I don't even think you have public opinion with you on this one, but even if you did, it still stinks."

"I don't blame you for being angry, Ted, but there's not a damned thing I can do about it. I've been told we're pulling out and my job is to make sure that policy is executed as smoothly and efficiently as possible."

"And when you're back home in a year, watching Afghan women in burkas get shot in the back of the head? How's that policy decision going to look to you then?"

Simmons started to leave.

"You will keep me posted if you learn anything new," Douglas said.

Simmons stopped at the door.

"Put up a fight, Preston. History records every injustice and when it records this one, it will note whose side we were on. You don't want to be remembered for selling out the Afghan people. Thanks for the Scotch," Simmons added before walking out.

Douglas had been sitting there for several minutes, sipping his drink and considering exactly what to tell the people back in D.C. about this Nuristan business when his secure phone line rang. Douglas answered it and promptly had Russ 'Rocky' Blackburn in his ear. Blackburn was a retired colonel and the current Under Secretary of State for Afghan Affairs. The new administration had held him over from the previous one, mostly because of his hardnosed, straight shooter style. It had worked well with earning Afghani respect and boxing ears. It just wasn't of much use in polite social circles.

Douglas thought of Blackburn as the Yanks had of Monty during World War II. The little British general. He was short, pink, dapper and wound tighter than a two-dollar watch.

Blackburn was calling from Washington and wasted no time in going ballistic.

"What the hell's going on over there, Preston?"

"To what are we referring?"

"The bombing!"

"What bombing?"

"The one down in Knost Province! The Taliban leadership put out a statement a short while ago, claiming we had broken the ceasefire and that the bombing was in retaliation! Christ, are you even watching the news!"

"I've had Simmons here for the past hour, bringing me up to speed on what he learned about that Nuristan business."

"Yeah? And so exactly what did happen up there?"

Douglas explained what he had learned from Simmons.

"Goddamn it, Preston. I'm smelling the Afghan government's greasy hand in this."

"How so?"

"Well, it's obvious, isn't it? Their leadership doesn't want us pulling out so they stage this raid to blow up the peace process."

"That might make sense, if not for the corpse. If the Afghan government was behind this, why would they leave a body buried up there as evidence? In army fatigues no less."

"Well, Christ if I know but you can't trust these bastards as far as you can throw them."

"I suppose."

"No, take my word for it."

"Very well. What would the administration like me to do?"

"Well, dig up that corpse, for starters. Have Simmons send his team back up there."

"And what would you like us to do with it?"

"Take it out to Bagram. They have a morgue. I'll get in touch with General Marshall and let him know to expect you. We need to track down this woman's identity. In the meantime, get in touch with Husaini over at Afghan Interior and see if you can squeeze anything out of him. I'm getting on a plane shortly and will expect some answers by the time I hit the ground tomorrow morning. Any questions?"

"No. I assume we're trying to keep this under wraps?"

"You bet your ass we are. I want a total media blackout."

"And if the press comes poking around, asking questions?"

"Just issue the usual blanket statement. 'We're looking into these Taliban claims but have yet to verify them. Blah, blah, blah...The same goes for Simmons and his team. Understood?"

"Of course, Russ. We'll do everything possible."

"Good. Then the minute I'm on the ground tomorrow, the two of us are going to sit down and see if we can figure out just what the hell is going on over there."

"Very well. I'll talk with you then."

Blackburn ended the call. Douglas immediately called Simmons and brought him up to speed.

"And we're still negotiating with those bastards?" Simmons said, referring to the Taliban bombing down in Knost.

"Well, we are where we are. The question is, when can you get up there to retrieve the body?"

"Oh hell, tonight. Darkness is our best advantage with the Taliban. I'll have my men airborne within the hour."

"Good, thanks...And put the grave back the way you found it. Probably best if no one knows we've been up there disturbing things."

"Consider it done."

"Thanks, Ted. I'm sure we'll be talking tomorrow."

"I'm sure we will."

Simmons ended the call and immediately called Clayton. Clayton had just walked up to the door of the women's shelter when his phone rang.

"Yeah, chief, what's up?"

"You know that package we were discussing earlier today?"

"Yeah?"

"I need you to go back up there and retrieve it."

"When?"

"Tonight. You got enough room up there to land two birds?"

"Yeah, plenty of room."

"Good. Then go grab the same team, plus four extra shooters. You're flying straight from Karzai and air mailing the package over to Bagram, special delivery. I'll make arrangements for two birds as soon as we get off."

"And they'll know what's going on out at Bagram?"

"Everything will be arranged on that end. You just make sure to get your hands on that package. And clean up after yourselves."

"Will do."

"Good. And let me know the minute you're back."

Clayton ended the call and paused outside the door. It had to be someone at State, wanting answers. Fair enough. Clayton wanted answers too, the very reason he was standing there at the door of that women's shelter.

After another moment, puzzling over things in his mind, he knocked. A few seconds later, a woman cracked the door. She was Afghani and not someone Clayton had seen on the night of the bombing. He introduced himself and explained his reason for being there.

"I'm just checking to see if the woman I had helped is okay."

"We not to talk about other woman here," she said in broken English.

"Is the director here?"

The woman stared. Then another woman appeared behind her.

"Hi," Clayton said and explained himself again. "Can you please ask the director to come down?"

The second woman nodded and closed the door. A minute later, Cylyse reopened it.

"Oh hi," she said. "Yes, I remember you from the night of the bombing."

"Yeah, sorry. I've been meaning to stop by and check on that young woman but there just hasn't been the time. Is she okay?"

Cylyse stared for a long moment before parting the door.

"Please, come in. We can talk in my office."

She looked up and down the block before closing the door and leading Clayton down a long hallway to her office.

"Please, have a seat."

Cylyse closed the door and went around to her side of the desk.

"That young woman's name is Saarah and we've been wondering if she's okay too. She disappeared two days after the bombing and we've not heard from her since. She left a note, saying not to worry, but of course we do. I've reached out to the Interior Minister on Women's Affairs and your State Department but no one seems to know a thing. Or if they do, they're not talking."

"I'm sorry to hear that."

"There's more," Cylyse said.

Clayton gestured for her to go on.

"Four other young women have also disappeared from local shelters. Three on the same day as Saarah and one more just two days ago now. Perhaps you can look into it for me."

"Do you have their names?"

"Better than that. I have their photos."

Cylyse opened a drawer and pulled out two sheets of paper.

"We put this one together the day after Saarah disappeared. And this one separately for the young woman who disappeared two days ago."

Clayton stared at the first 'missing person' flyer while taking the second one. He glanced quickly at that sheet and looked back at the first one. One of the women was Saarah. One of them was the woman in the grave. Her name was Kashm. The third woman on that sheet was named Veeda, the fourth one, Hajira. The woman on the second sheet was named Gulnoor.

"Do you recognize any of them?" Cylyse said.

Clayton looked up and shook his head.

"Saarah, of course, but none of the others."

"But you will look into it for us, yes?"

"I'll certainly try."

"It would be greatly appreciated. I can't help but feel like we're being stonewalled somehow. True or not, I've not been able to get one bit of help out of any of the agencies."

"May I take these?"

"Of course."

Clayton folded the two flyers and tucked them away.

160

"And you've not heard a single word from any of these women since they disappeared."

"Nothing. Our fear is that they've been snatched away by the Taliban. Possibly even the Islamic State people. I dread the very thought of it. You know what they do to women."

Clayton nodded and stood up.

"Sorry but I really do have to run."

"I'll walk you out."

Clayton stopped outside the door and looked back.

"You know, if they've been taken, as you fear, I'm afraid the odds of finding them are very slim. It would be a matter of pure luck, like if they turned up in a raid somewhere."

"And with the Americans planning to pull out now…"

Clayton bit his lip.

"Like I said, I'll definitely look into it."

"Thanks for that, and for stopping by. I appreciate your concern."

"Yes. I should have stopped by sooner."

He felt where the flyers were tucked away in his coat pocket.

"I promise to follow up on this."

"And let me know if anything turns up?"

"Of course."

Clayton waved and hurried back to his car.

The situation was riddled with even more mystery now. Saarah and Kashm knew each other. That was a given, based on his observations the night of the bombing. Then both of them disappear on the same day and Kashm turns up in a grave, dressed in battle fatigues and with bullet wounds in her neck and chest. So where did that place Saarah in all of this? And where the hell was she?

Clayton raced away from the curb and headed back towards Camp Eggers, his mind swirling with questions. One of them was just how much of this he was going to share with Simmons. It was Clayton's style to let things play out a bit before opening his mouth. Then there was the simple matter of discretion. If Simmons knew what Clayton knew, he'd be in a tough spot. It was one thing for Clayton to hold back evidence from the State Department and, by extension, the president. It was quite another for Simmons to be doing so.

Fourteen

It was well into the night and the women were gathered together in the back room of a sprawling, residential compound, the compound located in the northern district of Kahmard and tucked along one side of a fertile valley. It had been two days since their battle with the Taliban and the women were beyond restless. Their grief over Kashm's death had increasingly turned to anger and thoughts of revenge and those feelings only grew more fervent with every idle minute.

While awaiting their next orders, they had been told not to go out in the village, instructions that had only added to their frustration. Kahmard was ostensibly under government control, and was bordered by the Northern Alliance, but you only had to go over the next mountain to find the Taliban, or down the street to find locals who sympathized with them.

Afsoon, the woman who owned the compound, was an old friend of the woman who owned the one where they had trained and had known her own share of grief over the years, having lost her husband and two sons during the Soviet occupation, and seen her own freedom repeatedly stolen away, first by the mujahedeen and then by the Taliban. Life for women had actually been better before the Soviet tanks rolled back across the northern border.

In hearing Saarah's story, Afsoon had given her a book from her library, about the mythical women warriors of Afghan's past. Shah Bori, Nazauna, Malalai, women

163

renowned for having turned scarves into swords and roasting their enemies in fire. Saarah had found herself swept away by it all.

Veeda, who had been watching Saarah read the book, was driven to speak up.

"Why do you bother with these fairy tales? We should be emulating women like Commander Kaftar. Now there's a real woman, fighting real battles."

"Emulate Kaftar?" Hajira said. "She's a traitor."

"Who says?"

"Haven't you heard? She's now joined hands with the Taliban."

"Who told you this nonsense?"

"I saw it in the news when I was in the shelter."

"Eh. The news is full of nonsense."

"Is it nonsense when it comes from her own mouth?"

Veeda stared.

"I am speaking the truth," Hajira went on. "I saw her telling a British reporter that she's now working with Mullah Khodaidad to control the local drug routes. She announced this proudly. That woman does not stand for anything but her own self-interest."

"Eh," Veeda said.

"It is true," Mahvash said. "I saw it in the news too."

Veeda grumbled but said nothing more.

Suddenly, there were stirrings in the vestibule outside their sanctuary and every woman in the room grabbed her rifle. Then there was the sound of voices speaking softly and a light knock on the door.

Ariya, who had been away since the previous evening, entered the room. Irem was with her.

"I see you are all alert," she said to everyone there before turning back to address Afsoon. "Thank you again for your hospitality."

Afsoon bowed her head and disappeared. Ariya closed the door and joined Irem in greeting the women.

"I assume you have eaten."

There were nods all around. Ariya removed the scarf from over her head and sat down.

"All right, then. It is time to make plans."

"Finally," Veeda said.

Ariya gave her a frown and pulled out a map.

"You are a good commander, Veeda, but patience is as important as courage when going into battle. Always remember that."

Ariya spread out a map in the candlelight so everyone could see it.

"This is the latest map of controlled territory in Afghanistan. It is shifting day to day now so difficult to say how accurate it is. You will find Afghan government forces in Taliban areas and Taliban forces in government-controlled areas, but for the most part, the government-controlled provinces are relatively safe."

Ariya pointed to several widely scattered red areas to the north and east of Kabul.

"After consulting with all our supporters, we have decided that the best course of action is to try and clear these areas first. As you can see from the map, here to the southwest and southeast, there is much greater Taliban control and therefore a much greater challenge."

Ariya pointed again to the scattered areas of Taliban control in the northeast.

"If we can clear this section of Afghanistan, we will have near continuous control from Herat to Kunduz and Mazar-e-Sharif to Kabul."

Ariya looked from face to face.

"I did not share this with you before because it was not important. And even now, I cannot give out the names of the people involved, for their safety and yours, but we have built up a supply chain of food and weapons. It is only a question of where to attack first."

While still looking at the women, Ariya tapped her index finger on a red splotch, just to the northwest of Kabul.

"And this is where we have decided."

She tapped her finger on two more red areas.

"If we are successful in clearing that area, and these areas farther to the north, the Northern Alliance will have an uninterrupted supply chain and we can count on them to help us clear these additional areas to the east. Just in the past few days, with the Taliban gaining control of several more provinces, people have begun to realize that their freedom too will soon be lost if they do nothing. Warriors from the past are dusting off their old weapons so we may soon be part of a much greater movement."

Ariya paused with a somber look.

"We must never forget that we are talking about war. God willing, we will be successful, but just these small objectives will take months to accomplish and much blood will be shed."

Ariya tapped again at the red area just northwest of Kabul.

"But back to our first objective. We have chosen this area to start, which happens to include Saarah's home village."

Ariya looked up.

"I want you to know that this choice was made solely on the basis of supply chain considerations. However, if we do choose to attack here, Saarah's knowledge of the area will be invaluable. Does anyone wish to speak up on this matter?"

"I welcome any target if it gets us out of this room," Veeda said.

Ariya looked from face to face but there were no objections.

"Very well. Then that is our plan."

Ariya pointed at the map and turned to Saarah.

"We know the road east of this point is now under Taliban control. What can you tell us of this general area and the road up from the Turkman Valley?"

"I don't know what the Taliban control, beyond my village, but that road down the mountain to Surkh-O-Parsa, that is how I escaped."

Saarah pointed at the map.

"A river runs down through this canyon with the road mostly high above it."

"Then you think we could approach your village safely from this direction."

Saarah nodded.

"It is a difficult climb in places but most of the time you can only see the river from the road if you stop and peer over the edge."

"And I assume it will be even safer at night?"

"Yes. At the closest, the road is maybe two hundred feet above you. Most of the time, it is much higher."

"And do you think some of the villagers would be sympathetic and help us? As with food and such?"

"Yes. I'm sure some of them would."

"Good...Then we will take you as far as Surkh-O-Parsa and leave you with enough supplies to last a week. Veeda, you have the satellite phone. If you are successful in taking Saarah's village, we will rejoin you there with whatever fresh supplies you need. If for some reason you must retreat, we will meet you back in Surkh-O-Parsa. Remember, success in war means fresh ammunition and weaponry from your enemy. If you run out of rations from your packs, take only what the villagers are willing to give you. We are here to defeat the Taliban. We do not wish to leave behind any anger or resentment."

Ariya folded up her map.

"A few more things. Irem will be taking Kashm's place on your team. Kejal has taken a handful of fresh recruits up to Mazar-e-Sharif and is setting up a new training camp there."

"God help them," Veeda said.

Ariya smiled at hearing the women laugh.

"And I will remain here, attending to your supply lines and offering whatever help I can."

With a final look from face to face, Ariya held out her hand as a blessing.

"May God be with you. Now let's get ready to move out."

Veeda was the first to her feet.

"Finally. Any more being cooped up in this room and I would have turned into a mad dog."

The women were all business now, gearing up with their tactical vests and weapons.

At the gate to the street, Ariya stopped everyone and peeked out. The village appeared to be asleep but a dog had begun barking somewhere down the block.

Finally, Ariya waved and the women hurried out to the two, up armored 4Runners. Mahvash and Farzaneh had already been chosen as the drivers and climbed behind the wheels. Veeda sat up front with Mahvash. Irem sat up front with Farzaneh. Qammar was behind the wheel of the lead van and had two more armed men seated inside with him.

Ariya went over to Veeda's window.

"Qammar will drive ahead of you. Hold back and watch to see if there are any checkpoints. If there are, he will radio to let you know whether or not it's safe. If there is trouble, we will have to find another route into the Turkman Valley. If all goes as planned, these men will drive your vehicles to someplace safe until you need them again. Any questions?"

Veeda shook her head.

"Good. Then God be with you."

"The minute I can start shooting these Taliban dogs, God will be with me," Veeda said.

Ariya smiled and went up to speak with Qammar.

"Remember. The turnoff is two miles before Zarkharid."

"I know," he said.

"There is a checkpoint if you continue on into the town."

"I know."

"Then go."

Ariya waved for Qammar to move out and waved a final time to the women as they drove away.

It was a clear, star filled night and the snow-covered mountains glowed high up against the sky. The road down to Surkhdar was slow and poor and dangerous. It took them over an hour to navigate the thirty miles but they saw no one else coming or going.

The highway from there to Tupchi and from Tupchi to Zarkharid was in good condition and they made that forty-five mile trek in less than an hour. As they neared Zarkharid, they saw a checkpoint up ahead.

Qammar radioed back to them.

"They've moved the checkpoint closer to the turnoff. I will go forward and distract them. You take the turn and continue on a safe distance. If you see anyone leaving the checkpoint to go after you, then hurry forward and find someplace to hide. If there is no trouble, I will pretend to have missed my turnoff and go back. If there is trouble, I will find some way to warn you."

"Then mute your radio," Veeda said. "Otherwise we will be forced to maintain comm silence."

"Very well. Muting now."

"And prepare to slow down, rear vehicle."

"We will follow your lead," Irem radioed back.

Veeda motioned for Mahvash to ease off the throttle. The checkpoint was still well up ahead but close enough to make out the soldier's faces. All of them were turned towards the oncoming lights.

As Qammar slowed to a stop, one of the soldiers walked up to his window. The rest of the soldiers were staring back in the direction of the two 4Runners.

"Okay, go!" Veeda told Mahvash with a wave of her hand.

As they made the turn, Veeda saw a soldier head for his Humvee.

"Did you see if that soldier got into his Humvee?" Veeda called back to the rear vehicle.

"I could not tell," Irem radioed back. "I lost sight of him as we made the turn."

"We must assume that he did."

Veeda clicked off and thought for a moment before keying up her radio again.

"Okay, Farzaneh. Lights out and night vision goggles. And stay close so you do not lose us."

With both sets of headlights off, the night was utterly black around them. The dirt road quickly jackknifed north and up into the mountains.

They had snaked cautiously along steep slopes for several miles when Veeda had Mahvash stop. Farzaneh came to a halt behind them. Veeda got out and trained her night vision binoculars back in the direction of the highway. The other women climbed out too.

"Anything?" Mahvash said.

"Nothing."

"So many stars," Esin said, looking up at the sky.

"Perhaps someone is up there, looking back at us and saying the same thing," Noushineh said.

"Enough with you dreamers," Veeda said.

"And what is life without dreams?" Hajira said.

"It is not a life worth living," Noushineh said.

She had started to say something more when Veeda cut her off. A pair of headlights had appeared in the distance. Veeda watched through the binoculars as the lights slowly snaked up the mountain. The other women stood around her watching too.

"Can you tell if it's the van?" Irem said.

"Not yet."

Time passed with the lights slowly weaving up the mountain towards them.

"We should call him," Hajira said.

Veeda kept watching.

"Qammar told us to flee if they came for us," Esin said. "What if it's them and not Qammar."

"If they've taken Qammar captive then they would have his radio too," Mahvash said.

"If they have his radio," Tabaan said. "Then they would be trying to call, just to see who answered."

"I still say we should call," Hajira said.

Veeda kept watching through the binoculars and Hajira kept staring at her. The headlights had disappeared again behind a fold in the mountain.

"Fine," Veeda said finally. "Call him."

Hajira keyed up her radio.

"Qammar, are you there?"

The radio crackled without a response.

"Qammar, are you there?" Hajira said again.

There was still no response.

"I think we should go."

Hajira looked around at the other women.

"I agree," Tabaan said.

The women all shared a look and nodded, save for Veeda. She was still watching with the binoculars.

"Veeda," Irem said.

"All right," she said. "We will proceed as far as Lakhshan and find someplace to hide there while we wait."

The other women were quickly climbing back into the 4Runners. Veeda had one more look with the binoculars before joining them. Mahvash had started the engine when Noushineh turned her head and spotted the headlights. They were only half a mile back now.

"They're nearly upon us," Noushineh said.

"All right, go!" Veeda said.

The caravan had raced forward a hundred yards when they heard the radio crackle.

"Are you there?" Qammar said.

Veeda called back.

"Yes."

She motioned for Mahvash to stop.

"Where in God's name are you? We have been watching a pair of headlights come up the mountain for the past fifteen minutes. Is that you?"

"Yes. Where are you?"

"Just up ahead. We have our headlights off. And you might have answered our call."

"We tried calling you but it was too far for a signal."

"Eh. Sometimes this technology is useless. All right. We are here."

Veeda waved and Mahvash turned on the headlights.

"Ah, I see you now."

"Good. We will move out as soon as you join us."

"So many stars," Esin said again, looking out her window.

"I like Noushineh's thought," Hajira said. "Perhaps someone is up there on their own distant world with their own distant star, fighting their version of the Taliban."

"There are enough Taliban in this country for the entire universe," Veeda said. "Let us just focus on the ones we have."

"Yes, Commander Veeda," Hajira said.

Veeda grunted in response.

They had been sitting there waiting for another minute when the van's headlights finally appeared from around a bend and the caravan pulled out.

Surkh-O-Parsa was only twenty miles ahead now but the road was in poor condition and it took the better part of an hour to reach the outskirts of the village. The village appeared to sleep.

They drove on through farmland and came to a heavily wooded area. Mahvash pulled in among the trees and the other drivers followed. Quietly, everyone climbed out. The road continued up into a narrow canyon with the stream running below it.

"That way?" Veeda said to Saarah.

Saarah nodded.

"How far to your village?"

"It took me four hours to get from there to here on foot."

"All right. We had better move out. We will want to do some recon before it is light."

All the women were checking their gear outside the vehicles. Veeda turned to Qammar.

"We will see you up there or back here, depending on how the battle goes."

"God be with you," he said.

The other two men had climbed into the 4Runners and the three vehicles were soon turned around and heading back the way they had come. Without prompting, Saarah took the lead and started into the canyon.

At times the way up was easy. At times it was hard. They scaled alongside waterfalls and pushed through heavy brush with limbs slapping at their faces. Little was said as the hours passed but the frustration was palpable.

With only a few hours of darkness still left, they came to a small forest of trees and Saarah stopped to face the team. The road was only fifty feet above them now.

"At the far end of this grove, we will see the village. It is possible that they have someone watching the road."

"All right. Everyone be alert," Veeda whispered. "And you, Farzaneh, get out that drone."

While she did, Veeda turned back to Saarah.

"Tell us what you know."

There in the moonlight, Saarah took a stick and drew the lay of the land in the sandy soil. The women around her stole glances while keeping watch.

"But where we will find the Taliban in my village?" Saarah said, in conclusion. "I only know that their leader Akmad has taken up residence in my home. Or so I was told."

Saarah pointed with the stick to where it was in the valley.

"Beyond that I know nothing more than you do."

"Well, let us have a look," Veeda said with a nod to Farzaneh.

Farzaneh started the drone and gently tossed it up into the air.

"High enough to where we can't see or hear it before you start scouting."

The drone drifted up and up into the starry sky.

As soon it had disappeared from view, Veeda nodded and Farzaneh guided it out past the mouth of the canyon. Mahvash had opened the laptop and everyone crowded around the screen.

"We should not all watch," Veeda said. "Tabaan, Esin, Hajira and Darsameen, take the watch for now. If you stare at the screen it can take minutes for your eyes to readjust to the darkness."

Tabaan and Hajira grumbled but moved off to secure a perimeter with the other two women. Veeda looked back at the screen and immediately pointed.

"There, beside the road. It looks like one of the Taliban dogs."

The man was sitting with his back to a tree while looking this way and that.

"We will be sending you to the bowels of hell by tomorrow night," Veeda said.

She nodded and Farzaneh moved the drone farther into the valley. There were no signs of life until the drone came to the far end of valley, where the road started back up into the mountains.

"Another Taliban dog," Veeda said. "All right. I have seen enough. Bring the drone back. Saarah, take Irem and Noushineh and find a suitable place to camp. I'll stay here and cover the drone team. We will join you shortly."

Saarah already had a place in mind, down by the first falls, where a cluster of trees along the stream would keep the women hidden if someone looked down from the road above. Plus, it was far enough away from the valley to make a chance encounter unlikely.

174

"Go ahead and make camp," Saarah said once they had reached the spot. "I will keep watch."

Five minutes later, the other seven women came into view. Saarah tapped the butt of her rifle against a tree as a signal and stood up. Veeda had a look around the campsite and nodded approvingly.

"Are you good with taking first watch?" she asked Saarah.

Saarah nodded.

"Okay. Noushineh, you also take the first watch. Tabaan and Esin, will take second watch. Wake us in one hour," Veeda told Saarah and Noushineh. "Everyone else, try to get some sleep."

Fifteen

It was yet an hour before dawn when Saarah awakened Tabaan and Esin. Disturbed by the changing of the guards, Mahvash and Hajira awakened too, grumbled and turned over. The other women had not stirred at all.

Saarah drank from the stream and refilled her bottle before crawling into her sleeping bag. The familiar gurgle of the stream brought comfort to her heart.

She lay there staring up at the shimmering stars, thinking of what Noushineh had said. Perhaps someone was indeed out there wondering the same thing, wondering if their own planet was all alone in this universe, or if someone else was out there looking back. The idea seemed both miraculous and impossible to believe. Saarah closed her eyes, still thinking of these things, but was soon asleep.

Tabaan and Esin were just returning from their watch when Saarah awakened again. The first gray light of dawn was brightening the sky. Saarah very much wanted to sleep again but the entire camp had begun to stir.

Reminded of the impending battle, the gravity of it all suddenly seized her heart. How unreal to think this band of women warriors was about to go to battle and spill blood. If not for the blood they had already spilled, she would not have believed it at all.

She remembered Kashm's words. There were only two choices, to fight or grovel like dogs, and that made the choice easy. Saarah would not grovel before anyone. She remembered too what the Taliban had done to her father and her family and her heart boiled over anew with anger.

She got up and joined the others in prayer, then went looking for Veeda and found her with Mahvash and Farzaneh at the far end of the camp. The drone was up in the air, scanning the valley.

"Good," Veeda said, seeing Saarah. "I was about to call you. Let us see what these dogs will do at the break of day."

Together, the four women stared at the laptop screen. The drone was high enough to provide a view of the entire valley. Nothing seemed to be stirring in the grainy light, not even the two men on watch. Off in the distance, they heard a cock crow.

A few minutes later, four Taliban appeared on the porch of a building.

"What is that place?" Veeda asked.

"Our schoolhouse. The one for girls."

"Of course they would close it down," Farzaneh said.

"Of course," Veeda said. "Do you recognize any of them, Saarah?"

"No, but it is hard to tell from this height."

The four men climbed into a Toyota truck, two in the cab, two in the bed of the truck, and headed down towards the far end of the valley. When they reached the man who was on watch there, he traded places with a man in back. Then the driver turned around and headed towards the opposite end of the valley and the women's camp.

"Look," Mahvash said.

Four more men had come out of the schoolhouse. They climbed into a Land Cruiser and headed towards the opposite side of the valley. The women watched the truck cross over the bridge and stop at the first house. One of the men pointed his AK at the sky. A moment later, the report of his gunfire echoed down the canyon and every woman in camp grabbed her rifle.

"Is that spawn of Satan shooting at our drone?" Veeda said.

"No," Farzaneh said. "It is only the Taliban giving the villagers a pleasant wakeup call."

The other women drifted over and joined in watching the screen. The men in the Land Cruiser had continued down the valley, shooting off rounds.

One by one the village men began to appear at their front doors and make their way out into the fields. They walked as if all the hope and happiness had been drained out of their hearts.

"You will soon be dead, you dogs," Hajira said.

"Who are these people?" Veeda said.

"That is Bikram, and Aarshin. They are the men who saw me when I escaped."

Saarah went on pointing out everyone she knew and what she thought their sentiments would be if the women succeeded in liberating them from the Taliban. Her eyes were on her own house, hoping to see her family. The Land Cruiser had pulled to a stop out in front of it and moments later, the front door opened.

"Is that Akmad, their leader?" Veeda said, seeing a man appear.

"Yes."

"I am sorry," Veeda said, reaching out a hand. "Even if I have to die in battle, I will make sure that scum dies with me."

All of the women reached a hand and touched Saarah.

While they watched, Akmad took a seat up front in the Land Cruiser and the driver started off on a slow tour of the valley, stopping here and there to drop off armed men. The men in the fields went on working with rifles at their backs.

"Are there no women in this village?" Tabaan said.

"They are obviously inside with their burkas," Hajira said.

The men had been at work in the fields for some minutes when the first woman appeared outside, then another one, and another one. Most of them headed down to the river to do their wash.

Saarah remembered Maanika and searched for any sign of her. It was nearly impossible to tell who was who beneath the burkas, but just going by size and walk and mannerisms alone, Saarah did not believe that Maanika was among the women.

Saarah thought of Pazir, the young man from her village, but he was nowhere in sight. Perhaps he had been killed.

Saarah returned her attention to her own house. More minutes passed before her mother finally appeared from under the shed at the back of their house, wearing a burka. Paksima and Baddar were with her and together they herded their goats and sheep up into the nearby hills.

"Your family?" Veeda said.

Saarah nodded. Veeda looked back at the screen and continued watching for any fresh signs of the Taliban around the valley. When it seemed clear that there was nothing more to be seen, she motioned to Farzaneh.

"That is enough for now. Best not to risk them spotting the drone."

As Farzaneh turned the drone back towards their camp, Veeda faced the other women.

"Has everyone eaten?"

"No," Darsameen said. "We were just opening our rations when the gunfire went off."

"Then let us eat and discuss our plan of attack before we have more rest."

Saarah paused to watch her mother and siblings. Once they had herded their goats far up into the hills, Zeeana pulled back her burqa. Oh, Momma, she thought. Tonight I will free you and you will never have to submit to this scourge again.

Saarah returned to find all the women opening their rations. Hajira had the entire package spread out on her sleeping bag.

"What does this mean, 'First Strike Ration'?" she said.

"It's meant for teams like us," Irem said. "When you are out on patrol and there is no way to prepare your meals."

"Is it meant for me to eat all of this at once?"

"If you wish to be a pig."

Hajira stared back while the other women laughed.

"No," Irem went on. "It is meant to be your total food consumption for one day."

"What is French Toast?"

"It is bread dipped in egg batter. With syrup."

"So that is breakfast?"

"If that's what you like."

Hajira opened the package and tried it.

"It is sweet."

"That's the syrup."

"Hmm."

"Bacon Cheddar Breakfast Sandwich," Tabaan said. "Did they forget we are Muslims?"

"Pepperoni Pocket Sandwich," Darsameen said. "Does that have pork in it too?"

"I think so," Irem said.

"What a waste!"

"Don't eat what you don't like," Veeda said. "We are lucky to have provisions."

She took a big bite of her own Bacon Cheddar Breakfast Sandwich.

"Blasphemy," Tabaan said.

"Ah, yes. Let us not offend Allah! And where was this god while these dogs used me like chattel day and night for weeks? I prayed and prayed to be saved, and yet nothing happened. Nothing except that I remained a slave to these foolish superstitions."

"Blasphemy," Tabaan said again.

"Very well. I am blasphemous, and will remain so until this god comes down to earth and shows me otherwise."

Some of the women had smiled, amused by Veeda's rant, which only angered Tabaan more.

"Let us not waste time fighting among ourselves," Veeda said and looked from face to face. "We should only be thinking of our plans for tonight."

"It seems simple to me," Hajira said. "Let Saarah take out the two watchmen, then send one team after this dog Akmad and another team to take out that schoolhouse. We will be done in an hour."

"We will need to take out this nearer guard first, or we can do nothing," Farzaneh said.

"Veeda has that Glock and silencer," Darsameen said. "Maybe we can take out this nearer guard while Saarah takes out the other guard at the far end of the valley."

"Whatever we do, we need to take out this nearer guard first or he will alert the others."

"I agree," Irem said. "We should take out the nearer guard first but then surround both buildings before Saarah takes out the other guard. In case there is a problem and he somehow alerts the others to the danger. That way we are waiting when they stick their heads out."

Veeda had finished her bacon cheddar sandwich and was looking through the rest of her meal packet. She opened her chocolate protein drink and tasted that.

"Hmm, good."

"Are you even listening?" Tabaan said.

Veeda looked up at Tabaan.

"Of course I am listening. I was only allowing everyone to offer their thoughts."

"And so? What do you think?"

"I would agree with Irem. We take out this guard and surround the two buildings while Saarah moves into position to neutralize the other guard. I would only add, let the one team surround the schoolhouse and be prepared to neutralize the men inside, but let the other team take out Akmad first. As Darsameen had said, we have the Glock. Best to see if we can kill Akmad quietly, without arousing the others. If we try

181

to take out those eight men in the schoolhouse first, we will surely have aroused Akmad in doing so."

"And if we can't take out Akmad quietly?"

"Then, at the sound of gunfire, the other team should be prepared to breach the schoolhouse immediately with grenades and gunfire. We will still catch them asleep and confused."

Veeda looked at Saarah.

"It is only fair to Saarah. We do not want Akmad having a chance to hold her family hostage."

"I want to kill him myself," Saarah said.

"I know," Veeda said. "But the team needs you as our sniper."

"And what if there are more Taliban that we have not seen?" Esin said.

"It is a valid point," Veeda said. "We will fly the drone again towards the end of the day and see if we have missed anyone. I am sure they will have all shown their faces by then. For now, let us take turns on watch. And get that solar charger and battery pack out, Farzaneh. We should charge everything so that it is fresh for tonight."

Veeda grabbed her rifle.

"I will take the first shift towards the valley. Whoever feels most rested, take the first shift at the falls."

"I will do it," Irem said.

"Very well. Everyone else, get more rest. We will need all of our strength when the hour comes."

Most of the women were still eating and the jokes and complaints about the food continued. Then there were yawns and talk of their former lives and little by little, they all settled back into their sleeping bags and slept.

It was midmorning when Darsameen and Tabaan were awakened to take the next shift. The day had grown warm enough that all the women were now lying with their sleeping bags open. At noon, when Esin and Hajira climbed out of their sleeping bags to go on shift, the day had grown listless with heat and the buzz of insects.

The rest of the women had said their midday prayers and were either snacking or down by the stream washing their sore feet. Ariya and Kejal, in the manner of their Kurdish tradition, had helped all of them to paint their finger and toenails red. There were jokes about the Taliban going mad when they saw this horde of female Afghan Stars coming at them with weapons.

As sunset neared, a silence fell over the women. The battle was near.

Veeda had Farzaneh put the drone back in the air at a thousand feet and the women sat around watching the valley at the close of day. By the time everyone in the village had drifted inside for the evening, it seemed clear that there were only the eleven Taliban.

A woman appeared at a door and threw out some scraps to a dog. A boy came down the road, herding his errant goat. All else was quiet.

Later, they saw the Taliban make one last patrol of the valley and change guards. Then the driver of the Land Cruiser dropped Akmad back at Saarah's house. Akmad stood by the door and watched the Land Cruiser head off towards the schoolhouse before turning to go inside.

All eyes were on Saarah.

"I still wish it was my privilege to end his life."

Veeda nodded.

"Understood but we must do what is best for the team."

Veeda looked back at the screen.

"Farzaneh, see if you can find a suitable place in the hills to set the drone down. It will save battery life if we do not have to bring it all the way back each time. And Saarah and Irem, take first watch."

While Farzaneh worked to land the drone, the other women drifted back to their sleeping bags, and had been resting there but a brief minute when the lights of a car passed by on the road overhead. Everyone sat up to watch.

"Farzaneh," Veeda whispered. "Get that drone back up in the air."

Everyone quickly gathered around the laptop to watch. The vehicle was another Land Cruiser and eventually came to a stop in front of Saarah's house. Four men climbed out and Akmad came out of the house to speak with them.

They had talked for several minutes when their meeting suddenly broke up. The four men climbed back into the Land Cruiser and the driver turned around in the road, heading for the bridge and the other side of the valley. Akmad stood watching for several moments before going back inside.

Veeda cursed.

"Tabaan, quickly, go relieve Saarah and tell her she is needed here."

While they waited, the driver parked in front of a building and the four men went inside. Veeda motioned for Saarah to hurry as she approached.

"What is this place?" Veeda asked.

She pointed to the building where the men had gone inside.

"It is the boy's schoolhouse."

Veeda cursed again.

"So now we have fifteen Taliban and three targets to neutralize."

"So," Hajira said. "We split up into three teams instead of two."

"Eh," Veeda said. "I liked the odds better before."

"I can come back and help with one of the teams," Saarah said. "Once I have neutralized the other guard."

"We shall see. For now, Tabaan, plan on taking Farzaneh, Mahvash, Esin, and Darsameen with you and lead the assault on the girl's schoolhouse. Irem, you take Noushineh with you to the boy's schoolhouse. Hajira and I will join you there once we have neutralized Akmad. Remember, no one attacks until Hajira and I have returned."

"And if you fail to neutralize him?" Mahvash said.

"You have already asked me this. We will neutralize him."

"And if Akmad puts up a struggle and shots are fired?" Irem said.

"Then attack, of course. If we have lost the element of surprise, toss your grenades and engage the enemy."

The women turned their attention back to the laptop screen.

"Okay," Veeda said. "Everyone not on watch, make sure your gear is ready and get some rest. We will wait an hour, just to make sure everyone is asleep, then begin our attack. Farzaneh, bring the drone back down before we waste the batteries. And Saarah, go relieve Tabaan and position yourself so that you can see the guard. If someone comes to relieve him before we move out, let me know. Otherwise, we will come your way in one hour."

With everyone's sleeping bag already rolled up and tucked away, the women went down to the stream and stretched out on the sandy soil. Veeda lay on her back with them and looked up.

"So many stars," she said.

The other women had to choke back their laughter. Then they were all silent with their thoughts.

Before the hour had passed, Veeda got up and took Farzaneh and Mahvash with her. Farzaneh brought the drone back up in the air and they knelt there together, watching for any signs of movement in the valley. Here and there, they saw goats and sheep stirring in open pens. Two foxes came down from the hills. A dog barked, but all else was quiet.

"All right," Veeda said. "Bring the drone over to this side of the valley, closer to the schoolhouses, and lock the controls."

She checked her phone for the time.

"One hour has passed. We probably have at least one more hour before the guards change. Get ready to move out. I will gather the others."

Veeda returned to the stream and nodded. The women were quick to their feet.

"We should pray," Tabaan said.

"To the same God these dogs pray to," Veeda muttered.

"You do not have to join us."

"That much is true."

Veeda walked back towards the village and waited for the others to join her. The mouth of the canyon was three hundred yards away. They marched quietly forward to Saarah's position. She was up on a ledge with the barrel of her rifle resting on a rock. Veeda motioned for everyone to wait and climbed up with her. The guard was seventy-five yards away and Saarah had a clean shot.

"You can't miss," Veeda whispered.

"I won't miss."

"Then as soon as we hear your shot, we will move out."

Veeda climbed back down and signaled to Saarah. The women stood there looking from face to face, knowing to expect the shot but still flinching a bit at the sound of the muffled shot. It was quickly followed by the slap of the bullet into the man's skull and his gasp.

Saarah scrambled back down from her ledge and nodded.

When the team neared the body, Veeda signaled for everyone to get down into a watch and cover position while Irem went inspect it. Irem gathered the man's weapon and ammunition. She checked but he had no phone, only a radio. She took that and made sure it was off. He had been sitting up against a tree so Irem carefully set him back into that position.

With a signal from her, the teams moved out, Veeda and Hajira towards the north side of the valley and Saarah's home, the rest of the team members down the south side of the valley and towards both schoolhouses. Saarah went alone down the stream and through the woods.

Ten minutes later, everyone was in place.

"Are we good?" Veeda whispered to Saarah over the radio.

"We are good. The guard got up to urinate. I am waiting for him to sit back down."

"Sounds like the perfect time to shoot him to me," Farzaneh whispered.

"Ssshhhh," Veeda said.

Everyone sat there waiting again.

"The hostile is dead," Saarah whispered a minute later.

"Good," Veeda said. "Leave his weapons for now and move to where you can cover both schoolhouses. We will wait until you are in position before we breach your house."

"I am running that way now."

A minute later, Saarah reported in.

"I am here."

"Then complete radio silence until you hear from me again."

Veeda clicked off and glanced over at Hajira. The two of them were crouched up the hill a good distance from the back of Saarah's house, just watching and listening. When it seemed clear that no one was awake inside, Veeda gave the signal and the two women headed down the hill.

The sheep and goats stirred as they moved past the shed. A dog began barking off in the distance. Both women froze in place and waited until it had stopped barking.

At the front door, they lowered their night vision goggles. Hajira gave cover while Veeda carefully opened the door. The darkened room showed no sign of life so Veeda slipped inside. Hajira followed, still giving cover.

Based on Saarah's intel, Veeda headed for the last door down the hallway. The other two doors were both slightly ajar so she paused there to listen before moving on again.

When Veeda reached the last door, she got her Glock out and met Hajira's eyes. They had practiced this kind of breach and clear tactic hundreds of times over the past two months, enough to know that no two situations were ever alike. The hope was, they terminated Akmad before he awakened, but there were many possible scenarios in which things could go wrong.

Veeda was about to open the door when Hajira sensed movement behind them and quickly spun around. Veeda spun around too, having sensed Hajira's movement.

It was Paksima, staring with the guns pointed at her.

Hajira tapped a fist to her chest, put a finger to her lips and pointed at the room. Paksima stared for another long moment before going back in through the door.

Hajira and Veeda shared a look and took a deep breath. Perhaps it was a good omen. Paksima could just as easily have cried out.

With a final look at Paksima's door, Veeda nodded. Hajira got her rifle into the up and ready position. Veeda placed her hand on the door to Zeeana's bedroom and carefully parted it a few inches. When there was no response, she pushed it open far enough to have a look inside. Akmad and Zeeana were asleep in the bed.

Veeda had started to open the door the rest of the way when the hinges creaked and Akmad reflexively bolted upright in bed. Veeda pumped three bullets into him before his hands could reach his AK. His body collapsed there, half on the floor.

In all of this, Zeeana had awakened and screamed.

"Silence," Veeda whispered.

Hajira had already entered the room and was scanning it for any other threats.

"Clear," she whispered.

"Then go secure the children."

Hajira went out the door.

"It is okay," Veeda told Zeeana. "We are here with your daughter Saarah. Within the hour, the Taliban will be gone from your village."

Hajira herded the children in from the hallway. They both ran to their mother.

"Keep them quiet," Veeda said.

Zeeana nodded. Veeda spoke into her radio.

"Number one, here. All secure. We are on our way to join you...Saarah, your family is safe."

Veeda clicked off and waved to Zeeana.

"Come wait in the front room. We will leave the body where it is for now."

Hajira grabbed Akmad's rifle and ammunition and satellite phone and together the two women slipped back out the front door.

Sixteen

Veeda had barely closed the front door when her radio crackled and Tabaan's voice came over the air.

"Four of them just exited the girl's schoolhouse and are heading towards the east end of the valley in their truck. It must be to change the guards."

Veeda cursed under her breath.

"Esin, quickly, join Irem and Noushineh at the boy's schoolhouse. I am sending Hajira to join the three of you. That makes four on four at both schoolhouses."

Veeda motioned and Hajira took off running.

"Saarah, I need you back at that guard post. Everyone else, prepare to light up those two schoolhouses. There is about zero chance we will be able to neutralize these four dogs without others hearing gunfire go off. I am on my way there right now. And Saarah, if they get there first and find the guard dead, you have my permission to engage the enemy."

In the stillness of the starlit night, Veeda took off running. She could hear the hum of the truck off in the distance. Then it stopped and there was only the sound of her boots clomping across the wooden bridge.

A moment later, she heard men's voices, then a shot from Saarah's gun and all hell broke loose, first with return fire in Saarah's direction, then four nearly simultaneous explosions down at the other end of the valley. This was followed by a fierce exchange of gunfire in that direction.

Veeda reached the far end of the bridge and turned east up the valley along a row of mudbrick homes. Several villagers had poked their heads out their front doors but quickly retreated inside when Veeda waved her rifle at them. She keyed up her radio.

"What is our status, Saarah?"

"I have eliminated two of them. The other two are heading your way in the truck."

"Forgive me if I sound foolish for asking this but why did you not eliminate all four?"

"I tried but the other two escaped my line of sight. I am running your way now. You should see them any minute."

Veeda saw that an old man had come out to watch from his front porch. With a look over her shoulder, she also saw that the truck had come into view. It was well off in the distance but moving fast. Feeling she had no choice but to trust the old man, Veeda ran up to him.

"Quickly, we must get out of sight."

He waved at the front door and followed Veeda inside. She got down into a firing position and pointed her rifle back up the road. While waiting, she glanced over her shoulder.

"I am here with Saarah from your village and very soon, you will be rid of these dogs."

"I can help," the old man said.

Veeda searched the man's eyes before reaching for her Glock and handing it to him. When she looked back, the truck was some seventy-five yards off and the two men in the cab were now visible. Veeda aimed and waited until the last second before firing. Both bodies lurched violently backwards and then slumped forward. The truck careened off the road and came to a halt against a wellhead. The forward motion of the driver's body had left him pinned against the steering wheel. The horn was blaring and off in the distance, the sounds of the firefight were ongoing.

Saarah ran out from the woods just then and pointed her rifle at Salahuddeen. He raised both hands and let the Glock hang limply from one finger.

"So you are a warrior now," he said. "I am glad."

"He can be trusted," Veeda said. "Come. Help me clear these bodies from the truck so we can join the others."

Still wary, Saarah nodded at Salahuddeen and backed her way over to the truck.

With both bodies on the ground, Veeda grabbed the shemagh from the one on her side and used it to clear some of the blood and broken glass from the seat before climbing behind the wheel.

"Get in!" she told Saarah and jammed the truck into reverse.

Having backed away from the wellhead, Veeda jammed the truck into first gear and called to Salahuddeen through the shattered window.

"Is there anyone else here in the village that we must fear?"

"I believe Aarshin is sympathetic to these men. There may be others but I do not believe any of them are armed."

"Very well."

Veeda nodded at the gun in his hand.

"If it becomes necessary, please shoot them."

Salahuddeen nodded back. Veeda raced off down the valley, cursing at the sound of the ongoing firefight.

"Only the spawn of Satan could have survived those grenades."

Just then, they heard another explosion.

"Ah, good," Veeda said. "I would gladly use an atomic bomb on this scourge if I had one."

She keyed up her radio.

"Number one, here. All clear on this end. Saarah and I are headed your way in a Toyota truck. What is your status?"

Irem radioed back.

"The boy's schoolhouse is now cleared. One hostile had survived the first blast but we just now sent him on his way to hell. We are on our way to the girl's schoolhouse now."

"And your status, Tabaan?"

"We believe there are two hostiles still alive inside. They are returning fire in all directions so we have not been able to approach the building with more grenades."

"I have your answer," Irem called back. "We found an RPG in the other schoolhouse."

"Fine," Veeda said. "Just remember not to shoot when you see us coming."

Following the river, the road came around a bend and into view of the firefight. The other women had taken cover inside the woods, opposite the boy's schoolhouse. Veeda pulled the truck out of sight down by the river and climbed out with her rifle and those of the two men she had killed. Saarah now had the long gun slung over her back and the AK in her hands.

"Get to where you have a line of sight at this side of the schoolhouse," Veeda said. "I will give cover until you are in position. If you have a shot, take it. I am off to see about this RPG business."

Veeda opened fire at the schoolhouse while Saarah lit off across the open space. Once she had safely taken cover behind an adjacent wall, Veeda ran off through the woods and keyed up her radio.

"Coming through the woods from the east."

"Roger that," Tabaan called back.

Veeda ran up and found Esin dressing a wound on Noushineh's left arm.

"What is this?"

Esin looked up.

"She took a bullet."

"Where's the bullet?"

"It went through."

Noushineh was staring up at Veeda. Veeda reached out a hand.

193

"So now you are initiated."

"I can still fight," Noushineh said.

"Let us see how your wound is healing. If it becomes infected tomorrow, we will have to send you back to Kahmard."

"It will not become infected."

"All right. We shall see."

Veeda went off among the trees, looking for Irem.

"Where are you and this RPG?"

"Right here," Irem whispered back. "Ready to fire whenever you are."

Irem had a pile of AKs and ammunition lying next to her. Veeda walked over for a closer look at the RPG.

"You remember how to use this thing?" Veeda said.

"Of course."

Veeda looked off through the trees at the schoolhouse. The exchange of gunfire had stopped. Veeda knew from Saarah's description that there was one big classroom in front, with an office and small kitchen in back. Veeda hit the com button.

"Saarah, do you have a shot?"

"Nothing yet."

"All right. Here is the plan. I will send Hajira and Darsameen over to the opposite side of the building and while you distract those dogs with crossfire, Irem will send the RPG through the front window. Then we will attack from the front and sides until they are all dead."

Veeda motioned to Hajira and Darsameen.

"Call when you are in position."

They moved off through the woods to the west. The rest of the women stood back among the trees, watching and waiting.

"I do not like the feel of this," Farzaneh said.

"How so?"

"Someone among them must have called for backup. The longer we delay here, the more danger there is."

Veeda pulled Akmad's phone out from her vest.

"This is the only phone they had. If they have radios, they are only useful in this valley."

"That is an assumption," Mahvash said. "Should we not at least be sending a team to guard the road coming in and out of the village?"

Veeda scratched her neck while considering the question.

"It is a reasonable suggestion but I do not consider it wise to split up the team at this moment. Everyone, just keep a secure perimeter for now."

The radio crackled just then with Hajira's voice.

"We are in position."

Veeda nodded and the women eased up closer to the edge of the woods. Irem rested the RPG on her shoulder and nodded at Veeda. Veeda keyed up her radio.

"All right. Give us some diversionary fire and prepare yourselves for this RPG."

The second the gunfire began peppering the building, the two men inside returned fire and Veeda gave Irem a nod. The grenade screamed off towards the front of the schoolhouse with the gunfire inside continuing. Then, at the last second, there were the sounds of men shouting and scrambling for cover before the RPG exploded inside.

Then all was silent.

With smoke billowing out of the windows, Veeda called for more cover fire and led the charge. With Darsameen, Hajira and Saarah spraying the mud walls of the building from both sides, Veeda reached the front wall and pulled out a grenade. Tabaan and Esin raced up next to her and gave cover. Veeda made eye contact with them, pulled the pin, tossed the grenade in through the shattered window and ducked for cover.

A moment later, the explosion blew out all the remaining windows and sent a fresh cloud of smoke and debris billowing up into the sky.

Veeda stood up, pulled her night vision goggles down and waited until Tabaan and Esin had flanked her before she kicked the door in. Following a spray of bullets into the schoolhouse, she cautiously looked inside. When there was no response, she motioned with the barrel of her rifle for Tabaan to enter the building. Veeda covered her and Esin covered Veeda in a search and clear formation.

They quickly found four dead bodies but made no assumptions and cleared the back of the schoolhouse before letting their guard down.

"All known hostiles accounted for and dead," Veeda called over the radio. "Irem, take Mahvash with you and gather up all the weapons from the girl's schoolhouse, then make your way back here. Everyone, meet us here. We must talk and then confront the villagers. Farzaneh, bring that drone down. And all of you, watch your backs."

Veeda stood guard at the door while Esin and Tabaan stripped the mangled bodies of all their weapons and ammunition and anything else of value. Saarah arrived first, followed by Darsameen, Hajira and Noushineh. Noushineh shuddered at seeing the carnage and turned away.

"How is your arm?" Veeda asked her.

"It is fine. I can still fight."

Veeda smiled at her and turned to Darsameen.

"Please, find something to cover the bodies with if you can. And listen, everyone. We need to do three things before we leave this village, and we need to do them quickly. Gather up the bodies and decide where to bury them, gather up all our weapons and supplies and get them into the two Land Cruisers and meet with the villagers. I want all available intel while we listen to their grievances."

"Listen to what?" Hajira said. "We liberated them from this filth."

Veeda looked back from watching the door.

"Not everyone here will feel as we do. That village elder has already told me that some in this village support the Taliban. Is this not true, Saarah?"

196

Saarah nodded. Irem and Mahvash pulled up outside in the other Land Cruiser.

"Any trouble?" Veeda asked as they approached the front door.

"The villagers are starting to gather out in the road but we just kept moving."

"Is everything in the Land Cruiser?"

"Everything."

"Any phones?" Veeda asked.

Irem shook her head.

"Any phones here?"

Veeda shook her head.

"There is only the one I found on Akmad."

Farzaneh appeared out of the woods and walked towards the schoolhouse carrying the drone.

"Everyone is here?" Farzaneh said.

Veeda nodded. Farzaneh walked in and looked around the room. Darsameen was just then covering the last two bodies.

"They will have no need to cause trouble now," Farzaneh said.

"Beating these dogs is too easy, yes?" Mahvash said.

Veeda looked at her.

"It was easy because they were not expecting us. It will not be this easy next time, I promise you."

"What are we doing now?" Farzaneh said.

Veeda quickly explained what they had already discussed.

"And then?"

Veeda looked from face to face.

"I read once that when you have the enemy on the run, you should keep pursuing him and never let up."

"What are you saying?" Irem asked.

"The night is still young and the enemy is still unaware of our presence."

Veeda turned to Saarah.

"I remember you saying that they had come from the direction Ghowr Band."

"That is where we first heard their gunfire. From over the hills in that direction."

Veeda looked back around the room.

"Then let us take the fight to them before they learn of this massacre and have time to prepare."

"We have no intel," Tabaan said. "And Ghowr Band is ten miles away."

"We now have two Land Cruisers. We can meet with the villagers and still be there within the hour."

"I agree with Tabaan," Esin said. "We have no intel. We would need to set up camp and recon the area first as we did here. Otherwise, how will we know how many hostiles we face or where to attack?"

"So? We will go there and prepare."

Irem spoke up.

"If what you say is true and this massacre is not yet known to the outside world, then let us prepare an ambush. Surely when they are unable to communicate with Akmad, they will come looking to see what is wrong."

"And be doubly wary because of it."

"And we will be as quiet as mice, but strike like tigers once they have walked into our trap."

"I can see the upsides and the downsides to this strategy."

"There are upsides and downsides to any strategy."

"Some have more downsides than others."

Veeda turned to Saarah.

"What do you think?"

"I know this is not part of our mission, but I want to make sure that my family is safely out of this village. That is my first concern."

"You are right. It is not part of our mission, but your concern is understandable. We will do what we can to protect them."

"Did not Ariya instruct us to contact her before doing anything else?" Darsameen said.

"That is true but enough of this discussion for now. We waste precious time. Let us break up into teams. Hajira, Darsameen and Tabaan, you are the strongest. We will take you back to the truck. Use it to gather up all the dead Taliban and bring them back here to this schoolhouse. Noushineh, Farzaneh, Esin and Mahvash, take the other Land Cruiser and gather up all that remains in our camp. I will go with Saarah and Irem to meet with the villagers."

"I want to make sure my family is safe," Saarah said.

"Very well, but let us go retrieve the truck first."

Outside, Noushineh, Farzaneh, Esin and Mahvash took one of the Land Cruisers and headed for the camp. The rest of the women gathered at the other Land Cruiser and squeezed in together. Irem drove. Veeda and Saarah sat up front with her and the other three women took the backseat.

On their way to the truck, they came across a gathering of villagers out in front of the girl's schoolhouse. Veeda waved and Irem braked to a stop. Most of the people looked to be in a state of shock over what had happened, but a few were angry and Aarshin was among those.

"You?" he said at seeing Saarah. "You and these women have brought this blasphemy upon our village?"

"We liberated you, old man," Veeda said. "So shut up and listen."

"And you, a woman, would talk to me in this manner?"

He spat on the ground.

Veeda cursed under her breath, climbed out of the car and fired off a few rounds into the sky with her AK. That quieted Aarshin for the moment. Veeda turned to everyone else.

"Listen! We will be meeting at Salahuddeen's home shortly to discuss what has happened here and what to do next."

"We will all be butchered," Aarshin said. "That is what will happen next."

"And if you choose to live as a slave, rather than to live freely, that is your choice."

Veeda turned to face the others.

"All of you. We came here to free you from this Taliban scum and that is now done. They are all dead and it is time to discuss what comes next. Once we have gathered all the dead at the boy's schoolhouse, we will meet you at Salahuddeen's. Please pass the word to the rest of the village."

Veeda kept her rifle pointed at Aarshin until Hajira, Darsameen and Tabaan were in the truck and ready to drive off. Then she backed over and spoke to Hajira through the missing window.

"Follow us over to Saarah's house and we will throw that scum Akmad in the back while you are there."

Saarah had gotten out and was talking to one of the village women.

"Come, we must go!" Veeda called out to her.

Saarah lingered for a moment longer before joining Veeda and Irem back in the Land Cruiser.

"What was that about?" Veeda asked as Irem pulled away.

"I was speaking to my friend Maanika's mother."

"And? What of it?"

Veeda turned to stare at Saarah when she failed to answer.

"One of the Taliban violated her and she refuses to come out of the house now."

Veeda continued staring at Saarah for a long moment before looking forward again.

Approaching Salahuddeen's house, they could see more villagers had already gathered in front. Veeda waved for Irem to stop and rolled down her window. Salahuddeen sat on his porch, listening calmly to the agitated discussion around him. Again there was anger mixed in among the many voices.

Veeda called out.

"We are telling everyone in the village to meet us here. Expect us back shortly."

Salahuddeen nodded and went back to listening. Veeda waved and Irem drove forward.

Up ahead on the bridge, they passed more people drifting towards Salahuddeen's house. Seeing Saarah and the other women dressed for battle, there were the same stunned looks.

At Saarah's house, she jumped out and ran to the front door. Hajira, Darsameen and Tabaan climbed out of the truck and joined Veeda and Irem in keeping watch.

A minute later, Saarah reappeared at the door and waved for everyone to come in. Zeeana stood in the front room with Paksima and Baddar at her side. Saarah introduced everyone.

"These are my sisters," Saarah told her mother. "We live and die together."

"Forgive me, Mrs. Khalil," Veeda said, "but we must be on with our business."

She nodded and Hajira headed down the hallway with Tabaan and Darsameen. Veeda looked back at Zeanna.

"The village is meeting at Salahuddeen's house. Is it your wish to join us?"

Zeeana nodded.

"I will need to bring the children."

"Of course, but let us go."

The other three women came out carrying Akmad's corpse.

Seventeen

The gathering in front of Salahuddeen's house had swelled into a large, restless crowd and heads turned in unison as the truck and Land Cruiser rumbled across the bridge. Irem braked to a stop well back of the gathering and everyone inside the Land Cruiser climbed out. The truck turned right and continued down towards the schoolhouses.

At seeing the women in battle gear, there were grumblings among the village men, some of it in anger. Veeda and Irem pushed ahead through the bodies and made a path for Zeeana and her two young children. Saarah followed behind, ignoring the many denunciations hurled at her.

She had neared the front of the crowd when someone grabbed her arm. Saarah turned fiercely, ready to pounce, only to find it was Mrs. Farooq. Mrs. Farooq stared with a sad look in her eyes. Before Saarah could speak, Mrs. Farooq leaned into ear.

"I am so glad to see you have survived. But this. It is as if you have abandoned all of your dreams."

Mrs. Farooq pulled back and stared again. Saarah had started to reply when Mrs. Farooq motioned with her eyes, up to where Aarshin was glaring at them from Salahuddeen's front porch. Saarah gave Mrs. Farooq a brief hug and went up to join her fellow warriors. Aarshin had continued glaring at Saarah this whole time, then turned to Zeeana.

"Look at the shame and disaster you have brought upon our village, allowing your daughter to act in his manner."

"Shame and disaster?" Saarah said.

She turned to the crowd.

"The Taliban killed my father and violated my mother. That is shame and disaster." She turned to Aarshin. "While you blessed this blasphemy. You are an insult to the prophet, just like the Taliban you clearly admire."

When Aarshin moved angrily at Saarah, Veeda and Irem stepped between them.

"Enough," Salahuddeen said quietly and stood up. "We can argue all night and it will not change a thing. What is done is done. The only question now is what to do next."

"We can start by shooting ourselves," Aarshin said. "For if we don't, the Taliban will surely do it for us."

Incited by his words, the village men began arguing again.

"Stop!" Salahuddeen shouted and waited for the many voices to still. "I tell you again, there are only two choices now. Lie down like dogs and surrender, or fight."

"Fight with what?" a man called out.

"If you are willing," Veeda called back. "We will leave you the weapons we have taken from the Taliban."

"Yes, give us weapons and leave us here to die on our own."

Farzaneh pulled up just then in the other Land Cruiser and all attention turned that way as four more women in combat gear piled out. The villagers parted for them, but not without more grumbling.

Once the additional team members were gathered on Salahuddeen's front porch, Veeda spoke up again.

"We are not here to tell anyone how to live their lives. We are only here to fight for the freedom of the Afghan people. We are willing to die for our own freedom. Now you must decide if you are willing to die for yours."

"What freedom?" Aarshin said. "I tell all of you again, these women have brought only shame and disaster upon us.

The Taliban will be back like a swarm in the days to come and you will not know misery until they get done with us."

"Eh," Veeda said. "Listen to this man. We are only ten women but alone were able to rid this village of that scourge."

"What do you know of bravery? For ten years I fought to free this country of the Russian invaders."

"You fought for your freedom, not mine. Women were treated with respect by the Russians. And as soon as they left, you were quick to enslave us again."

"If you had any respect for Prophet Mohamed and the Quran, you would know that women have their place."

Being several inches taller, Veeda moved closer and glowered down at Aarshin.

"Would someone please shut this man up? I am sick of listening to him. I have never known such a coward in all my life."

When Aarshin went to strike Veeda, the rest of the team raised their rifles at him.

"Oh yes. You see how brave they are while holding these weapons."

In a flash, Veeda threw her rifle aside and went after him, and Aarshin quickly backpedaled, fending off her furious attack. When Veeda finally got hold of his collar and clipped him across the mouth, Saarah and Farzaneh rushed forward and restrained her from hitting him again.

"She struck me!" Aarshin said with a look at those around him. "There is blood!"

"Yes, I struck you," Veeda said. "You stupid old man. You think I am afraid of you? I will tear you limb from limb."

"Please, we are wasting precious time," Salahuddeen said.

"Yes, we are wasting precious time," Veeda said and shook her arms free. "First we must bury the dead, then all of you here must decide. Are you willing to fight or not?"

For a long moment, there was silence. Then Bikram spoke up.

"I will fight."

"Traitor!" Aarshin said.

"Me a traitor? You were quick to grovel before these dogs, when our first loyalty should have been to the village."

"Our first loyalty should be to the prophet and his laws."

"I will fight too," another man said. "In honor of Farzaad, if nothing else. Where in the Quran does it teach us to kill a man and take his wife?"

"I will fight too," another man said.

Many men surged forward now, echoing those words.

"You are all mad," Aarshin said.

"And you are a fool," Veeda said.

She looked out over the crowd.

"We will arm you and even stay here to fight with you, if that is your wish, but I must warn you right now, the minute you turn your backs, this man will betray us."

She looked back at Aarshin.

"I would surely never trust him with a weapon in his hands."

Salahuddeen came forward and spoke up again.

"Let us have a simple vote. All of you who are unwilling to fight, go home now. We will not consider you enemies, but we who are willing to fight must know who is with us and who is not."

In silence, the villagers all exchanged looks. Time passed but no one left. Salahuddeen turned to Aarshin.

"It appears that you are alone."

Aarshin looked from face to face with the entire village staring at him.

"You think I am a coward? You think I will not fight for my beliefs? Then you are wrong. I spent ten years with nothing but fighting. But fighting for a free Afghanistan, based on Sharia Law. So if you are asking me now to desecrate the laws of our prophet, then no, I will not fight with you."

"The times are changing," Salahuddeen said.

"The laws of Allah never change."

"You are right. Now go home and allow the rest of us to fight as we see fit."

With a scowling look for everyone there, Aarshin headed off towards the bridge with his wife following behind him. The villagers watched them depart before turning their attention back to Salahuddeen and the women. He turned to Saarah and Veeda.

"What would you have us do?"

They looked at each other.

"Go ahead," Veeda said. "It is your village."

Before speaking, Saarah leaned closer and whispered into Veeda's ear. Veeda pulled back with an intense look and whispered something to Irem, who in turn whispered to Farzaneh and Noushineh and those three quickly made their way to one of the Land Cruisers. Saarah waited until they had climbed in and raced off towards the north end of the valley before turning back to address the crowd.

"Until three months ago, I had spent my entire life in this village. And it was a good life. Were things not good here before the Taliban came?"

The villagers looked among themselves and nodded.

"Then tell me, how can I not hate what has happened to this village and my own life since they came? I am especially angry for what they have done to my family. I know in the past that some of you were resentful of the American presence and I confess. I too sometimes had those feelings, but did the Americans ever kill one of us? Did they ever force their ways upon our people? No...The day before I ran away, I spoke with two of their women soldiers and knew in that moment that they were only here to help us...Well, if we had doubts in the past, we have seen the difference between them and the Taliban now."

Saarah looked at Salahuddeen.

"As our elder has said, the times are changing, but freedom for women is nothing new in this country. I learned this from reading books while I lived in a Kabul shelter. When exactly did the men in this country decide that women should be slaves? I do not know but refuse to be one of them. I refuse to be married off to an unholy man like Akmad, just so the rest of you can live in peace. Many times, when I first ran away, I regretted my decision. I regretted that I brought this grief upon my family and my village, but I tell you now, I would do it all over again. I am prepared to die for my freedom, as I am prepared to die for yours. I know that we can keep this scourge from ever oppressing us again. It only requires courage and working together."

"And guns!" a man called out. "We cannot fight the Taliban with hoes and plows!"

Salahuddeen looked at Saarah and Veeda before turning back to the crowd.

"There is much yet to discuss, including guns and the proper defense of our village, but first we must honor Muslim tradition and bury the dead."

He looked back at Veeda.

"You say all the bodies are gathered down at the boy's schoolhouse?"

"I believe they are all there, yes. If not now, they will be soon."

Salahuddeen turned back to the villagers.

"The dead will be gathered down at the boy's schoolhouse so I ask everyone who is able, grab a shovel and meet us there. We will bury them out behind the building."

Most of the villagers began to disperse. A few came up to speak with Salahuddeen but Veeda took him aside first.

"I must call and talk with the person who supports us. Our plan had been to strike and move on."

She glanced at the villagers and back.

"I am certain that all of us are willing to stay here and fight, but it is not our decision alone."

Salahuddeen nodded and turned to the men now surrounding him. Veeda pulled Saarah and Zeeana aside.

"I must call Ariya. And you, Zeeana, must decide what you will do. Fight with us, or go to another village where it is safe."

"This is my home. Of course I will stay and fight too."

"But this is no place for children," Saarah said. "Not for now."

"But where would we take them?" Zeeana said.

Veeda looked down at Paksima and Baddar and back at Zeeana.

"We may know of a place where they can stay. At least until the danger has passed."

Zeeana shook her head.

"And do you really think that this danger will ever pass?"

"That I do not know. And is a question for another day. For now, I must go help bury the dead."

As Veeda turned away, Zeeana started to follow.

"No," Veeda said, stopping her. "This is nothing for the eyes of children. Go," she said to Saarah. "Take them home in the Land Cruiser. The rest of us will walk down to the schoolhouse on foot."

Zeeana kissed Veeda on the cheeks before leaving. Mahvash was staring at Veeda when she looked back.

"What?"

"Why is it that Irem, Farzaneh and Noushineh hurried off?"

Veeda explained her concerns about Aarshin.

"I do not trust that dog as far as I can throw him so I have arranged to have eyes on the road coming in and out of the valley."

"It is wise, with or without him."

As they spoke, Irem appeared in the distance and had soon pulled to stop in the other Land Cruiser. Veeda and Mahvash watched as she climbed out and joined them.

"Is it done?" Veeda said.

"As you asked."

"Good. Then go with Mahvash down to the burial site. I will be with you shortly. I must call and speak with Ariya."

The women drove off and Veeda drifted that way while calling Ariya.

"I am very glad to hear from you," Ariya said upon hearing Veeda's voice. "And everyone else?"

"One minor scratch. Otherwise all is well and that nest of vipers has been removed."

"Completely?"

"Completely…But there is more."

In coded words, Veeda explained the current situation.

"We had not expected this invitation to remain as guests," she concluded. "Do you think it is wise?"

"Do you?" Ariya said.

"It is not how we had planned things."

"That is true, but I have always found it good manners to accept an invitation when given. You can never have too many friends in this world. Do you agree?"

"I consider anything that furthers our mission to be good fortune."

"Agreed."

Veeda paused.

"There is another matter," she said and explained in more coded words about the children. "The question is, where would we throw this birthday party, and how would we get the children there?"

Ariya paused.

"I will have to get back to you on that question."

"Very well. I will report back as soon I know more."

"And supplies?" Ariya said.

"We have everything we need for now."

"Good. I will await your next call."

"I expect that will be sooner than later."

Veeda had steadily drifted down the road while talking and could see the villagers gathering around the schoolhouse in the distance. There were two tall trees and a large open area behind it before the land rose up into the hills.

Someone had parked the truck alongside the schoolhouse and people were carrying bodies from there around to the back. Before joining the burial, Veeda paused again for a radio check on the two guard patrols. All was quiet for now so she headed around in back too.

The dead bodies had been laid on white sheets and the women were busy washing them. Despite the gruesome condition of the corpses, the women went about their task without flinching. The men were digging a grave nearby. Veeda took a furtive photo of the enterprise, lest the Taliban tried to claim down the road that their dead had not been treated according to Muslim tradition.

It was well past midnight when the task was done. Salahuddeen had joined them and said a final prayer. The women took the cloths they had used to wash the dead and rinsed them out in the river before heading home. Saarah heard Salahuddeen inviting the village elders and her fellow warriors to his home for further discussions and had started towards the two Land Cruisers when she came face to face with Mrs. Farooq again. The two women stopped and stared.

"I am sorry," Saarah said.

"No, it is I who is sorry for you, my dear child. Sorry to see all of your hopes and dreams stolen away."

"But what hopes and dreams will I have if the Taliban come to power again?"

"No, you are right. There would be none, for any woman in this country."

Saarah heard Veeda calling and waved that way.

"I must go."

"Of course," Mrs. Farooq said.

She stood back and held out her hands towards Saarah.

"Look at you, like the warrior princesses of old. How do the Americans say? I did not see that one coming?"

Saarah had to bit her lip, lest she laugh out loud.

"Go," Mrs. Farooq said. "And know that I am proud of you. And will be praying for your safe keeping."

Saarah hugged Mrs. Farooq and hurried off, but not without a look over her shoulder, and again as Farzaneh sped off in the Land Cruiser, the words Mrs. Farooq had spoken turning over in her heart.

When the women entered Salahuddeen's front room a minute later, there were uncomfortable looks among the men. The women settled onto the floor and returned their looks. Sensing the discomfort, Salahuddeen spoke up.

"You must understand, it is customary for the women to leave the room when men discuss these village matters."

Veeda looked from face to face.

"If we leave this room, we will leave for good. The entire village. Do not ask us to risk our lives for you and then treat us like children."

"These are not normal times," one man said. "Let us quit bickering and discuss how we are to fight the Taliban."

"They have already shown that they can defeat them," Salahuddeen said with a wave at the women. "We should hear what they have to say."

He looked at Veeda. She looked at all the other women before speaking.

"I want to hear from you first. How many Taliban were here? How often did they come and go? Everything you know."

Over the next half hour, the men explained what had transpired in the village since the Taliban first arrived. Sometimes there would be twenty of them, sometimes only a handful. Once a man named Tajj Yusufi had come. He appeared to be Akmad's senior and they had spoken at length before Yusufi left. There was only one other thing the men knew for certain. The Taliban also had control of the highway to the east and the nearby villages in that direction. How far did that control extend and how many men did they have? No one knew for certain.

In the ensuing silence, Veeda pulled out Akmad's satellite phone.

"This belonged to Akmad. I have been waiting for someone to call his number. Sooner or later, they will, and when no one answers, we can be sure that the hour of battle is very near."

"You still have not told us how we are to protect our village," a man said.

"First of all, you will each have an AK to keep near you at all times. In your homes. Out in the fields. Wherever you go. It should remain out of sight but always within reach. We will also be here, but out of sight, watching from the hills and guarding the road in both directions. The Taliban will no doubt be wary when they arrive so it is best that you go about your lives as if everything is normal. We will even park their vehicles where they have been parked in the past, so if someone drives into the village, they will have no reason to suspect there is trouble. Only now we will all be waiting for them and the minute they walk into our trap, we will attack."

"It is all very good, this talk," a man said, "but what if one of them stops me in the fields and asks, 'Where is Akmad? We have been calling him the past few days and he does not answer'."

"Then you will say, 'Oh, yes. Akmad had mentioned that his phone was not working. You will find him where he usually stays'."

"And what of the schoolhouses? How are we to explain that? They look as if the Americans had bombed them."

"It is a reasonable concern," Veeda said. "But it is on the opposite side of the valley from the main road and the last thing they will see. And they will be under attack by us long before they do."

"I'll tell you what I fear," a man said. "That they will come in great numbers and bring even more powerful weapons. When Yusufi came, his men had machine guns mounted on the back of their trucks."

Veeda nodded.

"We now have an RPG launcher that we took from them. And I think nine or ten grenades?" Veeda added with a look at Irem.

"Eight now," Irem said.

"So eight, plus we have our own hand grenades. A machine gun is no doubt to be feared, but if can surprise them, it will be easy enough to terminate the men manning the guns."

"If," someone said.

Veeda shrugged.

"I did not enter into this struggle expecting guarantees. I entered it expecting to fight bravely for my freedom, and die if I must."

The men looked from face to face in the candlelight. The women sat there watching them.

"We do have other advantages," Mahvash said. "A drone, and radios for communication."

"You have radios."

Veeda looked to the other women before speaking.

"If you decide to fight, we can spare two of them. It would be up to you to choose two men who will be your leaders and help coordinate with us as the battle is unfolding."

Salahuddeen nodded at Veeda.

"I believe that is enough information for now. If you would leave us, we will take some time to discuss this matter on our own."

Veeda stood up and the other women joined her.

"We will be here and there around the valley, keeping watch. If we do not talk with you before then, we will see again you in the morning."

The women were not yet to the door when what sounded like a tractor drove up and stopped out in front. This was followed by doors opening and closing and angry voices. Given the commotion, the men in the room were quick to rise up and join the women outside. It was Aarshin being marched up to the house by Farzaneh and Noushineh with their rifles at his back. Aarshin's old flatbed truck was parked behind them.

"We caught this one trying to leave the valley," Farzaneh said.

"In which direction?" Salahuddeen said.

"To the east."

"I was merely leaving early for the morning market."

Veeda pulled her AK up over her head and handed it to Salahuddeen.

"We will let you decide what to do with him, but if the Taliban learn of our plans in advance, they will come in the hundreds, and none of us are ready for that fight."

"We will disable his truck for now."

"That is the very least you should do with him," Tabaan said.

Aarshin glowered at her. Tabaan looked ready to spit.

"This traitor is going to get us all killed."

"That is for their jirga to decide," Veeda said.

She turned to Salahuddeen.

"Do you still have my Glock?"

He pulled it out of his waistband and handed it to her.

"All will be lost if he betrays us."

Veeda encouraged the rest of the women with her hand.

"Come, let us make camp."

The men led Aarshin into the house. The women walked over to the two Land Cruisers and stood facing each other.

"I would like to stay with my family tonight," Saarah said.

Veeda looked from face to face.

"Does anyone object?"

The other women all shook their heads.

"Very well. Irem and I will take Saarah home and return by foot to the camp. It is best if we leave the one Land Cruiser parked out in front of her house. Take the other Land Cruiser and keep the additional weapons with you."

The women climbed into the two vehicles and went their separate ways. Veeda's satellite phone rang while they were crossing the bridge. It was Ariya.

"I received word on the children's party," she said. "You can have it here, but only if there are women from the village to chaperone it. And you will have to find your own way. That will be the most difficult part. The roads are not in good condition right now. You will have to decide if you can make the trip safely."

"We will discuss it among ourselves and call back."

Veeda thanked Ariya and ended the call. After a moment's reflection, she explained the situation to Saarah.

"We could not possibly spare anyone to escort them," Veeda said. "Besides, I would consider the journey foolish right now."

Saarah nodded. Her thoughts had immediately turned to Natalie. Saarah still had her phone number and Natalie had said to call if Saarah was ever in trouble.

She quickly explained the thought to Veeda and Veeda reluctantly handed her the satellite phone.

Eighteen

Russ Blackburn had been on the ground in Kabul for three days now but had yet to receive any meaningful intel with respect to that Taliban bloodbath up in the Nuristan Forest. Ambassador Douglas claimed to know nothing about it and ditto the Army and Afghan government. Even Simmons over at CIA said he was clueless. After knocking heads for three days, Blackburn had begun to wonder if anyone was telling him the truth. Meanwhile, the Taliban's reprisal bombing campaign was in full swing and the president's orderly withdrawal plans had been turned into a joke. Blackburn was growing more dyspeptic by the minute.

Station chief Simmons was just then hanging up from one more harangue by the Under Secretary when Clayton knocked on his partly opened door. Simmons looked up and waved for him to come in. Clayton closed the door and paused briefly before walking over to Simmons' desk. Simmons watched intently as Clayton sat down.

"What's on your mind? I can see it's something."

"Yeah, look. I was just going over the intel from last night and something caught my eye."

"Go on."

"It was a phone call made to an Army specialist named Natalie Montero. She and her team had been operating up in the Shaik Ali area until they were ordered to pull back towards Bamiyan a few months ago. I'm guessing as part of the larger withdrawal plans. Anyway, the call came in from a village in the Shaik Ali area, requesting assistance with transporting a group of village children over to the Kahmard district."

"Are we talking the village elders asking for help?"

"That I don't know. I haven't been able to source the outgoing call but whoever made it referenced having interfaced with this Specialist Montero previously."

"So? With the Army stationed up there, it wouldn't be unusual for them to give out a phone number."

"No, that's not unusual, but this business of getting the children out is. The Taliban's controlled that area for the past three months. They have to be watching every move."

"So you're thinking something went down up there."

"That's my thinking."

"Okay. Where are we going with this?"

"I'd like to take a bird up there and see for myself."

"You could get your ass shot out of the sky doing that."

"With your permission, I'd take a team with me and recon from five thousand feet. See what things look like on the ground before we drop in to investigate. If it's still a Taliban hornet's nest, that should be pretty obvious. We'll take note of their troop strength and move on."

"You think this has something to do with Nuristan?

"I don't know. Just something doesn't add up. You're not trying to get your children out of a village unless you're expecting trouble, but you wouldn't dare do it with Taliban guns at your back."

Simmons shrugged.

"Sure, go ahead. I'll take anything if it gets that SOB Blackburn off my back. He's like a Jack Russell terrier tearing at your pant leg."

Clayton smiled.

"You going now?" Simmons said.

"May as well."

Simmons glanced up at the clock on his wall.

"All right. Report back the minute you have something."

"Will do."

Clayton headed downstairs and out back to the barracks, feeling a bit guilty as he did. He had held back some of what he knew from Simmons, most critically, that the person making the call to Specialist Montero was named Saarah. Clayton's gut instinct told him that it was the same Saarah who had disappeared from that shelter three months earlier. If correct in that assumption, things were finally starting to add up.

He found Bradley, Palmer and Metcalf lounging around in their usual Club Med mode; tank tops and sandals, feet up and the music cranking. An operator named Kelley was with them. Kelly had rotated back on duty when Rosen went off on R&R. Palmer reached over and turned down the music.

"What's up chief," he said. "We going back up to bury that body again?"

"No. Gear up and let's go. All four of you. There's a situation up in the Shaik Ali area we need to recon."

"We expecting to see some Taliban?"

"Don't know. That's what we're going to find out. If there's a hostile force, we'll keep going. If not, we'll drop in and talk to the locals. See what they know. Come on. Sunny's waiting for us over at Karzai. Grab a rig and meet me out in front."

Fifteen minutes later, the five of them were climbing onboard the helicopter with Sunny.

"We expecting trouble?" Sunny asked with his usual smile.

"Don't know," Clayton said. "We'll soon find out."

"This flight come with a beverage service?" Palmer asked, settling in.

"The stewardess'll be around as soon as we reach cruising altitude."

"Make mine a Tanqueray on ice."

"Coming right up. Catch that door if you don't mind."

Sunny went about his business and was soon banking up and away from the airport, heading northwest. The sprawl of

Kabul rushed by below them. The Hindu Kush rose up off to their right with the Shemali Plain straight ahead. Between that plain and Mazar-e-Sharif lay a hundred miles of rugged mountain terrain, carved up by deep, precipitous canyons. Short of nuking the place, it made a joke out of anyone trying to conquer it. The closer you got to the enemy, the farther they slipped back into that labyrinth.

Fifteen minutes later, the remote villages around Shaik Ali were in view, five thousand feet below them. Clayton was scanning the terrain with binoculars. Metcalf came up and crouched between the two seats.

"Anything?" he said.

Clayton shook his head.

"Take us down to three thousand."

Sunny glanced over at him.

"You're sure these boys aren't sporting Stingers or SAMS?"

"There hasn't been anything in our intel. Take us down. You'll still be well out of range of any RPGs."

Sunny smiled at Metcalf.

"I guess if I'm going to go out, it may as well be with a bang."

With Sunny banking into a dive, Metcalf rose up to see the terrain for himself. There were village men out in the fields working, others herding their goats and sheep up in the hills. Some village women were washing clothes down at the river. Everyone stopped to look up at the helicopter. Otherwise, things appeared to be perfectly normal.

"What's that?" Metcalf said, pointing over Sunny's shoulder.

Clayton stood up to look.

"What are seeing?"

"That building. Looks like somebody blew the hell out of it."

"Bring us around," Clayton told Sunny.

Both Palmer and Bradley now came up to look.

"Well I'll be," Palmer said. "Somebody blew the hell out of both those buildings."

He looked at Clayton.

"Some serious shit definitely went down up here."

Clayton pointed towards the east end of the valley, where an old man sat alone on the front porch of his house.

"Bring us down in front of that hooch."

Clayton resumed scanning the valley for hostiles. The rest of the team returned to the back and did a final weapons check.

Before they were on the ground, Clayton joined them.

"Cover me, but give me plenty of space. I want this guy to know we came as friendlies."

As soon as the wheels touched down, Clayton threw the door open and jumped out.

"Kill it," he called over his shoulder to Sunny.

The rest of the team jumped out with Clayton and assumed a defensive posture around the helicopter. Clayton ran head down until he was safely away from the rotor blades.

The old man remained sitting on his porch, watching Clayton's approach without the slightest sign of emotion. Clayton offered a respectful bow of his head when he drew near.

"Do you speak English?"

The old man nodded.

"Clayton Dorn."

"Salahuddeen."

Clayton touched his hand to his chest.

"Would you happen to be the village elder?"

Salahuddeen nodded slowly.

"May I?" Clayton said, pointing at an adjacent chair.

Salahuddeen waved for Clayton to help himself. Clayton took the seat and stared.

"I'm with the American government."

Salahuddeen nodded again.

"It is said that your government is leaving."

Clayton stared while considering his words.

"Not all of us agree with that policy," he said.

"But you will leave anyway."

"That is the official policy as of this moment. There are those of us who are trying to change it."

"And what would it take to change this?"

"A number of things. Mainly, if there was a perception that the Afghan people were willing to fight the Taliban on their own. Do you understand the Vietnam analogy?"

Salahuddeen shook his head.

"In that war, when it became clear that the South Vietnamese were unwilling to fight for their own freedom, there was nothing for us to do but pack up and leave."

"Then you are looking for a sign."

Clayton nodded.

"I have been looking for that too."

Clayton looked off across the valley in thought. After a moment, he looked back

"May I speak freely?"

Salahuddeen waved his hand.

"Our intel suggests that something happened here in this valley. That someone has put up a fight but we don't know who that is or anything about their organizational strength. Frankly, we don't know anything about them."

The two men stared.

"And you are thinking that I know something?"

Clayton held up his palms with a look around.

"We know from our sources that the Taliban had taken over this area. But where are they now? And how did those two buildings come to be damaged back up the road?"

Salahuddeen studied Clayton now, nodding his head.

"And tell me, my American friend. If for some reason I came to know of these fighting Afghans you wish to find, what kind of help would you be willing to offer them?"

Clayton considered Salahuddeen's words before speaking again.

"Intelligence and weapons. Possibly even light air support. Aiding this force would have to be done quietly. Given the official policy."

"So you could help, possibly. But if the people responsible for this official policy were to find out, your help might quickly vanish."

Clayton stared, taking the measure of this old man.

"Yes, it's true. But that could change. If the American people see that your people are willing to die in defense of their own freedom, public opinion could shift, and that is a big thing in our country. Few politicians are willing to buck the sentiments of their voters."

"I see. Well, if I happen to learn of this force, I will surely tell them to get in touch with you."

Clayton looked from Salahuddeen over to the helicopter and back.

"Salahuddeen, you are a wise man, and right to be wary. If I may speak frankly again?"

Salahuddeen nodded.

Our sig intel picked up a communication last night. That you were trying to get all of the children out of this village. And that suggests to me that your village is in trouble. And that is why I came here today."

Clayton nodded at the helicopter.

"That helo can hold a lot of children. Perhaps two or three trips and we could have them all to safety in a matter of an hour or two."

"And you would be willing to do that."

"That I can do without asking."

Salahuddeen sat there playing with his beard and thinking.

"Let me ask you a question," he said.

"Please."

"Are you able to promise me this much. That no matter what happens, you will not betray what you have learned here today?"

222

"I can promise that I will never discuss our dealings with someone who would try to stop you. That is what we do in the CIA. Keep secrets."

Salahuddeen stared for another long moment before pulling the radio out of his pocket and pushing the com button.

"Veeda," he said in Pashto. "I am sitting here with one of the Americans and he wishes to speak with you. It is my belief that we can trust him."

"Alone?" she said.

Salahuddeen considered the question while staring into Clayton's eyes.

"No. Bring everyone. Whoever is not on watch."

"If you say it is okay, then we will be there."

Salahuddeen clicked off.

"We wait," he said.

The two men sat there side by side, watching the road. A minute later, one of the Land Cruisers appeared in the distance. The shooters instinctively brought their rifles up into a ready position. Clayton jumped to his feet.

"It's okay. It's a friendly force."

With everyone watching, the Land Cruiser pulled up and braked to a halt. Six women climbed out, all of them in fatigues, all of them with AKs slung over their shoulders. Saarah was among them. Clayton walked over to greet her.

"Do you remember me?"

Saarah nodded. Clayton glanced at the other women.

"My Pashto and Dari are limited. Do all of you speak English?"

Irem and Farzaneh nodded.

"They don't," Saarah said of Veeda, Tabaan and Noushineh.

"Who's in charge then?" Clayton said.

Saarah touched Veeda's arm.

"Then can we go inside and talk?" Clayton said.

Veeda searched Clayton's eyes while listening to Saarah translate. Finally, she nodded and the women moved towards Salahuddeen's front porch.

"Chill," he told the shooters and followed the women.

Salahuddeen welcomed everyone into the house.

"I shall make tea," he said.

"Please," Clayton said. "We don't have time for that."

Once everyone was seated inside, Clayton explained what he knew, from the battle up in the Nuristan Forest to the more recent intel. He said nothing of having exhumed Kashm from her grave, knowing it would deeply offend them.

Saarah again translated everything and looked back at Clayton.

"What is it that you want from us?"

"It's what I can do to help you. Tell me about your objectives."

Saarah answered Clayton's question while explaining everything to the other women in Pashto.

"Then you believe that another Taliban force will be coming here soon."

"Akmad's phone has not rung yet," Saarah said. "But we know one day soon it will. And then…"

She shrugged.

"And what did your friend in the Army tell you? About getting the children out of the village?"

Saarah tensed up at hearing this question.

"I'm sorry," Clayton said. "It is the way of our government. There are always people listening."

Saarah stared, still feeling violated, but ultimately went on to translate again. Then all six women spoke in Pashto at some length before Saarah turned back to Clayton.

"The soldier who gave me her phone number said she doubted she could help now. It was her desire to do so but they had strict orders to stay away from this area."

"Okay," Clayton said. "Let's deal with the children first. If you are willing, we can transport all of them in that helicopter."

Saarah paused before translating the offer. Another animated discussion in Pashto followed. Saarah looked back at Clayton.

"There is a total of sixteen children and we must send four women along to help care for them."

"Then it will take two trips, possibly three, depending on the size of the children."

"They are mostly small," Saarah said.

"Okay, then maybe just two trips. So are you ready to go?"

"This very minute?"

"Yes. My men will have to stay behind here and every second we waste is one more second they're at risk."

After another quick discussion among the women in Pashto, Saarah spoke.

"Then what shall we do? Bring the children here?"

"Whatever's fastest."

"The children are all down at the other end of the valley."

"Okay. We'll fly the bird over there. You take your Land Cruiser and lead the way."

With a final word in Pashto, the women stood up and Clayton joined them.

"I will be leaving my men here," he told Salahuddeen.

"They are welcome in my home."

The women were already outside and climbing back into the Land Cruiser. Clayton joined the shooters back at the helicopter and waved for Sunny to come out before explaining things.

"You sure about this, chief?" Bradley said. "Sounds like we're going way off the reservation here."

"Maybe?" Clayton said. "But those six women over there?"

Bradley nodded.

"That's who took on the Taliban up in Nuristan. Those six and four more like them."

"No shit?" Metcalf said.

Clayton nodded.

"And apparently they just wiped out another fifteen of them here last night."

"Damn," Metcalf said with a look at the rest of the team. "Just the kind of gal I've been looking for all my life."

"All right," Clayton said. "Let's get serious. But to your question, Bradley, yeah, when it comes to official policy, the company's going way off the reservation here. I do have the backing of Simmons but that's it. So any problem with maintaining comm silence on this?"

"Hell, I don't have a problem with it," Sunny said. "Just make sure I'm not taking hostile fire while we're dropping in and taking off."

"I've been told that we're clear on both ends."

"Okay, then let's get this show on the road. Are you coming?"

"I don't know. Let's see what the load is. The rest of you are waiting here. Salahuddeen is the village elder and welcomes you into his home."

"Okay, chief," Palmer said. "You'll know where to find us."

As Clayton climbed onboard, he heard Metcalf say, "Do you believe that shit? Women warriors."

"That is badass," Palmer said.

Clayton slammed the door shut with the two of them still jawing away about the women.

As Sunny was bringing the helicopter back up to full power, the women crossed the bridge and headed west down the valley. Veeda was on her satellite phone, explaining things in coded language to Ariya. Then she radioed the four women on watch to make sure they too were in the loop.

Saarah had Irem stop at Bikram's house. His wife Kaamisha and their daughter Maanika were watching half of the children.

"Go on to my home," Saarah told Irem. "I'll walk the other children down from here."

Saarah got out and waved for Sunny to follow the Land Cruiser. The men in the fields paused to watch as Saarah spoke with Kaamisha by the front door.

"Let me put together a bag then," Kaamisha said.

Saarah followed her inside and found Maanika alone in her bedroom. She had not left the house since being violated. Saarah knelt down in front of her and explained things.

"You must go with them."

In response, Maanika hid her face with her hijab.

"Please, my friend. I know you are hurt. I know you feel ashamed but this will be a safe place for you. A place where perhaps you can begin to heal."

Kaamisha appeared with her bag and knelt down with Saarah.

"Please, my daughter. The children need you. I need your help to."

After a long moment, Maanika stood up and walked out to the front room. Kaamisha joined her and explained things to the children. Saarah went outside to wait.

When Bikram saw them heading down the road, he came out of the fields. Kaamisha spoke aside with her husband and explained the situation. Bikram hugged his wife and daughter and watched them continue on their way.

At Saarah's house, they took the children in out of the heat. The other eight children were already gathered inside. When Clayton followed them in, Maanika disappeared down the hallway.

"My mother, Zeeana," Saarah said.

"A pleasure," Clayton said with a bow of his head. "You could be sisters."

Zeeana waved a hand at him.

"Has the situation already been explained to you?" Clayton said.

"Yes," Zeeana said. "And thank you greatly for helping."

"Glad to do so."

He looked around, assessing the situation. There were infants and girls nearing puberty and everything in between.

"If I don't go with you, we can do this in two trips," Clayton said. "You're sure that everything is safe on the other end."

Saarah nodded.

"Okay, let's divide the children up by weight, as evenly as we can. Some of the older girls in each group."

Once the children had been separated, Clayton turned to the women.

"Who's going as chaperones on this first trip?"

Saarah spoke to Zeeana and Kaamisha in Pashto before answering Clayton.

"Kaamisha and her daughter. Come. I will help the children onboard."

Clayton followed Saarah and the first group of children outside. With the children safely strapped in, Saarah took Clayton aside and explained about Maanika.

"She is so filled with shame, she does not want to be seen by anyone, but especially not by men. Can you tell your pilot not to look at her? And can you move away when she comes out?"

"Sure. But will anyone onboard know where this place is?"

Saarah shook her head.

"Is there an address or anything?"

"Perhaps, but I don't know it."

"Okay, one minute."

Clayton went forward and explained the situation to Sunny. Sunny looked over his shoulder and shrugged.

"Yeah...It'll be close but I can carry her too."

Clayton went back outside with Saarah.

"You have to go too. Just to show the pilot where it is. Are you all right with that?"

She nodded.

"Okay. Sunny knows not to look. Go ahead and bring her out. I'll get out of sight until she's onboard…And I'll see you back here in an hour or so."

"She's on her way out," Clayton called out to Sunny. "And do whatever you can to crank it. And comm silence. We are way off the reservation here."

"You got it."

Clayton retreated to the side of the house and waited while Maanika was being helped onboard. As soon as he heard the cargo door slam shut, Clayton stepped back into view and gave Sunny a thumbs up.

Clayton joined Zeeana and watched the helicopter take off. Once it had disappeared over the hills, he turned to her.

"Do you know who the other chaperone will be?"

"Yes."

"Okay. Please make sure she's here with you when they return."

"I will."

"Thank you."

"Thank you, Mr. Clayton."

Clayton nodded and joined the women back in the Land Cruiser.

"Let's go," he said.

Irem turned the vehicle around and headed back to Salahuddeen's house. They found the four shooters sitting on the front porch when they pulled up.

"You got this mission under control now?" Palmer said.

Clayton nodded.

"Get comfortable. We're here for at least another two hours."

"Oh, I'm plenty comfortable…What's with the bandage?" he asked Noushineh.

She stared, not understanding English.

"She took a bullet last night during the battle," Irem said.

"You mind?" Metcalf said.

Irem explained to Noushineh that Metcalf wanted to have a look at her wound. Once he had peeled the bandages back, he grabbed the first aid kit out of his vest.

"We'd better clean this up a bit."

Metcalf looked over at Irem with a smile while working.

"I hear you ladies kicked some Taliban ass last night."

"I need to make a call," Clayton said and wandered down the road a bit.

When he returned a few minutes later, the men and women were sharing war stories. Metcalf looked over at Clayton.

"I'll tell you what, chief. I'd go into battle with these chicks any day of the week."

"And I'd go into battle any day with these dudes," Irem said.

The shooters laughed, all of them except for Bradley. He looked from face to face, taking things in as serious as hell. But that was Bradley. He was almost always as serious as hell.

With the women chattering away in Pashto, Clayton settled down with his back to the wall and stared off to the northwest.

Nineteen

Clayton had been listening to the war stories for nearly an hour when he finally heard the sound of the approaching helicopter and jumped to his feet.

"Let's go," he said and headed for the Land Cruiser.

"We should change the guards," Veeda told Irem. "Take the others and have them bring the Land Cruiser back here.

"Hey," Metcalf said, seeing Irem go. "Any time you're in Kabul, look me up."

Irem gave him a haughty look.

"Any time you want to fight the Taliban, look me up."

"I'm here for you, honey. Night and day."

The roar of the helicopter exploded over the opposite hills.

"Come on," Clayton called out from the Land Cruiser.

Veeda said something and started around to the passenger door.

"She said for you to drive," Irem told him.

"Fine."

Clayton changed seats and raced off as soon as Veeda was onboard. Farzaneh, Tabaan and Noushineh had climbed into the other Land Cruiser with Irem and headed the other way. Salahuddeen sat there stoically watching all this from his porch.

Saarah was already helping her mother and the other chaperone to get the children onboard when Clayton pulled up. Veeda jumped out and gave them a hand. Clayton went forward to talk with Sunny.

"Any trouble?"

Sunny shook his head.

"Clear sailing. This old gal Afsoon has a big compound so I was able to drop down inside her walls. Can't say who saw what around that village or what they were thinking but no trouble so far."

"You know where you're going now. I could send one of the shooters with you instead of Saarah."

"Couldn't hurt."

"Okay. Meet me back over at the old man's house."

Clayton went around and explained things to Saarah.

"Go ahead and ride with them over to Salahuddeen's."

He helped her onboard and slammed the door shut.

"Let's go," he said to Veeda.

Clayton whipped the Land Cruiser around with the Sikorski kicking up dust. In the race across the valley, Sunny was quickly ahead. Clayton pulled up with the helicopter already on the ground. He jumped out and headed over to the front porch.

"What's up?" Bradley said.

"I want one of you to go with them in place of Saarah. Just in case."

The four shooters looked at each other.

"Hell, I'll go," Kelley said, getting to his feet. "It's been a month out of country and I'm kind of antsy for some action."

"Have at it," Palmer said. "We'll be keeping an eye on the harem here while you're gone."

Mahvash, Darsameen, Hajira and Esin pulled up in the other Land Cruiser just then.

"Looks like the A team just got swapped out for the B team," Kelly said, seeing those four women climb out.

"One of them's more like the D team," Palmer said.

Saarah stared down at him.

"The Taliban did that to her. For wanting to be a free woman."

"Oh, Jesus. Sorry," Palmer said.

He and Metcalf shared a sheepish look.

"Fucking Taliban," Metcalf said. "Just show us where we can find those bastards and we'll send their asses to hell real fast."

"Just show us some respect," Saarah said. "That is all we ask of you."

Palmer shrugged sheepishly again. Saarah went back over to say goodbye to her family.

"Shut your ass up," Bradley said.

"Yeah, damn," Palmer said. "You can't help but hate those bastards. And up yours," he added with Bradley still staring at him.

Metcalf got up and introduced himself to the other four women.

"Have a seat. We've been talking war and weapons with the other ladies."

Mahvash translated for Hajira and Esin. Hajira looked at the men and said something to Mahvash.

"She wants to know if you're special forces," Mahvash said.

"We are," Palmer said, pointing at himself and Bradley. "Metcalf here's just a special kind of fuck up."

Metcalf kicked him. Mahvash translated the comment as best she could.

"You show me how better to fight," Hajira said in her broken English.

Hajira took a stance as if preparing to engage Metcalf. He laughed and stood up.

Clayton had come out from talking to Sunny. Saarah was still standing by the cargo door, comforting the children.

"Everything okay?"

She nodded and kissed Zeeana and Paksima and Baddar before Clayton slammed the door shut. Clayton and Saarah backed off and shielded their eyes from the dust as Sunny took off.

"We need to talk," Clayton said. "With Veeda and Salahuddeen."

They went back to the house. Saarah spoke with Veeda. Clayton explained things to Salahuddeen and he stood up.

"We shall talk inside."

"Just like the CIA," Palmer said as Clayton headed inside. "Always keeping secrets."

Clayton glared at him going by.

"Uh oh," Metcalf said. "You said the magic word."

Clayton closed the door. Salahuddeen waved towards the kitchen.

"I will make tea," he said.

Saarah was quick to help him. Clayton took a seat at a nearby table. Veeda sat opposite him. Salahuddeen looked over his shoulder.

"You are free to speak."

"Okay. What I'm about to tell you, no one else knows about except for us and someone back at the station but I've positioned a drone over the valley. There's no air strike capability. It's only for reconnaissance, but at least you'll have advance knowledge of any Taliban movements."

Clayton looked at Veeda and waited for Saarah to translate.

"The same applies to our aerial support," he said when Saarah was done. "I can transport your team from place to place but we will not be able to engage the enemy for you."

Clayton waited again until Saarah had finished translating.

"I repeat," he said. "Other than for your team, no one can know about this. Even if there's a gun to your head, you have to deny our involvement."

Saarah translated again. Veeda stared at Clayton for a long moment before nodding.

Salahuddeen came with the tea and honey. Saarah brought four cups. With everyone's tea ready, they toasted and drank.

Salahuddeen said something to Veeda in Pashto and their conversation drifted off.

"I'm sorry for your loss," Clayton said to Saarah.

She nodded while staring at her tea.

"I'm sure this isn't what you had planned for your life."

Saarah shook her head.

"I had planned to go to college."

"To be what?"

Saarah looked up.

"An astronaut, perhaps."

Clayton smiled.

"A doctor, actually. Though there was a hope that I could be an astronaut too. And maybe even the president of Afghanistan."

The smile on Saarah's face quickly faded.

"I'm sorry," Clayton said. "I'm sorry this war has robbed you of your dreams. And your father."

"If the Taliban take power, there will be no point in having dreams. For me or any woman."

"Yes, I know."

Clayton watched Saarah play with her cup. Had it been appropriate, he would have reached out to touch her hand.

"I hope we can build an Afghanistan where all women are able to follow their dreams," he said.

Saarah looked up.

"Is that why you're here helping us?"

He shrugged.

"I hate injustice. In any form."

Saarah stared at him.

"And what of you? What kind of life do you have back in America?"

"Not much of one. I was in special forces for almost ten years. First in Iraq, then here in Afghanistan. And now I do this. My home is an empty apartment."

"Then you have no wife."

Clayton shook his head.

"Not even a girlfriend?"

Clayton shook his head.

"It's hard to start anything when you're always somewhere far away and on the move."

Clayton noticed Salahuddeen gesturing with the teapot and waved him off. He checked his watch. Sunny had been gone for half an hour. His impulse was to do something, but there was nothing to do until he got back.

Clayton had started to say something more to Saarah when a phone rang. Veeda pulled out the phone Ariya had given her but it wasn't ringing. She reached into the other side of her vest and pulled out Akmad's phone. It rang again and continued ringing.

Veeda said something in Pashto.

"She wonders if she should answer it," Saarah said to Clayton

He shook his head and reached out a hand, wanting to see the caller ID. It was a blocked number. He sat there waiting for the ringing to stop, and then to see if whoever had called would leave a voicemail. Time passed but nothing happened.

Veeda spoke again and Saarah translated.

"She asks if they will be coming now."

Clayton checked his watch. It was going on four o'clock.

"I don't think so. Not tonight. It would be dark by the time they got here and the Taliban don't like to operate in the dark. I suspect they will call again later, and if there's still no answer, they will come in the morning."

"Then what should we do?" Saarah said.

"Didn't you say that you had two members of your team who were tech experts?"

Saarah nodded.

"Both Farzaneh and Mahvash."

"And are they here?"

"One of them. Mahvash

"Could you ask her to come inside?"

Saarah got up and returned a moment later with Mahvash. Clayton already had a small laptop pulled out from his vest and was at work deleting all its sensitive programs and files. He waved for both women to sit down.

"Do you speak English?" he asked Mahvash while still working.

She nodded.

With the file deletion in progress, Clayton set up a guest access and password, copied and pasted a link to the home screen and turned the laptop so Mahvash could see it.

"This laptop has a satellite connection to a drone directly above us and this link on the home screen connects you directly to the drone feed."

Clayton showed Mahvash how to navigate the site.

"Just click on this tab and a drop down menu will show you options for the live aerial feed. When I get back to headquarters later, I'll have the pilot program in wide angle and zoom views of this entire area. Whatever the drone can see, you'll be able to see it. If the Taliban come, you'll know well in advance. It may be only dawn to dusk. The drones are brought in for refueling and servicing at night but I'll try to get authorization for a second drone. That will keep you going 24/7. If not, you'll need to stay on your game. Don't get caught sleeping after dark...Understand?"

Mahvash nodded.

"Do you have some way to keep this charged?"

"We have a battery pack and a solar charger."

"Okay, good. Your password to the guest access is *warrior*."

Clayton closed the screen but left the laptop on the table.

"I have a program running right now, deleting some files. I need you to let it run until it's finished. It should take about half an hour, okay?"

Mahvash nodded again. Clayton turned to Saarah.

"Please translate everything for Veeda."

Veeda stared at Clayton while listening. He pulled out a card when Saarah was done.

"That is my personal number. If you need to talk with me, call, but speak in code. 'We have considered your offer and would like to discuss it further with you' or 'We already have twelve guests at the birthday party and more are coming'. Never use words like 'war' or 'guns' or 'battle'. Please translate."

When Saarah had done so, Clayton held up Akmad's phone.

"I would like to take this with me. I expect we'll be able to extract some intel from it, based on who Akmad's been talking to. It's the kind of intel that could help us stay one step ahead of any Taliban battleplans."

Clayton waited while Saarah translated. Veeda nodded.

"Okay," he said. "We will have a good idea in advance of how many men are coming. If it looks like you're going to be overwhelmed, we can extract you and live to fight another day."

"No," Saarah said. "We gave our word that we would stay and fight with the other villagers."

Saarah translated for Veeda and looked back.

"We cannot abandon them."

"All right," Clayton said. "I'll do everything in my power to help you. Do you have plenty of weapons and ammunition for now?"

"For now, yes."

Clayton looked at his watch again.

"The pilot must be getting close."

He stood up and headed out the door, greeted to the spectacle of Hajira and Metcalf locked in hand to hand combat down on the ground. Metcalf smiled sheepishly at seeing Clayton.

"Sorry, chief. Just giving her a few pointers."

When Metcalf went to stand up, Hajira used this distraction to leg whip him and pin him to the ground. Metcalf lay there laughing.

Off in the distance, Clayton heard the drone of the helicopter.

"All right. Time to move out."

Metcalf gave Hajira a hand up and fist bumped her before dusting himself off.

"This is one badass chick," he said to Clayton.

"Kicked your ass," Bradley said.

"It's all right. If the men in this country were willing to fight half as hard as these women, the Taliban would run screaming for the hills with their tails between their legs."

Salahuddeen came out and sat in his chair. Clayton stared off to the west, waiting. The day had grown long and some of the men were drifting out of the fields.

Moments later, Sunny burst into view from over the western hills and was quickly dropping in for a landing. Kelly opened the back door and jumped out. Metcalf gave Hajira another fist bump and a one armed hug. Bradley and Palmer acknowledged the women too.

"Any time the chief here gives us the word," Palmer said. "We'll be here to join the battle with you."

Clayton turned back to Saarah and Veeda and Salahuddeen.

"Remember, not a word of this to anyone outside the village."

He saw some of the village men approaching.

"You must tell these men the same thing. My involvement cannot be acknowledged. If that gets out, I can no longer help you."

Clayton started to leave but Saarah threw herself at his chest.

"Thank you," she said and pulled back. "I say this for everyone here in my village. Thank you for helping us."

Clayton noticed the village men staring and held his hand to his chest in a show of respect before turning to leave again. With the team increasingly surrounded, Bradley, Metcalf and Palmer reverted to their natural instincts and assumed a defensive posture around the helicopter.

"Any trouble?" Clayton asked Kelly while climbing onboard.

"Not really. Saw what looked like a few hostiles on our way back, about ten miles outside that village, but we were already well out of range, if anyone had thoughts of taking a shot at us."

"But the children are safe?"

"Oh yeah. Nice old lady. Reminds me of how nice this whole country used to be."

"Before the fanatics took over," Palmer said, climbing onboard.

As Metcalf climbed in, he noticed Hajira staring at him and tapped at his heart before slamming the door shut.

"Christ. What happened to her?" Kelly said.

"A Taliban warlord threw acid in her face for rejecting him."

"Goddamned bastards. I'd shoot them all."

"Metcalf's in love with her," Palmer said.

Metcalf threw him the bird but smiled.

"A real shame," he said. "Such a beautiful woman before they did that to her. And she's totally kick ass inside."

"Shit," Kelly said. "Marry her, take her back to the States and get her some plastic surgery."

"Yeah," Metcalf said. "I just might do that. If they survive the coming Armageddon."

Clayton settled in up front, aware of the conversations in back but with his mind far away and on other things.

Dusk had settled over Kabul as they touched down at Karzai International. Clayton had been silent the whole way back. As he unbuckled his seatbelt, he locked eyes with Sunny.

"Remember, strictly classified."

"You got it. You can't help but admire those women, huh?"

Clayton nodded and climbed out. The five men drove back from the airport in silence. Bradley pulled to a stop out in front of the station. Clayton climbed out and paused with his door open.

"No need to repeat it," Bradley said. "Strictly classified."

Clayton nodded. Metcalf called out from the back.

"Anytime those chicks need help kicking some Taliban ass, you just say the word."

"I'm sure they'd appreciate it," Clayton said and closed the door.

Back inside the station, he went down to check with the analysts. Simmons knew nothing about the drone yet. He was even clueless about the helicopter escorts but Clayton had called him during the first trip and asked him to hang around until Clayton got back.

Scottie looked up from his bank of computers when Clayton walked in. To look at Scottie, you naturally thought liberal arts college professor. That or a tech geek. The pile of fluffy hair on his head was accented by a week old beard and tortoise shell glasses.

"You the only one here?" Clayton said.

"Just me. You expecting dancing girls?"

Clayton sat down and pulled out Akmad's phone.

"I need a quick analysis of this. It belonged to a Taliban chief. I'd like to know who he's been talking to."

"That's a find," Scottie said, taking the phone and hooking it up to one of his computers.

He quickly downloaded all the contacts and recent calls and then cross checked them against a data base.

While the computer crunched the data, Scottie leaned back and looked at Clayton.

"This guy dead?"

Clayton nodded and stared at the computer screen.

"Ah, here we go," Scottie said once the software was done.

He scrolled down through the list.

"Abdul Qahhar, your Kunduz region's favorite warlord. And Khan Zada, he's part of the Taliban's leadership council up in Baghlan."

Scottie kept scrolling.

"Looks like the usual nest of vipers…Whoa. What's this? Naseefa Durrani? You know who he is?"

"Yeah. He won a seat on the Afghan National Security Council last year."

"Yeah, and funny thing, his main political rival just happened to turn up beheaded two days before the council vote."

Clayton stared at the screen without answering.

"Want me to print this up?" Scottie said.

"Yeah. And delete the file."

Scottie hit 'print' and rolled his chair over to the printer. Clayton disconnected the phone and stuck it in his pocket.

"You're now read into the operation so this is all classified."

Scottie held up his hands.

"You know me, boss. No loose lips here."

Clayton took the printed copies, headed up to his office and sat down to go over the list more thoroughly. The last man to call Akmad was Tajj Yusufi, one of Akmad's fellow Taliban commanders in the region, probably a notch above him in the pecking order. Whatever his reasons for calling Akmad, it suggested some kind of operational connection.

Clayton locked the report away in his desk and headed over to Simmons' office. Simmons was reviewing a dispatch when Clayton knocked and walked in.

"You just get in?"

"A minute ago. I wanted to double check on some intel before coming over."

"So what's the word?"

"The word is, we have a maverick female fighting force on our hands."

242

"Really? Doing what?"

"Doing what we found up in Nuristan. Kicking Taliban ass."

"You're telling me that the Taliban got their asses kicked up there by a bunch of women?"

Clayton nodded.

"Not only up there, they just got their clocks cleaned again up in the Shaik Ali area."

"No kidding. So that's what's going on up there?"

Clayton nodded.

"And you met with them?"

Clayton nodded.

"Well, I'm going to take this as an encouraging sign, but ten women? That's not likely to save Afghanistan."

"I was told they're currently training another team up in Mazar-e-Sharif. And they're planning to keep training them"

"You're still talking dozens against a force of thousands."

"You have to start somewhere."

Simmons took off his glasses and rubbed his eyes.

"Go on," he said.

"Well, my thought is, keep this to ourselves for now, lend them whatever support we can and let it play out. Maybe even get someone from the press up there to do a feature story. You get this all over the evening news back home and public support for the president's withdrawal plans could quickly go south."

"Yeah, I could see the dynamics changing...That's if you can keep these women alive long enough for things to take root."

"That's my hope."

Simmons had a look at the lens of his glasses and put them back on.

"What kind of support were you thinking?"

"Aerial reconnaissance for now. Weapons if necessary. Maybe give them an air lift from here to there as needed."

Simmons leaned back in his chair.

"We could probably do that much without attracting attention. You thinking to position one of our drones over the area?"

"I already took the liberty of doing that."

Simmons raised his eyebrows.

"Sorry I had Rick move one out over the valley while I was there and left them my lap top."

Simmons looked askance at him.

"It's okay. Their team has a couple of tech savvy gals and I deleted all the sensitive files before setting up a guest sign in...Anyway, they can now watch the drone feed and hopefully stay one step ahead of the Taliban."

"And what if the Taliban make a move at night?"

"That's what I was going to ask you. Is there any chance we can keep eyes on this situation 24/7?"

"That would mean pulling a drone from one of the other operational areas."

Clayton stared.

"What the hell," Simmons said. "There's nothing terribly important about Adelman's mission right now."

"Yeah, well, just make sure you're the one telling him that. I don't need him in my face."

"He'll probably be in your face anyway...but he'll live. I'll call around to Fenty and Bagram and see about borrowing one of their drones...What about weapons and ammunition?"

"They appear to have enough of both for now. They've been adding to their cache from the dead Taliban as they go."

Simmons shook his head.

"I'll be damned. So these women really are kicking ass."

"That corpse we exhumed up in Nuristan?"

Simmons nodded.

"It was one of their own."

"Well, like I was saying the other day, I'm surprised the women of this country haven't taken up arms sooner."

Simmons rubbed his eyes again and yawned.

"Well, we'd better get our ducks in a row on how we're going to game this. Once word gets out, you can bet that State and the Pentagon will be all over our asses, wanting to know what we know. And I can just hear the Taliban leadership squawking, once they get wind of this ass whipping. They're already on a rampage for the last one. Set off another roadside bomb outside of Kandahar this morning. A family on the way to a wedding, half the clan wiped off the face of the earth. And another gang of those bastards dragged three men off a bus up in the Kunduz region this afternoon. Shot them dead on the side of the road, just for the sin of being Hazara."

"I know it's a small start, but I have a gut feeling that this thing could go viral. These women come from all stripes. A couple of college students. A mother who lost her husband and children in a Taliban attack. A couple of them used as chattel. One of the women had acid thrown in her face. It's bound to resonate with the other women in this country. You link them up with the Northern Alliance and it could be a game changer. The Taliban are so locked into their medieval thinking, they can't imagine women actually being willing to fight back."

Simmons sighed and shook his head.

"You know, if the bastards showed one shred of decency, you could turn your back and walk away from this country and still sleep at night, but not like this...Speaking of trouble, I'm due over at the embassy in fifteen minutes. Blackburn wants to shake me down again. Swears I'm holding out on him."

Simmons smiled slyly and stood up. Clayton stood up with him.

"What are you going to tell him?"

"I don't know. I have to give him something to chew on. I already have his teeth at my pant legs. I'm doing my best to keep him away from actual flesh...But I won't say a word about our band of lipstick warriors."

Simmons waved for Clayton to go ahead of him out the door.

"Plausible deniability," Simmons said. "You know I've always trusted your instincts. That's why I give you plenty of rope, but we can't get too far off the reservation here. Try to make it look like the usual op. We picked up on some intel and were just chasing down leads. That way, if the whole thing goes sideways, we cut these women loose and come out looking clean. One assumes they can't be any worse off for us having tried to help them."

"I'll be discreet."

"Okay. Let me go see about fending off this Jack Russell Terrier."

With Simmons smiling, the two men went their separate ways.

Twenty

Clayton went from Simmons' office directly down to sig intel, hoping to find Emily Grayson on duty, a British ex-pat with a pretty face and an apparent aversion to sunlight. She had skin like rose petals and the color of milk.

The station looked a bit deserted at that hour but Clayton knew someone was always hanging around in sig with a set of headphones on. Thankfully Emily was one of them. She looked up from her monitor when Clayton walked in, as serious as hell. She always had that look about her. We had five minutes to find the guy with the nuclear bomb codes. The survival of the entire planet was in her hands.

"You have a minute?" Clayton asked her.

She nodded.

"I need you to keep an eye on this target."

Clayton jotted down Naseefa Durrani's name.

"Who he's talking to. Who he's meeting with…"

"Who he's sleeping with?"

"Well, not that so much, but sure, if it's relevant."

Emily stared.

"Any particular reason why we're surveilling him?"

I think he's Taliban, or at least sympathetic. Whichever it is, I'm pretty sure he's working against Afghan government's interests, particularly when it comes to the peace process. This is an op so you're read in."

Emily continued staring, serious as hell.

"Okay. Anything operational comes up, call me. Night or day."

She nodded and turned back to her bank of computers. Clayton was halfway out the door when Akmad's phone rang in his coat pocket. He pulled it out. It was Tajj Yusufi.

Emily was staring when Clayton returned.

"Here," he said, handing her the phone. "Trace that call. I need to know where it originated."

Emily plugged the phone into one of her computers and worked with machine like efficiency, typing in code and crosschecking coordinates. A few moments later, a map popped up on her screen with a red pin. It looked to be some kind of compound ten miles east of Ghowr Band.

"What you were expecting?"

"Yeah. Give me those coordinates."

Emily scribbled them down on a Post-it. Clayton grabbed that and the phone.

"We may need you in the TOC later on," he said on his way out the door.

Clayton headed out back to the drone pilot command trailer and used his ID to let himself in. There were four men inside at separate controls and all four of them turned their heads when Clayton appeared.

He closed the door and pulled up a chair next to Rick Corso, the pilot Clayton had tasked with positioning a drone over the Shaik Ali area.

"Did Simmons call you?" Clayton said quietly.

"Yeah. I got Adelman's drone moved into position before bringing yours back for refueling. He should be down here any minute now going ballistic."

"Tell him to see Simmons."

"I'll tell him to see you."

Clayton leaned in towards the screen.

"We still up and operational?"

"Yeah, you're looking at it right now."

"Okay. Give me a zoom shot right here."

Darkness had set in so they were seeing things through an infrared camera, but a group of men were gathered inside the walls of a compound, having what was clearly an agitated conversation. Several more men walked up as they watched.

"What are we looking for?" Rick asked.

"Any kind of troop buildup and movement in the direction of Shaik Ali."

"You expecting an attack tonight?"

"No. I'm expecting they'll make a move first thing in the morning, but there's likely to be an uptick in battle preparations before then. When are you supposed to be off?"

"At eight in the morning."

"I'll probably need you to pull a double."

"How did I know you were going to say that?"

"I'll bring down some Desoxyn later on."

"That would help. In fact, that will be imperative."

"Okay. In the meantime, I want wide angle and close up views of that compound, this village and everything in between."

Clayton pointed.

"And keep them running full time. If anything changes, call me immediately."

"You got it."

Clayton was on his way back up to his office when his phone rang. It was Simmons.

"You still at the station?" Simmons asked him.

"Yeah."

"Okay. I need you over here at the embassy. Blackburn wants to hear it straight from the horse's mouth."

"Hear what, exactly?"

"What you found up there at Nuristan."

"Anything else?"

"Basically, no."

"Okay. I'll be over there in about ten."

Clayton called down to the barracks while heading up to his office. Bradley answered.

"It's Clayton. I've been called over to the embassy and need a transport."

"And that's it?"

"That's it."

"Okay. I'll come get you. I'm going off duty shortly but the other guys are grabbing some grub."

"Thanks. I'm heading down to the front right now."

Clayton paused long enough to text Veeda's phone.

> Second call came in. Same client. Check your visual feed. Expect you'll have company by tomorrow morning.

Clayton locked Akmad's phone in his top drawer, grabbed his briefcase and headed out the door. Bradley was already waiting when he stepped outside. Clayton climbed in back and Bradley sped off. Once he was out on the main boulevard, Bradley looked in the rearview mirror.

"Anything new on that mission up there?"

Clayton met Bradley's eyes and shook his head.

"And I repeat, complete com silence. You don't know anything. You were never there."

"Oh, got that part loud and clear. Just figuring, if the shit hits the fan, those chicks may need some help. You get fifty battle tested Taliban soldiers descending on that place and you'll have Custer's Last Stand on your hands."

Clayton nodded while staring out the window. Bradley was probably right, but Clayton wasn't about to stick his neck out any farther than he already had, at least not yet. The best he could hope for at present was an evac if things went south, and that might not even be in the cards.

Bradley pulled to a stop in front of the embassy and looked over his shoulder.

"You good with getting back on your own?"

"Yeah. Simmons is here. If I end up needing a ride back, I know where to call."

Clayton climbed out, his mind on Russ 'Rocky' Blackburn and the grilling he was about to face.

Inside, the Marine manning the desk went through the usual protocols, crosschecking IDs against his list.

"They're waiting for you upstairs in the ambassador's study, sir."

The Marine buzzed Clayton through the steel door and into a long, empty hallway. Clayton pushed the elevator button and waited. A minute later, he was exiting onto the residence level. An aide to the ambassador stood outside the study door.

"They're expecting you, sir."

Clayton walked in to find Simmons, undersecretary Blackburn, Daniel Silva and Naseefa Durrani with Ambassador Douglas.

"Ah, here he is," Douglas said.

He got up to shake Clayton's hand.

"I believe you already know Under Secretary Blackburn."

Clayton nodded and shook his hand.

"And of course, Daniel."

The two men nodded.

"And Naseefa Durrani," Douglas said. "Mr. Durrani sits on the Afghan National Security Council. But I believe you know that?"

Clayton nodded.

Durrani stared from the other side of the coffee table, suave in that Middle Eastern sort of way, with oily hair combed back on his head and eyes that Clayton wouldn't have trusted from here to across the room. Rather than awkwardly reaching across the coffee table, Clayton settled for a wave and a strained smile.

"Something to drink?" Douglas said.

"Scotch and soda if you have it."

"Coming right up."

Clayton took a chair beside Simmons and opposite Blackburn and Durrani.

"Well, let's get right to it," Blackburn said. "I want to hear everything you found up there on that mountain."

"Here you go," the ambassador said, handing Clayton his scotch.

Douglas took a seat on the other side of Simmons. Clayton had a sip, set the glass down and proceeded to give a description of his mission up there, keeping it as brief as possible.

"And that's it?" Blackburn said.

"That's it."

"Given that it was effectively a crime scene, I'm still trying to figure out why the hell you reburied her."

"Exhuming a body is considered a sacrilege by Muslims, so I did what I felt would represent the least possible insult. And provide us with deniability."

"Hmm. Well, I can tell you this, with that body and a bit of old fashioned legwork, I've already established who she was. *And* where she came from."

Clayton stared.

"You don't seem to be much interested in that fact," Blackburn said.

"I was sent here to help the Afghan people, sir, and I can't really see how her identity does anything to assist towards that mission."

"Well, for the record, her name was Kashm Julid and she had been staying in a women's shelter just down the street from here. It appears that she was going to be married off to a Taliban leader and fled her village."

"Have you told her family about digging up the body?" Clayton asked.

"Of course not!" Blackburn said. "And that's not the point!"

"Then what is the point, sir?"

252

"The point is, in tracking down this Kashm further, I learned that she had been seen in the company of a Kurd named Ariya Suleman, and this Ariya had been seen frequenting the compound of an old blood Afghani by the name of Shabana Wali. And guess what? It turns out that Shabana just happens to own the retreat facility where you found that body. Of course she's denying any knowledge of what went on up there but come on."

"Again, sir, I don't see how any of this helps to explain that skirmish up in the mountains. Or why there's so much animus over a dead woman's identity."

"What the hell is that supposed to mean?!"

"Just that, I thought we were trying to defeat the Taliban, and since it appears that they just got a good ass kicking, why are we so concerned about one dead Afghan?"

"We're trying to get the hell out of this goddamned country! Not get stuck here for another twenty years!"

Blackburn's face had turned red.

"So, all the better, don't you think? That somebody else is doing the ass kicking for us?"

"If you haven't noticed, a fairly orderly withdrawal has been turned into another Taliban bombing campaign!"

Clayton shrugged.

"I'm still not sure what it is that you want from me, sir."

He glanced again at Simmons.

"From us?"

"Some answers, that's what! Like who's behind this uprising and how in hell do we put an end to it!"

Clayton calmly looked around the room and stopped his gaze on Durrani.

"What do you think, Mr. Durrani?"

"I'm asking the questions here!" Blackburn said.

Ambassador Douglas reached out a hand.

"No, no. Let's hear what our council member has to say. It is your country, Naseefa. What would you propose we do about this rogue element? After all, as Clayton has suggested, it does seem that they're doing your government a favor."

"Trust is everything in Afghan culture," Durrani said. "If I give my word, it must be like gold. It can never be tarnished, so when the Taliban see this unauthorized campaign against them, of course they will see it as a betrayal."

"If I may speak freely," Simmons said, "when has the Taliban ever honored its word? Let alone a ceasefire?"

"I can only speak in the context of this current situation, but they have generally been honoring the peace agreement until now."

"Generally," Simmons said. "Not a day goes by without those son of a bitches setting off a bomb somewhere in Afghanistan."

Durrani shrugged.

"We generally accept that the Taliban does not have a centralized chain of command, so there will be exceptions."

"Let me put it to you in terms that I understand," Simmons said. "A few indiscriminate killings here and there and we have to look the other way, but god forbid if they take one on the chin. We all have to sit around here wringing our hands."

"Oh for Christ's sake!" Blackburn said, looking at Simmons and Clayton. "We're getting completely off point here! It's your job to find out who the hell is behind these rogue operations and where the hell we can find them, and it's my job to send the Army in so we can put an end to this bullshit. Now what is it?"

Clayton felt his phone vibrate in his right coat pocket, had a quick look and saw that it was a text from Veeda's phone. He read the message with a sense of alarm.

Had two early visitors. They are now resting here peacefully. Aarshin was able to take that planned vacation. Now expecting a large family visit tomorrow.

Clayton put the phone away and looked back up.

"Anything you'd like to share with us?" Blackburn said.

Clayton shook his head.

"No. Just one of our shooters checking in."

Blackburn kept staring.

"Well?" he said. "What are we doing to get to the bottom of this? I'm due back in Washington in two days and expect to be telling the president that we've gotten this situation under control."

Simmons glanced at Clayton and back at Blackburn.

"If you have any leads, we'll be happy to follow up on them."

"That's your damned job!"

"Well, the truth is, we simply don't have any reliable intel. Perhaps you'd like us to follow up with this Shabana Wali."

"I already told you! She's claiming ignorance! What I want from you is to find that Kurdish woman, Ariya, whatever the hell her name is, and figure out why she's in this country and not in Iraq or Syria or wherever the hell she belongs! That would be a good place to start!"

"Very well," Simmons said. "We'll look into it right away."

Simmons looked from face to face.

"Anything else you'd like from us at the moment?"

"Just do your job! Christ, the incompetence."

"It's a wild and unwieldy country, Blackburn."

"I don't need to be reminded that it's a wild and unwieldy country!"

"Well, I would encourage you to go stand at the mouth of one those innumerable canyons, that leads off for hundreds of miles into other canyons just like it, and shout to the Taliban, 'Come out, come out, wherever you are,' because that's what you're up against here."

"Goddamn it, Simmons! I don't need to be lectured about the Afghan countryside! I just need you to go find me this Kurdish woman!"

"We'll work on that as soon as we get back to the station."

"Good! As usual, I have a funny feeling you folks aren't being completely forthright with your intel."

"It's the nature of our business," Simmons said.

"What? Bullshitting?"

"No. Making sure that we get our facts straight before opening our mouths."

Simmons stood up and Clayton with him.

"Mr. Secretary...Daniel...Mr. Durrani...And thanks again for the scotch, Preston."

"Not at all. Here, I'll walk you out."

Clayton nodded to everyone there before following Simmons and Douglas to the door.

"Don't make too much of it," Douglas whispered out in the hallway. "Russ has his feet to the fire back in D.C. so he's understandably a bit on edge."

"Frankly, Preston, I'll be damned if I know what we're arguing about here this evening. This administration's so eager to walk, regardless of what state we're leaving this country in. Meanwhile, we've finally found someone willing to punch the Taliban in the nose and their answer is to snuff them out like a bug? Yeah, we're running full speed to fulfill that assignment."

"Just find this Kurdish woman and let's see what she knows. At least humor him that much. I'm afraid if you don't, he's going to be gnawing on my leg next."

"Why don't we just perform an actual sacrifice for him?"

"Just find this woman and I'll guarantee her safe passage back to Iraq or wherever she wants to go."

"Safe passage. That's a joke. If Blackburn gets his hands on her, she'll disappear into a black hole."

"Just bring her to me and I'll make sure she's transported safely out of Afghanistan."

"We'll look into it. In the meantime, maybe you'll search D.C. for one person who sees the good in this thing, rather than having us throw them to the dogs."

The ambassador pursed his lips in consternation and headed back into his study. Clayton crossed the hallway and pushed the elevator call button.

"I assume you need a ride," Simmons said, joining him.

"Yeah. I sent Bradley back."

The two men did not speak again until they were safely back inside Simmons' office. Simmons settled into the seat behind his desk and waited until Clayton was sitting opposite him.

"All right, spill it. Everything you haven't told me already. If I'm going to take a whipping, I damned well want to know what I'm being whipped for."

"You pretty much know it all. The only thing I haven't told you is what I just learned about Durrani."

Clayton explained about Akmad Husseini's phone and the calls Durrani had made to it.

"Why that son of a bitch. He's a Taliban plant?"

"Sympathizer, in any case. It definitely looks like he's working against official Afghan government policy."

Simmons scoffed.

"And to see him sitting there tonight, smug as an Iman. 'Trust is everything in Afghan culture. My word must be like gold'...I'll definitely enjoy watching him swing in the wind when the time comes. You have that phone, right?"

"It's locked away in my desk."

"Good. Let's give Durrani a bit more rope and pull it out the next time he gets self-righteous...So, what else? Exactly where do these women stand in terms of troop strength and battlefield preparedness?"

"Going by their current success, they obviously know how to handle themselves in a firefight. But as to troop strength? I'm afraid they're about to be overwhelmed."

Clayton explained about the text from Veeda's phone and what he personally knew of the Taliban's nearby force.

"Frankly, I don't give them much of a chance tomorrow. Not on their own. They'll probably be outnumbered five to one. I'm afraid this thing is going to get snuffed out before it really gets off the ground."

"Well, if you're thinking to intervene, the question is, how? Whatever we do, we need to maintain plausible deniability? You have any ideas?"

"Well, I know those two Kurdish women are training a new team and that they're personally battlefield tested. Even just a handful more bodies would help. Beyond that, we could possibly bring in an independent contractor. Ten men and a couple of .50 cals. If we can get the troop strength down closer to 2 to 1 and throw in the extra fire power, I think they'd have a fighting chance."

"Who do we have for freelancers these days?"

"With this planned pull out, it's getting pretty thin. Probably best to ask the shooters. They always have their finger on who's in country."

"You think they'd want to get involved in this?"

"I know Palmer and Metcalf are all in. They made that perfectly clear today. Plus they've already been up there."

"All right. Let's drag them up here and see what they have to say."

Simmons reached for his phone.

"One other thing," Clayton said.

Simmons paused with the phone in midair.

"I still think we should bring in a reporter on this thing."

"I don't know. That's all we need. Getting a reporter killed up there and having it all over the news."

"Win or lose, this shouldn't go down in darkness. The world needs to know that these women were willing to fight and die for their freedom."

Simmons sat there fidgeting with the phone.

"All right. Who do you have in mind?"

"Megan Newburg."

"Oh Christ, Clayton. That woman? She's a thorn in the side of half the armed forces on this planet."

"She's a thorn because she's good, sir. And she's battle tested. Over fifteen years now covering Iraq, Syria and Afghanistan. Plus, I think it should be a woman. Who better to sympathize with what's at stake up there?"

"All right, but you tell her for me, the coverage better be good or it's the last scoop she'll ever get out of this office."

While Simmons called down to the barracks, Clayton went out into the hallway and called Megan's number. She answered after several rings.

"Hey, Clayton. What's going on?"

"I've got a scoop for you, but here's the rub. You have to be ready to board a bird in about fifteen minutes."

"Sorry, no can do. I'm on my way to Doha in a couple of hours. The word is, something big's about to blow with the peace negotiations."

"Look, what I have for you will make the peace negotiations seem like covering the PTA for metro."

"Come on, Clayton."

"All right. I'll just call the next person on my list. And you can spend the rest of your life knowing you blew off the scoop of the decade."

"Okay. Spill it. What's this all about?"

"I can't discuss it with you over the phone. You're just going to have to trust me."

"Jesus, Clayton. You're killing me here."

"Look, let me put it to you this way. Where we're going? We're not even supposed to be up there, let alone you. Now are you in or out?"

"All right, goddamn it. This better be good. And there better not be anyone telling me how to write the story."

"No one's going to tell you how to write it, but just so you know. Simmons said if he doesn't like the coverage, it'll be the last scoop he ever gives you."

"That crusty old fart...Look, you know me, Clayton. I'm good with what you boys do but I'm going to tell it straight, so if that's a problem."

"No, no. It's okay. I called because I trust your professionalism. Just get yourself ready and maintain complete com silence in the meantime. I'll call when we're on our way to the airport."

"I'll be waiting for you at the gate. I'm slipping out of my nightie right now."

Clayton ended the call with Megan's comment stuck in his brain.

Twenty One

Simmons had the drone feed of the Taliban compound up on his computer screen when Clayton walked back in.

"You see this?"

Clayton went around to Simmons' side of the desk.

"Looks like they're getting ready for a Road Warrior sequel. I'm counting over fifty men and at least four .50 cals."

Clayton watched the men and vehicles moving around with a sick feeling.

"Somebody's obviously pissed those boys off," Simmons said.

"Yeah, they probably figured out they're up against a bunch of women by now and that would tend to do it."

Clayton went back around to other side of the desk and sat down.

"So?" Simmons said. "Did she promise to give us good coverage?"

"She'll tell it straight."

"I want more than straight."

"She'll tell it straight. Once this story hits the press, it wouldn't surprise me to see Afghan women lining up around the block to enlist."

"Yeah, we'll see. It's a nice thought."

"So what's with Palmer and Metcalf?"

"They're on their way up. In the meantime, what are we doing about the Kurds? And these additional troops they're supposed to be training?"

"It's probably best if I maintain comm silence until I'm on the ground up there. Once we're face to face, I'll make an assessment. With the bird, it's a two hour ride, max, wherever we're going. We'll have plenty of time for troop movements before morning if it comes to that."

"Your call."

Simmons sat there drumming his fingers and staring at the door.

"Okay. Here they come now."

Palmer and Metcalf walked in and plopped down.

"What do we have here, chief? Code Red?"

"I'll let Clayton explain it to you."

"So, you remember Akmad's phone?"

Both men nodded.

"Well, there's been a who's who of dicks calling it over the past twenty-four hours. Meanwhile, I just received a text from Veeda, and if I'm reading her coded message correctly, the T-men sent a couple of scouts out to see what was going on. They're now dead but there's a major hornet's nest building up over the next hill."

"So the shit's about to hit the fan," Palmer said.

"Looks that way. I'm assuming they'll launch their attack at dawn. We have a drone keeping eyes on the situation but that's it. Those ten women are about to be overwhelmed."

"Just like I said."

"Hell, just send us up there," Metcalf said.

Simmons held up a hand.

"I've already got my neck stuck out there far enough, gentlemen. One of you gets killed and there goes my plausible deniability right out the window."

Metcalf looked at Palmer and shrugged.

"Drake and Gurney just rotated back on duty and we're due some R&R ourselves. We'll just clock out and go up there freelance."

"Let's just talk private contractors first, all right? That's why I brought you up here. I need someone in country who can get his ass up that way pronto. And knows how to keep his mouth shut."

The two shooters looked at each other again.

"Connelly," Palmer said.

Metcalf nodded. They both looked back.

"He specializes in private security so he's mostly off the grid."

"And he's here in Kabul?"

"Somewhere, yeah?"

"And what kind of platform can he provide? Clayton's thinking we'll need at least a couple of .50 cals up there. And the vehicles and men to go with it. Think that's doable?"

Palmer and Metcalf nodded at each other.

"That's definitely doable."

"Okay. Make the call and see how fast he can roll."

"You want him to come here?"

"Hell no. That's all I need, more exposure. Your call Clayton. Where do you want to meet him?"

Clayton looked from face to face, thinking.

"There's an alley behind the Zaynab Cinema. Tell him to rendezvous with us there in fifteen."

"Go ahead," Palmer told Metcalf.

Metcalf had Connelly on the phone a few moments later.

"Got time for a little rodeo for the company tonight?"

Metcalf listened for a moment.

"Something in the order of two ponies with fifties and ten cowboys to go with it."

Metcalf listened again.

"Yeah, like I said. It's the company calling."

Metcalf shared the rally point.

"Fifteen minutes. They'll explain whatever you need to know when you get there."

The other men could hear Connelly talking again.

"No, this is all going down tonight partner."

Metcalf listened again and ended the call.

"Is that it?" he asked Simmons.

"Yeah. Just remember to keep this under your hats for now. Down the road a year or two and you're having a beer in a local tavern, I don't care what kind of tales come out. The story will have written itself by then, one way or the other. I just don't want a word said while you're still in country."

"You got it, boss."

Palmer and Metcalf threw a wave on their way out the door.

"What am I offering him?" Clayton said.

"Whatever the hell he wants. Just get him and his team up there. I'll have Sunny waiting for you at Karzai...You got Newburg on call?"

"She's already waiting for me at the airport gate."

"All right. You'd better get rolling...and keep me posted."

Clayton was reaching for the door when it opened for him. It was Palmer and Metcalf again.

"Hey chief," Palmer said. "We decided to go ahead and take that R&R. If anyone asks, tell them you have no idea where we went."

Simmons started to say something but let it go. If this thing blew up, they had left him with enough wiggle room.

Metcalf gave a thumbs up.

"See you in a couple of days."

Clayton shrugged at Simmons and closed the door on his way out. Palmer and Metcalf were waiting at the elevator.

"You serious about this?" Clayton said.

Palmer nodded his chin at Metcalf.

"He's in love with that Hajira. Going to marry her and take her back to the States and get her a facelift."

"I'm asking you again. Are we being serious here?"

"Serious as hell."

"Okay. Get geared up and meet me out front with a rig."

"You got it, partner. See you in a few."

Back in his office, Clayton quickly got into his vest, grabbed his Glock, his AR-4 and extra ammo, unlocked the drawer with Akmad's phone and shoved that into his go pack, along with his spare laptop, and headed downstairs to wait.

Palmer whipped around the corner a minute later, Clayton jumped in and they sped over to Sulh Road. A mile farther on, they passed the hospital and slipped into an alley on the far side. That led them back through a maze of buildings.

Once both Butcher Street and Sulh Road were blocked from view, Clayton had Palmer stop. Palmer hit the lights and left the engine running. Metcalf brought his rifle into the up and ready position and did a quick press check. In the silence, they could hear voices from around in front of the cinema. Traffic came and went. The lights from passing cars flashed on the walls of the building opposite them.

They had been waiting a good five minutes when an up armored Land Cruiser crept around the corner with its lights off. Palmer flashed his lights twice and the other driver did the same. Everyone sat there without moving for several seconds before doors started opening.

A man with the physique of a body builder and facial hair befitting ZZ Top got out from the passenger side of the Land Cruiser. An equally chiseled man with a goatee got out from the driver's side. Palmer and Metcalf joined them.

"Connelly," Palmer said. "Good to see you."

"Good to see you, Palmer…Metcalf."

Connelly did a double take on the M-4.

"You boys expecting trouble?"

"Not from you," Metcalf said.

Connelly smiled.

"And where's your major?"

"Right here."

Palmer looked over his shoulder and waved. Clayton climbed out and came forward.

"Clayton Dorn. CIA."

Connelly nodded at him.

"Okay, number one. It's your show. Tell me what you got."

Clayton explained.

After listening, Connelly looked from face to face.

"I'm going to guess this is majorly off the reservation. Otherwise those pricks in Washington would just send in the cavalry."

Clayton nodded.

"So win or lose, this shit never happened."

Clayton nodded again.

"And you boys are coming along for this rodeo?" Connelly said to Palmer and Metcalf.

They nodded.

"But off the reservation too."

Connelly looked from face to face while nodding.

"Okay, I'll need $500K cash up front for this death march, plus another $500K upon completion. Ain't nobody going to join me for anything less...You got a problem with that?"

"What kind of package will you be bringing?"

"Two Afghan Army Hummies, both with .50 cals, ten men and a shitload of other toys."

"Consider it done."

"I'll consider it done when I see the money."

"We don't have time for that tonight. You'll have it in the morning."

"If I'm alive in the morning."

Connelly turned to Palmer and Metcalf.

"You vouching for this?"

"You're good," Palmer said. "This just came down from the station chief."

"Okay. Whoever's still alive in the morning, they'll be waiting for the dough." Connelly pulled out a card and handed it to Clayton. "Just call this number."

"Consider it done."

"Very well, gentlemen. Where are we going and how are we getting there?"

Clayton waved back towards their Land Cruiser and got his laptop opened up on the hood.

"This is your target area," he said, pointing at the map on his screen. "And this is the fastest way of getting there, but you'll run right into the teeth of the Taliban going in that direction."

Clayton pointed at the map again.

"It's the long way but you're better off going up through Tupchi. There's a possible choke point here, at Zarkharid. The Afghan Army keeps an eye on that crossroads, but the US forces have been keeping A77 open from Tupchi east through to Shaik Ali...Beyond Shaik Ali, it's hard to say. You may or may not run into the Taliban."

"Fuck it," Connelly said. "We'll just blast our way through. Just tell me about this Afghan post."

"I'll drop in with our bird on my way up and make sure they're expecting you. I also have a drone scouting A77 so if there's any potential trouble, I'll send you advance intel."

Clayton pulled out his satellite phone.

"Give me your number again."

Connelly rattled it off while Clayton dialed. Connelly's phone rang a moment later.

"There. If anything comes up on your end, you call me."

"You got it, chief."

Connelly looked from face to face.

"Okay, let's get this show on the road. You coming with me," he said to Palmer and Metcalf.

"We'll be bringing up the rear. As soon as we drop off number one at Karzai."

"You remember where to find my hooch?"

"Out on AH76, at the ass end of Tilai Town."

"You got it."

Connelly checked his watch.

"It's a bit past 2100 hours. We'll be rolling at 2200."

"We'll be there."

Everyone climbed back onboard the two vehicles and went their separate ways. While they were driving, Clayton sent a text to Veeda's phone.

> Heading your way now. If I should expect any trouble on the ground, let me know immediately.

A message came back a few moments later that all was clear.

They passed through both checkpoints at the airport with Palmer flashing his ID. A few hundred yards farther up the road, Clayton spotted Megan off to the side, leaning against her car. He waved for Palmer to pull over.

"You didn't tell me that Newburg was joining the party."

Clayton rolled down his window without answering him. Megan strolled over and leaned on the door. Palmer looked over his shoulder with a smile.

"Long time no see, beautiful."

"I thank my lucky stars every day."

"Come on. It's not my fault that we had to ditch you down in Helmond that day. If it had been my call, I would have carried you."

Clayton cut him off with a gesture.

"Yeah. Let's just stick to business here," Megan said. "What are we doing?"

"Just follow us," Clayton said. "You can leave your car on the tarmac."

"You got it."

Palmer whistled as Megan strutted by. She flipped him off over her shoulder.

"She loves me," Palmer said to Metcalf.

"You should see what women do when they don't."

"All right. Let's roll," Clayton said.

"She loves me," Palmer said as he pulled back onto the road.

A minute later, he was braking to a stop alongside the Sikorski. He looked over the seat.

"You're sure you're going to be all right without a shooter onboard, chief?"

"Just get in gear and make this happen, okay? I have enough on my mind already without you two guys screwing off."

Clayton paused with the door open.

"I'll be on the ground up there in under an hour. If there's anything you need to know, I'll call. If anything comes up on your end, call me."

"Will do."

Clayton closed the door and walked over to join Megan. She was grabbing a valise and camera case out of her back seat.

"This everything?" he said.

"I was thinking to drag a suitcase along but figured you'd frown on that."

"If we're more than forty-eight hours where we're going, nobody's going to need a change of clothes."

"That's encouraging."

"Come on. Let's go."

Clayton grabbed the valise and ducked his head on the way over to the helicopter. Megan was right on his heels.

"Welcome aboard," Sunny said to Megan.

"Good to see you, Sunny. You have any idea where we're going?"

"You'll have to ask the boss, here."

Clayton slammed the door shut and went up to the passageway next to Sunny's seat.

"Our first stop is Zarkharid. You'll see an Afghan Army checkpoint somewhere near the north end of town. I need you to drop in there so I can relay a message."

"You got it."

Sunny eased up off the tarmac and banked over his shoulder, going west. Clayton went in back and sat facing Megan.

"What kind of chatter have you been hearing about the Taliban lately?"

"I know they've got their shorts in a knot about something but no one seems to know what it is. Is that where we're going?"

"We're going to join a band of Afghan women warriors."

"Wow, okay. Do tell."

He did. Megan sat there listening to his account, spellbound.

"Still wish you were on your way to Doha?" Clayton said when he was through.

"Oh god, no. This is a to die for scoop. Thank you. I just worry that these women have set themselves up for a terrible fall."

"That's why I'm here. To give them whatever support they need. And you're here to make sure the whole world knows about it."

Megan shook her head, smiling.

"Lipstick and fingernail polish. Those Kurdish women sure are something, aren't they?"

"Yeah. They appear to have trained these Afghan women well, going by the results."

"Yeah, that is something. You know, this has blockbuster written all over it."

"Yeah, well, while we're making movies, let's shoot for a happy ending. Here, let me show you what's going on."

Clayton got his laptop out, linked up to the drone and showed her the zoom shot of the Taliban compound. It was even more of a beehive now.

"That's the Taliban and we assume all this activity is preparation for an assault tomorrow morning."

Clayton clicked on the drone feed for the village.

"And this is where the women are, and where they're preparing to make a stand."

Everything looked quiet in in the village so Clayton checked the highway on the way to Tupchi. It looked deserted but that was to be expected at night. The Taliban were fond of lobbing mortar rounds after dark, but they rarely stuck their heads out.

Sunny called back to Clayton twenty minutes later.

"I think I see your checkpoint."

Clayton went forward. There were two Humvees with .50 cals, two trucks and an SUV. There looked to be about ten men on the ground.

"What do you want me to do?"

"Give them a friendly signal and ease down in that open field."

Sunny rocked the helicopter side to side and started his descent. The soldiers on the ground were all up armed and watching, but no one appeared to be taking their approach as hostile.

As soon as they were on the ground, Clayton grabbed a carton of Camel filters from his brief case, opened the back door and hurried over to the waiting soldiers.

"Who's in charge here?"

"I am. Captain Noorzai."

"Clayton Dorn."

Clayton showed his ID and handed Noorzai the carton of cigarettes.

"A little gift from the American government."

That won him a smile.

"So, listen, captain. Just wanted to give you a heads up. Some of my men will be passing through here in about an hour. I need them up north."

Clayton gestured at his chin.

"Look for a long beard. Connelly's the name."

Clayton looked from face to face and back at Captain Noorzai.

"Are we all good then?"

"We are all good Mr. Clayton," Noorzai said.

"Good. Then I'll be on my way."

Clayton held his hand to his chest and ran back to the cargo bay.

"Back to the village," he said to Sunny while slamming the door shut.

Clayton texted Connelly.

> The Afghans are expecting you. A77 looks clear all the way through to Shaik Ali but can't swear to it. Will keep eyes on the road for any hostiles.

A thumbs up came back a few moments later.

Clayton went back to sit with Megan.

"Do you know the area?"

"Nope, never been there. Nice village?"

"Yeah. Wars aside, it's a lovely place."

Clayton stared out a window into the darkness, lost in thought. They were passing over the Turkman Valley.

Suddenly, a phone rang. Clayton looked at Megan, then checked his own pockets, then realized it was Akmad's phone ringing in his briefcase. He quickly opened it and looked.

It was Durrani. Clayton sat there watching the phone and Megan sat there watching him.

"What's going on?" she said.

Clayton held up a hand. A minute later, a voicemail came through, but in Pashto. That was followed quickly by text, also in Pashto.

The man's a fool, Clayton thought. That or brazenly arrogant. Either way, he hadn't the slightest sense that he might be in trouble.

Unable to speak or read Pashto fluently enough to decipher the messages, Clayton put the phone back in his pack. It would have to wait until they touched down in the village.

"You going to tell me what that was all about?" Megan said.

Clayton thought for a moment before deciding to explain.

"Wow. That's a shit storm waiting to happen...And I'm free to write about this?"

Clayton nodded.

"Just remember. I'm not in the story. The CIA's not in the story."

"You're sure?" Megan said with a smile. "You'll be famous."

"Yeah, famous and in the stockade."

Megan smiled again.

"Don't worry. I know how to play this."

"Yeah, I'm counting on that."

Sunny was just then clearing the mountains above the Turkman Valley. The village was straight ahead. Clayton went up front.

"Drop us back in front of Salahuddeen's place."

"You got it."

As soon as they were on the ground, Clayton jumped out and gave Megan a hand getting down. Salahuddeen had come out to his front porch. Clayton led Megan over and introduced them.

"Megan's a reporter. She's going to get this story in the news."

Salahuddeen bowed his head at her.

"What's our status?" Clayton asked him. "Am I safe having Sunny park here for now?"

"For now, I believe so, yes. We had two visitors but they are no longer with us."

"Yeah, I heard."

Clayton looked back and waved at his throat. Sunny cut the turbines and the whirl of the rotor blades started to slow.

"So Aarshin was one of them."

"Yes."

"And how is his wife taking it?"

"She's in mourning, but she did not share his sympathies."

"I'll make sure she gets some kind of bereavement…And the women? Where are they?"

"Here and there, keeping watch."

"I need to speak with Veeda. Where can I find her?"

Salahuddeen keyed up his radio and called for her. Veeda's voice came back. Salahuddeen listened and responded before ending the call.

"She is on her way…Have you eaten?"

"No, but there's no time for that right now."

Clayton got out Akmad's phone and pulled up the voicemail.

"I need you to listen to this."

Salahuddeen did.

"What did he say?"

"He speaks of the CIA. That he thinks they are helping the women."

Clayton showed him the text.

"This too?"

Salahuddeen read it and nodded.

"Okay. It's good to know but it doesn't really matter. It's not going to affect anything we're doing here."

Clayton took the phone and put it away.

"Now look. I have a team of men coming. They should be here in about an hour, assuming they don't encounter any trouble. If I'm gone, I need everyone to cooperate with them. Whatever they suggest you do, do it. They've been to war and know how to prepare for it."

Salahuddeen nodded.

"I'm also suggesting that you get the village women out of harm's way. If they're left hiding in houses somewhere and things go wrong?"

Clayton shrugged.

"And where would you have us take them?"

"I don't know. That's one of the reasons I wanted to speak with Veeda."

Clayton looked off in the direction of the bridge, expecting to see one of the Land Cruisers coming from that direction. Instead he heard a vehicle approaching from the other end of the valley and turned to watch. Veeda was driving with Saarah riding shotgun. They stopped in front and climbed out with AKs slung over their shoulders. Clayton greeted both of them and introduced Megan.

"Megan is going to tell the world your story."

Veeda stared as Saarah translated and Megan got a recorder out of her valise. Clayton stopped Saarah.

"Listen, before you get going, I received your message so explain to me again what happened."

"A truck came from the east. We saw it with the help of your drone. There were two men and they stopped a few kilometers away from the valley and came this way through the hills. Hajira and Irem killed them and then saw that one of them was Aarshin. We buried him in the village cemetery. The other we buried behind the schoolhouse."

"And their truck?"

"We brought it here."

"Okay, good. Now I need you to translate something else for Veeda. I have a team of twelve men coming to help you. Americans. Special Forces, with more weapons. Better weapons, but I still don't think it's enough so I want to talk to Ariya. It would help if she has more bodies to spare. Anyone trained well enough to fight. Go on. Tell Veeda that much."

Veeda stared at Clayton as Saarah translated. When she was done, Saarah turned back to Clayton.

"If you wish for more women to help us, they are training in Mazar-e-Sharif. Ariya is alone in Kahmard."

"Okay, we'll figure it out. Just ask Veeda to get Ariya on the phone so I can talk to her."

Having heard Saarah's translation, Veeda got her phone out and made the call. When the conversation went on and on, Clayton waved at her.

"Saarah, tell her I need to speak with Ariya myself."

Veeda looked perturbed but handed Clayton the phone.

"Hello, Ariya?"

"Yes."

"It's Clayton. I was telling them that I'm still worried our birthday party tomorrow won't be festive enough and wanted to see if you had anyone else who could attend."

"Possibly. Were you able to provide transportation?"

"Yes. Absolutely. I can come get them right now."

"It would be best if you came here first."

"Of course. I can be there in twenty minutes."

"Very well. I will be ready to leave as soon as you arrive."

"I'm on my way."

Clayton ended the call and handed the phone back to Veeda.

"I want to take you with us," he told Saarah. "It will give Megan a chance to interview you on the way. Tell Veeda."

Veeda listened and said something back.

"She says she would rather have you take Irem. I'm the sniper."

"Look, we don't have time to argue. Tell her we'll be back in two hours max."

Saarah did and Veeda stared with a venomous look.

"Look, nothing's going to happen here tonight."

He dragged Saarah towards the helicopter and shouted back.

"Just keep your eyes open for my team! The man's name is Connelly! He'll be coming from the west."

Salahuddeen walked up to Veeda and translated for her. She remained staring. Clayton helped Saarah and Megan into the cargo bay and pointed to the west.

"Just keep an eye out for them!"

Clayton climbed onboard, waved one more time and slammed the door shut.

Twenty Two

Clayton paused there in the cargo bay with Saarah and Megan.

"This is Saarah's village, by the way."

"Oh wow," Megan said. "So where should we start?"

"You two go ahead. I need to check in with Sunny."

Clayton went forward and crouched between the seats.

"Just wanted to make sure you knew where you were going."

Sunny glanced over with a smile.

"Got my coordinates locked in, chief. I could find it in a sandstorm."

"Good. I need to interface with Saarah and Megan for a bit and then get my eyes back on the intel. Just give us a shout when we're getting near."

"Will do."

Clayton returned to the cargo bay. Megan paused from the conversation and looked up at him.

"Saarah was just telling me how she escaped."

"Did she tell you how we met?"

Megan looked at Saarah, shaking her head.

"No. I guess we hadn't gotten that far."

He looked at Saarah and she gestured back.

"Please. You know it better than I do."

"Okay. So I was having dinner in the Blue Zone a few months back and Saarah just happened to be standing on the

277

sidewalk in front when that bomb went off. The concussion knocked her to the ground and I ran out to help. And eventually gave her a ride back to the shelter where she was staying."

Clayton turned to Saarah.

"Then we got word of something going on up in the Shaik Ali area and I flew up to have a look. And out comes this women's fighting force, Saarah among them."

Clayton looked at Megan.

"The night of the bombing, Saarah had been talking with another young woman but they parted ways a minute before it went off."

Saarah looked away, suddenly wiping at tears. Megan reached out a hand to her.

"What Saarah? What's going on?" she said with a look back at Clayton.

"She'll have to tell you."

"What?" Megan said again.

Saarah wiped away more tears and looked back.

"Her name was Kashm and she was killed in our first battle with the Taliban. Up in the Nuristan Forest."

"Awwww...I'm so sorry to hear that."

Saarah sighed deeply.

"She was the one who convinced me to join the fight so..."

Seeing Saarah's continuing grief, Megan leaned forward and gave her a hug.

"Trust me, Saarah. I know how it feels."

Megan pulled back and waited until Saarah looked at her.

"I've lost several of my friends in war. Fellow reporters and you never get used to it. You..."

Megan looked at Clayton and back.

"There's really nothing anyone can say. There's just time and the pain eases somehow. The important thing is to believe in what you're doing. Believe that you must go on doing it. I know my fallen colleagues would never want me to stop being a reporter and I'm sure your friend Kashm would feel the same. That you must go on fighting for the freedom of Afghanistan. For the freedom of women all over the world."

Saarah nodded with a brief and miserable smile.

"Oh god, Saarah," Megan said. "You can't imagine how incredibly brave and courageous I think you are and we're going to make sure the whole world knows about it. The world is going to know that you ladies are out here fighting bravely for your country, okay?"

Saarah nodded.

"I need to get back to my intel," Clayton said.

He touched Saarah's shoulder, settled into a rear corner of the cargo bay and pulled up the drone feed on his laptop. Simmons was right. The ongoing Taliban battle preparations had that furious Road Warrior madness to it.

He turned his attention to A77 and was just zooming in on a gathering of vehicles near Tupchi when his phone rang. It was Connelly.

"Is this number one?" he said.

"Yeah. What's going on?"

"Well, we have ourselves a bit of a situation here. We just ran into a US patrol and they're telling us they have orders to turn back anyone trying to come through this way. You know, anyone packing toys like us and looking for a party."

Clayton cursed under his breath.

"All right. Whoever's in charge there, please put him on the phone."

"You got it."

"This is Sgt. Rodriguez," a voice said a moment later.

"Sgt. Rodriguez, this is Clayton Dorn with US intelligence and those men are traveling under my orders."

"With all due respect, sir, but how do I know that you're who you say you are? And that's setting aside the fact that I've been given orders not to let anyone armored up like this to pass through here."

Clayton stood there with his brain churning.

"All right, where do I find you?"

"We're just west of the road down from Ghandak."

"All right, hang on."

Clayton muted the phone and rushed forward.

"Sunny, I need you to turn this bird around."

"Hell, we're almost there, chief. I was just about to give you a shout."

"I know, but this can't wait."

Clayton pointed at the map on his laptop.

"I need to you to drop in right here, on A77. And hurry. I'll be back with you in a minute."

Clayton headed back to his seat.

"What's going on?" Megan whispered.

"Hang on."

Saarah grabbed Clayton's arm and whispered.

"I think I know this man. There was a Sgt. Rodriguez in our village and he was there the day I escaped. The phone number I called about the children?"

Clayton nodded.

"It was one of the women in his patrol."

Clayton pursed his lips, staring back, not quite sure what to make of all that.

"Okay, I need to get back to this guy. And please keep quiet until I'm through with the call."

Clayton unmuted the phone.

"Okay, Sergeant. I'm on my way to you right now. Please stand by until I get there."

"Your ETA?"

Clayton checked his watch.

"Ten, fifteen minutes, tops."

"Roger that. We'll be here waiting."

"Sergeant. I'd appreciate complete radio silence on this until we've talked. This is a very delicate situation."

"I can keep quiet until you get here but I can't make any promises after that."

"Fair enough. I'll see you shortly."

Clayton ended the call and paused there in thought again before turning to Saarah.

"All right, tell me everything you know about this Sgt. Rodriguez."

Megan began furiously scribbling notes as Saarah did. When Saarah got to the part about Natalie and Leanna helping her escape, she stopped and looked from face to face.

"I am worried for them."

"Why?" Clayton said.

"Because Sgt. Rodriguez spoke of punishing Natalie and Leanna that day."

"What? For trying to help you?"

Saarah nodded.

"And I do not think he is aware of this other call I made."

"Okay. That's easy enough. I won't bring it up. If Natalie and Leanna decide to, that's their call…Anything else?"

Saarah shook her head.

"Okay, I'd better get up front."

Clayton paused.

"You two need to stay out of sight. I don't want them knowing you're here. I'll close the door behind myself when I climb out but there's always a chance one of their soldiers will come snooping around so lay low."

Clayton went forward. Sunny looked over at him with his usual smile.

"We expecting fireworks down there?"

Clayton shook his head. A77 had come into view off in the distance, like a ribbon weaving its way through the rugged terrain. Clayton checked his watch. It was ten minutes shy of 2300 hours.

"There," he said, pointing to an open field on the north side of the highway. "Bring us down with the cargo doors pointing away from the patrol."

Clayton studied the patrol as they drew closer. It consisted of three Humvees, two with .50 cals up top and eight soldiers that Clayton could count. All of them were bearing arms and staring up at the helicopter.

Connelly's two Humvees and Metcalf's up armored Land Cruiser were parked back up the road a few hundred feet. Connelly and his right-hand man Jake were leaning against the grill of the lead Humvee. No one else had gotten out of the three vehicles.

The minute the wheels touched down, Clayton opened the cargo door.

"Leave it running," he told Sunny before jumping out and slamming the door shut.

Sgt. Rodriguez was staring as Clayton ducked under the rotor blades and ran over to the Army patrol. Clayton shook the sergeant's hand and showed his ID.

"Thanks for holding your fire. Now how are we going to clear up this situation?"

"I don't know, sir. You tell me. My orders are to stop anyone armed up from going in that direction, and immediately report in to my superiors if anyone even tries."

"Sergeant. You know how these things work. I can't always tell you what kind of ops I'm running. All you need to know is that we're both working on the same side."

"Orders are orders, sir, and I have yet to hear one good reason why I should start disobeying mine."

Out of the corner of his eye, Clayton noticed two of the soldiers drifting out into the field and circling around the Sikorski. Rodriguez noticed too before turning his attention back to Clayton.

"The way I see it, sir. This should be easy enough to clear up. Make a call up your chain and have them get in touch with my superiors. Then if someone calls and tells me to stand down, I'll stand down."

"I wish it was that simple, sergeant, but it's not."

"Well, it's simple enough to me, and the only way I'm going to back down."

Clayton was staring at Rodriguez and weighing how to respond when one of the soldiers hurried back across the field.

"What's up, Dundy?"

While listening to Dundy whisper in his ear, Rodriguez' eyes drifted off in the direction of the helicopter, then suddenly snapped back with a laser focus on Clayton. Rodriguez whispered something to Dundy, who raced back over to the helicopter.

"All right, Mr. Clayton. You have about one minute to explain the nature and purpose of your cargo before this situation gets totally fubar on you."

Clayton glanced over and saw that Dundy and the other soldier now had their rifles in the up and ready position, aimed at the helicopter. Clayton looked back.

"And like I told you, Sgt. Rodriguez, I am not at liberty to discuss the nature of my mission with you."

"All right," Rodriguez said and called over to the two soldiers. "Politely get that pilot to cut the engine and get all three of those bodies in that helo over here in front of me!"

Clayton heard the distinctive slowing of the turbine and watched Sunny jump down to the ground. Then the legs of both Saarah and Megan appeared beside him. Then all three were being marched around the helicopter and across the field. Rodriguez kept staring at Clayton until everyone was standing in one place. Then he had a look at the two women.

"So, let's see here. We've got your obligatory CIA guy, a war correspondent, a contracted pilot and one runaway village girl, who just happens to be wearing combat fatigues. It sure looks like someone's trying to cook up something to me."

"Hi Rodriguez," Megan said. "Nice to see you again."

"Yeah, right. Great seeing you. Thanks for the coverage."

"I told it straight."

"Yeah, sure. You always tell it straight, and leave us Americans looking like shit."

"It's the American policy towards Afghanistan, sergeant. Nothing personal...I put in that part about you saving a mother and her child."

"So you did. So you did...All right, let's get back to the business at hand. I'm going to give you one more shot at coming clean, Mr. Clayton, before I key this up to command."

"What is it that he wants?" Saarah said.

Rodriguez looked at her.

"Answers, that's what I want."

"Answers? For what? Why you have left us here in Afghanistan to fight on our own but still want to get in the way? Two days after you left, the Taliban came and killed my father. And violated my mother."

"Leaving your village was not my call."

"No. You blame it on your new president. *Fighting a war over women's issues. How is that going to work?* I heard him say that on the news one night. Well, good. Then please go home and leave us to fight this war in the way that we choose."

Back on his heels a bit now and not quite sure how to respond, Rodriguez noticed Natalie heading their way.

"Specialist Montero, you are to stay right where you are!"

She kept coming.

"With all due respect, Sergeant, fuck off."

"I will duly note your opinion when I report your insubordination to command. In the meantime, you are to return to your position and keep your eyes on those two Humvees."

"Fuck you. Fuck this whole situation, sergeant. I'm sick of pretending that we're here to help these people when all we're doing is getting in the way."

"You are really seriously out of line, Montero."

"Yeah? And you must be blind not to realize what's going on here. These people are just fighting for their freedom and we're going to tell them how to go about it doing it?"

"You know something you're not telling me, Montero?"

"I just know this is fubar, Sergeant."

"Well, I have my orders, Montero, and that's that."

"To hell with our orders. I'll take the article 15s if need be"

Natalie tilted her head at Saarah with a smile and gave her a hug.

"How are you?"

Saarah nodded.

"Okay." She glanced at Clayton. "But it will not be that way for long."

"Why? What's going on?"

Saarah looked at Clayton now. He looked at her and at everyone else standing there and finally threw up his hands.

"Fine. Go on. Fill him in."

Clayton turned to Rodriguez.

"Permission to check in with my assault team."

Rodriguez nodded and looked back at Saarah. Clayton heard her voice trailing off as he headed down the highway.

"This is looking like one major fuck up," Connelly said as Clayton drew near.

Doors started opening and the rest of the men climbed out.

"How are we looking?" Palmer said.

"I don't know. Saarah's back there telling her story. She knows this patrol team from back in her village."

"Let's just go around the bastards," Metcalf said.

"There is no going around them. The only other way's back to Kabul and up through Taliban controlled territory. That or off through those mountains for a hundred miles. We'd be lucky to get there by next Tuesday"

"So? Drop us in with the bird."

"I ain't going nowhere near this fight without these two .50 cals," Connelly said.

"Just unpin them and we'll take them with us. Someone must have a tripod we can use."

"I ain't going nowhere near that place without these .50 cals mounted to these two Humvees. I've got 1/2" ballistic steel plates welded on front, back, sides, top and bottom and bullet proof glass."

Connelly looked back at Clayton.

"Either you get this shitshow straightened out or we're turning around. I won't bust your balls about the original quote but you're definitely going to be compensating us for some time, no matter what happens."

Clayton looked back and saw Natalie waving to him.

"Looks like you've got an invitation to the party," Connelly said.

"I'll take that invitation any day of the week," one of his men said.

Clayton started off on his own.

"Good luck," Connelly called after him.

Rodriguez was staring as Clayton walked up.

"All right. Show me this Taliban build up."

Clayton led Rodriguez and his team back over to the helicopter. All eyes were on Clayton as he got his laptop set up on the cargo deck and pulled up the drone feed. The men in the compound were all gathered together praying now.

"Looks like there must be a hundred of them son of a bitches," Dundy said.

Rodriguez looked at Clayton.

"And you say they've been gearing up for battle?"

"Going on two days now. And there's more bodies since the last time I looked. I'm sure this village defector Aarshin told them that they're up against a bunch of women and it's really got them pissed off."

"I'll tell you what's really them pissed off," Dundy said. "That someone else would break the ceasefire."

"Whatever it is," Clayton said. "They're clearly coming for blood."

"And you say your force is how strong?" Rodriguez said.

"These twelve men plus ten women in the village. We were on our way up to Kahmard right now to grab another handful of bodies."

"You'll still be outnumbered five to one."

"The villagers are armed too. And if we have enough time before morning, we can command the hills and have them in a shooting gallery when they pull into the valley. We should be able to pick off enough of them to even up the odds a bit. That's if we can get back up there before morning."

"All right, Mr. Clayton. I need to talk with my team before I make any decisions. Can I trust you not to make any trouble while I do? And ditto with those dudes up the road there?"

"Their hands are in the CIA's wallet. You won't have any trouble with them, or us."

"Okay. You stay right here and we'll be back."

Rodriguez walked around to the front of the Sikorski and waved to where the rest of the patrol was manning the two Humvees and .50 cals.

"Becket and the rest of you, get your asses over here."

Mason looked reluctant to abandon his post.

"It's all right," Rodriguez said. "I've been assured that those gentlemen up the road won't give us any trouble."

While the patrol huddled together in the road, Clayton leaned against the edge of the cargo deck, restlessly checking his watch every ten seconds.

"If you don't mind, I think I'll continue my interview with Saarah," Megan said.

Clayton waved a hand. They climbed in and sat on the rear seat of the cargo bay. Sunny sat down next to Clayton and smiled.

"Don't worry, chief. We'll get this show back on the road."

Clayton nodded. The minutes passed.

Finally, Clayton heard footsteps and stood up. It was Rodriguez.

"All right, first thing, I need everyone here read into this game plan. No second hand rumors...Go on, grab the rest of your people and meet us out on the road."

Rodriguez peeked into the cargo bay.

"That goes for you two ladies, too. Come on, let's do this."

Once everyone was gathered around him, Rodriguez looked from face to face.

"Okay, here's what's going to happen. You dudes are going to take your two Humvees and Land Cruiser and head back down the road a few miles. Then you are to wait fifteen minutes before heading back this way. We're going to disappear and stay disappeared long enough for you to pass through. This gives us deniability if some analyst in Quantico or wherever happens to be looking through drone feed and sees this deal go down. I sent you back the way you came and waited to make sure you didn't come back and then chased some gunfire we heard up the road towards Ghandak. Are we all good with this?"

Connelly smiled.

"Sounds just the way I would have planned it, partner."

"Yeah, well. This ain't no joke. All our asses and careers are on the line here so I need everyone's word right now. I don't care what cantina you find yourself in down the road, you never tell a soul what we did here. Are we all good with that?"

There were nods and thumbs up all around.

"All right. Then you get that bird back in the air and you boys head on down the road and we'll pretend this encounter never happened."

As everyone was parting ways, Leanna reached out to Saarah.

"Go get 'em, girl."

"Yeah," Natalie said. "Go kick some Taliban ass. I wish we could be there with you."

They both gave her a hug before turning away.

Clayton was waiting at the helicopter and gave Saarah and Megan a hand getting back onboard.

"Let's go," he said to Sunny and slammed the door shut.

Clayton checked his watch again while heading forward. It was now past midnight. They had lost well over an hour and would be lucky to get everyone back on the ground by 0300 hours in the morning.

Sunny had the turbine whining and pulled the helicopter into the air.

"Push it," Clayton said. "Whatever extra muscle you can get out of this thing."

He pulled out his phone and called Ariya's number.

Twenty Three

Ariya stood behind the main house of the compound, staring up at the approaching helicopter. She was wearing fatigues and had an AK slung over her shoulder.

As soon as they were on the ground, Clayton jumped out and ran over to greet her.

"Sorry for the delay."

"Please, my friend. We owe everything to you. What can I do?"

"Get us some more bodies."

Ariya gestured at herself.

"I had assumed as much."

"But you said there are more up in Mazar-e-Sharif, right?"

"Yes. Kejal my fellow Kurd will join us. She is a well-trained warrior and there are two or three more."

"Then let's go. Are you ready?"

"Yes. I have this case of ammo here and two more AKs."

"I'll grab the rounds, you grab the rifles."

Clayton picked up the box and followed Ariya back to the helicopter.

"Ah," Ariya said at the open cargo door.

"Ariya!" Megan said. "Jesus, it's been what? Six or seven years?"

They quickly embraced.

"I no longer remember. Everything becomes a haze when you are at war with Daesh."

"Come, we need to hurry," Clayton said.

He helped Ariya onboard and slammed the door shut.

"You'll have to tell us exactly where we're going."

"Dawlat Abad. It is northwest of Mazar-e-Sharif. Bring us to Sharif and I will show you from there."

"All right, let's go," Clayton said to Sunny, going forward.

Clayton got his laptop open and checked the drone feed again. He heard the women chatting away in back. Sunny had his eyes fixed on the black, starry night up ahead.

A text came through as they raced through the night. Connelly had arrived to the village and was coordinating with the women on their best defensive posture.

Clayton checked the news. Durrani had made a statement to the press, chastising the Americans for not negotiating in good faith. Clayton could imagine Blackburn's indigestion. Simmons too. No doubt Simmons was dying for an update but Clayton wasn't about to break comm silence. A full report would have to wait until he got back to Kabul.

Forty-five minutes later, Clayton saw the lights of Mazar-e-Sharif up ahead and called to Ariya. She came forward.

"Do you want my seat?" he said.

"No, I am fine."

She crouched down and Clayton showed her his laptop.

"It is fine. I know the area well. Follow these valleys to the left. We will see the village at the edge of the flood plain."

They passed the lights of many villages but Ariya kept gesturing forward.

"There," she said some minutes later. "Do you see the compound?"

"Got it," Sunny said.

It was roughly a mile back from Dawlat Abad and up on a hill, with woods surrounding it. Sunny was quickly touching down inside the compound walls. Someone had fashioned a crude version of a French garden, divided up into four quadrants by walkways and hedges. It was a modest but not altogether lousy job.

Five women stood there in fatigues, one of them Kejal.

"Are they all coming?" Clayton said.

"If you can carry them, yes," Ariya said.

Clayton looked at Sunny.

"We'll be fine," he said.

"All right. Let's do this."

Clayton opened the cargo door, jumped out and helped Ariya down. She ran over to greet the five women and after a brief exchange escorted them back.

"This is Kejal," Ariya said as she climbed onboard.

Clayton shook her hand.

"Thank you for coming."

"It is we who should be thanking you for your courage. We know your government no longer wishes to be involved."

Clayton acknowledged her comment while helping the other women to get onboard. With everyone inside, he closed the door and went forward. Sunny waited until everyone was seated and buckled in before lifting off.

"Back to where we started?" he said.

Clayton nodded and checked his watch. It was just past 0130 hours and they had an hour flight ahead of them. They were making better time than he had expected but it still left only a few hours before dawn for preparations, a task that seemed increasingly impossible and overwhelming.

His mind had gone to work on all that needed to be done when he stopped himself. Connelly, Palmer and Metcalf knew what to do. The best way for Clayton to help was to drop these women off and get back to Kabul. Someone had to control things behind the scenes. There were sure to be fires that needed putting out along the way.

He texted Connelly to say that he had six extra bodies and left it at that. Everything looked quiet in the Taliban compound. No doubt they were resting up before battle.

As they got close, Clayton texted again, asking Connelly to have the team leaders meet at Salahuddeen's house. ETA was five minutes.

Coming in over the village, Clayton spotted one of the Humvees, Palmer's Land Cruiser and seven people gathered around Salahuddeen's front porch.

"Leave it running," Clayton said as they touched down.

He quickly had the cargo door open and was on the ground, helping Ariya out.

"Help the others," he said and dashed over to the front porch.

Connelly stood there watching the women get out. Hearing the noise, some of the villagers had come out to the front of their homes.

"I take it you're not sticking around," Connelly said.

"Yeah, I'm heading back to Kabul. Durrani's been shooting his mouth off in the press. And that's just one fire I need to put out."

"I kind of had my heart set on some air support."

"Not going to happen. The best I can do is some fresh ammo and another bird if extraction becomes necessary."

Clayton looked from Connelly around to the others.

"I don't mean to tell you people how to go about your business but man those hills around the road coming in from the east. You lose control of that and you're on the wrong side of the eight ball."

"I got it covered," Connelly said. "Worst case scenario, we hold the other end of the valley and evac back the way we came in. Lead them right back into the teeth of that Army patrol."

"All right. The women have a link to the drone feed. That should keep you one step ahead of any attack plans. I'm half an hour away if evac becomes necessary. Anything else I can do, just give me a call. I'll be ready to go airborne the minute you need me. I would absolutely stay here and fight but nothing we do is going to matter if someone at State bring the hammer down on us."

Clayton held up his hands and looked from face to face.

"We got you handled," Connelly said. "Get on with your mission and we'll get on with ours."

"Thanks."

Clayton pulled Megan aside.

"I'm hoping to see something in the press by tomorrow evening."

"It'll be out on the wire by morning, D.C. time. Assuming I'm still alive to tell the tale."

"You'll be all right. Just don't play hero. I know it's your style to be down in the trenches but getting this story out to the world is the most important thing right now. I'm counting on you."

On his way back to the helicopter, Clayton stopped to talk with Saarah. She was fielding questions from some of the villagers.

"Excuse me," he said to those around Saarah and dragged her aside.

Both of them stared.

"There's always a chance I'll never see you again, and if that should happen, there are things here in my heart, things that I have wanted to say to you...Things that I'm not even sure are appropriate to say in your country. Or if this is even the right time to be saying them, but if that were the case, I'm sure I would miss you every day for the rest of my life."

Saarah stared for a long moment before throwing herself at Clayton's chest.

"I would miss you too," she said and pulled back.

After another long stare, Saarah gave Clayton a discreet kiss on the cheek.

"You must go. I know you have much to do."

Clayton made sure that no one was watching and handed her Akmad's phone. The phone had a note tied to it with a rubber band

"I am leaving this with you for safekeeping. If you receive a message from me, you will know to give it to Megan. The note will tell her what to do. You may have to translate a couple of voice messages for her but she can take it from there. Okay?"

Saarah nodded.

"Okay, be careful."

Clayton touched her hand before turning to leave. Moments later, Sunny was lifting off and everything on the ground quickly grew small, Saarah included.

Clayton noticed Sunny glancing at him and looked over.

"Pretty lady."

"Yeah. Pretty lady."

Clayton sent Simmons a text. He was on his way back. Please have a transport waiting for him at the airport. His ETA was twenty minutes.

The miles flew by with a thousand things rushing through Clayton's mind.

Seeing the airport come into view, he began gathering up his things.

"You're on call," he told Sunny. "If you want a bite to eat, hit the airport lounge. Grab some sleep in the back. Whatever. Just don't get any farther than five minutes from this helo. The odds are, we'll be rolling again soon. Maybe before dawn but definitely at some point tomorrow. You can figure, if I'm not at Camp Eggers or the embassy, I'll be on my way back over here so be ready."

"You got it."

As soon as the wheels hit the ground, Clayton jumped out and dashed over to the waiting transport. He checked his watch. A few ticks after 0300. He needed sleep but there wasn't any time for that. He texted Simmons to let him know he was on his way.

Back at the station, Clayton dashed up to his office and took two Desoxyn before heading over to see Simmons. The chief was stretched out on his couch and looking groggy.

"Let's hear it," he said.

Clayton gave him the run down.

"So, as good as can be expected."

"As good as can be expected. How about on your end?"

"As far as I can tell, Blackburn's still one step behind us. I'm sure he's busy tracking down every lead. CSI Kabul."

Clayton smiled.

"Yeah, he seems especially obsessed with whatever the hell went down at that retreat up in Nuristan. I expect he has a forensics team scouring the place right now...Oh, and he wants us over there at the embassy again. 0800 hours. He's jumping on a plane back to D.C. this morning and expects some answers before he leaves."

"I take it the Taliban have yet to say a word about this latest ass kicking."

"No, but if what you told me is true, about that defector from the village, they really must be in a state. They have to be thinking now that this represents an existential threat. A whole country of women rising up in arms against them? They'd be screwed."

"Remember, Aarshin saw me there. Meaning, the Taliban do have reason to think that the Americans are meddling behind their backs."

"Well, you can be sure they'll play it that way, once things get out in the open. Always the victim with those bastards."

"I'm still concerned about this battle. Maybe I've underestimated their troop strength. With enough men and the right strategy, this could quickly turn into a rout."

"What more can we do, short of calling in air support?"

"Call in air support."

"And that is not going to happen. Hell, we may as well drive over and confess everything to Rocky."

Clayton nodded.

"I did promise them air evac, if it comes to that. It's one thing to have egg on our faces. Quite another to be answering for a complete massacre."

"Where would you take them?"

"Up to their base outside Mazar-e-Sharif. Win or lose, they'll need to get out of sight for a few days. Nuristan happened in a vacuum, but once the smoke clears on this battle, every agency bloodhound will be on their trail."

The two men stared.

"What about Durrani?" Clayton said. "When were you thinking to play that card?"

"Not quite yet. Let's give him a bit more rope first. See how far he'll hang himself. What do you think?"

"How much rope does it take to hang a man?"

"I want to make sure it's a good long drop."

"I appreciate the sentiment but how much good will an extra foot of rope do us? It would be one thing if he were the prize, but he's just a pawn in a bigger game."

"How would you play it?"

"Give the phone to Megan and let her blow the lid off his betrayal in her story."

"And when they ask how she got her hands on that phone?"

"From the women. I already told her to keep us out of it."

"You really trust her that much."

"Yeah. She's known for protecting her sources."

"Yeah, I suppose she'd quickly be out of business if she didn't...And you left her the phone?"

"With one of the women warriors, with instructions to give it to Megan if she got the okay from us."

"Sure, go ahead. You have my blessing."

Simmons took his glasses off and rubbed his eyes.

"You wouldn't be getting emotionally involved up there, would you?"

Simmons put the glasses back on and stared at Clayton.

"Look, whatever's going on with me personally, I just don't think this story can wait. We need to win the news cycle. Empathy for the women while Durrani is outed for stabbing Afghanistan in the back. Like I said before, Durrani now has good reason to suspect that the American government is mixed up in this thing. It's only a matter of time before he plays his cards with the press."

"Yeah, he would. He's worse than the Taliban."

Simmons looked at his watch.

"Going on 0400. It'll be getting light soon. Have you checked the drone feed lately?"

"I did on the flight back. Last I looked, the Taliban appeared to be getting some shuteye."

"And how about you?"

"No. I just took a couple of Desoxyn. I couldn't sleep with World War III about to go down."

Simmons stood up.

"Well, guess I'll head back to my apartment. Take a shower and freshen up a bit. You ought to do the same."

Clayton stood up too.

"No, I'm going to hang around and keep an eye on things."

"All right. I'll be back by 0600. We'll get things up on the board in the TOC and see how things look."

"I have Sunny waiting on call up at Karzai but I want a second bird, just for back up and in case we need that evac."

"I'll arrange it."

"Thanks. How about Adelman? Did you give him the news about borrowing his drone?"

"Yeah and he stormed out of here, madder than hell and looking for you. He finally went out back to cop some sleep about an hour ago."

Simmons paused with Clayton out in the hallway after locking his door.

"There's going to be some blood spilled today but I guess I have to agree with you. Better to get this story out there. Let the world know about these brave women and see if the suits back in Washington can still explain away their Afghan policy...I'll see you back here at 0600."

Simmons patted Clayton on the shoulder and headed for the elevator.

Back in his office, Clayton pulled up the drone feed on his desk top. The Taliban were stirring. It was like morning anywhere, men splashing water on their faces, wandering out into a field to relieve themselves. Vehicles were jockeying around into position everywhere he looked. It was just as Clayton had figured. They were planning to strike at dawn.

His impulse was to call Connelly but assumed he had his eyes on this too.

While Clayton continued staring, the Taliban drifted as one towards a central place in the compound and knelt to pray. It was the age old story, their god against ours.

Restless, Clayton went downstairs and out in back to the drone pilot command trailer. There were only three pilots working when he slipped inside. Clayton sat down with Corso and spoke quietly.

"Was Adelman down here making a scene?"

"Yeah. I told him to have it out with Simmons if he didn't like it. That really pissed him off. I'm guessing he wore himself out because I haven't seen him in about an hour."

"Yeah. Simmons said he finally crashed...So what's our status?"

"I was about to call you. The new drone's in place. I was just getting ready to bring the other one back for refueling."

"All right. Give me the uplink code."

Corso scribbled it on a piece of paper. Clayton wheeled his chair away a few feet, texted Veeda's phone with the new code and wheeled back to have a look at the screen. Dozens of vehicles were now lined up in the compound, ready to go. He checked his watch. It was pushing 0430. In half an hour, the eastern horizon would start to blush ever so faintly above the dark hills.

"Looks like the Road Warrior," Corso said,

Clayton smirked.

"That's what Simmons said."

"I can picture it. Some haji on the front of a Humvee with his sitar and a Marshall stack."

Corso pretended to be playing the part.

"You're forgetting. They hate music," Clayton said.

"Oh yeah. Well, maybe just a mullah preaching Sharia Law at 150 decibels. *If you don't obey Allah, we're going to cut your head off and feed it to the pigs.*"

Clayton shook his head. His own thoughts had turned dark again suddenly. A premonition that Saarah would die that day. He nearly jumped out of his seat, fearing he would never see her again. If not for Blackburn and his nonsense, he would have raced to the airport that very second. It was hell, knowing he could not be there to fight by her side.

Clayton stood up.

"Just make sure you keep that UAV aloft and in position. Lives are depending on the intel down there."

"You got it…And hey. Don't forget my Desoxyn."

"I'll drop it off at 0800. Simmons and I are being dragged back over to State for another show and blow session."

Corso gave him a thumbs up. Clayton went outside and looked to the east. The sky was still dark.

Back up in his office, he pulled out his phone and sent Veeda another text.

> Please give that phone and note to Megan. Those men are getting ready to move out. I assume you are watching too. I hope to be there later. Good luck. Waiting for word from you until then.

Twenty Four

The last thing before moving up into the hills, the women gathered in the front room of Saarah's house to put on their makeup, with each woman helping another one. Megan sat at the outskirts of the throng, taking in this ritual and writing furiously on her laptop.

Ariya stood back from doing Saarah's eyeliner and eyebrows.

"You look beautiful."

Saarah's effort to smile looked more bleak than not. Ariya crouched down in front of her.

"What is it, my little sister?"

"I don't know. I had this vision just now that I will die here today and that this is the last time I will see this world."

"No. Do not worry. I have an equal vision that you will be alive for many years to come."

Saarah fell into Ariya's arms and lingered there for a long moment before pulling back.

"It is not that I fear dying, but I will miss this life. There are so many things I still wish to see. So many things I still wish to do."

"And you will see them, and do them. Everything will be all right."

"I don't know…I was thinking of a poem my teacher Mrs. Farooq shared with us last year. It was from a novel given to her by her Russian teacher when she was a schoolgirl."

"And? What did it say?"

"I do not remember the exact words but it was about a soldier who lay dying from a bullet. In a dale in Dagestan. And as he lay dying, he dreamed of his loved one at a feast, and at the feast she was wearing a crown of flowers on her head, dreaming of him, lying in a dale in Dagestan with a bullet in his chest and his blood growing cold."

"It sounds very beautiful, but sad. And you do not remember the name of this novel."

"I know it," Megan said, looking up from her laptop. "*A Hero of Our Times* by Mikhail Lermontov. He wrote the poem and then died in a gun duel, just like in his poem. It was very prophetic."

"You see?" Saarah said. "Perhaps we can all sense when it is our time."

"Nonsense," Ariya said and frowned furtively at Megan.

Ariya resumed doing Saarah's eyeliner.

"I saw you with Clayton today. You're in love, aren't you?"

"I don't know that I understand what love is."

"Of course you do. It feels as if you have been swept away by a great wind...Anyway, he is a good man and you will have a long life together. Now quickly, let us do your nails."

There was the sound of a vehicle pulling to a stop outside. A knock on the door followed. Hajira went to answer it. Connelly stood there with a Humvee and three of his crew members parked behind him.

Connelly had a quizzical look around the room.

"Are we doing battle today or having a beauty contest?"

"Both," Ariya called back.

"Look, you're the ones who told us that the Taliban force was on its way."

"Yes. Mahvash and Farzaneh are still watching."

The laptop was open in front of Mahvash as she did Farzaneh's nails.

"Look, these dudes are not going to wait around while we get pretty."

"Are they here yet?" Ariya asked with a look up from Saarah's hand.

"No, but they'll be spraying this place with rounds soon enough, so whenever you ladies can get your cute little asses in gear, it would be greatly appreciated."

"Have you forgotten that we sent Daesh running for the hills? This scum is nothing to us."

"Yeah? Well this particular form of scum is armed to the teeth and will look like a swarm of locusts coming at us once they get here."

"They will not be a swarm for long."

"Look. I ain't fixing to die here today so..."

"And neither are we...Five minutes more and we will be on our way."

"Very well. Any time you're done with your spa shit, I have some hills that need defending so let's get moving. And remember what we discussed about this comm business. Veeda's TL 1, I'm TL 2. Saarah's sniper 1, my man Rocco's sniper 2. Everything short and sweet and in English. And anybody who doesn't have some seriously important tactical intel to relay, stay off the airwaves. Okay?"

"Roger that," Ariya said.

"Okay, ladies, we'll be waiting on you."

Connelly had another look around the room before closing the door. Ariya translated what he had said while taking Saarah's other hand.

"A very insolent man," she added with a smile.

"But he is right," Veeda said. "Enough with the makeup."

"The better to anger the Taliban," Irem said. "Here, your lipstick."

"I do not wish to have lipstick!"

"No, you must."

Veeda stood there defiantly while Irem applied it.

"Now I look like a clown," Veeda said.

"Actually, you look very sexy," Farzaneh said.

Veeda pretended to be seductive while pointing her rifle and the other women laughed.

"Okay, enough!" she said. "Where are they now?"

She went to look at the drone feed on the laptop.

"They are nearing Babor. We must go."

"It's still ten miles of difficult road," Kejal said.

"Eh, always an answer with you. And your lipstick is already smudged."

Esin checked Kejal's lipstick.

"Come," Veeda said again. "All of you. It is time to go!"

After a last minute check in the mirror, the women pulled on their vests, grabbed their rifles and headed for the door.

"Radios, everyone?" Veeda said.

"Roger that," Farzaneh said on her way out.

Those who had radios tapped them as they passed by Veeda.

Palmer and Metcalf were driving by on the dirt road just then and stopped to whistle. Metcalf jumped out and ran over to Hajira.

"Remind her again, Irem. I'm taking her back to the States with me when we're done here so don't go getting herself killed today."

Irem translated and Hajira answered.

"She says, remember what she told you. We will not be done here until all the Taliban have fled back to their caves in Pakistan."

"Okay, baby. Whatever it takes." He tapped his heart. "I'm with you."

"All right, let's go!" Palmer called out.

Metcalf gave her a hug and ran back to the Land Cruiser. The other women had already started up into the hills behind Saarah's house and Hajira hurried to catch up with them.

"Hajira's in love," Farzaneh said.

"You're crazy. He's crazy. Let us focus on this battle."

The women climbed up and up among the rocks and brush until they reached a wooded area. The trees continued on for several hundred yards before they met a sheer cliff face. The mountains were visible above the cliffs. Off to the east, the sky was growing lighter. Somewhere above them, bells rang, where two of the villagers had herded the village sheep and goats up to safety.

There at the tree line, the women stopped and gazed out across the valley. The road from the east entered on their left but their view of it was broken by a towering carapace of rock. In the other direction, the hills funneled the road west into the steep canyon, back to where the women had originally camped. The only way for the Taliban to attack the women was a head on assault up the hill.

As the sky continued to brighten, a handful of village men drifted out to work in the fields. That was part of the plan, to make things appear as normal as possible to the Taliban, then slip away into the woods once the attack began.

The women commanded the hills on the north side of the valley, Connelly's men to the south, in what they hoped would be a fairly straightforward pincer movement. Of course all hell would break loose once the firing started and who knew what would happen then. Murphy's law, most likely. If something could go wrong, it usually did. From years of battle experience, the Americans knew this all too well. If the women didn't, they would find out soon enough.

Before spreading out into a defensive formation, they gathered around Mahvash's laptop and watched the convoy drawing closer. It had come to within a half mile of the valley when all the vehicles stopped. A number of men got out and a discussion ensued on the road. Then four of them crossed over into the woods alongside the road and started towards the village. Veeda had Mahvash relay the intel over the radio.

"They are coming through the woods along the road."

"TL 2 here. Roger that. I have eyes on them."

With the comm button off, Veeda whispered to the other women.

"All of you, spread out. And take your position, Saarah."

Saarah ran along the tree line and scrambled up onto a knoll, a hundred yards west of the other women. Of everyone on their team, she now had the clearest line of sight and saw the four Taliban scouts come into view before the others. She keyed up her radio.

"Sniper 1 to TL 1. I now see the four scouts and they have seen the men working in the fields."

"Sniper 2 here. Copy that."

Moments later, Mahvash came on for Veeda.

"TL 1 here. Copy that but waiting until entire convoy has entered the valley before engaging the enemy."

Saarah watched the men hoeing among the rows of crops, wanting to yell at them. "Run!" But they didn't. They looked over their shoulders once and kept working as the Taliban drew near.

"Are they being fools or courageous?" Saarah whispered.

Irem called back.

"Clearly they have reasoned that if they run, it will alert the scouts to the danger and the rest of the Taliban will not enter the valley."

"I am sick to think that they will lose their lives over this bravery," Saarah said.

"TL 2 here. Did I not advise to stay off the airwaves unless you had some seriously important intel to convey?"

Saarah clicked off and watched the four scouts walk up to the village men. One of the scouts spoke to the villagers while the other three stood guard warily.

You could almost tell what the village men were saying by their gestures. We don't know anything. Everyone left and we're just here taking care of our crops.

The man questioning them quickly grew agitated and pointed back towards the east end of the valley. The villagers were marched off with rifles at their backs. Saarah had her scope trained on the Taliban who had done the talking. Then she heard Mahvash break the radio silence.

"TL 1 here again. Do not fire yet."

"I am waiting for the one with a radio to use it," Saarah radioed back.

"TL 1 repeats. Everyone wait."

"I am waiting."

Go on, Saarah thought. Get your radio out and make the call. Get the rest of your scum to drive in so I can kill you and save the villagers. If she did not take the shot soon, the men would surely be dead.

"Sniper 2," Saarah whispered into her radio. "This is sniper 1."

"I'm listening."

"I'll take the one with the radio and the one with the black turban next to him."

"Roger that. I'll take out the other two."

The men had walked another twenty feet when the one with the radio finally brought it up to his mouth.

"Is the convoy moving now?" Saarah whispered.

"Don't shoot," Mahvash said.

"Are they moving!"

There was a long pause.

"Yes, the convoy is coming in but don't shoot yet."

"Permission to disobey orders, sir."

There was another long pause as Saarah watched the man put his radio away and shove his rifle into the back of the nearest villager.

"Permission granted," Mahvash said finally.

"Ready, sniper 2?"

"Ready to fire when you are."

"Now," Saarah said and gently squeezed the trigger.

Almost simultaneously, two of the heads rocked back violently and those men slumped to the ground. Reflexively, the village men had also dropped to the ground.

Saarah quickly refocused before the other two Taliban could take cover and dropped her second target with a shot in the back. In that same split second, the fourth man's head exploded in a spray of brain parts.

Saarah stole a quick look towards the east end of the valley. The convoy had yet to come into view. When she looked back, the man she had shot in the back was belly crawling between the rows of crops, trying to reach the man with the radio.

"All clear, sniper 1?"

"No. My second shot wasn't fatal."

"Where is he?"

"Between the rows of crops. You can't see him."

"Are you able to finish him?"

"One second."

With the man lying prone, it was a difficult shot. Saarah rubbed her eyes and refocused. He was five feet from the radio and reaching out his hand when she fired. The shot hit him somewhere in the arm or shoulder. He yelped and tried to roll out of sight. Saarah quickly refocused and fired again. This time, the man went limp. She wasn't sure where she had hit him but he was no longer moving.

She began searching for the villagers and saw them scrambling for safety among the rows of crops.

"Sniper 1 here. Alert to all team members. The village men are making their way towards the woods. They are friendlies so do not shoot."

"Sniper 2 here. Roger that. Meanwhile, game on. I see the rodeo's finally riding into town."

Saarah had heard the sound of the approaching column for the better part of a minute but only then saw the lead vehicles roar into view. Without access to the drone feed, she was blind to how far back it went but the line of up armored SUVs, pickups and stolen Afghan Army Humvees kept pouring into the valley. A handful of them quickly broke off and crossed the bridge towards the opposite side of the valley but the main column continued along the road below her and began to disappear from her line of sight.

"Sniper 2 to sniper 1. I've got your side of the valley, you take mine."

"Sniper 1 here. There is not much to shoot on your side and on this side, most of the column is now out of my sight. I can only see the trailing end. I may have to relocate."

"This is TL 2. You just make sure those long guns are focused on those dudes manning the .50 cals first."

"Sniper 2 here. Roger that."

"Sniper 1 here. How many more vehicles are there?"

"Mahvash for TL 1. The last vehicle should be coming into your sights in a moment. It is a white Land Cruiser."

"Sniper 2 here. I'm going to guess it's their team leader. Permission to take out that puke before I start hitting those .50 cals."

"TL 2 here. Permission granted. And then I want to see those RPGs lighting up trucks like a Fourth of July fireworks show. If anyone starts spraying .50 cal fire up into these hills, we'll be sitting ducks.

As Saarah watched, the convoy slowly came to a halt, with vehicles angling off to one side of the road and the other. The men inside quickly piled out and began to search the area with weapons ready. Saarah had her scope focused on a truck with a machine gun mounted on the back.

We have only seconds now, she thought, before the alarms go off. The four dead Taliban scouts were lying out of sight among the crops, but it would soon become apparent that something was wrong.

"Sniper 1 here. Waiting for permission to shoot."

"TL 2 here. Wait until everyone of those motherfuckers gets out into plain view."

"Sniper 2 here. I just seen their TL climb out of the Land Cruiser and have my sights on his pumpkin. Anytime you're ready to get this show on the road."

"How does it look with TL 1?"

Connelly heard Pashtun being spoken, then Mahvash said, "We are a go."

"All right. On the count of three, let's bang this drum. One…Two…Three!"

In response to the hail of small arms fire, the Taliban scrambled for cover and fired wildly in all directions. Connelly's two Humvees burst out of hiding and began to rake the rear of the column with their .50s, cutting off any hope of escape in that direction. Then two RPGs rocketed towards the convoy, leading to another wild scramble.

The grenades hit and exploded and two plumes of smoke rose up into the sky. As the smoke slowly drifted downwind and dissipated, it revealed what was left of the two trucks with their .50 cals. They were both on fire and reduced to twisted hulks of metal.

In the ongoing exchange of gunfire, screams of pain rent the early morning light.

Pinned down and with few choices, a sizable group of the Taliban made a charge towards the nearest row of houses. They were quickly out of Saarah's sight but many more of them had made a break for the woods and Saarah picked them off as she could.

Hearing a fresh barrage of bullets below her, Saarah looked that way with her scope. The men who had found shelter in the houses were spraying the hills from two back windows. The rest of her team quickly peppered the buildings with return fire and the men inside retreated from the windows.

Then, as if someone had flipped a switch, the gunfire stopped and the early morning grew eerily silent. Saarah surveyed the wreckage with her scope. In less than a minute, half the convoy had been reduced to rubble, all four of their .50 cals had been disabled and the hundred or so Taliban foot soldiers had been whittled down to sixty or seventy.

That was the upside. The downside was, they were now scattered all over the valley, hidden inside houses and down in the woods and among the fields.

Connelly's voice came over the radio

"TL 2 here. Any casualties to report?"

"TL 1 here. None with our team."

"Jake here. Copy that."

"Okay, TL 2 here to sniper 1 and 2. I need some cover. We're going to gather up a few of these vehicles, drive them down to where the road comes in from the east and blow them sky high. We do not want any potential reinforcements riding in here unimpeded."

"Sniper 1 here. Roger that."

"Sniper 2 here. Good copy."

"In the meantime, can anyone confirm how many of these hostiles retreated into the woods?"

"Sniper 1 here. I counted roughly fifty."

"Okay. I want one of my .50 cals and half my team members to go assist the villagers with holding that canyon to the west. If those pecker heads in the woods decide to stage an assault in that direction, the women hiding down there are going to get slaughtered."

"Jake here. Roger that. Consider one .50 cal on the move"

"All right. Once we've blocked the eastern access to this valley, I want to meet with TL 1 and her interpreter and her drone team over at the elder's house. Is that doable?"

After a pause, Mahvash came over the radio.

"That is doable."

"Okay, see you there in fifteen. In the meantime, I want all remaining firepower focused on where the hostiles are known to be hiding, long guns included. The enemy still outnumbers us three or four to one and sooner or later they're going to figure that out. Our job is to keep them right where they are. This situation is close enough to a cluster fuck already."

"Roger that."

"All right. I'm off to engage in some fireworks. Then I will expect to see TL 1 and her team at our agreed rendezvous point."

The silence in the valley was broken moments later by the sound of engines turning over and vehicles moving away to the east.

A few minutes later, a huge explosion rocked the morning and a flock of birds rose up from the fields.

"Mission accomplished," Connelly radioed back.

He arrived to Salahuddeen's house with no sign of anyone there.

"Let's clear the inside," he told his driver.

Their gunner manned the .50 cal while they went inside.

Connelly was back out front and leaning against his Humvee when Salahuddeen came down from the hills with an AK cradled across his chest.

"God be with you," Salahuddeen said.

"I'll take the devil if it keeps everyone from getting dusted today."

Salahuddeen smiled a bit.

"Tea?" he said.

"Sorry, boss, but we don't have time for tea and cake."

Connelly looked at his watch and then off in the distance, waiting. Veeda, Irem and Mahvash appeared a minute later, driving an Isuzu SUV they had taken from the back of the convoy.

"We'll be running a used car lot once this show is over," Connelly said to chuckles from his team.

He waited until all the women were gathered around him and nodded at Mahvash.

"Let's see the drone feed of that Taliban compound."

She set the laptop up on the hood of Connelly's Humvee and clicked on the zoom shot. Everyone gathered around as he studied the situation. There were a dozen or so more Taliban hurriedly loading munitions into three vehicles.

"All right," Connelly said. "The D Team's obviously been alerted. We'll have to keep our eyes on that situation. Let's zoom out and see what we got coming in from the east."

Veeda searched up the road in that direction for fifteen miles but there were no other signs of hostiles coming.

"All right, ten four on that shit," Connelly said, backing away. "I understand we've got some hostiles pinned down inside a house somewhere?"

"Two houses," Irem said.

"And how many hostiles are you figuring are in there?"

"Maybe twenty."

Connelly looked from face to face.

"All right, here's the deal as I see it. We'd be fools to go after those dudes with fifty hostiles at our backs so we need to do something about clearing the woods first thing."

"Good luck with that," his driver said. "We go in there trying to force the issue and we'll get our clocks cleaned."

"Point taken," Connelly said. "But on the other hand, we sit around here trying to starve these pricks out and we're likely to have haji and his forty thieves riding up our ass by the end of the day. And way better prepared."

Connelly waved at Veeda.

"I suppose you'd better translate all this shit for her."

Veeda listened to Mahvash and said something back in Pashto.

"She says we have our drone and should use this advantage to take these men out. Surgically, I believe you call it."

Connelly nodded, smiling at Veeda, then keyed up his radio.

"I'm here with TL 1, trying to come up with a plan of attack. In the meantime, if one of these hostiles goes to scratch his ass, I want to know about it. The day is still young and there's still a whole shitload of fighting left to do so keep your eyes peeled."

Connelly ended the comm and turned to Veeda.

"All right, honey. I'm all ears."

Twenty Five

Clayton was shaving in his office bathroom when a text came through from Veeda's phone. He paused and read the news, both relieved and concerned by how the battle had played out so far. No one on their team had been killed, but it had left a horde of majorly pissed off Taliban soldiers alive and cornered. This was where a few Apaches would come in handy. Two or three Hellfires and some M230 rounds pounding the woods and you'd be down to a handful of stragglers.

Clayton was determined to press Simmons on the air support issue. There had to be something they could do.

He finished shaving and made do with a splash bath before getting into a fresh shirt and pair of pants. His insides felt hollow from the lack of food and sleep but the Desoxyn had his brain humming. While brushing his teeth, he noticed the dilated pupils. The drug made you feel immortal. You could go on like this for a thousand years, or until your heart gave out.

Before heading over to Simmons' office, Clayton went out back to the drone pilot command center.

"I was about to send out a search party," Rick said, seeing Clayton come in.

Clayton furtively handed him the two Desoxyn.

"This should get you through to the end of your shift."

Rick quickly downed them with a swig of his Coke.

"I hope you got more of this shit."

"There's plenty more where that came from."

Clayton nodded at the screen.

"Show me what's going on."

Rick did, pointing out how the skirmish had unfolded and who was where.

"The last I saw, some of the friendlies had gathered together outside of this hooch, and then they split up, some of them heading across this bridge and up into the hills and some of them down the road in this direction. It's been pretty quiet since then. You want me to replay the feed?"

"No, that's okay."

Clayton glanced at his watch.

"I need to run. Simmons and I are expected over at the American embassy shortly. As soon as we're back, we'll get all this back up on the board in the TOC."

Rick yawned. Clayton patted him on the shoulder.

"You'll be feeling immortal in about twenty minutes."

"That won't be soon enough."

Back upstairs and on his way down the hallway to Simmons' office, Clayton popped into sig intel. Scottie was still busy at his station. Clayton sat down next to him

"Anything new with Durrani?"

"You must be kidding? That dude has either completely forgotten we can listen in on him or he just doesn't care. He's been on the phone about twenty times already. Talking in code mostly so it's kind of hard to tell just exactly what he's up to, but he's definitely up to something."

"Talking to whom?"

"Abdul Qahhar and Khan Zada again. And Khan Zada has been on the phone with Qammar Wali in Doha. There's another dude, Shahpur Sikander. Durrani's been on the phone with him a couple of times. Emily would have a better handle on his profile but I know he's the undersecretary of some kind of shit in the administration."

"What's he been saying?"

"Sikander or Durrani?"

"Both of them."

"Durrani's done most of the talking, speculating about what he thinks is going down and who's behind it. I heard him say *alphabet* several times so I think he's lasered in on the idea that the CIA is playing them. Or someone like us."

"And Sikander?"

"He mostly just listens and agrees."

"All right. I've got to run. You have a print out of this?"

"Yeah. Right here. I figured you'd want it."

"Thanks. Assuming we make it back from this meeting in one piece, Simmons is planning to get this operation up on the board. When are you off?"

"In about ten minutes."

"Can you stick around for another hour or two?"

"Yeah. That long. I'll pry my eyes open with another Red Bull."

"All right. See you in a bit."

Clayton had stopped by his office to grab his briefcase when Adelman cornered him outside the door.

"Hey, Dorn." Adelman pretended to paper over his anger with a smile. "I guess you already know I don't appreciate you appropriating my drone for your op. You think you're the only one around here with important shit going on?"

Seeing Adelman try to read the print out in his hand, Clayton turned it over and unlocked his door.

"Did you take this up with Simmons?"

"Oh sure. But I know he's just covering for you...Look, if you're going to fuck with my shit, the least you could do is read me into your op."

Two other operatives came down the hallway and lifted their eyebrows going by. Clayton acknowledged them and looked back at Adelman.

"I'm not trying to be a dick, Adelman, but maybe you've forgotten how this works. Like, you get read in if Simmons wants you read in. That's not my call."

"Yeah, right. Like I'm a mole for the Taliban or something?"

Clayton opened the door and started in. When Adelman tried to follow him, Clayton held a hand up.

"I already told you. If you've got a problem, go talk to Simmons."

"I think I will."

"Fine. You know where to find him."

Clayton slipped through the door and closed it in Adelman's face.

When Clayton walked up to Lauren's desk five minutes later, she darted a furtive glance in the direction of Simmons' office. Clayton could see Simmons talking on the phone through the partially opened blinds. Adelman was standing on the other side of his desk.

"He's in a state," she whispered.

Clayton nodded, touched Lauren's hand and tapped on the door before opening it. Simmons waved him in. Clayton took a seat and tried to ignore Adelman. It quickly became apparent that Simmons was talking to his wife.

"Hang on a second," he said and cupped the phone. "What do you want, Adelman?"

"I want to know why you took my drone without reading me into the op."

"Because I don't trust you to keep your mouth shut."

Adelman stood there staring.

"If you want a few more reasons, I can give you those too. Otherwise, get the hell out of here and back to work."

After a long moment, Adelman stormed off. Once he was gone and the door closed, Simmons pushed a one page report across his desk towards Clayton.

"What a pain in the ass...Anyway, have you seen what these son of a bitches have been up to?"

While Clayton scanned the report, Simmons got back to his call. The report was a list of Taliban bombings over the past twenty four hours. Herat, Faryab, Badakhshan and Balkh Provinces.

Simmons ended the call and quickly gathered up his coat and briefcase.

"She has an uncanny knack for calling at the worst moment. Let's run," he added. "Our transport's waiting. You can bring me up to speed on our way over to the embassy."

Clayton stood up with the report still in his hands.

"Go ahead and bring it."

Clayton followed Simmons out into the hallway.

"Do you believe that?" Simmons whispered while locking his door. "One of the worst foreign policy decisions ever made. Give those bastards a departure date with no conditions and what did people think they were going to do...Oh, Lauren. If Adelman comes down here again making trouble, you have my permission to shoot him."

She smiled her upside-down smile.

Downstairs, the two men climbed into the back seat of a black Suburban. Bradley was behind the wheel and promptly sped off. Kelly was riding shotgun and nodded over the seat. Clayton was still holding onto the report. Simmons took it from him.

"Better tuck this away. I'll wait until old Rocky gets on his high horse again about leaving Afghan matters to the Afghanis before I drag it out."

Simmons opened his briefcase and snapped it shut.

"What's going on up there?" he said quietly.

Clayton related everything he knew about the battle.

"So, so far, so good," Simmons said.

"From what I understand, not as good as Connelly had expected. Not counting the villagers, they're still outnumbered more than three to one. I gather the Taliban don't know that yet, but once they figure it out, assuming they ever do, this thing could still get fubar."

"Believe me, Clayton. If I could send in a couple of Apaches to pummel the son of a bitches, I would."

"Have you tried reasoning with General Blake?"

"Look, I trust him as much as I trust anyone. Definitely more than I trust anyone else at Army, but if I let the cat out of the bag, I've left him with his back to the wall. I may as well say I'm planning a coup. He'll have no choice but to key it up the chain of command."

Clayton looked out his window. Simmons studied him for a moment before speaking up again.

"Listen, I'll see what I can do but let's get back to this meeting. Where do we stand with Durrani hanging himself?"

Clayton turned back and explained what Scottie had told him.

"And the press? When's that story supposed to hit?"

"She said this morning, D.C. time. I'll see if I can get an update."

Clayton texted Megan.

When exactly?

As they sped over to the embassy, a huge cloud of smoke appeared in the sky, but well off in the distance.

"What the hell is that?" Kelly said. "A fire?"

Clayton's had been thinking that too when a massive shock wave rocked the Suburban and nearly blew it off the road.

"Jesus Christ!" Simmons said. "Another bombing?!"

Bradley stepped on the gas and Kelly got his rifle into the up and ready position. Clayton had reflexively pulled out his Glock too. The sound of wailing sirens carried across the city.

"Looks like the Sixth Police District," Simmons said. "Always one of the Hazara neighborhoods with those bastards. Never miss a chance to stir up a little more sectarian hatred."

Bradley careened up to the front of the embassy and braked to a stop. The entire compound was bristling with security in response to the bombing. Smoke from the explosion had begun to drift overhead.

"You want us to wait here?" Bradley said.

"You think maybe?" Simmons said.

Clayton glanced at his phone while holstering his handgun and climbing out. A message had come through from Megan. The Post had made her column a lead story. He hurried around to Simmons' side of the Suburban.

"Megan said the Post has made her piece a lead story."

"What's that mean to us?" Simmons said.

Clayton shrugged.

"The Post updates its internet feed every few hours. It should be live by the time Washington's sipping its coffee."

"Well, it can't be soon enough for me."

Simmons stopped Clayton well short of all the hubbub around the embassy entrance.

"Let's stay mum on what we know about Durrani. Wait until the story hits the press. The more that son of a bitch lies in the meantime, the worse he'll look."

Clayton nodded. Simmons patted him on the back.

"We'll see if we can give Rocky a quick bone to chew on and get our asses back to the station. We need to keep an eye on this op before it runs off the rails."

Simmons had opened the door for Clayton when two Marine officers rushed by on their way out. And with that, Clayton's grim premonition returned. Someone was going to die that day and he feared again it would be Saarah.

He heard the receptionist speaking at the front desk and came back to the moment.

"The ambassador is waiting for you in the main conference room, sir."

Simmons signed in and walked over to the security door. Clayton did the same and joined him. The receptionist buzzed them through and Simmons stopped once they were alone.

"You all right?"

"Yeah."

"Come on, Clayton. Get focused. I need you here 100%."

"I'm here."

Simmons stared hard at him for another moment before heading down the hallway.

Going into the conference room, all the heads turned their way. Simmons was caught a bit off guard by the presence of General Blake and Shahpur Sikander. Blake was the one place Simmons had hoped to turn if these lipstick warriors ever found themselves with their backs to the wall, and having him read into this meeting tended to work against that game plan. As for Sikander, Simmons had always found him inscrutable. His dark, watery eyes hid well whatever he was thinking. The man was definitely thinking, whatever else you could say about him. Thinking and calculating.

Durrani was also there, along with Blackburn, Daniel Silva, and two secretaries taking notes. The mood was somber. Douglas stood up to greet them.

"Thanks for coming, Ted. I suppose you heard about the bombing."

"Which one?"

"Yes, well. We'll no doubt be discussing all that...Clayton," the ambassador added with a shake of his hand. "Please have a seat."

Simmons shook General Blake's hand and nodded to the others.

"There's coffee," Douglas said. "And some delicious pastries the French Embassy sent over this morning."

Simmons and Clayton both poured themselves a cup of coffee.

"No thanks," Clayton said when Douglas offered him the plate of pastries.

Simmons also declined.

With everyone seated, Blackburn looked from face to face around the table and settled on Simmons.

"Let's not beat around the bush here. What do you know that you didn't know the last time I saw you?"

"The intel's still vague on that skirmish up in the Nuristan."

"I don't want to know about the skirmish up in the Nuristan! I asked you to find me this Kurdish woman!"

321

"Actually, I was able to put together a dossier on her activities in the Kurdish resistance, but we know very little about her beyond that."

Simmons opened his briefcase and offered Blackburn the dossier. Blackburn practically swatted it away.

"I don't want to know what she was doing in Iraq and Syria! I want to know what she's doing in Afghanistan and where the hell to find her!"

Douglas cleared his throat.

"I believe you had something to say on this, General Blake?"

"DIA intercepted some comms that suggested she was operating out of Kahmard, but when we sent a team up there to poke around, the woman who owned the compound said Ms. Suleman had left weeks ago and the locals we questioned all claimed ignorance. We do have satellite imagery of several birds flying in and out of that compound in recent days but nothing specific on who it was...or why. For what it's worth, the team we sent up there heard a number of children inside the compound so we questioned the owner about that too and she said she ran a shelter for abandoned children and we have no reason to believe otherwise."

"I don't give a damn about homeless children! All I want to know is, where do we find this Ariya Suleman?!"

"Well, that's all I know, sir."

"Christ. Forgive me for saying so, general, but you folks are about as useless as the CIA here."

"It's a wild and sprawling and often impenetrable country. It's not like tracking someone down in the U..."

"And I don't want to hear that it's a wild and sometimes impenetrable country! Simmons has already reassured me of that! I just want my hands on that Kurdish woman! She's the one who's giving this administration a big headache!"

"Yeah," Simmons said. "I witnessed one of your headaches on the way over here this morning. Fifteen Taliban bombings over the past three days, from one end of Afghanistan to the other, but of course we don't give a damn about that, do we?"

"Their renewed bombing campaign is the direct result of the broken ceasefire!"

"Honestly, Mr. Undersecretary. I don't know how you can be so damned naïve."

"Naïve?! I'll tell you what's naïve! Thinking we can ever win this war!"

Douglas cleared his throat again.

"Perhaps we should hear from our Afghani counterparts. Mr. Sikander? Would you care to offer an opinion? What do you think can be done to get the peace negotiations back on track?"

"If I may speak frankly, Mr. Ambassador."

"Of course. That's why we're here."

"Then I would say, the Taliban will never trust in the process as long as various agencies within the American government are working at odds with each other. We hear one thing from the administration and something completely different from the military."

Sikander settled his gaze on Simmons.

"And then there are those agencies with which, quite frankly, it is impossible to tell who's doing what or why."

Simmons looked around the table with a sarcastic smile.

"I welcome Mr. Sikander's frankness. In fact, if there's one thing we're in agreement on, it's that it's becoming harder and harder these days to tell who has Afghanistan's best interest at heart."

Simmons' gaze shifted from Sikander to Durrani.

"And who's ready to stick a knife in someone's back. Of course, that assumes we're all in agreement that the Taliban is our common enemy. If not, then I too have no idea what we're doing here today. Or why we're even in this country."

Blackburn slammed his palm down on the table.

"Gentlemen! We're just going around in circles here and I'm no closer to finding this Ms. Suleman! Or throwing her on a plane and jetting her off to somewhere other than Afghanistan!"

He looked at his watch.

"Now I have a plane to catch back to Washington and by the time it lands, I want to be able to tell the president that we have this situation under control. Find Ms. Suleman and put an end to this mischief or some heads are going to roll!"

Blackburn stood up and headed for the door. His secretary quickly gathered up her laptop and papers and hurried off in his wake. Simmons waited until both of them had disappeared before turning to the ambassador.

"If that man put half as much energy into kicking some Taliban ass as he does trying to find that woman, we might just win this war."

Douglas looked at the Afghanis with a strained smile.

"The rough and tumble of diplomacy, gentlemen. It's never easy, but trust me, America remains committed to a free and fair Afghanistan."

He sighed.

"Well, we will endeavor to find this woman. In the meantime, please do whatever you can to placate the Taliban and get them back to the negotiating table. This endless bloodshed does no one any good."

Simmons stood up.

"Christ, Preston. I know it's your job to be diplomatic but I have had it up to here with this spineless foreign policy of ours. Negotiating table? You just had a taste of the Taliban negotiating tactics half an hour ago. They're going to bomb their way back into power and we'll have left this country exactly the way we found it in 2001."

He paused with a long look at Sikander and Durrani.

"And to think of all the blood and treasure we've wasted. It makes me sick."

With Clayton and Simmons heading for the door, General Blake stood up.

"If you don't need me for anything else, Mr. Ambassador, I'll be on my way too."

"No no, that's fine. Thanks for being here, general."

"Gentlemen," he said to the Afghanis before going out and closing the door.

Simmons paused to let General Blake catch up with them.

"Blackburn needs a job where he's safely removed from the general public."

The general chuckled.

"I get a sense that there's some lingering bad blood between you two."

"Yeah. He was already chewing on my ankle and when I refused to give him the rest of the leg, he got his dander up."

The general chuckled again.

He waited until they were outside before speaking again.

"And you honestly have no idea where this Ms. Suleman is."

Simmons stood there with his fingers twitching at his side.

"You going to be around the office today, general?"

"As far as I know."

"And if for some reason I needed to run something by you?"

"Feel free to stop by, Ted. Any time."

"I may just do that…You know, it's in both our bloods to do the right thing. To help these people make this a better country so when somebody asks me to consciously do otherwise, my system revolts. Frankly, to hell with the consequences, general. If the choice is between doing what's right or selling these people out, they can have my job."

The general smiled and patted Simmons on the shoulder.

"You know where to find me if something comes up."

The general's transport pulled up and he climbed in. Simmons turned to Clayton.

"Did you alert Bradley that we were on the move?"

Clayton nodded. Bradley and Kelly whipped around from the side of the embassy moments later.

Clayton waited until they were back in the privacy of Simmons' office before speaking again.

"Are you considering that air support now?"

Simmons dropped his briefcase and grabbed a mint from his desk.

"I'm considering it. Let's get over to the TOC and see what we've got. Stop by and grab Emily and Scottie on your way."

Simmons already had the drone imagery up on the big screen when Clayton walked in. Emily sat down and opened her laptop, as serious as hell. Lauren darted a look at Clayton and pretended to be Emily. Her deflated mouth gave the 'serious as hell' look an especially comic touch to it. Clayton had to stop himself from laughing.

Scottie came in and looked around like he was expecting a frat party.

"What's this place?" he said with a nod at the screen.

"Probably best if we don't give it a name," Simmons said. "Just one more little village in Afghanistan. What you need to know is this. There are sixty to seventy Taliban cornered in that valley. Most of them in that wooded area, and the rest of them somewhere in two of those mud huts."

Simmons pointed at the woods.

"I'm seeing movement right here," he said with a look over his shoulder at Clayton. "You thinking they're friendlies?"

"It's hard to tell through the trees but I doubt it. The last I heard, they were discussing a strategy to flush the Taliban out of there."

"Go ahead and text your connection. See if we can get an update."

"What are we doing here?" Emily said.

"Oh. What more do you have on Sikander and Durrani?"

"Sikander put a call in to President Rahmanzai early this morning."

"About what?"

Emily opened a page on her screen and turned it towards Simmons.

"Here's a transcript of the call."

Simmons leaned over the table and read it.

"Well I'll be a son of a bitch. Rahmanzai's definitely placed his bet on the Taliban taking power. Just as long as he has a seat at the table, he couldn't care less how this mess plays out."

Simmons stood there staring at the screen and shaking his head.

"I just can't tell if Sikander is with him. What do you think, Clayton?"

Clayton came over and read the message.

"I don't know. You could read what he said in several ways."

"He's a cagey one, isn't he? I'd like to get a scope inside his brain...All right, you two," Simmons said to Emily and Scottie. "I want to know where both those SOBs are in real time for the next twelve hours, and everything they do or say."

Simmons looked at his watch.

"Washington should be waking up to Megan's piece about now."

Simmons took off his glasses and rubbed his eyes.

"Then the shit should start to hit the fan all right."

He put his glasses back on.

"All right, another thing, you two. The last man to call Akmad was Tajj Yusufi. I suspect he was the one commanding this operation. Try to find out if he's dead or alive."

Simmons and Clayton had turned back to stare at the big screen when the signature of an explosion billowed up at the edge of the woods. This was immediately followed by the Taliban mounting a charge, some of them heading for the convoy and their cache of weapons, the rest of them heading up into the hills towards the women.

Clayton's phone buzzed a moment later. It was a text from Megan.

The Injuns have just broken out. Can't see down to the west end of the valley but hearing all kinds of excitement from that direction too. The women are in retreat. May need SOS. I'm giving this a 50/50 chance of turning into a rout. Hope you have eyes on this situation.

"Son of a bitch," Simmons said, seeing the text. "All right, make sure those two birds are on the tarmac and waiting, in case an evac becomes necessary." Simmons started for the door. "And text me with any updates. I'm on my way down to see General Blake."

Twenty Six

Connelly was crouched with Mahvash and Veeda behind a line of rocks alongside the river, a hundred yards back from the south edge of the woods. The drone feed was up on Mahvash's laptop with all three of them watching it.

Connelly keyed up his radio.

"Drone pilot. I can't see a damned thing through these treetops. Motor on down a little farther to the east."

Farzaneh was up in the hills with the other women and slowly eased the drone in that direction. While Connelly and the two women watched the feed, fresh gunfire broke out at the west end of the valley and Jake's voice came over the radio, shouting above the din of their .50 cal spitting out rounds in the background.

"TL 2! We've got a pretty serious force trying to push out in this direction! I can hold the road okay but can't speak for those village dudes down in the canyon! If they turn tail and run, those women down there are gonna to be toast!"

"TL 2 here. Am I hearing this straight? You are unable to hold that road and also reinforce the villagers?!"

"Affirmative. Not without that other .50 cal running up their tails! These motherfuckers are coming at us from six different directions!"

"Sorry, partner but no way I'm leaving the other end of this valley unattended, not with those hostiles sending fresh reinforcements our way. I'll head your direction with two more bodies and we'll see what we can do to assist. Drone pilot, get me a tighter shot on that situation."

"Let's go ladies!" Connelly shouted and raced back to the Land Cruiser.

He was busy backing up as Veeda and Mahvash climbed in. The second they were turned around and headed down the road, Connelly keyed up his radio again.

"Palmer and Metcalf! Where the fuck are you?!"

"Still positioned out here in cropsville," Palmer radioed back. "Our eyes on that convoy. You want us to assist?"

"Possibly, but hold tight on that thought for now...Sniper 2, do you have a line of sight on this shitshow?"

"I got nothing. Want me to relocate?"

"No. You keep your sights on that convoy too. And team 1, keep your eyes trained on the north edge of the woods. I want word the second anything moves over there. I have a funny feeling those hostiles are about to execute a major breakout in your direction...What's your status, sniper 1?"

"I can see the road to your west and the .50 cal but nothing below it. Even if I relocate, the trees will be in my way."

"All right, screw it. You keep doing what you're doing with that long gun. And hold those hills, ladies. I'll be back at you as soon as I've assessed this situation."

Connelly had barely ended his comm when a hail of bullets sprayed the shotgun side of the Land Cruiser and the women hit the floorboards. Connelly ducked too while cursing up a storm. He tried to out run the gunfire but quickly realized it was hopeless and jerked the wheel hard to the left, coming to a stop at the side of a house.

"Grab your weapons, ladies! Looks like we're making a stand right here!"

The three of them dove out and belly crawled towards the back of building. Bullets were slapping off the mud walls above their heads. As soon as they were safely out of sight, Connelly shook the glass out of his hair and beard and got back on the radio.

"TL 2 here. Remind me never to go anywhere again without my armored up slick. I'm still spitting out glass here."

"Jake here, TL 2. Are you saying you are unable to assist?"

"Roger that, partner. We just took heavy fire and had to seek cover. What is your status?"

"Scooter and Bly scrambled down from the road and are assisting the villagers. Gauging from the vector of gunfire, their position is holding. For now. Copy your funny feeling. I think this is mostly a diversionary maneuver. The main force is still back in the woods somewhere. I wouldn't be surprised to see them push out hard and try to take the hills to the north."

"Roger that! Everyone on that side of the valley! Do not let those pricks reach that line of abandoned vehicles! They clearly did not have time to grab their heavy weaponry so maintaining that status is your number one priority!"

Connelly clicked off.

"Let's move inside and get eyes from the front of this hooch."

Connelly used the butt of his rifle to bust out a makeshift window above their heads and climbed in.

"Come on," he said and held out his hand to Veeda.

With her inside, Connelly headed for the front room while she helped Mahvash climb in.

"Let's see what we got here," he said when the two women joined him.

Mahvash opened her own laptop and pulled up the drone feed. Farzaneh still had it hovering over the skirmish down at the west end of the valley.

"Drone pilot," Connelly said. "Pull back and give me a view from the north edge of the woods. I'm looking for any sign of hostile activity."

He quickly peeked out the window and ducked down again. Other than for the gunfire down at the west end, it was eerily quiet. He didn't like it. Something didn't smell right.

"Sniper 2 here. I'm not doing anything where I am. Why don't I move down to the west end and help them engage?"

"You stay right where you are, high speed. I'm giving it about one minute before this place explodes."

Connelly looked back at the drone feed and quickly pointed.

"There! At the edge of the trees!?"

He clicked on his comm button.

"Sniper 1 and 2, are you seeing this shit?! These cheesedicks are about to launch their version of D-Day!"

"Sniper 1 here. I have them in my sights. Permission to engage."

"Permission?! It's a goddamned order, soldier! Start shooting and keep shooting until every one of the son of a bitches is toast or you're out of ammo! Whichever comes first!"

Saarah took the first shot and the instant that man went down, it was like she had hit a trip wire. The Taliban came charging out of the woods like a wild horde, firing their weapons in all directions. Ten or so of them headed east through the fields, in an apparent effort to reach their line of abandoned vehicles. The rest of them headed north towards a row of houses at the base of the hills.

Connelly keyed up his radio again.

"Can somebody up on that hill please start putting these assholes out of their misery?!"

"We killed some of them but the rest are now hidden in the fields and among the houses."

"Well isn't that dandy. How about you, Palmer and Metcalf. What is your status?"

"Fire and retreat! There's too many of these hostiles for us to hold our ground! We're going to try and circle around and reinforce the women up in the hills!"

"Roger that. Sniper 1, what is your status?"

"I dropped several of those heading for the houses but they are now out of my sight. I am now repositioning to the east."

"Sniper 2, do you still have a visual on this circus?"

"I'm laser focused on those hostiles trying to reach their weapons cache. Every time one of them pops up his head, I'm giving him a free Uber ride back to hell. It's like shooting pumpkins…Oh shit! Taking fire! Someone must have spotted me! Repositioning now! Better get a .50 cal on this situation, TL 2, and watch yourselves up in those hills, ladies. I've got my money on the pukes in those hooches pushing out your way any minute."

"Okay, Dunbar! TL 2 here! Permission to move that .50 cal from the valley entrance over to that weapons cache! Meanwhile, we will be attempting an evac from our current position. Any luck and we'll be joining the battle shortly!"

He clicked off and turned to Veeda and Mahvash.

"I'm going to try and reach our ride out there. The minute I go out that door, I want to hear some serious cover fire through this window."

He paused against the door.

"Ready, ladies?"

They nodded. Connelly nodded back and kicked the door open. He hadn't gotten five feet when he was forced to turn around and dive back inside. While he rolled out of sight, Veeda kicked the door shut. Bullets continued to shred the front room.

"Motherfuckers!" Connelly screamed and sent a wild spray of gunfire out the window.

Some seconds later, the oncoming finally stopped. Dust was settling and the door was mostly gone. Connelly had a quick peek out the window and got back on the radio.

"Dunbar, do you now have your sights trained on that weapons cache?"

"Roger that. I count eight Taliban pinned down in the fields but still trying to reach those vehicles. Every time one of them pops his head up, I gun him down. As you probably know, they don't mind dying."

"Yeah, well, if you could spare a moment, I'd greatly appreciate you killing me some Taliban over here. They've got *us* pinned down and we will be unable to evac without some serious cover fire."

"Sniper 2 to Dunbar. Repositioned and got your back. You are free to go extricate TL 2 from his Barcalounger."

"Roger that. Heading that way right now."

"Much obliged, gentlemen."

Connelly paused to think before keying up his radio again.

"Palmer and Metcalf, what is your present location?"

"Climbing up this hill before heading west to rendezvous with the women. We can assist with covering that convoy until the .50 cal gets back."

"Hold that thought. TL 1, what is your status?"

Irem's voice came over the radio.

"There are many Taliban coming at us from many directions. We are retreating up through the woods. Hoping to find a more secure defensive position before they have our flanks. Much farther and we will have our backs to that cliff. Sorry but unable to assist with covering that convoy."

"All right. Palmer, Metcalf. Proceed with reinforcements. As soon as we can get out of this hole, we will attack from their rear and at least carve out an evac route. Waiting on Dunbar for now. This location has absolutely no strategic value but we can't do diddly squat to assist until we get our asses out of here…You still have eyes on that convoy, sniper 2?"

"Roger that. It's like a roach hotel. You can go in but you ain't never coming back out."

"Roger that. And Jake, what the hell is going on down there in that canyon? You have those assholes in retreat or what?"

"No. There's still six or seven of them pinning us down."

"Shit. All right, we can't afford to waste any more time or firepower on saving those villagers. Get a message down to them. They need to retreat down that canyon and keep retreating if necessary until they reach the next valley. We need your .50 cal up here in this fight."

After a moment, Jake called back.

"Scooter's going to stay down there and help them stage a retreat. He says he has enough firepower to do it in an orderly fashion."

"Roger that. Whatever it takes to free up your .50."

"Give me two minutes. I'm waiting for Bly to get his ass back up here and we'll join you. You still need help?"

"No. I see Dunbar coming down the road right now. Goddamn. The sweet sound of a .50 cal first thing in the morning."

Jake laughed.

"All right," Connelly said. "We should be on our way over to the north side in about one mike here."

Dunbar raced up and did a donut with the gunner tearing into the adjacent woods.

"All right, girls," Connelly said with a peek out the door. "Time to move."

He let loose with a spray of cover fire as they dashed around to the side of the building and jumped into the Land Cruiser. Connelly quickly had the engine turned over and the vehicle careening out onto the road. Dunbar led the way east up the valley with every available firearm pumping rounds into the woods on their left.

Once they were clear, Connelly keyed up his radio.

"All right boys and girls, what's our current status?"

"Metcalf here to tell you that this situation is quickly turning into an extract operation. My best estimate, there's roughly fifty Taliban now spread all over the hills below us. We'll be lucky to get out of here alive."

"I told you we should have flattened those two hooches when we had the pricks cornered," Palmer said.

"You never make a frontal attack with a superior force at your rear," Connelly said. "You think this is fubar. We would have been annihilated out there in the open."

"Jake reporting in. We're on our way. What do you say we quit the bullshit and just concentrate on getting those women safely down from that hill?"

~~~~~~

While heading down towards the entrance to Camp Eggers on foot, a squad of soldiers ran by Simmons, going the other way. The base went off in all directions on Simmons' right, tan, stucco and drab. A low-income apartment complex came to mind. That said, everything was crisply painted.

The entrance to the general's headquarters was around to the back of an administration building. A snappy looking sign at the door announced his rank and presence.

Simmons went inside.

"The general's expecting you, sir."

He knocked on General Blake's office door and opened it for Simmons. Blake stood up and offered his hand.

"Have a seat, Ted. Anything I can get you? Coffee? Tea? A donut?"

Seeing the general's coffee, Simmons accepted a cup.

"Anything with it?" the aide said.

"No, black's fine. Thanks."

General Blake sat back down with a smile.

"So, what's going on?"

Simmons leaned forward and spoke in a hushed voice.

"Look, Bill. We've known each other for going on twenty years. The last thing I'd want is to put you in a tight situation but..."

"Ah, here we are," the general said, seeing his aide come in with the coffee. "Thank you, Biggs, and please close the door on your way out."

The general waited until Biggs had gone out before raising his eyebrows expectantly.

"Look, Bill. Can we talk completely off the record for a minute? Just friend to friend?"

The general waved a hand.

"Well, I know you feel the same about these withdrawal plans. You tell the Taliban that we're going to leave on such and such a date and without any conditions? We may as well have handed the damned country on a platter."

"I've done my share of bitching, Ted, but it's over now and there's not a damned thing anyone can do about it, other than to be good soldiers and carry out their orders."

"Look, I understand the position you're in and I'm not about to start breaking the china here, but something came up, a little seedling of resistance and I'll be damned if I'm just going to sit around and watch it get snuffed out."

The general smiled ever so slightly again.

"Go ahead, Ted. Get to your point."

"Okay, well, the truth is, I've had Clayton lending logistical support to a band of women fighters and I'm afraid without some intervention in the next few hours, the whole lot of them are going to be wiped off the face of the earth."

The general started drumming his fingers.

"Explain."

Simmons did.

"And you want from me?"

"Air support."

The general stared.

"That would represent a direct violation of my orders."

"I understand, but let's just say for the sake of argument that you had a unit patrolling nearby, and they just happened to hear gunfire and went to investigate and saw a village under siege by the Taliban, and felt additionally that their own safety was at risk, it would not be unthinkable for them to call in and request an airstrike."

"That's a lot of *ifs*."

Simmons nodded. General Blake leaned back and looked out his window.

"Speaking theoretically, strictly theoretically, it wouldn't be out of the question, no."

"Well, it just so happens you do have a patrol operating nearby."

General Blake looked back.

"How did I know you were going to say that?"

Simmons stared.

"Okay, Ted. What's their posture?"

"I believe it's an eight man team, three Humvees, two with .50 cals."

"And they're familiar with this situation?"

"Peripherally. They stopped one of our contract teams last night. Clayton had to fly up there and untangle the situation. They're also familiar with the village and one of the women. It was part of their patrol before they were ordered to pull back."

The general looked off into the empty spaces of his office, drumming his fingers again. After some moments, he looked back.

"Okay. Here's what I won't do. Order this patrol up there to start poking around. However, if they should somehow find themselves in the area and for whatever reason felt an airstrike was necessary, I would authorize it...Mind you, a drone strike only. I can't afford to risk one damned life in this scenario, and that includes this patrol. I don't want them anywhere near this battle, or directly engaged in it."

"Understood."

"And this conversation never happened."

"Understood."

The general smiled with a raise of his eyebrows.

"So how's everything with the wife and kids?"

"Kids are fine but I think the wife is going to divorce me if I don't retire soon, or find an assignment stateside."

"Yours and mine both."

Simmons' mood turned somber again.

"I'd throw it all down the drain, Bill. I really would, if I thought there was one damned thing I could do to save these people. I toss and turn at night, trying to sleep and wake up every morning, filled with the same anger. With ISIS, at least you knew what you had. With these Taliban bastards?"

Simmons shook his head.

"It's a damned wolf in sheep's clothing."

The general nodded.

"You'd better get moving, Ted. I hate to think of these brave women getting slaughtered."

"Thanks, Bill."

Simmons stood up.

"I'm going to assume that you just happen to have an armed drone operating in that theater."

"You go deal with this patrol and leave the rest to me."

Simmons reached for the door and paused there.

"At the risk of sounding melodramatic, Bill, but you're a good man."

"Back at you, Ted. Hell, when you boil it all down, we're just trying to do the best we can as human beings, and don't think for a second that it doesn't piss me off when I see the rules getting in the way of our better angels."

"Amen to that...I was going to say, I'll keep you posted, but this conversation never happened."

"Go. Before this thing really does turn into a disaster."

Back outside, Simmons wasted no time in getting Clayton on the phone.

"What's the word?" Clayton asked.

"Call Sunny, tell him to get that bird warmed up and get your ass in a transport, armed and ready for battle. I'll meet you at the front gate and explain everything on our way to the airport."

Simmons called Camp Sullivan while he was walking and cleared the flight. Bradley braked to a stop alongside Simmons about fifty yards shy of the front gate. Simmons climbed in back with Clayton.

"Did he give the okay?"

Simmons gestured with his hand to say, keep it down, and leaned in closer to Clayton's ear.

"You know that Army patrol you met with last night?"

Clayton nodded.

"Well, you need to locate them ASAP and lay our cards on the table. The women are surrounded and facing a massacre. But you have word from high up that if that patrol happens to have its eyes on the situation and decides to call in a drone strike, it will be approved."

"He said that."

"Completely off the record. The conversation never happened and he can't be seen ordering the chess pieces around himself. However, if the request comes in from someone in the field?"

Clayton stared.

"That's if I can find them."

"Just scan the road near where you saw them last night. There's no reason to believe they'd be anywhere else."

"And the drone?"

"I was told to leave that to the general."

Bradley had come to a stop at the Afghan checkpoint. IDs came out and the guard quickly waved them through.

"What's the latest on our status up there?" Simmons asked.

"Grim. The Taliban broke out and got the women pinned up against a stone cliff with their retreat blocked to both the east and west. They were able to back into a shallow canyon but now the only way out is right back into the teeth of the Taliban."

They came to the American checkpoint and were waved right through. Simmons looked back at Clayton.

"Go on."

"Oh, the women do have the high ground but they're running out of ammunition. Meanwhile Connelly and his men have mounted a rear attack and are trying to carve out an escape route. Which is the only thing preventing this situation from turning into a total disaster."

Bradley braked to a stop a hundred feet back from the helicopter. Sunny was in the cockpit and had it ready for takeoff. Simmons jumped out with Clayton.

"Keep me posted, but not a word about that patrol over the airwaves…You want me to send this other bird up there right now? See if we can resupply them with ammo or whatever?"

"Yeah, do that, but tell the pilot to stay well back when he gets up near the valley. Let me assess things on the ground first. I'll have Sunny radio him as soon as I know more."

"All right, go. And if anything else comes up, just let me know."

Clayton nodded and dashed over to the cockpit door.

Twenty Seven

Clayton had Sunny start at Tupchi and follow the highway back towards Shaik Ali. The dirt road snaked along at the base of a deep gorge with towering ridges rising up on their left like the backs of great beasts. Farther off to the east, the snowy peaks of the Hindu Kush glimmered beneath a starry sky.

They were clipping along at a hundred miles an hour with Clayton searching the terrain for any sign of that Army patrol. Halfway to Shaik Ali, he jumped forward in his seat.

"There! I saw them parked under those trees!"

Sunny had blown past the spot a good mile and torqued the helicopter hard back over his shoulder.

One member of the patrol was lying on the hood of his Humvee and immediately sat up at seeing the helicopter come back. The other team members were stretched out on the grass beneath the trees and quickly got to their feet. Sunny rocked the helicopter to indicate friendly but that did not stop the soldiers from arming up as it came in for a landing. When they saw Clayton jump out and run their way, they relaxed a bit but not entirely.

"Sgt. Rodriguez," Clayton said with a nod to the entire patrol.

"What brings you back our way, Mr. Clayton?"

"We have a situation and need your help."

"What kind of help?"

Clayton looked from face to face again.

"Let me start with acknowledging that this is a delicate situation. Involving a conversation between my station chief and someone high up in your chain of command. A conversation that I am to pretend never happened, but if it had, it would go something like this. If one of my patrols found it necessary to call in an airstrike, and I just happened to have a drone operating in that theater, I would approve the strike."

"And why would I want to call in an airstrike?"

"To save a friendly force...and a village."

Rodriguez stood there staring.

"Go on. Explain."

Clayton did.

"You mean, that's what that shit was all about last night?"

Clayton nodded.

"Well, the problem is, Mr. Clayton. I still have my orders. Which is to keep my ass strictly away from that area."

"I understand. And no one is saying that this won't become an issue at some level of command, but if you did happen to find yourself in the vicinity of that firefight, and you did find it necessary to call in an airstrike, that airstrike would be approved. That's all I know."

"Come on, sarge," Natalie said. "We're out here in the middle of nowhere. Who's going to ask why we ran up towards Shaik Ali? And even if they did, all we have to say is, we were pursuing some hostiles, took fire and ordered the airstrike. It's not like we're going to end up on CNN."

"Specialist Montero, you're still on my short list for an article hearing, along with a demotion, so I'd be treading real fucking lightly here."

"Fine. You can toss in a treason charge if you want but this is real life shit here, Sergeant."

She looked around at the rest of the patrol.

"Come on. Ask yourselves. Are we going to sleep easy tonight, knowing we could have saved those women and did nothing? Like, what? Just shrug and have another donut? How about you Mason? And you, Dundy? All of you?"

Without saying a word, the entire team turned its attention back towards Rodriguez.

"Are you serious?" he said. "We have orders."

"No one left behind," Leanna said.

"That applies to our fellow soldiers, Becket."

"And they're not?"

"They're a band of rebels and totally off the reservation. And we'll be totally off the reservation if we go off trying to save them."

"Sometimes it's just about doing the right thing," Natalie said.

"And like I already told you, Montero. You're on seriously thin ice with me already so don't push it."

The rest of the team kept staring.

"Aw, come on, man. Are you people really going to put my balls in a vice here?"

With everyone still staring at him, Rodriguez cursed under his breath and turned to Clayton.

"All right. Let's just say for the sake of argument that I agreed to this bullshit. And I'm talking totally for the sake of argument, how would this plan work?"

"As I understand things, they still hold the road going west out of the valley. We get in that close and I can show you the battlefield posture with our drone feed. Get you on the phone with someone in the field to establish the enemy coordinates and you call in an airstrike. And remain safely out of harm's way in doing so."

Rodriguez looked around at his team.

"Sounds all neat and pretty, right? Except that's never the way these ops go down. There's always the unexpected and I can think of a half dozen ways that this thing could get fubar."

"Why don't we just get in that close?" Dundy said. "What's it going to hurt?"

Rodriguez looked from face to face and settled back on Clayton.

"And you're saying this is authorized from the top."

"The word I got was unambiguous. This general's not going to start moving chess pieces around in the field, but if those chess pieces did happen to call in to Camp Eggers and request an airstrike, he'd authorize it."

"So we're talking General Blake here."

"As I said, that conversation never happened."

"Yeah. Everyone's going to have plausible deniability in this situation but me."

"Come on, Sarge," Leanna said. "No one's going to bust our chops for just driving up there to have a look."

Rodriguez looked back at Clayton.

"Time's wasting, Sergeant. For all I know those women are already dead. But if not, it probably won't be long."

Rodriguez shook his head.

"All right, fine. We'll go have a look. But that's all I'm agreeing to at this point. Where are we supposed to find you?"

Clayton handed him a card.

"That's my number. You get in that far and I'll find a way to hook up with you on the ground."

"All right. Let's roll, team."

Clayton gave them a thumbs up and ran back.

"That was short and sweet," Sunny said as Clayton climbed in.

"Yeah. The sergeant was having a fundamental disagreement with the rest of his team. Let's roll. I don't even know if we still have a force left to save."

With Sunny pulling up and away from the ground, Clayton called Connelly. Connelly came on the line with a serious firefight going on in the background.

"I was just wondering what happened to you."

"I've been working on something. Help is on the way."

"What kind of help?"

"I can't discuss that with you over this line but I'll be on the ground in about five minutes. What's your current status?"

"One of ours wounded but nothing life threatening. With the women it's a different story. Apparently one of them took a pretty serious hit."

"Who?"

"Don't know. Didn't ask. Too many bullets flying around for me to bother. All you need to know is this. They're running low on ammo and I'm unable to resupply them. We pretty much have an endless supply from that Taliban convoy but the Taliban have a serious rearguard keeping us at bay while the rest of them go after the chicks...And I mean, with a vengeance. Those fuckers are clearly pissed off to think a woman would pick up a rifle and shoot back. Our best hope at this point is for the Taliban to run out of ammo first. And if not?"

Connelly left that thought hanging in the air.

"You still have somebody down at the west end of the valley?"

"Yeah. One man. Can't say where he is right now. He was helping the village men to evac their women."

"Does he have a radio?"

"Yeah."

"Okay. Touch base with him. He should see my bird overhead shortly and my asset will be arriving ten, fifteen minutes later, tops. As soon as they're in place, I'll call back...Should I be worrying about RPGs?"

"No. I have one .50 cal keeping an eye on their convoy and shredding up any fuck who is dumb enough to get near it."

"All right, over and out for now. I'll be back at you in under five mikes."

As Connelly hung up, he heard a serious intensification of the running battle farther up the hill and immediately got on his radio.

"What the hell, ladies. What is your status?"

Irem called back, shouting over the gunfire.

"Retreating to the last line of trees. Farzaneh's bleeding badly and we're nearly out of ammo. Will report back once we've reestablished a defensive position. If we can't hold this tree line, there's nothing left but some open space and a jumble of rocks at the end of this canyon."

Irem went offline and joined Tabaan and Veeda in providing cover fire as they backpedaled through the trees. The Taliban seemed to be coming from behind every tree. Irem spotted one climbing the canyon walls and picked him off.

"Quick! Go join the others!" Veeda told her and Tabaan.

They took off with their heads down. Veeda peeked out from behind her tree, sprayed one last bit of cover fire and turned tail with tree bark and limbs being shredded above her head.

Veeda saw the remaining force hunkered down behind a fallen log and dove in with them. They were at the edge of the woods now with rounds zipping by overhead.

Veeda looked over to where Esin was treating Farzaneh's leg wound. She had applied quick clot and a compress. It was obvious from the ashen color of Farzaneh's face that she needed an IV but there was no way they had time for that right now.

"Someone keep eyes on these canyon walls," Veeda called out. "Irem just shot one of those dogs trying to take the high ground."

"I've got this side," Tabaan said.

"I've got the other," Noushineh said.

Veeda looked around again.

"Where is Saarah?"

"She got cut off from us," Ariya said. "I thought you knew."

"No. I heard her voice on the radio and assumed she was with you."

"I will check."

347

Ariya hit her comm button.

"Sniper 1. Ariya here. What is your status?"

"On the move. They know there's a sniper so every time I pick one off, they send out a patrol in the direction of my last shot and I have to move again."

"Where are you now?"

"Up the hill and to the east of you."

"And what is the hope of you terminating some of these dogs on our trail?"

"I am killing them as I can but I can't see inside the canyon. Not from where I am."

"And is it possible for you to move to a better position?"

"Not unless you wish me dead."

"No. I am only hoping for that not to be our fate."

Before Ariya could speak again, there was a torrent of gunfire and Saarah's radio went silent.

"Sniper 1. Arriya here. Can you read me? Sniper 1."

There was no answer.

With the Taliban mounting yet another charge, Ariya got low and fired wildly over her head.

"Son of a mongrel!" she said as one of them broke through and came flying at her.

She sprayed him with gunfire and rolled to one side before his body could land on top of her.

"Eh! This foul beast smells like the ass of a bull!"

She kicked him for good measure and resumed firing over her head.

Amidst the bedlam, she heard the sound of a helicopter and shielded her eyes to look up in the sky. The helicopter had crossed over the sun, leaving behind a momentary shadow. Then the helicopter was gone.

Her phone started ringing but she had no time to answer it. The Taliban kept pushing forward, tree by tree in a relentless barrage of gunfire.

"A curse on this spawn of Satan!" Veeda shouted over the noise. "They seem to be multiplying before our very eyes!"

She scrambled over to where Esin was treating Farzaneh's wound. Farzaneh was unconscious."

"What is her status?"

"Not good. The bullet hit an artery and she's lost a lot of blood. If I can't start an IV, she'll go into shock."

Veeda cursed to herself while thinking.

"Watch out!" Tabaan shouted and began firing to her left. "They're trying to flank us!"

Kejal scrambled that way and helped Tabaan in fighting back the assault. Every woman was firing furiously into the trees but the Taliban kept coming.

Ariya crawled over to Veeda.

"We can't hold this line! We have to retreat!"

They both glanced back towards the end of the canyon.

"They will gun us down as we run!" Veeda said.

"They will gun us down if we stay here. There are too many of them...Listen, let's spread out across this entire tree line and then melt away one by one. From our flanks left and right. Kejal and I will hold the center until everyone else has taken cover."

Hajira scrambled over.

"I will help you."

Ariya looked down at Farzaneh.

"What are we going to do with her?"

"I'll carry her," Veeda said.

"Okay," Ariya said. "You go first and get Farzaneh to safety."

Ariya hit her comm button and passed the word.

"Spread out our line of defense and prepare to retreat! One by one from our flanks inward while the rest of us give cover fire!"

Mahvash crawled down to Tabaan's position.

"You go left!"

"Then cover me!"

Mahvash sprayed the trees while Tabaan ran head down to Irem's position.

Darsameen nodded at Mahvash and scrambled to their right.

Once all the women had spread out into formation, Ariya turned to Veeda.

"As soon as you hear this grenade go off, you run!"

Veeda nodded. Ariya pulled the pin, waited three seconds and yelled, "Grenade!" before tossing it.

The second Veeda heard the explosion, she threw Farzaneh over her shoulder and ran. There was a hundred yards of open space in front of her and bullets zipping by over her head. In her mad dash, the end of the canyon seemed to be receding rather than growing closer but she finally reached the jumble of rocks and carried Farzaneh over to safety.

Ariya turned to Esin.

"You go next! You need to take care of Farzaneh!"

While laying down another blanket of cover fire, the team heard what sounded like a landslide off to their left and looked over to find two men tumbling down the steep wall of the canyon. Both of them landed with a thump and with a cascade of rocks and debris crashing down on their heads. One of the new recruits had been holding the end of the line and was about to shoot them when Irem called out.

"No! Hold your fire! They are friendlies!"

Palmer and Metcalf rolled to safety behind a tree, dirty and bloodied but smiling. Palmer pulled a fresh ammo magazine out of his vest and held it up like a prize before slamming it into his rifle. While he peeked around the tree for a target, Metcalf waved at Hajira. She rolled away from the log and crawled down to him.

"Hey, beautiful. Glad to see you're still alive. What's the game plan?"

Hajira stared.

"Okay, either you have to learn English or I'll have to learn Pashto. Or we can just do the grind a lot."

With gunfire still slapping into the trees above their heads, Irem scrambled over to them.

"Nasty Americans...I will not tell her what you said."

"Please do...But seriously, what are we doing here?"

"Staging a retreat. To those rocks at the end of the canyon."

He glanced over his shoulder.

"I guess that's as good a place as any to make a stand."

"Farzaneh was shot and Veeda and Esin are down there now caring for her."

Hajira said something in Pashto and Irem translated.

"She says you should have been here sooner."

Metcalf laughed.

"Tell, her, sorry, darling but we had a bitch of a time getting in here the back way...So, are we ready to do this?"

"We are supposed to be covering for the next one retreating."

"Look, Palmer and I got this. Just get this retreat in motion."

He grabbed a couple of extra ammo magazines and handed them to Irem.

"Take this with you."

He winked at Hajira and pinched her cheek.

"Go on. Get your pretty little ass in gear."

Hajira listened to Irem's translation and slapped him gently across the face.

"Go on," he said again and turned to Palmer.

They exchanged hand signals before Metcalf scrambled thirty feet to his right. The Taliban seemed to sense the retreat and began firing with renewed fury. Metcalf glanced once over his shoulder to make sure Hajira had made it to safety, then signaled to Palmer and they scrambled another thirty feet to their right. Metcalf had reached the fallen log and dove in behind it before reloading.

"We're wasting time here. The longer this evac takes, the more trouble those bastards are going make for us."

"We can only go one at a time," Ariya said.

"Screw that! Just get your asses in gear! Three at a time! Whatever! Just do this!"

"You Americans are brash...But it was kind of you to come."

"Yeah, we may be a lot of things, but we don't leave our own behind. Go on. Let's get this done. I'll feel a hell of a lot safer behind that pile of rocks back there."

Metcalf let off a burst of fire while Palmer scrambled over and dove in behind the log with him. Ariya got on the radio.

"Irem, you retreat with Noushineh and Darseema. Then you go next, Tabaan and take two more with you. Kejal and I will follow with the rest."

Metcalf and Palmer were laying down more cover fire when they heard a woman cry out and looked back to find Irem sprawled on the ground. Noushineh and Darseema quickly got Irem to her feet and dragged her the last fifty feet to safety.

Ariya was glaring at Metcalf when he looked back.

"Three at a time," she said.

"Hey, it's just as easy to get picked off one at a time. Even easier. Just keep this evac going before we're completely overrun here."

Metcalf handed Ariya an extra ammo magazine and scrambled over to Tabaan's position.

"Go on! Take your recruits and move out! I've got you covered."

With another burst of gunfire at their backs, the four women ran for the end of the canyon.

When it was time for Ariya and Kejal to retreat, Metcalf scrambled back to them.

"Palmer and I will be retreating from the flanks, left and right, and you are to lay down some serious cover fire as we do. Right down center alley here, okay?"

Palmer and Metcalf provided more cover fire while the rest of the women retreated, then paused with their backs to a tree. Metcalf signaled and sprayed the woods one more time as Palmer dashed head down to the far side of the canyon. Then

Palmer did the same while Metcalf repositioned. They were now looking at each other from a hundred yards apart.

With a nod and a thumbs up, they both tossed a grenade and sprayed the woods before lighting off in gallop. There was a brief lull before an exchange of gunfire zipped past them from both directions.

The two men's paths had nearly converged at the end of the canyon when Palmer took a bullet in the calf and went down.

"Ahhhh! Fuck me!"

Palmer was struggling to his feet when Metcalf ran up, grabbed him by the vest and dragged him the rest of the way. They tumbled hard into a space that was roughly fifty by thirty feet and looking like a trauma ward. Esin had Farzaneh lying in the shade with an IV and was treating Irem for a bullet wound in her shoulder.

Esin looked with concern at Palmer.

"I got this," Metcalf said.

He quickly had his knife out and cut away the pant leg.

"You want me to take the leg off with it?"

"Fucker...Ow! Son of a bitch!"

Palmer looked down at his now exposed wound.

"At least they could have hit me in the thigh."

"All right. Shut up and let me get a tourniquet on this."

Metcalf did that, applied some quick clot and packing gauze and wrapped the leg with an Ace bandage.

"There. Good as new."

"Yeah, right."

"You want some morphine?"

"Yeah, I'd love some of that shit but this battle ain't over with yet...Where's our fearless war correspondent, by the way?"

"Ariya said she took one of the Taliban vehicles and headed west."

"Yeah, conveniently out of harm's way."

"I guess she couldn't get a signal on her laptop to file her story."

"Okay then. I guess forgiven."

Palmer peeked over the rocks and was immediately met with a volley of bullets. Metcalf had a more cautious look.

"Look at those cockroaches. Amassed all along the tree line and just waiting to pick us off...Watch this."

Metcalf took aim, fired one shot and the head of a Taliban snapped back with a spray of blood. That led to a lot of shouting and return fire but the Taliban quickly retreated back among the trees.

"How bad is it?" Metcalf said with a look at Irem.

"The bullet missed the lung but it hit bone and she's bleeding internally, like Farzaneh."

"And the bullet's still in there?"

Esin nodded.

"Damn, okay. Something has to give here or we'll soon be counting dead bodies."

Afghan's Lipstick Warriors
First Chronicle

Twenty Eight

Metcalf gestured at Ariya, took her radio and hit the comm button.

"TL 2, this is Metcalf. We're going to need a medevac here real soon. We have three wounded, two of them pretty seriously. What is your status?"

"The same as you. Pinned down. There's just way too many of these fuckers to make a push. Our best hope is for them to run out of ammo. Meanwhile, Clayton called."

"About what? Was that who zipped by in that bird?"

"Roger that."

"So what's his game plan?"

"Don't know. He wouldn't discuss it with me over the airwaves."

"Well, that's fucking great. Did he give you any idea when he was going to start revealing his secrets?"

"Don't know that either. I think he saw the warzone around here and went back up the road a bit, looking for some place to touch down without taking incoming."

"Well, good for him. Meanwhile, T-man is using us for target practice."

Bly cut into the call.

"Hey, TL 2. I have Mr. Clayton down here and an Army patrol just pulled up behind us."

"Well put his ass on."

Clayton was on a moment later.

"Connelly?"

"All day long."

"First, I'd like an injury report. Who's been hit and how seriously?"

"My man Danny took a bullet in his left arm. You'll have to ask TL 1 on their status."

"Ariya?"

"No, Metcalf here, Dorn. Farzaneh was hit in the upper leg and has lost a lot of blood. And Irem just took a bullet to her shoulder. She's bleeding badly too. And Palmer was shot in the calf."

"And that's it?"

"That's it...for now."

"Okay, we're working on your evac...So, back to you, Connelly. I need you to talk to a Sergeant Rodriguez."

"I'm all ears."

After a moment, Rodriguez came on.

"I understand you're pinned down by a Taliban force."

Connelly held the radio up to the gunfire for a moment.

"You hear that? That shit's happening in real time."

"Are you able to provide me with coordinates for an airstrike."

"Sir. I will drop my pants and shoot your bird the moon if it means I'm going to see some fireworks around here."

"Hey, Metcalf here. Can you put Clayton back on for a sec?"

There was a shuffling sound and Clayton was back on.

"Yeah, Metcalf. What's up."

"Look, can you access your shot of this valley right now?"

"Hang on a second...Okay, what am I looking for?"

"You see those cliffs up on the north edge?"

"Yeah."

"And that canyon splitting them about a mile to your northeast?"

"Got it."

"Okay. We're at the far end of it, behind that jumble of rocks and the hostiles are in the woods, directly opposite us. That's your coordinates. The woods. Just make damned sure you've got it straight. There's only about a hundred yards separating the two of us."

"Okay, I will relay a danger close strike."

"And a little heads up before it hits would be appreciated. I'm not fond of surprises in the form of a Hellfire missile."

"I'll double back...And how about you, Connelly?"

"We're on the south end of those woods. Will retreat a hundred yards down the hill and you just pound those trees to your heart's content."

"Got it."

The radio went dead. Metcalf looked around from face to face.

"Okay, ladies and gentlemen, looks like we're about to have ourselves a little fireworks so get ready to grab your crotch."

Ariya shook her head and translated. Then they all sat there blind to what was coming. Then Clayton was back.

"ETA thirty seconds. Expect two strikes. One on your end of the woods first, then one back down Connelly's way."

"Okay. Thanks for the heads up, chief."

Metcalf ended the comm and called for everyone's attention.

"Heads down and tight to the ground. We've got about fifteen seconds!"

Esin used her body to shield Farzaneh. Ariya did the same with Irem. The seconds ticked by with everyone waiting.

Then a concussion shook the earth beneath them and the explosion mushroomed up into the sky. Everyone reflexively pressed their bodies tighter to the ground for several seconds and were just starting to look up again when debris began to rain down on their heads. Then the second strike hit off in the distance and shook the earth a second time.

With the sounds of wounded men screaming down in the woods, Metcalf cautiously peeked over the rocks to have a look. Then he was back on the ground and jamming a fresh magazine into his rifle.

"Okay, ladies. Whoever survived that hit is going to be plenty pissed off so don't let your guards down. I wouldn't be the least bit surprised to see what's left of them come charging up this way."

He placed his rifle in the cleft between two rocks and took aim. Palmer grunted and got up to join Metcalf.

"Don't think for one second that I'm going to miss out on this fun."

All of the uninjured women besides Esin joined them in searching for targets. When Hajira let loose with a spray of bullets, Metcalf put his hand on her forearm and held up one finger.

"One shot at a time, honey. Just look for a target first, then shoot. You ain't doing nothing spraying bullets around like that."

Hajira listened to Ariya translate and made a face at Metcalf, then stared down the barrel of her rifle again.

Tiny Noushineh had crawled up on the rocks to take better aim when a report echoed from down in the woods and she fell backwards onto the ground. Hajira rushed over to her. Blood was quickly pooling up next to her head in the dusty soil.

Metcalf and Palmer exchanged a look.

"Damn," Metcalf whispered. "Those assholes must have someone with a decent scoped long gun."

"Well, somebody sure as hell survived that hit."

Both men had been staring at the tree line and waiting when a good twenty Taliban came charging out into the open with rifles firing.

"Son of a bitch!" Palmer said with bullets splintering off the rocks around his head.

"All hands on deck, ladies!" Metcalf said. "We don't have time for more grief!"

He was busy firing the rifle over his head and hadn't noticed Hajira climbing up on top of the rocks. She stood there cursing away in Dari and spraying fire at the advancing Taliban.

"Jesus Christ, woman! Get your ass back down here!"

Metcalf was just pulling Hajira back down to safety when she took a hit and tumbled into his arms. The bullet had passed through her throat and severed the carotid on its way out. She lay there in Metcalf's arms, choking in blood.

"Esin! Quick! Get me some clot and gauze over here!"

Seeing the women stare at Hajira, Palmer barked out at them.

"Goddamn it, ladies! We still have a battle going on here!"

Metcalf heard the sounds of the Taliban charging and the women firing back but did nothing. He just sat there staring down into Hajira's eyes. They had glazed over but still appeared to be staring back at him.

"Oh, you beautiful stubborn little woman, you. We almost had our ticket punched and you had to go and do some stupid crazy ass shit like that. Why?"

It seemed as if Hajira's eyes had crinkled up ever so slightly into a smile and Metcalf felt her hand squeeze his, and then she was gone. Metcalf hung his head.

"The fucking bastards. They couldn't be satisfied with stealing everything else from you. They had to take your life too."

Metcalf kissed her bloody lips and closed her eyes. Her lipstick had gotten smudged so he wiped at it as best he could.

"Okay, baby. This one's for you."

Metcalf got to his feet, packed his vest with a handful of fresh ammo magazines and jumped up on the rocks where Hajira had been.

"All right, you cocksuckers. I've had just about enough of this shit!"

With bullets whizzing around him, he mowed down the last five Taliban still charging their way, jumped to the ground and went running back towards the trees, spraying gunfire as he did.

Palmer hopped up on his good leg.

"Fucking Christ! Will somebody go help that crazy son of a bitch before he gets himself killed!"

Ariya had already grabbed the pack of magazines and threw several of them at Palmer's feet.

"Stay here with Esin. Somebody has to watch over the wounded."

With a last nod his way, she waved to the rest of the women and they were over the rocks and running together down towards the tree line. Palmer heard what sounded like Metcalf's rifle firing in the distance and hit his comms button.

"TL 2, Palmer here. The Taliban are in retreat but watch for Metcalf and the women. They just headed down this canyon in pursuit."

"TL 2 here. Roger that."

Palmer was about to hit his comm button again and explain about the dead but stopped himself. The others would find out soon enough. For now, the news just seemed too goddamned sad to relay.

He had been standing there on his good leg, alternately watching Esin treat the wounded, stealing glances at the dead and wishing he could join the fight when he heard Connelly come back over the radio. The sounds of battle were ongoing in the background.

"TL 2 here. I don't know what you boys and girls did but this is a sight to behold. The Taliban are fleeing right into the arms of death...Oh well. We all have our time to die...Oh yeah, Clayton told me to tell you. The bird's on the way to evac the wounded right now. See you on the other side."

Palmer was staring down at the trees and waiting for further word on the battle when the helicopter popped out from behind the hills. Palmer waved and watched Sunny ease down a hundred feet on the other side of the rocks.

Clayton jumped out and ran over. With a quick look over the rocks, he turned to Palmer.

"Just didn't seem like a great idea, announcing this shit over the airwaves."

"Where's Saarah?"

"I don't know. The last I heard, some of the Taliban were on her trail."

Clayton grabbed Palmer's radio.

"Clayton here, calling Saarah. Are you there?"

There was no answer.

"Clayton here. Does anyone know where Saarah is?"

"Connelly here. That's a negative."

"Ariya?"

Clayton waited. Finally, Ariya answered.

"We're still helping TL 2 with mopping up the Taliban stragglers. Have not heard from Saarah in over half an hour."

Clayton's heart sank.

"All right. Just so everyone is read into this operation. I'm extracting the wounded first thing."

Clayton glanced over at Palmer.

"They will be transferred to a secondary bird and evacked to the nearest hospital. As soon as that package is transferred, I will rendezvous back here and await further instructions."

Clayton clicked off and looked down at the dead. Sunny ran up just then and saw them.

"Bummer."

"Yeah. We'll have to deal with the bodies later. We're just taking the wounded for now. Once the shooting stops, I'll coordinate with Ariya on where to take them...You coming with us?" he asked Palmer.

"Naw. I'll catch a red eye. I couldn't sleep if I booked a ticket out of here now."

"You at least want a ride to somewhere safer?"

"Yeah. You could drop me off at that elder's place."

"All right. Let's go then."

Clayton squatted down in front of Irem.

"Are you able to walk?"

She nodded. Clayton got his hands around her waist and helped her to her feet.

"Sunny. Find somebody to give you a hand. We need to get the one with the IV into the bird too."

"I can help him," Palmer said

Clayton went ahead, helping Irem to climb over the rocks. Palmer and Sunny gently picked Farzaneh up from opposite ends and followed behind with Esin holding the IV.

With Farzaneh and Irem finally onboard, Clayton turned to Esin.

"How about you?"

"She doesn't speak English," Irem said and translated.

Esin waved a hand at Clayton while speaking to Irem.

"She says she'll stay to treat the wounded."

"All right. Tell her it's safe down to the end of this canyon but beyond that, I don't know, so be careful."

Esin listened to the translation, nodded and began to gather up her pack and medical supplies. Clayton slammed the door shut and gave Sunny a thumbs up. He rose up a hundred feet and banked hard over his left shoulder.

The last of the battle came into view as they climbed higher. The Taliban appeared to have hidden somewhere among a row of houses and the two teams were slowly closing the circle around them. Sunny ran downwind half a mile to get clear of any gunfire and banked towards the south side of the valley.

Salahuddeen's front porch was empty when they touched down in front of his place. Clayton opened the cargo door and helped Palmer climb out, then handed Palmer the radio. Clayton had been trying repeatedly to reach Saarah during the flight.

"Keep trying her," he said.

"You got it, chief."

Clayton waited until Palmer had hobbled over to the front porch before slamming the door shut and giving Sunny the go sign. He quickly rose over the hills and headed south.

Palmer sat down and hit the comm button.

"Palmer here. Still looking for any word from Saarah."

The calls all came back negative, one by one.

Saarah had wanted desperately to answer them but didn't dare. She had been evading a patrol for the past half hour and sensed them closing in on her. Hearing a snap in the brush, she jumped.

With nowhere else to go, she crawled into some heavy undergrowth, hard up against the rock cliff face, lay on her back and covered herself in dead leaves and branches as best she could. She had the long gun pointed with the AK in her lap. If they came her way, she would see them first. Whether she could kill them all before they killed her, she wasn't sure. She only knew that if they were spread out far enough and she shot one with the long gun, there was a chance the others would not hear the report. There would be no hiding once the AK went off. Her best case scenario was for them to pass by without discovering her. Then she could get on their tail instead.

She had been lying there for several minutes when something moved down the hill. She pointed the long gun in that direction. Then something snapped in the brush to her left and she pivoted it that way.

The footsteps stopped five feet from her head. She suppressed her breath and waited. Then whoever it was crouched down and started to part the branches. Out of options, Saarah put a bullet into his head and his body fell forward, half into the bush and nearly on top of her.

Sensing movement somewhere down the hill again, she pivoted back in that direction. The sound of hands and feet climbing over sandstone grew louder. Then a head popped up from below and she knew she had no choice but to fire again. Whoever it was had seen the dead body and was aiming his rifle.

She clicked off one round and the man and his rifle fell out of sight with a clatter. Saarah's mind raced through her options. Staying hidden no longer seemed to be one of them. If only she knew how many men were pursuing her, but she didn't.

She heard the man move again down below. Then it was silent. So was he dead? Or simply waiting to ambush her?

As the seconds passed without any further sounds, she decided her only choice was to move forward and peeked out through the branches. With no one in sight, she crawled out and inched towards where she had shot him.

About to look over the edge, she stopped herself. No. That would be foolish. He could be waiting with a gun pointed at me. Instead, she moved laterally a hundred feet past an abutment of rock, slipped down to his level and headed back slowly, hoping to come in unseen from his flank.

Saarah had just rounded a corner when the man suddenly came into view, sitting with his back against the rocks and his chin at his chest. Seeing her, he tried to raise his rifle and point it her way. She put another bullet into his chest and he slumped forward. The rifle had dropped from his hands. She rushed over and kicked it away.

While she stared down, he took a pained breath. Blood had gathered at the corners of his mouth. When his eyes came up and slowly focused, his head jerked back in surprise.

"You?" he said.

It was Pazir, the young man that Saarah had once loved as a girl, the young man she had imagined marrying long ago.

"You?" he said again.

"Yes, me, and I am sorry to have killed you, but at least you will be free now. It is more than you would have granted me in this world."

Pazir made a feeble lunge for the rifle but Saarah quickly took it in her hands.

"I will leave you to die in peace. You will soon be with God. When you see Him, please repeat these words that I say…I forgive you."

Saarah threw the long gun over her back, checked to make sure the magazine in her AK was loaded and reached for her radio.

Twenty Nine

Connelly and Palmer were sitting in the shade of Salahuddeen's hooch when the helicopter appeared from over the western hills. Out in the hot sun, a man knelt alone with his hands clasped behind his head. Connelly had his rifle pointed loosely at the man's chest. Several of the village men were also sitting nearby, talking among themselves, a conversation that paused with the helicopter approaching.

Connelly's phone rang and he answered it.

"This the number one cheese?"

"Yeah. What's our status?"

"We've got a bit of a situation here. Why don't you drop in and join the party? You see us?"

"Is that you in front of Salahuddeen's place?"

"That's us. We've got a surviving hostile and an ongoing debate about what to do with him. Plus a number of other problems we need to address…See you in a few."

Connelly clicked off before Clayton could inquire any further. The village men, seeing Connelly end the call, went right back to arguing. Besides the question of what to do with the man kneeling before them, there was a major kerfuffle over what to do with all the dead Taliban bodies.

As the helicopter touched down nearby, the men shielded their faces from the wind and dust. The man kneeling closed his eyes and turned his head.

Clayton opened the cargo door, jumped out and started helping the village wives and mothers to climb down. Seeing their women return, the village men got up to assist.

With that situation under control, Clayton walked straight over to Saarah. He had a long look in her eyes and gave her a hug.

"I'm so glad to see you alive."

He pulled back and looked at Megan.

"Good to see you made it back safely too. Is everything a go?"

She nodded.

The two Land Cruisers pulled up just then and the remainder of the women warriors climbed out, Ariya among them. Clayton went around shaking their hands.

"Where's Metcalf?" Clayton asked Palmer.

"He hiked back up to be with Hajira. Esin went with him."

Clayton nodded and turned to Salahuddeen.

"There's a lot to discuss but I need to retrieve the two dead women first."

"May God be with them."

Clayton started to leave but the village men were promptly in his face, talking a mile a minute.

"What's this about?" Clayton asked Ariya.

"About this Taliban and their dead bodies."

"All right. Tell them we'll discuss everything when I get back."

The men kept talking."

"They also want to know what happened to the other village women and the village men who helped them escape."

"The healthier women are hiking back with the men right now. They'll be here soon. The half dozen or so women who were too exhausted to hike back, we'll go down to grab them as soon as I'm done with retrieving Hajira and Noushineh."

The men listened to Ariya's explanation but were quickly back in Clayton's face.

"Goddamn it!" Clayton said. "We've got too much to do here to be arguing! Now tell them to hang loose and I'll address all their concerns when I get back!"

The tone of Clayton's voice alone had stopped the men in their tracks. He nodded at them and went over to check on Connelly. The young man still had his hands clasped behind his head. He couldn't have been more than eighteen years old. Clayton waved for him to put his hands down.

"What are we doing here?" he said to Connelly.

"Well, first question is what to do with this dude. He gave himself up and I figured, rules of engagement and all, it wasn't my job to shoot him."

"Yeah, thank you for that. There's been enough killing already for one day...Anything else?"

"Yeah. Like those village dudes were just ranting about. All the dead bodies. I guess the general consensus is, they're tired of turning their valley into a Taliban shrine."

Connelly glanced up at the hot morning sun.

"Better do something with them quick. They'll be rotting soon."

"All right. Let me grab the two women and we'll sort things out when I return...Let this guy sit down in the shade somewhere. Maybe a little kindness will help us get something useful out of him."

"Your call, boss."

"And those additional forces you saw mobilizing in that compound earlier in the day? What happened with them?"

"Oh, I had Jake unpin one of those .50s and sent him down there to give them a little welcoming party. The poor souls never knew what hit 'em."

"So the bodies are still out on the road?"

"Right where we dusted them."

"All right. We'll have to get that cleaned up too."

Clayton had started for the helicopter but stopped and pulled out his phone.

"By the way, I'm looking for this man. Tajj Yusufi."

Clayton showed Connelly a photo.

"Any chance you've seen him here?"

"Sure did, chief. He's back down there at the end of their convoy with his head half blown off."

Clayton nodded and hurried over to the helicopter.

When he returned five minutes later, the women warriors were waiting for the dead bodies with white sheets and shovels.

"We've decided to bury them in the woods, down by the stream," Saarah said.

Clayton nodded.

"Can you deal with this then? I need to get the other village women back here and deal with the dead Taliban."

"Go," Saarah said. "We will bury our own sisters."

"Okay. Please explain to the village men. I need one of them to go with the pilot while he retrieves the rest of the villagers."

Saarah talked to them while Hajira and Noushineh were being carried over to one of the Land Cruisers.

Saarah returned.

"Bikram will go with him."

"Good. You're sure you don't need help with…"

"No. We will be fine. He is coming with us," she said, pointing to Metcalf.

"Okay. I'll talk with you again before I leave."

Saarah touched Clayton's hand tenderly and turned to join her fellow warriors. Clayton went over to Palmer.

"As soon as Sunny's back, I'll fly you to a hospital and get that bullet out of your leg."

Palmer thumbed his chin at the collection of trucks and SUVs gathered along the road.

"I was thinking to grab myself a new rig and just drive back."

"I'm flying you out. I need there to be a zero footprint around here within the hour. My neck is out there far enough already."

"Just messing with you, chief. Esin gave me a shot of morphine but I'll be feeling the pain before long, so anytime you're ready."

"Yeah, in just a minute."

Clayton went over to Salahuddeen.

"I understand the villagers don't want to bury any more Taliban in the valley."

"Yes. I believe it is a wise course. Anymore Taliban buried here and it will become a place for pilgrimages."

"Yeah, I suppose so. Well, let's go deal with this prisoner."

They walked over and joined Connelly. The young man was sitting in the shade now but Connelly still had his rifle pointed at him.

God only knew what had led the young man to his zealous beliefs. Faced with death now, he didn't appear to be quite so zealous. He just looked lost and afraid.

Clayton turned to Salahuddeen.

"Is Aarshin's flatbed truck still in the valley?"

"Yes. It is parked over by the boy's schoolhouse."

"Okay. How does this sound? We load all the dead Taliban into the truck and let this kid drive it back to that Taliban compound. I don't know of anyone here who's willing to kill him. And I wouldn't allow it anyway. So we get rid of our prisoner problem and the bodies all at once."

Clayton looked back at the young man.

"I can't see how letting him go will make this war any worse. Might even help. Somewhere in his heart, he'll have to know that we were decent people."

"I too think that is a wise course," Salahuddeen said. "But first I must talk it over with the other elders."

As Salahuddeen walked away, Clayton crouched down beside Connelly.

"You ready to pull out?"

"Yeah. Wouldn't mind grabbing a free rig or two from that used car lot over there."

"Yeah, why not. Just don't get too greedy. I'm sure the villagers have their hearts set on them too."

"We'll go easy."

"Okay."

"And my dough?"

"You've got my number. Call me later this afternoon and I'll meet you with the cash."

Clayton heard footsteps and looked over his shoulder. Several of the villagers had returned with Salahuddeen.

"It is agreed. He may take the bodies with him. All of them except for Pazir. As much as he betrayed us, he is still our brother."

"All right. Tell him what's going on, and make sure he understands that the American government had a hand in his freedom."

Clayton turned to look at the young man.

"I want him to have that knowledge. Perhaps he will tell others that we never meant the Afghan people any harm."

The young man stared at Clayton as Salahuddeen explained, then bowed his head in gratitude when Salahuddeen was done. Clayton nodded back and turned to Salahuddeen.

"Okay. He's in your hands. As soon as that bird gets back with the rest of the women, I'll be pulling out."

The two men stared.

"I basically need you to deny my part in this. With all of this. Do you understand?"

"We have much practice at playing dumb for the Americans."

Clayton smiled.

"Yeah, well, you're likely to have a bit more practice here in the coming days...Oh, and about these Taliban rigs, Connelly and his boys are planning to take a few. I figure they've earned it but the rest are yours. The villagers can do whatever they want with them."

"We will make good use of them."

"Good.

Clayton touched his heart.

"I'm heading down to check on the women before I leave."

Turning west, the village road passed alongside the fields and the fields ended where the woods began. A path led down through the trees to the stream. Clayton found the women still digging. Metcalf stood there with dirt on his clothes and hands. Clayton gave him a hug.

"Sorry, brother. I know you had come to care about her very much."

"Yeah. I'm figuring I'm going to miss her for the rest of my life."

"Yeah. I know that feeling…Are you going to be okay with driving back to Kabul?"

"Yeah. I'll caravan with Connelly and his boys."

"Okay."

Clayton looked over to where Tabaan and Kejal were digging the graves.

"Better touch base with him. I know he's getting ready to pull out soon."

"I already told him to wait for me."

"Okay."

Clayton touched Metcalf's shoulder and pulled Saarah aside.

"I brought this for you."

He handed her a satellite phone.

"My personal number is in the contacts. Anything you need, any time you need to talk, call me, okay? I'll be around."

"Will you?"

He nodded.

"I have no idea if and when they'll try to pull us out, but if they do, I'll retire and stay on as a private contractor. I'll be here. I have to be here. I wouldn't sleep if I left you alone."

Saarah threw herself at Clayton's chest, then pulled back and searched his eyes for a moment before kissing his lips.

"Are you going now?"

"As soon as the bird is back. Actually, I have a second one nearby, if you need me to fly all of you up to Mazar-e-Sharif."

"Thank you but we are planning to take a few of the vehicles and drive there. Sgt. Rodriguez has promised us it is safe as far as Tupchi and the roads should be clear from there."

"Okay."

Clayton looked around at the woods.

"Beautiful place."

"It is where I always came to dream as a young girl...And where I decided to become an astronaut."

Clayton smiled.

"It's a nice place to dream...Be safe."

Clayton turned to the rest of the women.

"All of you. Anytime you need my help, call."

He went around hugging them and then gave Metcalf the soldier's handshake before turning to leave.

The helicopter came out from over the hills as Clayton walked back up the road. The village men were carrying dead bodies down from the hills. The back of the flatbed was already half full. By the time Clayton arrived back, the last of the women were on the ground and greeting their loved ones.

Clayton joined Salahuddeen.

"If you need anything, you have my number. Just let me know."

"What we need more than anything right now is peace. And time to heal."

"Okay. As soon as Sunny drops us off in Kabul, he'll fly up to Kahmard and start bringing the children back."

"Thank you."

Clayton nodded.

"Stay vigilant. They are gone for now, but not forever."

"I think the villagers understand that now."

Clayton touched his heart and went over to help Palmer. Connelly and his men were lined up on the road and ready to go.

"Don't forget Metcalf," Clayton called out.

Connelly signaled with two fingers.

"And make sure to get that boy a pillow."

Palmer flipped him off and there was laughter. Clayton helped Palmer onboard. Moments later, Clayton was watching the valley grow small below him. His heart was down in the woods along the stream with the one he loved. Then the valley was gone and they were racing south towards Kabul. The morning had long ago turned to afternoon.

Kelly and Bradley were waiting on the tarmac when Sunny touched down. Clayton unbuckled and turned to him.

"You know where you're going."

"Sure do."

"Okay. Anything else comes up, give them a hand."

"Sure will."

"Thanks."

"Yeah, thanks for the memories."

"Sure."

Clayton opened the cargo door and helped Palmer out. Bradley and Kelly were having a laugh as Clayton helped him into the back of the Land Cruiser.

"Step on a tack, did you?"

"Yeah. I'll give you a tack."

"All right, let's go," Clayton said, closing the door.

"Where are we taking numb nuts here?"

"The emergency hospital on Sulh Road."

"Got it. I take it this shit's still on the classified side of the ledger."

"Veering towards top secret at this point."

Kelly smiled over the seat.

"Yeah, but seriously don't forget that," Clayton said.

Back at the station, Clayton went straight to his office. There were two options. Take two more Desoxyn and keep going, or crash on his couch and sleep for eight hours. He took two more Desoxyn, had another splash bath, changed into some fresh clothes, grabbed his briefcase and headed down to sig intel. Scottie pretended to collapse face first onto his keyboard when Clayton walked in.

"You're free to go," Clayton said. "Just give me the latest print out. Anything interesting going on?"

"That Durrani can't keep his mouth shut but. He tried reaching Tajj Yusufi several times, and when Yusufi didn't answer, he called Abdul Qahhar and then Khan Zada again. And they both told him to quit calling. He did reach Sikander but as usual, Sikander never seems to say anything, just let's Durrani do all the talking."

"Yusufi's dead," Clayton said.

"Yeah, well, that would tend to explain why *he* wasn't answering."

Clayton took the print out.

"Remember. This is all classified."

"My lips are sealed."

Clayton nodded.

"Go home. You look like hell."

"Yeah. So do you."

Clayton headed down to Simmons's office. Lauren was there and smiled with her mouth that went the wrong way. But today, Clayton felt nothing but caring and compassion for her. She was a good and decent soul and this mad world badly needed more of those.

"How's the chief doing?" he asked.

"Not sure but he came through here a few minutes ago, looking like he was walking on air."

Lauren made a face.

"And I'm guessing you know why."

"Yeah but I'd better let him tell you."

Clayton touched her hand and went in through Simmons' door. Simmons was sitting at his desk, beaming.

"Close that and come take a look."

Clayton did and went around to Simmons' side of the desk. Megan's feature story was up on the screen. She had titled the story *Afghan's Lipstick Warriors*.

"Have you seen this?"

"No. Hell, I haven't had time to stop and look in the mirror. Is it good?"

"Yeah, great. She references all that Afghan warrior princess stuff from the past and tied it all to the present."

Simmons looked back at his computer screen.

"Let old Rocky Blackburn try to stuff this toothpaste back in the tube."

"Has he called yet?"

"No."

Simmons checked his watch.

"I'm sure everyone in Washington's already out of bed. I'll give it about thirty minutes before the shit hits the fan...So how did it go up there?"

Clayton explained.

"Damn, that's too bad about the ladies."

"Yeah."

"Yeah, a damned shame...Well, I trust you got things tidied up nice and neat."

"Yeah, I wiped our prints clean as best I could."

"Good. With this story out there, let someone make a big stink. The Taliban got their asses kicked by a bunch of ladies."

Simmons had to chuckle.

"Oh, by the way. If anyone drags us before a judge, our line is, Blackburn told us to get some answers and that's why we flew up there. End of story."

Clayton nodded.

"You worn out?" Simmons said.

"I don't know what I am. I just took two more Desoxyn so I'm good for a spell."

"Yeah, check with Rick. Did you already have him shoot that drone back to Adelman's care?"

"No. I'll run down there right now...Oh, by the way. I need $500K in cash for Connelly."

Simmons eyed Clayton while spinning around to his safe. Clayton opened his briefcase and turned it around facing that way. Simmons spun back around a moment later, stacked the cash neatly inside the briefcase and Clayton snapped it shut.

"Tell him thanks for me."

"I will."

Clayton looked back once on his way out the door. Simmons was staring at his computer screen again, beaming.

"Just like the good old days, Dorn. Riding saddle with the Northern Alliance and chasing the Taliban up into the hills."

Clayton nodded and closed the door. Lauren made a face as he passed by her desk.

"Someone better tell me what's going on around here."

"Check the Washington Post online. That's all I can tell you for now…And you didn't hear it from me."

Out back in the drone command trailer, Rick looked up from his monitor when Clayton walked in and checked his watch. Clayton sat down next to him and looked at the drone feed.

"No need for me to go home, dude. I could keep doing this shit for a thousand years now."

"I know. You're immortal. Blow up that zoom shot of the village for me."

Rick did.

"I've been watching them pile bodies into the back of a truck for the last hour. Something gnarly definitely went down up there. Did you get your gun out?"

Clayton shook his head. All looked calm in the village. He had hoped to see Saarah but it appeared that the women were still down in the woods.

"You can go ahead and reassign that drone to Adelman now. Or bring it back to the corral. Just get it out of the area. We need to cover our tracks."

Clayton stood up and patted Rick on the shoulder.

"Thanks, and feel free to finish your shift, if that's what you want."

"Hell, I may as well. I try to crash now and I'll just be bouncing off the walls."

Clayton patted his shoulder again and left.

Back up in his office, he sat down at his desk and started making a mental list of things he had to do that day. It was a short list. Get Connelly paid. Make sure Metcalf got back to the reservation all right. Sit around and wait for incoming from Blackburn. Go back to his trailer and bounce off the walls.

This was normally when you would write up a report, only there wouldn't be any reports written up today. It never happened.

He sat there unable to do a thing but think of Saarah.

Restless, Clayton dashed across the street to the market for an espresso and pastry and headed back up to Simmons' office.

"Wow!" Lauren said as Clayton walked by her.

Her mouth turned down even more dramatically. He had to keep himself from laughing.

"Remember, mums the word," he said going by.

"Yeah, but wow."

"By the way, if you see Adelman, raise the drawbridge and drop the hot oil."

The mouth tried to come up the other way in a smile but it just couldn't do it.

Clayton went in and found Simmons on the phone. He pointed at the receiver and held it up so Clayton could hear. It was Blackburn, on a rant. Clayton sat down and bit into his pastry. Simmons got back to listening to Blackburn.

"Yes, no problem," Simmons said finally. "We'll both be on the conference call. Yes, I got it. 0900 hours, D.C. time."

Simmons listened again.

"I can't imagine what else could happen between now and then."

Simmons held the receiver away from his ear with Blackburn screaming. Then the line went dead. Clayton had a sip of his coffee, waiting.

"So?"

"Oh, the little general wants us on a conference call. The president's national security advisor and the head of the NSC will be joining the party, among others."

"When?"

"Five thirty, our time."

Clayton checked his watch. That was a little over an hour away.

"Hell," Simmons said. "I'm hungry. Think I'll order a pizza. You want some?"

Clayton held up his espresso and pastry. Simmons hit his comm button.

"Lauren. Order a pizza. Make it a large deluxe, in case anyone else around here wants some."

He had just clicked off when the door flew open and Adelman stormed in. Lauren stood behind him, shrugging repentantly.

"Adelman, if you give me any shit right now, I'm going to shoot you. I'm not in the mood."

Adelman held up his iPhone.

"I just saw this Newburg story. I mean, really? Woman warriors? Is that what you guys have been hiding from everyone around here?"

"No. Just from you," Simmons said.

"Yeah, that's great, chief. All for one and one for all."

Simmons opened his top drawer, grabbed his Glock and slammed it down hard on the top of his desk.

"You've got five seconds to get your ass out of here before I start shooting."

"Come on, chief. All I'm saying is, how am I supposed to do my job if you don't keep me in the loop?"

"Five…"

"This is important shit. *Everyone* around here should have been read in."

"Four…"

"Oh, this is bullshit."

"Three…"

379

When Adelman started to speak again, Simmons grabbed the gun and did a press check.

"Fucking bullshit," Adelman said and hurried out.

Lauren was still standing there, looking petrified.

"It's all right," Simmons said. "Just get me that pizza before this conference call starts or I may have to shoot you too."

Very slowly, she closed the door.

Afghan's Lipstick Warriors
First Chronicle

Epilogue

Clayton and Simmons got down to the TOC shortly before nine and had been logged into the virtual meeting for several minutes when Dan O'Brien, the president's national security advisor, appeared on the screen. He was urbane, Ivy League and exuded all the warmth of an inquisition. McReynolds, the head of the NSC, was there too, along with Blackburn and one of his staff. Like Blackburn, McReynolds was retired military and more than a bit flinty.

O'Brien greeted everyone coolly and started the questioning.

"Chief Simmons. Let's start with Ms. Newburg's piece in the Post this morning. Do you have any idea how she managed to get embedded with these..." O'Brien looked down at his notes... "Lipstick warriors, as she's calling them?"

"Not sure, beyond saying that that's what reporters do."

"And by that, you mean?"

"Dig up the truth."

"I see. So you're telling me that a Washington Post reporter has more intel on these women than our own intelligence people?"

"To be completely frank with you, it did catch us a bit off guard. With this ongoing troop withdrawal, our eyes have been laser focused on ensuring our boys get out of country without the Taliban clipping their heels."

"And you, Mr. Dorn?" O'Brien said. "I understand you've been CIA's point man on this issue."

"To the best of my knowledge, sir, they're operating out of Mazar-e-Sharif area. But as to their exact location, current status and future plans, I have no firm intel."

"And this Ms. Newburg. Do you happen to know where we might find her at present?"

"No…I suppose we could check with the Post, though I doubt they'd divulge her whereabouts if she's still embedded."

"Oh, hell," Blackburn said. "Let's just call a spade a spade. The agency has its hands all over this thing but they're not about to tell us."

"Well, whatever else it is," McReynolds said. "It sure sounds like one hell of an intel failure to me."

"It's not like these women were advertising themselves," Simmons said.

The several faces on the conference call were left staring at each other.

"If I may speak frankly," Simmons said.

O'Brien waved a hand.

"Why does anyone back there in D.C. care? About Newburg. About these woman warriors. About any of it. You want out of Afghanistan? Fine. Then get on with turning your focus to the Sahel or the South China Sea or wherever it is this administration feels it has more pressing interests and let these people fight as they see fit. Hell, we should be thankful these women are taking it to the Taliban. We should be trying to help them. The last thing we should be doing is hunting them down like common criminals."

Blackburn turned red.

"If you haven't noticed, they've made a complete mess of what was once a fairly stable ceasefire! Christ! Just this morning, we got word that another half dozen private militias have jumped into the fray! At this rate, the entire country will have descended into civil war before the last C-130 can draw up its loading ramp!"

"And what did you expect, Mr. Secretary? That everyone would just lie down and willingly accept tyranny again?"

"What I expect is for you to execute this administration's policies!"

"And that would be?"

"Make sure this withdrawal goes smoothly! How many times do I have to repeat myself?!"

The several faces on the conference call were left staring at each other again. O'Brien cleared his throat.

"Emotions aside," he said. "It *does* sound as if you're struggling to execute this administration's foreign policy goals."

"Sir, I came to Afghanistan to help the Afghan people build a free, fair and democratic society, and once that ceases to be our policy goal, frankly, I no longer know what the hell I'm doing here."

"Well, back to the purpose of my call. Do you have any thoughts on how we might get this situation back under control? It's not doing anyone any good to have these militias and the Taliban at each other's throats."

"Setting aside the premise of your question, that your unconditional withdrawal from this country was ever going to be remotely *under control*, I'll be damned if I'll do the Taliban's dirty work for them. I'll hand in my resignation before I start gunning down anyone who's brave enough to fight those SOBs."

O'Brien stared.

"Very well. Please pass along whatever intel you can gather on these militias, especially the women."

"You can be sure I will."

"And Ms. Newburg too."

"I'll see if we can find her."

"Thank you."

With the call ended, Simmons turned to Clayton.

"I don't think if I've ever seen a bigger bunch of educated fools."

Clayton nodded.

"It does seem like we keep ending up on the wrong side of history."

"That's because we keep ending up on the wrong side of justice."

"Yeah, you may be right about that…"

Clayton stood up.

"Well, if you don't mind, I'm heading in back to get some sleep."

"Go right ahead," Simmons said. "You've more than earned it."

"Thanks…I'll see you sometime tomorrow morning."

Clayton had stopped back in his office to grab a few things when his phone rang. He looked, saw the number was blocked and hesitated before answering the call.

"Clayton Dorn here."

"Mr. Dorn. This is Shahpur Sikander."

Clayton tensed up.

"Yes, Mr. Sikander. What can I do for you?"

"In fact, Mr. Dorn, I called to see what we can do for each other. Is there a chance we could meet someplace quiet this evening? I'd like to discuss the future of Afghanistan with you."

Clayton remained wary, not at all sure he could trust the man, any more than he could trust Durrani.

"Perhaps the Kabul Star?" Sikander suggested. "I'm sure we can find a quiet spot in the restaurant to lay our cards on the table."

"All right. When?"

"I can be there in five minutes."

"I'll see you there."

Feeling as if he was about to be had somehow, Clayton headed downstairs and grabbed his personal car from around in back.

The hostess looked up and smiled for Clayton when he walked into the restaurant. It was a quiet Tuesday evening out on the town.

"Mr. Clayton?" she said.

He nodded.

"Mr. Sikander told me to watch for you."

He was led to a corner booth in back.

"Ah, there you are," Sikander said, standing up to shake Clayton's hand. "Have you eaten?"

"No, but I..."

"Please," Sikander said and promptly ordered several dishes. "And a glass of Scotch for starters?" he asked Clayton.

"Sure."

With the hostess gone, Clayton looked back at Sikander, still wary of this out of the blue evening soiree.

"Let me guess," Sikander said with a charming smile. "You suspect me of being a double agent. In public, I'm an honest broker for the Afghan people, but behind the scenes I'm busy working for the Taliban and stabbing everyone in the back."

Sikander's smile lingered briefly before melting away.

"Please, Mr. Dorn. Let us be frank here. Of course you have listened in on my conversations. It is the way of your government. But I would challenge you to go back and find one instance where I explicitly agreed to sell out my country."

Sikander had started to lean forward when a waitress arrived with Clayton's scotch. When she was gone, Sikander leaned forward again.

"Let me be perfectly clear. I humor Durrani with good reason. The man would not confess all of his sins to me otherwise. There is an old saying. It is better to be in the den with a fox than to be alone in the woods with a wolf."

"And what does that mean in this instance?"

"Mr. Clayton. I can assure you that the Taliban are our common enemy. It is only a question of how to defeat them."

"And how would you propose we go about doing that?"

"Well, somewhat sadly, I must admit that the militias are our best hope now. Perhaps you heard the news today. That the Northern Alliance has sworn allegiance to the Afghan government and army. All the militias have."

"No. I had not heard that."

"Yes, no doubt you have been distracted with more important matters."

Sikander smiled again.

"But, yes, it seems the Afghan people are finally coalescing around a common cause of defeating those fanatics."

"Not all of the Afghan people feel that way."

"No, not all, but most. Far more than not. Anyway, that is why I asked you to come here this evening. To discuss how we can best coordinate our resources to achieve that goal."

"Who is we?"

"Ah yes. There are many of us still dedicated to the freedom of the Afghan people...particularly to that of our women. But like you, we must tread carefully. There are wolves among us...Plausible deniability. Isn't that how you say it?"

Clayton nodded. Sikander raised his eyebrows in return.

"And so?"

"Fair enough. Let's discuss how we can best defeat the Taliban. As long as that involves securing complete freedom for the women of Afghanistan, I'm all ears."

"Trust me. We are in full agreement on that issue. My wife would have my head if my goals were anything less."

"For better or worse, you chose your wife wisely."

Sikander laughed.

"Very clever of you. I'll have to remember that line the next time she's putting me in my place."

The food came and the two men sat there eating and talking until late.

When Clayton finally arrived back to his trailer, he poured another Scotch and bounced off the walls for a couple of hours. Saarah was there with him, as if she were a red rose glowing in his empty heart. So much beauty, he ached to possess it, though he knew full well that the beauty of a woman could never be possessed, only admired and adored.

The next day passed by without a call from her, and the next one, and the next one. Somewhere in all of that, Clayton recalled the words of a sage old man he once knew. I am reasonably calm amidst unresolved circumstances. And so, amidst the many unresolved circumstances of his personal and professional lives, Clayton forged ahead, quietly praying for Saarah's success and safety.

On the morning of the fourth day, a new piece by Megan appeared in the Post. The women had hit the Taliban hard again, this time thirty miles east of Kunduz, up near the Tajikistan border.

And, just as quickly, they had vanished into thin air.

Clayton was in Simmons' office that afternoon when Blackburn called from D.C., on another rant.

"So, for the hundredth time, I'm asking you people. Just what the hell are you doing to get this militia business under control? And I especially mean these women."

"To be perfectly frank with you, Mr. Secretary, nothing. I believe I made myself abundantly clear the other day. I'll resign before I start hunting down anyone who is willing to fight for their own freedom."

"Goddamn it! You folks at CIA really are useless!"

"Well, if you think you can do a better job, please feel free to hop on a plane and come join the battle."

Blackburn screamed something about having Simmons mop floors back at Langley and hung up. Simmons put the phone down and shrugged at Clayton.

"You think there's any chance Connelly's hiring?"

After a moment, Clayton laughed.

About the Author

The product of an Irish/Italian family, Mr. Corcoran was transplanted from the clapboard New England of his youth to the cookie cutter, stucco subdivisions that increasingly littered the old ranches and disappearing orange groves south of Los Angeles in the 1960s. Ever rebellious, and true to the folk music/coffee house idealism that helped shape his early worldview, he chose to resist the Vietnam War, was a man without a country for several years and can count incarceration in a Mexican prison as one of his many colorful experiences from that era.

Having pursued a love of reading and writing in various forms all his life, Mr. Corcoran finally took that passion seriously around the turn of the millennium and has dedicated the remainder of his days to authorship. In completing the circle of destiny, he has returned to the New England of his youth and presently resides along the shore of Rhode Island.

www.ingramcontent.com/pod-product-compliance
Lightning Source LLC
Chambersburg PA
CBHW051058030726
47504CB00006B/1684